# THE EMPRESS

## BOOK 2 OF THE DIABOLIC TRILOGY

# S.J. KINCAID

SIMON & SCHUSTER

First published in Great Britain in 2017 by Simon & Schuster UK Ltd
A CBS COMPANY

First published in the USA in 2017 by Simon & Schuster BFYR,
an imprint of Simon & Schuster Children's Publishing Division

1 3 5 7 9 10 8 6 4 2

Simon & Schuster UK Ltd
1st Floor, 222 Gray's Inn Road
London WC1X 8HB

www.simonandschuster.co.uk
www.simonandschuster.com.au
www.simonandschuster.co.in

Simon & Schuster Australia, Sydney
Simon & Schuster India, New Delhi

A CIP catalogue record for this book
is available from the British Library.

PB ISBN 978-1-4711-6914-4
eBook ISBN 978-1-4711-6915-1

Printed and bound by CPI Group (UK) Ltd, Croydon, CR0 4YY

Simon & Schuster UK Ltd are committed to sourcing paper
that is made from wood grown in sustainable forests and support the Forest
Stewardship Council, the leading international forest certification organisation.
Our books displaying the FSC logo are printed on FSC certified paper.

To Sophia, Grace, Madeleine, and Estelle—
I can't wait to see you live your dreams!

# OUR MOST CHERISHED SENATOR

*Alectar von Pasus:*

*May the light of the stars illuminate your every venture. I apologize for the crude medium of a discreet-sheet with my handwriting, but I dare not send you a transmission. You are likely receiving this note from my trusted messenger ten to twelve days from now. I implore you to crumple it to powder immediately after reading, and if need be, put this bearer to death to preserve these contents. He will not object to a death in service of our Living Cosmos.*

*I hate to impose upon you at this time of grieving for your beloved daughter, Elantra, but I must. I am the Vicar Primus now, but I sense I will not be for much longer. As the foremost Helionic at this imperial center, I am compelled to send you my desperate plea for assistance!*

*We of the faith are all alarmed by the last hour's events here at the Chrysanthemum. The Senators von Pasus have always been ardent champions of the Living Cosmos. Now, it is your hour to show you are no exception! Our divine Cosmos requires your zeal and your strength. I will be displaced from my position soon, so I will not have the power to act myself.*

*I know you to be a great man, Senator. The day you denounced the late Senator von Impyrean for his heretical and unseemly interest in the sciences, I felt most astir with joy. You were instrumental in striking down blasphemers set on breaching the sacred mysteries of our divine Cosmos. An entire faction of the Senate sought to destroy the foundation of our empire in the name of the "sciences," and they might have succeeded, but for your words in the Emperor Randevald's ear, your steadiness driving his striking hand.*

*So I must ask you to be brave once more.*

*Like a two-headed viper, our enemies have reared a new pair of fangs to poison this galaxy once again. And I tremble to tell you who this new head is, though you must have guessed.*

*It is our young Emperor Tyrus von Domitrian.*

*You are aware that I have served as the Vicar Primus at the Chrysanthemum for over a century. I have been the voice of the Living Cosmos for those Grandiloquy who exercise power in this galactic court. I've ensured this center of our Empire remained untainted by those outdated faiths that should have been abandoned on old Earth. I am instrumental in maintaining the spiritual welfare of this court, and I am as much a fixture here as any of the*

*Grandiloquy, so I speak with authority. Two Domitrian sovereigns have sought my counsel!*

*Young Tyrus, though, looks elsewhere. And I am not writing as an old man, peevish at being overlooked. I could accept being thrust aside if I knew the proper reasons lay behind it, but at the time of this writing, I know an unholy plot is afoot. I do not know what narrative will be propagated about the recent events, but I will tell you my truthful, firsthand account of the Emperor's coronation.*

*The Emperor Tyrus smuggled Luminars—a particularly fractious, heathen sort of Excess (you know better than anyone!)—onto the Chrysanthemum. With their help, he ambushed his own grandmother, our beloved and faithful Grandeé Cygna. He united planet dwellers against his fellow Grandiloquy, but it was the least of his misdeeds.*

*You surely have seen his Convocation transmission. He speaks of a new era, of restoring the sciences so he might solve malignant space. This is ludicrous! But I know the dreadful influence putting such ideas in this young Emperor's mind.*

*The creature he means to take as his wife.*

*It pains me to speak of this to you, to a father so new in his grief, but I must: Tyrus von Domitrian means to wed the Diabolic, Nemesis dan Impyrean, who murdered your daughter, Elantra.*

*You must think these vile words to be false. I wish they were!*

*Nemesis was intended to be the fire sacrifice at the new Emperor's coronation. His grandmother, Cygna, demanded it, and Tyrus agreed to it. Instead the Emperor liberated the creature Nemesis and condemned the Grandeé Cygna in her place. Then—and I shudder to recount this—the Emperor killed his grandmother and expressed his intent to make this Diabolic his Empress.*

*An Empress!*

*You have not misread this. I can hardly fathom it.*

*A Diabolic, a subhuman, an abomination—to be our Empress!*

*The rumors always spoke of young Tyrus as a madman. Then, other rumors: he was feigning madness all along to escape the malice of his own family. Well, I fear he must be mad after all. He must be! We all know what Diabolics are!*

*These are* not *people. Nemesis dan Impyrean is not a person. She is a genetically engineered monster. She was only fashioned to appear human, yet she is not. Diabolics are stronger and faster and crueler than we are, merely for the protection of a master. We know this. Nemesis should have been killed the moment it became known she wasn't Sidonia von Impyrean, her mistress, but rather an imposter posing as her.*

*And all the violence that followed . . . The death of your beloved Elantra, the murder of our Emperor, now this . . .*

*This cannot be tolerated. This cannot stand.*

*I was aghast. I refused to anoint the Emperor if he clung to this creature. If I lose my position—which seems likely—it is because I made a stand for you. The Emperor spoke to me with such insolence upon my refusal: he informed me that this was a new age and I was not necessary. I've advised the Domitrians the entirety of my life, and this*

4

*bastard of some Excess speaks so to me! Then he embraced Nemesis and kissed her before all our appalled eyes.*

*I do not know how to stop this. I do not know how to act. So I beg for your help. The Emperor Tyrus von Domitrian means to wed Nemesis dan Impyrean. A "dan." A subhuman. He is mad to entertain the idea.*

*I know his cousin Devineé has been afflicted with grievous damage to her mind, but she is also the single living Domitrian who can take Tyrus's place. To you, Senator von Pasus, the foremost territory holder of this Empire, I plead for this: stand against this new Emperor. He must be made to see reason, or he must be replaced with an Emperor who does not spit in the face of the Living Cosmos. If he will not change course, and naturally, restore me to my position as Vicar Primus, then he must be replaced with a Domitrian who will.*

*And before you think I propose something daunting, I will tell you: Tyrus does not have my blessing. He does not have the blessing of the rest of the body of the faith. You, Senator, know the implications of this! Tyrus is a clever boy, but he was appointed Successor Primus by the last Emperor merely due to familial tensions; Randevald took no care to cultivate him, to teach him what a successor must know.*

*Tyrus von Domitrian is totally unaware of the weakness of his position.*

*Now is the time to strike.*

*—Fustian nan Domitrian, Vicar Primus*

1

SOMEONE had poisoned me. I knew it with a single sip.

That someone was about to die.

I glanced around the crowded presence chamber, hoping to spot the doomed idiot who thought to poison a Diabolic. This was hardly the first attempt on my life in the harried days since Tyrus's coronation. There'd been the young Grande Austerlitz, who tried to stab me in a surprise attack. I'd been bemused enough to tolerate his clumsy slashes for a few moments.

It seemed wise to be diplomatic, so I gave him a chance. "Stop this at once," I told him, dodging his next slash, his next.

He just bared his teeth and dove at me. I sidestepped him and hooked his ankle in mine to flip his legs out from under him. He screamed out as he tried to launch himself back to his feet—so I delivered a kick to his head that broke his skull open.

Days passed before the next attempt. This one had been a fanatical junior vicar. She gave away her intentions with the shout of, "Abomination!" just before she tried to pull me into the air lock with her.

I tore from her grip and batted her away, knocking her into the air-lock shaft. The blast doors sealed closed behind her—clearly some automated timer she'd set up in advance—and I met her eyes in the split second before the door to space popped open behind her and vented her into the darkness.

When criminals were vented to space for execution, the onlookers were supposed to turn their backs and look away. It was a gesture of deliberate disrespect. The condemned were so unworthy, even their deaths wouldn't be watched.

For this bold woman who'd attacked me, I felt a strange desire to watch her float away. She'd seen the fate of Austerlitz and still mounted a direct attack. This was the least I could do for one of such daring. There were a great many Grandiloquy who loathed me, a great many Helionics who scorned me with every righteous fiber of their being, but few were bold enough to act upon their malice.

Helionics viewed creatures like me as subhumans. The "dan" in our names meant we were beneath them in status, yet now their new Emperor meant to wed me. They would have to kneel to a creature. A Diabolic.

The assassination attempts weren't a surprise to me; the infrequency of the attempts was. A mere three attempts on my life in ten days? It was actually somewhat disappointing.

I welcomed the familiarity of feeling in danger. It tightened my focus, made my heart pick up a beat. My gaze swept the crowd as I drew the goblet to my lips, because surely my would-be assassin was fool enough to watch me drink this poison.

Yet I realized in moments that too many eyes were fixed on me to guess which pair might belong to my poisoner. I should have realized it at once. After all, everywhere I went now, I was watched, I was scrutinized, I invited discussion and opinion.

"Do they ever tire of staring?" I'd wondered the first night after the coronation, when I'd noticed the unnatural degree of scrutiny.

"This is just life as a Domitrian," Tyrus told me.

So my assassin . . . There were too many candidates. The crowd for the Day of Pardon was simply too thick, and there was no guessing who'd meant to end my life. Too many of these people watching me probably wished to do it.

Then a familiar pair of pale eyes met mine, and Tyrus inclined his head toward the exit, telling me silently that we needed to part ways with this company of Grandiloquy. It was time for the ceremony, which we would spend with the Excess.

I dipped my head in acknowledgment. The Day of Pardon would be held in the Great Heliosphere. It was an important imperial holiday, one of the few aimed at pleasing the Excess, who lived on planets, rather than the ruling Grandiloquy space dwellers.

On this day, Tyrus would enjoy the Emperor's privilege of commuting the prison sentences of several Excess who'd converted to the Helionic faith. I aimed for the exit, knowing Tyrus would meet me there. Then my steps stilled as I passed a cluster of revelers gathered before Tyrus's cousin and her husband.

I always took note of those who flocked to the Successor Primus, Devineé. She was Tyrus's last immediate relative and consequently heir to his throne. In my eyes, she was the greatest threat he faced. I'd damaged her mind beyond healing, so she couldn't plot on her own behalf, but others could use her as a puppet. Had it been up to me, she'd be dead already. It was Tyrus's decision, though. She was the last of his family, and I'd disabled her. He'd view her murder as monstrous.

And then . . .

Then the realization crawled into my mind: there was a weapon of murder in my hand that could not be blamed on me or traced back to me.

I made up my mind. I walked over to my intended's sole living relative. As my shadow slid over her, her foggy gaze rose to mine.

"Hello, Your Eminence. Are you enjoying the festivities?" I said pleasantly, looming above her.

Devineé blinked up at me dully, unable to comprehend me. I set down my goblet seemingly offhandedly, just beside hers. I made a show of unwinding my elaborate twist of currently chestnut brown hair, then arranging it anew (unnecessary with the hair stilts that arranged my locks in any style, but many women fussed over hair anyway).

"Fine conversation," I said to Devineé. "We must speak again."

Then I plucked up her goblet, leaving mine behind. And so quickly, so easily, it was done. I headed out to meet Tyrus for the ceremony, hoping that by the time it concluded, we'd hear news of it: confirmation of the death of his deadliest foe.

"You look beautiful," Tyrus murmured to me as we neared the heliosphere.

"I know," I said.

We were both wearing reflective garments of silver, interwoven with veins of liquid crystal. Though I'd gone with auburn hair and a darker skin tone, Tyrus looked the same as always, pale and lightly freckled, with clever pale eyes and light, sharply angled eyebrows crowned with tousled red hair.

Just outside the Great Heliosphere, I hesitated. It wasn't like me to be nervous, and I wasn't, per se. . . . But I just knew I was about to commit an obscenity, marching into the Great Heliosphere and taking an honored place during the ceremony.

Tyrus guessed the turn of my thoughts. He leaned in closer to me, dropping his voice. "There will be no issue with zealots today. We're not broadcasting this live, so we can edit any incidents out of the transmission. We've also borrowed a vicar. This is a holiday for the Excess, so they comprise the audience. They will be more favorably disposed toward us."

He meant toward *me*.

Of course he did. Tyrus had been careful with every move of his reign so far, since he was the sort to think ten steps ahead before making a single one. I'd been eased slowly into public life over the last weeks.

First the galaxy was transmitted glimpses of me from the dramatic scene at the coronation, when Tyrus declared his love for me and embraced me before all, consigning his grandmother to death in my place. My prisoner's garb had been modified in the transmission to a lovely, tasteful set of rags, and my unpigmented hair to a mane of effervescent gold. I looked a lost princess from a tale, not a Diabolic.

The transmission was effective in one respect: Cygna had received all the blame—rightfully—for the late Emperor Randevald's death.

The galaxy received just that glimpse of me, enough to set the Excess on their planets across the empire wondering who I could be, wondering what story lay behind my appearance in public life. Tyrus believed the best way to strip a secret of its power was to glare a shining light on it from the angle of choice, to exhibit it fearlessly rather than seek to hide it. He followed up on that first glimpse by introducing me as his future Empress—and a Diabolic—at his first Convocation.

Thousands gathered in person on the *Valor Novus*, the central starship of the Chrysanthemum, and avatars from light-years away appeared to fill the rest of the seats in the Grand Sanctum. It was the greatest chamber on the vessel and only used on such occasions as the first time a new Emperor addressed the powerful of his realm.

Tyrus planted the question about me with one of his allies, and then gave his prepared answer: "My fiancée will be a symbol of the new era we begin here today. Her name is Nemesis dan Impyrean. Some will be scandalized that I have no intention of wedding a member of this Empire's elite. I say, let them be scandalized, for I love Nemesis above any other. She is the most honest, courageous, and worthy candidate I can imagine as the Empress of this galaxy, and I know you will come to admire her as I have."

He'd had the sound dampened in certain parts of the chamber in advance, anticipating the stir of voices. Many of the traditional objectors, though, dared do nothing but cheer. Tyrus had taken Helionic prisoners at his coronation. He intended to release them now that the danger of his grandmother was past—provided their relatives in the Senate showed themselves cooperative in this transmission. Thus, those few objections were squelched, whereas sound was amplified from those allies Tyrus could count on to cheer and applaud.

Every major figure in the galactic media of Eurydice received a personal message from Tyrus. He'd greeted each of them, and his words included the "coded language" indicating they were to support me cheerfully in public.

Before more questions could be asked, he forged onward to his lofty hopes about restoring the sciences to tackle the menace of malignant space. This time he selectively muted the Grandiloquy so the cheering of the Excess could be heard. Airing both of his most scandalous intentions at once divided the outrage, as he'd hoped.

Then, on a final note, when cheering swelled at the conclusion of his first Convocation speech, Tyrus reached out, took me by the hand, and drew me to his side to exhibit me at the very finest. Far from my natural, colorless albinism, I appeared hued with brilliant black hair and bronzed skin, stenciled with effervescent glow over the cheekbones, in a gleaming dress of cascading gold sheets.

A beautiful woman, not a Diabolic. That's how I appeared.

Yet illusion could only get us so far. I knew that in my heart.

Now, here we were at this first real test of whether my public image was being received as Tyrus hoped. With Excess in the audience, they'd hopefully be too amazed to find themselves at this great event to bother dwelling on who—or rather, what—I was.

Tyrus and I stepped into the Great Heliosphere. I was painfully conscious of every single flicker of my lashes, every twitch of my muscles. Now that everyone knew how human I was not, it had become more essential to seem human than ever before.

The crowd within the Great Heliosphere lapsed into silence as we drew into the sacred chamber of diamond and crystal, and then they were dropping to their knees, hands to their hearts in salute to the Emperor.

"Rise," Tyrus said. He never kept them lingering on their knees as Randevald had been wont to do.

We moved through the parted sea of bodies, and Tyrus glimpsed Astra nu Amador, a nervous young vicar who worked for Senator von Amador.

Tyrus inclined his head in silent thanks to Astra. She returned it with a smile. She was ambitious enough to see that she might become Vicar Primus if she impressed us, replacing Fustian nan Domitrian. Tyrus and Fustian had been at odds since the coronation, when Fustian refused to bless me. Fustian would not have performed this ceremony with me present.

Now, as I raised my eyes to take in our surroundings, the sheer force of the light blasting in through the windows truly registered, though it cast only a faint warmth over my skin. The heliosphere was designed to refract starlight in myriad ways for services. No mirrors were needed to amplify the starlight this close to the red hypergiant star, Hephaestus, for the Ritual of Pardon.

So large, so bright was Hephaestus that the distant, smaller stars of the Cosmos were drowned out against the black. The crowd would have appeared but silhouettes against the great blaze of its light, but for the glowing pigment under their skin that set their features in stark relief. I didn't recognize any of the faces.

We stood alone in the innermost circle as the Vicar Astra set about placing sacred chalices throughout the chamber.

The Excess prisoners shuffled inside in a silent line. They'd all converted to the Helionic faith in prison, and they were the fortunate dozen due to be pardoned this year as reward for their penitence.

Tyrus's role in this ceremony was brief. He stepped forward, and the men and women knelt before him, displaying their pitifully bared heads, where they'd shaved away their hair to exhibit their faith. He spoke the short litany of pardon, and then the vicar took it from there.

Astra moved between the converts to aid them in shedding their clothing. Then she led each of the converts by the hands to the window to position them in the glare of the sacred hypergiant. The naked men and women pressed up against the window, spreading their arms, their fingers, soaking light into every square centimeter of their skin.

Tyrus took my arm, nudged me gently, and we stepped back, and back, as the vicar slowly adjusted the optics so more light from the hypergiant could seep into the chamber.

Then the hypergiant's light grew so bright, it seemed to lance into my pupils. The white skein of starlight scorched my eyes, and my hand flew up instinctively to protect my face. Through the veil over my vision, I heard the rustle of other people raising their hands to do the same. Then heat followed, a great, terrible wave of it that pummeled the air about us, stinging my skin, and I knew it was too much heat.

Something was wrong.

The pardoned men and women scrambled back from the windows, dark silhouettes contorting as their terrible screams knifed the air. The vicar's garb flared ablaze and the oil chalices spouted columns of heat.

I comprehended several things all at once: flames, hundreds of bodies all about me, and one exit.

This was a death trap.

# 2

I REACTED before anyone. Tyrus was in my grasp before I gave it conscious thought, and then I hurled him directly over the heads of those between me and the exit. It was strength I hadn't had since being whittled down to a normal woman's size.

I leaped over the heads of the people now stirring, beginning to turn, to react, to shout. They moved as though in a swamp, but I shot past them. Tyrus caught his balance and then I was there, and he couldn't have stopped me from forcing him forward if he'd tried.

We broke out of the now sweltering and oppressive air of the sacred chamber as flames swelled out behind us. The mass of bodies I'd anticipated now swept toward me, saturating the air with screams and shouts and the pounding of trampling feet.

The human tide spat out the first handfuls of lucky ones. The others filled the doorway and then filled it more, arms and legs and fright-ened, screaming faces stuffing any gap. Then the logjam, and hysteria edged the cries of terror as they found themselves trapped.

Tyrus pointed at a nearby Excess. "Call for help! NOW! Tell every nearby vessel to send med bots!" Then he surged forward toward the jammed doorway.

Trapped people reached for him.

He vaulted forward to pull them free and I thrust aside the pitiless thought that there would be more to take their place. I joined him in his efforts to wrench the people free. In their panic, their grasping hands latched onto my arms, yet it was difficult to rip them free of one another. Each one I dragged clear never loosened the clog to enable escape. Instead others wedged into the place of those freed and trapped everyone. Then we began to make progress and gaps expelled the dark smoke from within the heliosphere, but there was a cost. The grasping hands were no longer clawing at me, at anything. . . . Screams dimmed and then were silent and the great wedge of people were now blue of lips, glazed of eyes.

Long after some of those we pulled out were scanned by med bots that floated away—determining them beyond revival—Tyrus worked to drag others out. I just stepped back to survey the survivors. A med bot soared over to me and neutralized the radiation exposure.

Finally, I laid my hand on Tyrus's shoulder.

His hands fell to his sides.

He turned about, his pale gaze skipping over the survivors, lips moving as he silently counted them up.

"How did this . . ."

His face was smudged with ash. He raked his hand through his hair, setting it askew, smudging it.

A bot hummed over to him, and he started when its red beam flared out to treat him for the radiation exposure.

"You did all you could have done," I told him.

He just seemed dumbstruck. "I don't understand what happened."

I counted up the survivors too. A mere eighteen. Hundreds still in the heliosphere. Mostly the dead were servants and employees of Grandiloquy. People held each other, others lay on the ground on their backs . . . or wherever they'd been deposited as they died. Burns had left ugly, blistered red skin. I gazed at a bot hovering over the head of a boy on his hands and knees, puking from the radiation exposure.

More med bots had been floated in with us, but the number—a mere dozen—was starkly low. And Tyrus had that Excess call for more. The med bots should have flocked here as soon as the system noticed a breach.

And the breach . . .

I turned to gaze back toward the Great Heliosphere, bewildered. It was as though the star reached straight through the Great Heliosphere and burned us. It was a catastrophic structural failure, the sort repair bots should have caught long before it took place.

Then a cold thought came to me: *The Helionics will point to this. They will say it is a rebuke from the Living Cosmos.*

Stars were the expression of the will of the divine Cosmos, and was there any show of displeasure more stark than this one? Even I felt a superstitious shiver at the thought.

I couldn't say I knew for certain whether I believed in the Living Cosmos, but I knew that the Cosmos didn't believe in me. Every vicar had told me as much.

When I turned to Tyrus, he'd withdrawn his Imperial Scepter and now just gazed at it.

"I think I did this," he said, so quietly I barely made out the words.

"Tyrus . . ."

But we couldn't speak. Already, there were political allies and foes who'd flocked to the *Valor Novus* at the first hint of tragedy, and there were dead bodies to be dealt with and families to be notified. I backed out of the way so servants could gather the dead, and my heel met something solid.

My gaze flew down.

A dead girl. Young, the skin of an arm riddled in ugly blisters, dark eyes open to the ceiling with that sludgy and fixed gaze of the dead. . . .

*Sidonia.*

I blinked and it wasn't her. It was not.

Yet the specter of her seemed to rear up into my mind, reminding me that she would never exist in this universe again. Whenever I pondered this, all in this galaxy seemed dark and empty. I drew in a breath of the acrid air to force myself to stay in this moment. So I made out the words being told to Tyrus.

Another tragedy. One we'd missed.

". . . think it was poison . . ."

My head swiveled toward them. *Please* . . .

"Salivar is dead?" Tyrus said.

No. No, *no.*

Devineé's husband. He had drunk the wine.

She lived. She would threaten us *still.*

I'd missed my target.

For a month, I'd been trapped in solitary confinement, awaiting my impending death at Tyrus's hands. I passed that month loathing myself for the longing I still felt for him, though I'd been certain—so certain—he'd been the agent of Sidonia's death. He knew I believed that of him.

Though he'd overcome his grandmother, forced a confession from her about deceiving me, and though we'd kissed before the entirety of the most powerful in the Empire . . .

There was still a thread of uneasiness between us.

And I still had those treacherous doubts.

I'd both welcomed and dreaded the evening we'd planned to spend entirely alone together after the Ceremony of Pardon, for the duties of an Emperor had kept him so busy, it was our first time to ourselves.

Now, it would not happen.

Of the dead, most had perished from crushing or trampling injuries, not so much the burn of the star. Senator von Amador's replacement vicar was dead.

And when Tyrus's servants began to investigate, they discovered that one victim was my would-be assassin. They showed us the surveillance of the poisoning. Tyrus and I watched the images of the gathering of Grandiloquy before we'd departed. . . . I saw myself moving through the crowd, looking toward a stumbling Grande hanging off the shoulder of his wife . . . while a Grande from a minor offshoot of the Rothesays poured several droplets into my drink.

Then, that Rothesay watched me. He clearly hadn't noticed my drink swap with Devineé, but he had followed me into the Great Heliosphere. The better to see me succumb to his poison.

"That certainly backfired on him," I noted, recognizing his face from the corpses. I felt Tyrus's gaze pinned upon me, and added, "I was totally unaware my drink was poisoned. To think, I unwittingly passed it along. . . ."

"Yes," Tyrus said knowingly. "I am certain that is devastating knowledge." To his servants, "Make it known this Grande poisoned Salivar. Leave Nemesis out of the account." His gaze returned to that video, and he gestured for it to replay.

"What?" I said quietly.

"Question that man, too," he said, jabbing his finger at the one who'd stumbled, who'd drawn my gaze while my drink was doctored. "Frighten him if you must. Make sure he wasn't helping."

"Good thinking," I told Tyrus with a smile.

He didn't return it. He was gazing down at the list of dead from the heliosphere once again.

Tyrus and I retreated to the *Hera* as planned, but there was no pleasure to be had in these stolen hours. He'd given me this magnificent asteroid starship crafted by his grandmother; it was an engagement present, a Domitrian starship for a future Domitrian.

Now we sat together in the great jade chamber Cygna had intended to turn into a shopping promenade, but never lived to do. So there was a gurgling fountain feeding a stream that meandered across the garden of bronze trees and plants.

Tyrus and I sat alone in the middle of that great, echoing promenade. He reached into the sheath attached to his waist, pulled out a rod of palladium. A flick of his fingers, and the end jutted into six pointed spikes.

The Imperial Scepter. I'd caught him staring at it with a strange intensity ever since his coronation. It appeared but a decorative rod, yet it was a powerful machine in its own right. It was the device that made the Domitrians the foremost family in the galaxy.

"What is it?" I finally asked him.

He dragged his gaze over to mine. "You know what this is, I presume?" At my nod, he said, "I received this as all other Emperors have. My uncle died. I ascended." He raised a palm, hovered it over the six spikes. "These penetrated my skin to sample my blood. They registered me as a Domitrian, and this became my scepter. With possession of this scepter, I received possession of the Chrysanthemum. Every single machine fell into my control."

It wasn't just every machine in the Chrysanthemum. It was every single machine within several light-years and even some quite far across the Empire. The Emperor controlled them all. This was the reason the Domitrians were the imperial royals.

"Not every Domitrian is skilled with this," Tyrus said. "My great-grandmother, Acindra, could give orders to the machines about her with a thought, but my uncle . . . he was clumsy. He needed to make hand gestures. Vocalize his command. I was certain I'd do better than that."

I hadn't seen him use it yet. "And how are you with it?"

Tyrus looked at me. "Nemesis," he said very quietly, "I can't get it to do anything at all."

I stared at him.

Then, "What?"

He shrugged, and spoke to the air: "I need a security bot here now."

We waited.

Nothing.

"Oh," I said.

"I've tried to avoid showing this in public until I figured it out," he told me. "This is a big problem, Nemesis. This scepter isn't just the way I control the machines. It unifies the Chrysanthemum. This is why two thousand individual ships form one large super-structure." He tightened his fist about the scepter. "This is why a tiny structural instability can lead to a catastrophe in the Great Heliosphere. The only repair bots that mobilized to fix the breach were the ones already on board the vessel, not the ones on other vessels nearby. That breach needed a hundred repair bots, not a handful."

"That's what happened today," I surmised. "And that's why the med bots only came after you called for them."

He nodded. "I can't control any of these machines, and right now we are sitting on one ship amid two thousand individual ships with nothing linking them. There's no network sensing potential problems in need of repair, and triaging the repair bots for the most important places. That heliosphere would have been tended long before it breached, especially this close to a hypergiant star. This shouldn't have happened. Repair bots aren't doing their job, and external security bots are offline. . . . This is a very serious problem."

The other safety implications hit me.

"Tyrus, do you think others realize you don't have control of it?"

"I think after today, it will be glaringly obvious."

If Tyrus didn't have security bots at his command, if he didn't have control over every ship in the same star system, why . . . he was as vulnerable to attack as he'd been before he'd become Emperor.

More vulnerable, in fact, because there was a target on his back.

"If any enemy means to move on you," I realized, "or . . . or on us, they'll do it now. That's what you're saying."

Tyrus nodded.

There were many threats to us, but one man posed the greatest threat of all.

He wasn't merely the most powerful Senator in the Empire and the leader of the Helionic opposition to everything Tyrus meant to do— he was also father to a girl I'd recently killed.

"How long before Senator von Pasus hears about this?" I said to Tyrus.

He opened his mouth to answer me—and that was when his palladium glove began to vibrate with an incoming transmission. He turned his hand over to see the sender's name, and I knew it without looking.

"Not long at all," Tyrus said with a sardonic smile. Then he answered Senator von Pasus.

# 3

WHEN I'D LAST SEEN Senator von Pasus, he'd adopted the look of a dignified elder, perhaps in deliberate contrast to his daughter, Elantra, whom he wished to wed to Tyrus. Most Grandiloquy used false-youth, but sometimes they selectively adopted signs of aging, whether to give themselves a different look, or more likely, to deal with the Excess in their territories. Planet dwellers had no access to beauty bots, so they associated visible age with experience. So Pasus had not seemed too odd, with that gray hair, that short beard.

Now he appeared before us in holographic form, lacking those former ravages of age. His hair had become a stark coal black that seemed to devour the light, his eyes an icy blue, his now-unlined features even and seemingly cut with the precision of a beauty bot that aimed to lend him not handsomeness so much as grandeur.

He dipped to his knees with a perfunctory grace before rising just as swiftly. "Your Supreme Reverence."

I'd retreated so I wouldn't appear in the holographic image on Pasus's end.

"Senator," Tyrus said icily, "your alteration is most surprising."

"Your Supremacy inspired me," Pasus said. "I felt as though I would be truly meeting my new Emperor for the first time, so I should follow suit and present myself anew."

Yes. He was one of the many Grandiloquy who'd known Tyrus only as his assumed persona—the mad heir to the throne. Not the clever young man he actually was. Tyrus turned his head and offered me his hand.

So he wanted me in the transmission. Though I'd be inflammatory, he wished Pasus to see me.

I moved to Tyrus's side and appeared on Pasus's end.

"Your call is most unexpected," Tyrus said, taking my hand. A message. Very deliberate.

Pasus stared downward a moment, and I knew his cold gaze was fixed on the image of those linked hands.

"You must forgive me for abstaining from attendance at your Convocation speech, and your coronation before that. I was most distraught over the recent death of my daughter, as well Your Supremacy knows."

"Everything about that situation was most regrettable," Tyrus returned with the same remote courtesy, "including the circumstances that directly led to the tragedy."

Pasus had to know what Tyrus was pointing out: Elantra had killed Sidonia, and that was what led to me killing her. His jaw ticked, but then he smiled—or rather, bared his teeth like an angry animal. "I have just heard word of the unfortunate death of your brother-in-law."

Tyrus was granite-faced. "Have you."

"I offer my condolences. What a terrible tragedy that is. And your cousin, left without a husband . . ."

"As she will be for a very long time," Tyrus said.

Something in me grew cold, for I didn't like the way Pasus was smiling—as though he'd just spotted something he meant to have, and he would allow nothing to get in his way.

"You must be very uneasy. How could your security bots have permitted a toxin so close to Your Supreme Reverence? And the heliosphere—why, repair bots are not what they once were, it seems. So coincidental, two separate systems failing on the same day."

Tyrus's eyes narrowed a fraction. I realized it too: Pasus knew. He knew why Tyrus's scepter was not working.

"Then again, things happen." Pasus's smile was knowing. "Perhaps it was a one-off."

"Perhaps."

"But in the case it is not so temporary, Your Supreme Reverence is in a most awkward situation, are you not? You will require very powerful friends about you. And yet, your allies all appear to be new Senators, replacements for those killed along with Senator von Impyrean during your uncle's reign. Novices."

I could feel Tyrus's heart racing in his palm. His voice, though, came out perfectly controlled: "I am ever so grateful for your concern. I assure you, all is in hand."

"Hmm. Yes. Though if I were in your position, and forgive me for offering unsolicited advice, but I have known you since you were a young boy, dear Tyrus, so I feel compelled to suggest . . . I would look into restoring my favor with our Living Cosmos. And such favor cannot be won with the help of those you've gathered about you." His eyes moved to my image. I knew that for sure, because raw hatred blazed over his face, though he had the same perfect mastery of voice Tyrus did. "I would look to longtime friends of your family.

And the means by which you might win back what you've lost."

"I thank you for the advice, Senator. Do feel free to come and give me more in person."

Pasus just smiled, for he knew to come in person would be to fall into Tyrus's power. "I am always glad to offer it. And if Your Supremacy wishes more, do but come to my territory—and seek it again."

Tyrus smiled too. That was not going to happen.

But then after the transmission ended, he blew out his breath, pulled the scepter out of his waist sheath again, and gazed down at it with frustration.

"He knows something. That's what he was hinting about. And the gall . . . Salivar is freshly dead, and he's already angling for my cousin's hand."

"That can't happen," I said.

Pasus was threat enough as it was, being the most powerful member of the Helionic faction of the Senate, and one of the wealthiest Grandes in the Empire. If he wed Tyrus's heir, Devineé, then I wouldn't give Tyrus a week before he'd meet an untimely death.

"Of course it won't happen," Tyrus said, tightening his fist about the scepter.

My eyes sought his, saw the stormy cast of his features, and I knew in my heart that a disaster loomed on our horizon. He shoved the scepter back into its sheath, where it might as well remain, for all the good it was doing him.

"Tyrus."

He looked to me distractedly.

"Perhaps it's time."

"Time . . . for what?"

"Let me kill those who pose a threat to you." This. This was one thing I could do—one strength I could bring him that no one else could. I had no pity, and if they threatened him . . . I couldn't lose him as I had Sidonia. "I'll start with your cousin."

He strode over to me, took my cheeks in his hands. "Nemesis, no."

"But—"

"You are not my Diabolic. I am never going to ask you to be my Diabolic again. This is a setback. I will figure this out."

He said that, but he didn't know how. He did not.

And so I waited until Tyrus had to surrender to that need to sleep, the one I had so little of, the one he needed far more than I did.

Then I determined to go find the reasons for his weakness for myself. There was one man in this superstructure who had the answers. And he would give them to me.

# 4

THE PENUMBRA was a tiny vessel, a fixture of the Chrysanthemum, and intended to be a domain solely of the vicars who served the imperial family. It had been donated to the faith by a long-ago sovereign, the pious Empress Avarialle.

I had no right to board it, but a threatening look toward those servants at the entrance stopped them from reaching out, from interfering. So I barged right into the vessel of holy sanctuary and found myself surrounded by clear walls that gazed upon the bright stars of the Cosmos, and tangled canopies of plants climbing over every surface.

Through that corridor of starlight and nature I strode, until I came upon the great central garden, lovingly tended by hand, not service bot. Hedges were crafted to mimic the traditional shape of stars—like circles with pointed rays jutting out from them.

And in the center of it all, the massive crystalline statue that gazed down upon it all. A depiction of a man, his bare feet so large that his ankles were at the same height as my hips. My gaze wandered up the crystal expanse and lingered on those features. A broad nose, heavy-lidded eyes. Flattened hair like a bowl over the head.

A distinctly ordinary-looking man, for his towering size.

Yet this was the same depiction I'd always seen of the Most Ascendant Interdict, the chief vicar of the Helionic faith. He was rumored to be immortal and dwelled in the Transaturnine System at a wondrous starlight realm called the Sacred City.

Donia had recited the accounts to me when we were both little, at first with reverence. And then, as she grew slightly older, with a tentative hint of uncertainty.

"Is it very bad of me if . . . if I doubt whether he really exists?" she'd asked me fearfully several times.

Nothing Donia could do was bad. That had been my belief, so doubting whether there was an actual Interdict seemed like it had to be a fair and just thing to do.

After all, no man was immortal.

"I should have expected you would have no respect for this sanctuary," spoke a voice behind me.

Fustian nan Domitrian carried a jar of oil and a liquisilk rag past me, aiming for the statue.

"This is a holy space, and you are an abomination. From what I've heard, your disrespect has already been rebuked once today by our Divine Cosmos."

"In fact, Vicar," I said, watching him anoint those big toes with oil, "that's what brought me here."

"I do hope our young Emperor is well?"

I narrowed my eyes. "Quite," I said between my teeth. "In fact, he meant to speak to you. But I wished to see you first. Alone."

"And why would that be?" said Fustian, looking back at me contemptuously.

I smiled broadly. "Because Tyrus is often kind. I am not."

Fustian's hand stilled where he was anointing the toes. His gaze trailed past me, and I asked him, "Are you contemplating calling for help? Do you truly know anyone suicidal enough to protect you from me?" I shook my head. "No, no, Vicar. This is the time when I ask questions, and then I get answers. And if you will not talk at first, I will convince you in the myriad ways abominations are skilled at using."

The vicar was trembling. I could detect that, practically sense his terror, and there was a part of me deep down that exulted, gloried in it. I'd been fashioned for just this, and every predatory fiber of my being enjoyed causing sickening fear in this old man who'd made himself my foe.

He'd abandoned the statue and now was on his feet, his back pressed against it as though the unmoving crystalline Interdict could shelter him. "What happened was the judgment of the Living Cosmos. You may harm me if you wish, you monstrous thing, but it won't change anything."

"I don't think it was a coincidence that you were soon to be replaced as Vicar Primus," I said quietly, "and suddenly a Great Heliosphere's worth of people—including your replacement—end up scorched by a star. And I don't believe that's divine intervention."

He paled. "You believe I did that."

"I believe after I tear out every one of your fingernails and teeth, you will be able to tell me honestly."

With that, I feinted toward him, and he shrieked, cringed back.

"It wasn't me!" His hand flew up over his face. "The scepter. It was the scepter."

He did know. He knew.

My blood raced with the need to lash out, to hurt. I circled him, keeping my aggression in check, and watched his shaking hand lower as he realized he wasn't being physically tormented just yet.

"Explain it all to me. Now."

He drew and released several breaths, gathering his courage. "This is not for you to know—"

"But I will know," I roared at him, "whether now or after I've hurt you." Then I drew so close to him, he backed into the statue.

I decided to test my theory. "Pasus betrayed you, you know." It was a lie, but I meant to test him. "He told us you were the one to ask about the scepter. I know you are in communication."

His eyes flew open. "He dared to share my words?"

So. So Pasus had been alluding to something this man knew. I just nodded, never blinking.

His mouth dropped. Then, "I was only partially responsible. It wasn't me."

"Keep talking."

"Do not hurt me."

"Tell me all you know, and I most likely will see no need." I retreated a few centimeters, just to free him somewhat from the oppression of my physical presence.

His shaking hand reached back, touching the bare foot of the statue, as though it could lend him strength. "These are all ancient vessels. They fall into disrepair on their own and require constant mainte-nance. I sabotaged nothing. And . . . and if today there was a tragedy, it was the will of the divine Cosmos *and*"—he added that part quickly, eyes wide, for I'd stepped toward him again—"and because the Imperial Scepter requires more than a Domitrian's blood to key into that Emperor. It needs the consent of the faith."

"Your consent."

"Not just mine! Of the body of the faith. And . . . and . . ."

At that moment, the stars outside must have shifted in just the right way, or perhaps the angle of the Chrysanthemum to the six-star system adjusted with gravity. . . . For the light struck the crystal-line statue above us, and an eerie glow ignited from the top of that head, seeping down through the veins of crystal, striking out vibrant rainbows.

And Fustian nan Domitrian whirled about to see. The brilliant display seemed to ignite some fire of courage in his heart, and his face lit with pure joy. He dropped to his knees in reverence, and I knew then that he'd overcome his terror of me.

Yet as I, too, looked at the statue of the Interdict, a strangeness settled over me. My heart stilled, for there was something wondrous about how brilliantly it shone above me, like an apparition or a glimpse of another universe.

A moment later the light blinked away, the subtle angle of the stars having shifted once more, and the spell was broken. Fustian wore a beatific smile, his eyes aglow with a fanatic's blind belief.

"How interesting it is, Nemesis dan Impyrean," he said in a dreamy voice, "that so rare a moment—but a few occasions in a month—should happen while you were here. I think there is a portent in this. Perhaps the Living Cosmos is telling me I am at liberty to reveal this sacred mystery, even to the likes of you. Now I will do so: not out of fear, but out of duty."

*Whatever you must tell yourself, Vicar,* I thought darkly. "Go on."

My vision still was hazed by the light of the statue as Fustian straightened to his full height before me, smiling, transcendentally happy.

"I have been honored to carry a diode of fealty." He spread his palm

33

between us. "It was implanted in my hand by an aged vicar, who was given it by an elderly vicar before him. Upon every Emperor's ascendance, the ones with these diodes must speak the words of consent to the rule of the new Emperor. A majority of those chosen to bear this honor must do so."

I stared at his palm. "And how many of you are there?"

"I don't know. There may be hundreds, there may be thousands of us. . . . Who is to say? All of us will join our voices and agree to the ascendance of this current Emperor. But each one of our voices is a small droplet in a larger body of water. Will it spare me pain to demonstrate now?" Then Fustian pressed his hands together and spoke: "May infinite stars bestow their blessings upon our new Emperor."

I cast a gaze about, wondering if something more would happen. But the old man just looked at me, his eyes twinkling.

"And there you have the consent of *one* voice. But you need so many more. Far more. And no one can tell you how many, or who they are. The only means of securing support from these vicars lies in removing their grounds for objection." His gaze lingered on me, the "grounds for objection." "Now I ask you, Nemesis *dan* Impyrean, how many vicars do you think will approve of a union between an Emperor and a creature who does not even carry the divine spark of our Living Cosmos? An Emperor who, moreover, has openly spoken of his desire to propagate heresies. . . . How many voices will rise in consent?"

Few. None. I wished to strangle him, but there was no use in it now.

Fustian's smile widened. "If you love the young Emperor, you will urge him to see reason. To right his ways. And then you will walk away from him and let him rule in peace. Otherwise, this tragedy today is the first of a great many to come."

"Tyrus is clever. He can rule without that scepter."

"Tyrus is a Domitrian, and the only strength of a Domitrian lies in the command of the Imperial Scepter—and all the machines it will control in his name. Without it? He is no Emperor. He is merely a boy in love with the wrong girl."

# 5

IN THE TWO WEEKS since the coronation, Tyrus had been busy.

For so long he had passed by, shifting with the wind, hiding his true beliefs behind a show of madness or whatever facade he required to evade death, that he seemed to explode with frantic activity upon reaching this destination.

He had become the Emperor of this galaxy, and he couldn't move fast enough.

However late he'd been up the evening before, he was always awake by 0600. He no longer had two hours to exercise, so he threw himself into an hour of intense exertion, whenever he could snatch it. Then he attacked some other task over a hasty breakfast—listening to transmissions he'd received, sending off instructions to distant provinces, setting up meetings for the day. He read over reports from advisers as machines prepped and polished him for appearing in court, or recorded propaganda broadcasts to reassure the farthest domains of the Empire that their new Emperor was not, in fact, the madman of rumor.

Then, hours of wrangling with Grandiloquy, all vying for something from him, with the Luminar allies who'd aided him, all aiming to secure favors for their planet immediately, not content to wait. He fit in those social occasions undertaken less for pleasure than for practical reasons: events that meant to be entertaining, but were really more episodes of maneuvering relationships within his new court.

He partook of every narcotic offered rather than insulting those gifting them with refusals, and if necessary, he subtly extended his arm to a med bot to clear them from his system—without the giver's knowledge. His watchful eyes always fixed upon those he spoke to, silently gauging their sentiments, their knowledge, their loyalty, all while wearing a disarming smile as though he were but a foppish young Grande enjoying the decadence about him.

Favor seekers dogged him everywhere. Grandiloquy sent messages and invitations, hundreds each day, always seeking a meeting, a discussion, following up on promises they claimed his predecessor had made, or referring to debts Randevald had incurred on behalf of all Domitrians.

Soon, even Tyrus's single hour of exercise could not be done in peace. As exertion-averse as the Grandiloquy were, preferring to fashion muscles using bots rather than through actual physical use, a great flock of them suddenly took to adoring exertion. Steroids and amphetamines became the favored narcotics at court for these, and each Grande or Grandeé scrambled to create the best high-gravity exercise chamber for his or her ship. There was also a thriving trade in gravity reduction bands, rather defeating the purpose of these exertion chambers.

I was thankful Tyrus had given me the *Hera*, so I might avoid so much of the bewildering and chaotic activity, and yet it had effectively separated us at a time when we were on uncertain terms. The fleeting minutes we could snatch were devoid of the old familiarity and intimacy, almost as though we were strangers joined in a cause, and I could see from the frustration on his face that he was as much at a loss over it as I was. . . . But he had too much to occupy him to apply his mind to this scepter dilemma.

Now I ran with him through the wooded track spanning the lower deck of the *Valor Novus* during that scant hour of exercise in the morning. Usually he alternated between sprinting and jogging, but today the crowds in pursuit had driven him to favor sprinting. Even those Grandiloquy abusing steroids couldn't keep up with us, not yet, so it was a rare moment of privacy . . . though the pace left Tyrus too breathless to speak much.

Me? It was quite easy. So I told him everything Fustian had told me.

Tyrus digested it with no words, just ragged breaths, that damnable scepter now in a cross-sheath over his back. An Emperor's first year in power meant it accompanied him everywhere; even here. Even useless as it was.

His sprint lagged, and Senator von Locklaite appeared behind us, in sight. Tyrus clenched his jaw and launched forward at full speed once more. I matched him effortlessly, and we kept our distance from Locklaite.

"Fine," Tyrus said.

"Fine?"

"We . . . can't get the support . . . of the vicars. Forget it, then." He concentrated on breathing for a moment as we reached a high-gravity section of the track, then said, in a great rush, "The vicars become obsolete sooner than I could have hoped. I can control this Empire without . . . without the scepter."

"How will you do that?"

"Kings . . . in ages past . . . relied on goodwill . . . good judgment . . . alliances. I'll do that."

"What of service bots, Tyrus?"

He began to slow, needing a rest from this pace. An idea came to me, and I took his sweaty arm, dragged him with me off the path into the overhanging mass of trees, and there we settled against the rough bark of a large oak tree beneath the yawning expanse of the sky dome above us. Tyrus leaned his head against the tree to recover his breath. He was pushing himself too hard. In every possible sense.

Even with this new plan of his.

"The problem with . . . service bots," he said, his breathing growing steadier, and I detected distant footsteps scuffling past, people striving in vain to catch up to their young Emperor, "lies in the centralization, right? No scepter means two thousand ships are all two thousand separate systems. So . . . so we can't rely on service bots to find problems and triage them as one great mass of bots." He grinned at me. "So we have people do it."

"People?"

"Employees. We hire them. Excess who will work for the Empire. They can . . . they can survey each ship using their eyes. Inspect them. Once . . . no, twice a day. They report any problems, and that way, we just . . . we just fix the most urgent problems by assigning bots to them ourselves. Problem solved." He spread his hands

Problem far from solved. "That will require a great many employees."

"I know."

"The Grandiloquy will feel uneasy with so many Excess about."

"They will. Perhaps uneasy enough to pressure the vicars of their acquaintance to render more employees unnecessary."

I eyed him dubiously, thinking of that mass of security machines ringing the Chrysanthemum, and the security bots that should be buzzing over our heads right now. All should be protecting us, all were outside his control.

And then there were enemies like Pasus, lurking like vultures, never taking their eyes from him. They tolerated Tyrus at the moment, but if Pasus wed Devineé, he would most certainly kill the current Emperor to secure her throne.

Tyrus was young. His coronation speech must have seemed quixotic, full of goals unlikely to be realized. If he ever began to make true progress toward his goal of reinstituting the sciences, empowering the Excess, the Grandiloquy would panic. As long as there was another Domitrian, they could kill him.

Footsteps were rustling our way, and voices exclaimed, "Ah, here are the two lovebirds!"

"We quite lost Your Supremacy!"

"Such a pleasurable run!" said Grande Stallix. "Shall we take refreshments together?" He had water ready. "There are electrolytes and amphetamine within this bottle."

"This is water from the purest springs of the third moon of Sillaquarth," said another, with water in his hand as well.

"Not stopping yet," Tyrus said. Then he heaved himself away from the tree and picked back up into a run. I didn't follow this time. I stood there and watched him, then that mass pursuing him, falling to ten steps behind him. . . . They were all abusing narcotics or secretly wearing low-gravity bands, and Tyrus relied only on brute strength. He was but one person and there were so many of them, all vying to catch up to him, with varying advantages he lacked. Today they did not—but one day someone would.

And when that day came, all the will and drive and cleverness in the world would not give Tyrus the edge he needed to stride out of their reach once more.

Love was a selfish thing, and I knew that, because I craved him so fiercely, I could ignore my misgivings, my doubts, and even that ruthless voice of reason within me that knew the truth: *I* was the root of so many of his problems. How easily I could solve them by simply leaving. He would not keep me if I convinced him I felt nothing for him, if I set off into the unknown that was life outside this place.

But I couldn't. I couldn't bring myself to do it.

There was one thing I could do for him, the thing I could always do for him: I could murder his enemies for him.

So that was what I would do.

Impaired or no, Devineé was the greatest threat to Tyrus's life. Her mere existence provided an alternative for the throne, and though Tyrus could live with that, I could not.

Luckily, her life was one of predictable routine now that she had to be ushered through it by outside forces.

I could take advantage of that.

Easily.

In this precarious time, I could not be known as her murderer. The last accident I'd engineered for her hit the wrong target. This one— this one would not fail.

I stood on the rampart above the animal pens of the *Tigris*, where I'd been imprisoned for a month, and watched Devineé Domitrian being led by a tether attached to a service bot. Three times a day, she was walked around her ship in this manner to circulate her blood. Salivar used to be led about as well, before he perished. How much better if it had been her!

Today it would be.

My gaze slid about the chamber. These were the long-term pens, not like the cramped ones directly below the arena. I'd passed enough time in here to know exactly which creatures were confined, though the force fields were all set to full opacity at the moment. The animal fights had ended under Tyrus, but the fighting beasts remained, just as I had been, since only this place could contain a Diabolic.

My confinement here had also intimately acquainted me with the habits of the animal attendants. I'd timed this carefully, and now I watched the one on duty depart from the chamber to retrieve food for the dead Emperor's manticore, usually a small cow. That gave me five minutes.

More than enough time.

I thrust myself over the railing and landed amid the force fields. Each computer console controlled the power of six surrounding force fields. I needed to depower only one panel to free the animals in six pens. They'd been born and bred to kill. Devineé stood no chance.

I fastened my ears on the sound of Devineé's humming service bot, strode over to the nearest console in her path, and waited.

Then I hooked my heel in the web of wiring, and thrust my leg down to snap it.

The console blinked out.

The opaque fields about me faded away, revealing a pair of empty cells, a serpentine creature coiled in sleep. Then a promising one in the fourth—a horned bull with snake eyes that lifted its head to sniff the air.

A series of clicks from the fifth one as a hybrid of bear and reptile, befuddled by liberty, began to paw at the dropped force field. Movement out of the corner of my eye from the sixth.

I looked sharply toward it.

Nothing.

That gave me pause. I could sense something watching me. The humming of the service bot was nearing me now, so I backed away slowly, knowing something, *something* would set these predators astir, and it was best to be clear of them before that. . . .

Then my back collided with a broad chest, and I whipped about to see the largest man I'd ever beheld, glaring down at me with black eyes and a faint smile, and I knew him. I knew him.

Cygna's Diabolic, Anguish dan Domitrian.

"You didn't expect me, I see," he said.

Oh no, I had *not.*

My fist flew at his face. He caught it and shoved me back so hard, I hurtled to the ground. I rolled in the same movement to my feet, terror and a swell of malice propelling my muscles. The first instinct I always had, the first one, was to attack—and so I did.

But I was smaller. Weaker. I'd been made weaker still to pass as Sidonia. . . .

And the power of the fist that met my face jolted my skull, knocking me back. He charged as I caught my balance, and this time I dodged the fist. Then I vaulted toward him and delivered a cruel kick to his groin . . . that weakness of male Diabolics.

He grunted with the pain of my blow, but his great hands snagged my leg and I kicked and twisted to escape his grasp. His hands anchored about my head. I knew then that it was coming, I knew it, oh stars no. . . .

Anguish snapped my neck.

# 6

## "IS THAT ONE DEAD?"

The voice, familiar but not, swam through my head, and I roused slowly, certain I was dreaming, for I didn't feel real.

Hazard dan Domitrian leaned in above me.

For a moment I stared up at the face that couldn't be there looming above me. Cygna's Diabolic. Another face appeared in my sight. Anguish.

Then I remembered.

Then I noticed what was so wrong and why the world was off.

All I could feel was my face. My neck. . . . My neck!

Horror swamped me in a great sickening crash and I was suffocating, for I couldn't feel my own breathing and the Diabolics were above me and free and this was it, the end, my fatal mistake.

Oh. Oh no, I'd freed Anguish, so he'd freed Hazard. . . . And now I was as good as dead. Hazard stared down at me, and Anguish told him: "I severed below the fifth vertebrae."

"You did not paralyze her respiration?"

"Not yet."

Raw panic flickered through me, clawed at me, and there was nothing I could do as the world swam above me, and even the scream I fought to voice wasn't rising, and it was a nightmare come to life. How were they even here? How were they alive? How was this happening? The thought came to me. Cut through the storm of terror. *Tyrus spared them. He spared them. But he didn't tell me.*

I had just freed them.

I was dead. I was dead, I was dead—and Tyrus. Helios, Tyrus. . . . What would happen to Tyrus? The air was too thin. Anguish's heavy footfalls moved him out of my sight, and then I heard a voice in the distance. . . .

"Not another word after this," Tyrus said. "You have your instructions. Not one word more."

He knew how good their hearing was. He still underestimated it. And the silence was thick and terrible and how I wished I were already dead, for anything would be better than bearing helpless witness to what was to come.

"Go outside the force field," Anguish rasped, "and close it about us. Security bots won't be able to fire on us."

They didn't know Tyrus had none to command. Tyrus had no scepter.

Hazard's boots thumped away.

Then Anguish was above me. He reached down, gripped the back of my neck, and sat me up. He kept my neck steady in place, though it was already broken.

A futile voice of hope within me pointed it out—*it can be fixed if I am treated soon.* . . .

But oh, I had to survive and Tyrus had to survive. I strained my eyes to the side, searching his face desperately for some hint of his plan. His dark features were set with a cold, lethal resolve. I wish I'd been conscious to hear whatever he'd said to Hazard.

Now that I could see, I ascertained that we were within an animal pen. And then Hazard flipped up the force field to surround us, locking the two of us in the cell while he remained outside it.

A humming mounted on the air, and then, above us, a platform slid into view.

And standing alone on top of it was Tyrus.

Just Tyrus.

Sickness churned through me. Sickness and dread. He was too close. Eight meters above us at most.

"Your Supreme Reverence." Anguish's voice flared out.

"Hello, Anguish." Tyrus entered my line of sight. With his light blue eyes and hair, his lashes pale, his skin perfect for the coronation, he appeared almost a creature of ice. No emotion touched his face or colored his tone as he said, "She is still alive. You spared my cousin as well."

"We had no use for her. We drove your pets back to their pens. This one is another matter."

*Devineé is still alive*, I thought with despair. I should have risked the opprobrium of murdering her outright.

"They told me you were holding Nemesis. What is it you want?" He spoke with a preternatural calm, and folded his arms so he might exhibit the Imperial Scepter, loosely grasped in his hand.

Although Hazard gave a growl at the mere sight, Anguish remained calculating, calm. He tilted his head, assessing the foe above him. "You remind me that you spared us as though you expect gratitude. Surely you know better, Your Supremacy."

"Tell us of our master!" Hazard roared.

He was not so calm as Anguish. He jerked back and forth in restless steps, as though desperate to rip something apart. The one stroke of good fortune for me was the fact that Anguish was in here with me, not out there with Tyrus. . . .

*Leave here, Tyrus. Please!*

"You know exactly what happened to my grandmother," Tyrus said, eyes on Anguish.

"You killed her!" rasped Hazard. "And we will tear you limb from limb—"

"Quiet," said Anguish.

Hazard fell silent.

Anguish gathered me closer to him, keeping my neck carefully steady as he angled me into Tyrus's sight. The indignity of this! Why hadn't he simply killed me?

"Strange," noted Anguish, "how no security bots are mobilized."

"I have no wish to escalate this situation," Tyrus said calmly, in such a fine show of confidence, I began to think there had to be a reason. . . . Or was he simply so skilled at faking it?

"Really." Tyrus spread his arms. "You don't think the *Emperor* stands here alone above you, defenseless, do you, Anguish? Be realistic. Now tell me what you want."

"Your blood." Hazard's voice shook. "Your pain. Your life."

"Surely you understand," drawled Tyrus without looking at him, "my reluctance to offer that. There must be something else."

Anguish shifted his gaze to me, studying me with an intent, predatory interest, and with a jolt I knew—he was trying to gauge from my face the emotions he could not read from Tyrus's.

"Perhaps," he said, lips breaking into an eerie smile, "I simply want you to watch her die."

Above us, Tyrus's hands flew forward, seizing the railing. It was his only reaction—but enough of one. Enough of one to betray that Anguish had hit upon a point of vulnerability, and no Diabolic could miss that.

Anguish stroked his finger over my cheek. "A pity," he said, "that she has no sensation below the neck. What pain I could inflict before she dies. . . ."

I glared at Anguish, wishing my rage could lacerate him, for I was a *Diabolic*. Just as he was. I could bear pain just as he could. Yet he meant these words for Tyrus, for the human and unwisely-in-love Tyrus, and my mind, attentive to all tiny details that relayed distress, noticed Tyrus's knuckles white where his hands still gripped the railing. He attempted to show nothing and in doing so, revealed everything.

And he must have realized it, because Tyrus suddenly changed tack: "Look at her, Anguish. Just look into her face. She is so like Enmity. She could be her twin."

"She killed Enmity."

"No," Tyrus said, face lighting up with hope at this single route of appeal.

*Don't tell him this! DON'T!*

"No, Anguish," Tyrus said, "*I* killed Enmity. As I killed your master. Your quarrel is entirely with me."

My view jolted, as though shock had loosened Anguish's grip on me. I could have torn Tyrus apart for telling him this, for giving him this! And yet Anguish looked at me swiftly, and I could see he was less willing to kill me now.

A bitter trade-off for increasing his incentive to murder Tyrus.

And Hazard's.

I'd forgotten him until he roared out, and even Anguish's shout couldn't stop him. A scuffle, and then he flashed into the corner of my vision as he leaped up onto a panel and propelled himself from there. Tyrus's eyes flew wide, and he jerked back as Hazard careened toward him. . . .

A frantic swing of his scepter crashed into Hazard's face. Hazard's own momentum turned his enemy as he hurtled, spinning, back to the floor. I didn't see his impact but heard it, the ugly *thunk* . . . his skull. The silence that followed, and a low sound in Anguish's throat . . . a cry aborted.

Tyrus gasped raggedly for breath.

Then Anguish pressed us against the side of the force field. "Hazard. HAZARD!" I saw it now—Hazard's leg. No movement.

I cast my gaze up frantically, and Tyrus's face seemed to electrify with an idea.

*Don't*, I screamed inwardly at him.

But he hurled himself over the railing and hit the ground in a roll. He was on Hazard in a moment, and Anguish bellowed at him. If Hazard stirred, Tyrus was dead. He was *dead*.

Yet Tyrus's face was wild as he dragged the unconscious Hazard into our sight, a blade at his throat, pressed so hard blood welled at its bite. "Here's the incentive now, Anguish," he rasped at him. "One for one. Let her go, I let him go. One wrong move and I open his throat, I swear."

"Why should that concern me?" rumbled Anguish's voice. His hand warningly brushed my neck. "Your Supremacy doesn't realize just how much blood loss a Diabolic can endure. And besides that—why would that ever prove an equal trade?"

"He's all you have left," Tyrus said quietly. "You have passed decades side by side. I know you care for him. I've seen it. Let her go, he lives. You live. We are all satisfied."

"You believe I love him, do you?" said Anguish in an odd tone. "As I

49

did my master? As you love this one?" A strange, ominous note in his voice. "As she loves you . . . ?"

Silence. Then, "I do."

"Prove it. Walk in here."

Tyrus didn't say anything.

"Prove yourself by coming in here and retrieving her, Your Supremacy."

*No,* I thought furiously.

Tyrus swallowed. "You'll kill me," he said hoarsely.

*He will. HE WILL.*

Anguish's voice dripped with the taunt of his words: "You believe we Diabolics love. Then show me. If I love Hazard—if I am capable of that much—then I will have reason to spare you and you will have gambled correctly." His grip tightened. "If you are truly certain she loves you—then you must be certain I can love him."

*Don't,* I thought. *Tyrus, do not do it. Back off. Regroup. Think of another plan. . . .*

Tyrus withdrew from my sight. His jagged breaths reached my ears, and I hoped he was figuring something out, I hoped he was leaving, anything, anything but do this. . . .

Then the force field dropped about us.

Anguish would kill us both.

# 7

HORROR THUNDERED inside my mind as Tyrus swept into my view, hands up, edging toward me.

He'd lost his mind. He'd committed suicide.

"I am proving it, am I not?" Tyrus said softly.

"Come and take her," Anguish said. "But first drop the weapon you are hiding."

"W-what?"

A rich, cynical laugh. "Come now. You have observed us? I have observed you. That is all we do. Now drop it."

A rustling of clothing, then a clatter.

"All of them," said Anguish. "You have more."

"That is all of them."

"*All of them*," Anguish said. "Lie to me again and I will kill you both."

A low sound in Tyrus's throat. Then . . .

Another clatter. Another.

Abruptly, Anguish wasn't supporting my weight anymore. My body flopped to the side.

"Then take her." I saw Anguish's boots step back from me. And Tyrus . . .

Edged toward me closer, closer—eyes on Anguish. Then I saw it ripple over his face, the moment Tyrus decided trust was not enough, that he couldn't take the risk of being wrong. "Now!" Tyrus shouted.

He threw himself over me just as Anguish shot toward me in response to betrayal, but Anguish's legs sank beneath him as a low tone filled the air about us, and then Tyrus drove his boot into the Diabolic's face, knocking him back. He bundled me up into his arms, lurched to his feet, and jolted us out of his reach.

"Raise it!" cried Tyrus, and the force field was snapping back up. . . .

Then confused faces washed into my sight as Tyrus turned, as he addressed his people: "Grab Hazard, get him back in a force field. Send a med bot *after*. Do it!"

And then Tyrus dropped down to the ground, still grasping me, and bodies were surging past us, people scrambling to follow the instructions. . . . We were safe, we were safe, and I was dizzy with the air I couldn't feel myself breathing as Tyrus pressed his lips to my hair.

"Hypocrite."

Anguish's voice was low, a taunt. He'd pulled himself to his feet and leaned his weight on the force field.

"You don't believe. You never believed."

Tyrus didn't answer him. Only now that he'd escaped did he begin to tremble, and then I knew he'd been afraid all along.


Pain awoke me. It was the scream of all the nerves below my neck registering sensation again, and my eyes snapped open, took in a bleary glimpse of Tyrus pacing at my bedside, before the dark swallowed me once more.

The next time my eyes opened, and my vision focused, it was to his hand on mine, his mouth wide open where he'd fallen asleep with his head against the bed. For a moment, I just looked at him, all the recollections of what had come to pass filtering over me. I wasn't sure how much time had passed, but I could envision Grandiloquy clamoring at the door, transmissions mounting in number, so many vying for the Emperor's time.

I must have completely disrupted his routine. I lifted my arm, and though it sent a slight twinge up my shoulder, it pleased me to know I could do so. My fingers hovered over his skin, so close I could just feel the warmth radiating from it. Then, the slightest touch to his pale, angular brow.

It startled him awake.

"Nemesis," he exclaimed, breathless. "Are you— Should I get—"

The scepter must've been in his lap, because I caught a glimpse of it clattering to the floor, and he didn't seem to notice as he leaned over me.

"Tyrus." My voice was hoarse. My mouth felt bone dry. "How . . . how long?"

"Three days. You had to be unconscious and totally still to re-fuse your spinal cord." He looked me over, worry shadowing his face. "The Doctors nan Domitrian say you should recover."

I closed my eyes, processing it. Licked my dried lips as my sluggish mind wrapped about what had transpired.

He'd spared the Diabolics. He hadn't told me he'd spared them. Then he'd very recklessly risked himself at their hands.

"Tyrus," I told him hazily, "I just remembered how angry I am with you."

"You are very calm in this anger."

"I am building up to it. I am too weary to illustrate it properly right now. You should not have risked yourself. You shouldn't have done that. It was foolish."

His lips crooked. "And I would not have done so had you not gone to kill my cousin. Or rather, to contrive another accident like Salivar's."

"An accident that would have succeeded had there not been surprise Diabolics within the pens!"

"Yes. About that . . ." Tyrus's smile faded. He rubbed his hand over his forehead. "It's called a 'neural suppressor.'"

"What?"

"The device attached to Anguish's spine. To Hazard's as well. I used it to cripple Anguish. I might've used it sooner, but I had never seen one in action and I wasn't sure how quickly it would work." He regarded me a moment. "I assume you were about to ask about it? The suppressor has a sonic activator, meaning all one needs is the right tone playing in the air and a Diabolic's muscular impulses slow, rendering their strength much more manageable."

"Did you . . . Where did you get it?"

"I didn't put it in Anguish. One of the Domitrian employees found it in the manticore's leavings. Just the tiniest device. I had someone look into it. It was in Enmity's body, attached to her spine. And it had been placed there early in her life. I tried bribing any former corral masters I could contact for an explanation of the device, but it wasn't until the evening of my coronation that they grew eager to supply an explanation to their new Emperor. Apparently, it's a trade secret. They used suppressors to protect themselves from their own Diabolics. That device had been attached before birth. It couldn't have been removed."

I remembered so little of those fearful, early years of my life. The corral masters had seemed imposing and enormous as a child, but I was certain they'd be small, easily breakable men to me now. I couldn't even recall how they'd protected themselves from me.

Tyrus scraped his fingers through his hair. He wasn't looking at me for some reason. "I understand why they kept it a secret. Anyone could have used it to overcome a Diabolic bodyguard. There goes the value of Diabolics as bodyguards."

Understanding clicked into place. "That's why you spared Anguish and Hazard's lives. You had a means of neutralizing them. You also didn't tell me." I watched him closely. "You kept it all from me."

He didn't speak.

But I figured it out. Telling me of their survival meant I would learn of the suppressors.

All Diabolics had these suppressors.

Including me.

"Why did you hide this from me?"

He let out a slow breath. "Because I considered the possibility I would need to use it. Use . . . yours."

"Ah."

"Had you known it was there, and had you meant to kill me—"

"No suppressor would have stopped me, unless it remained your surprise advantage," I said. "That's true."

"I wasn't sure if you'd take my hand at the coronation, or break my neck. I knew you could be biding your time, or you could doubt me still. . . ."

"I see."

"I know why you believed my grandmother," he said. He met my eyes now, his pale lashes fringing gray blue. "I once lied to you about those electrodes. Then I swore to you I wouldn't do such a thing again. I meant it then, but I've made a liar of myself once more."

"Yes," I ground out. "You have." Once again, he'd shown he hadn't trusted me.

Then again, I had gone behind his back to strike at his cousin twice now. I hadn't merited trust.

And I'd believed his grandmother's lie.

Tyrus surged to his feet and paced away as I carefully trusted my strength, pushing myself upright. I gazed at his back, my mind returning to the horror of knowing he'd let the force field down.

I'd feared he was reckless. Insane. Suicidally stupid. But he'd been underhanded, and he was even underhanded with me. And not without reason. I had posed a genuine threat to him. The part of me that wished to be his partner seared with the knowledge he hadn't trusted me, and yet the part of me that scorched with love for him knew this was the instinct that would preserve him.

"Tyrus," I finally said, my thoughts growing clear. "It vexes me. I'm offended you clearly don't trust me. I resent knowing you are underhanded and a liar with me at times and I'm also . . . I fully understand why you do it. I believed Cygna's fabrication. I believed her—and not you. I was *foolish*. So . . . so what am I to say? I'm glad you keep yourself alive and safe. Even if it's against me. I've warranted your mistrust."

He let out a groan. "Ah, but everything you believed, what you did . . . I know why, Nemesis! I have done it yet again—offered you excellent grounds to doubt my every word. I can't say anything to excuse it. I trust you more than anyone else in this galaxy, and yet even with you, I do this. All I can say—and I know how little it may be worth—but all I can say is I would never have hurt her if for no other reason than because you loved her, Nemesis. You loved her, and however inconvenient she may have been to me, I would never have stolen her from you."

"That's where we differ," I said quietly. "Because I would not hesitate to kill someone you loved." I looked at him. "Or a member of your family too disabled to fight back—who poses a threat to you with her mere existence."

"I've asked something difficult of you," he said.

"Yes. You have. You want me to just turn my back to a threat. Tyrus, I'm a Diabolic. This is what I am. Your grandmother knew it. I believed you were capable of engineering her destruction because it's exactly what I would do—in your position. Don't lament being manipulative or underhanded. You are still fundamentally better than I am."

Tyrus's lips quirked. "Do you recall the first time I saw you? Truly saw you? It was the day you jumped into an arena to stop a beast from tearing apart a helpless Exalted. How many of us sat there in the crowd, disgusted and repulsed by what we were about to see, yet did nothing to stop it? I was the Successor Primus and I did not utter a word or lift a finger to stop something wrong, and you did. You acted. It's the rarest quality there is, to actually move to stop something wrong and immoral. I've never had that. You are the better of us."

"That's ridiculous. You care for an ideal. I care for no such thing."

"Many care for high ideals, Nemesis. I pursue lofty goals only now after years of turning my eyes from evils just to stay alive. I've told myself I would become Emperor if I but survived long enough, and none of my inaction would matter. I'd one day reach the throne and vindicate myself with my doings. . . . Yet I was paralyzed and I didn't realize it. I think about things over and over. I revisit plans a hundred times. It wasn't until I knew you that I saw what I had neglected to do in all this planning and biding of time. . . . I hadn't *acted* and it was past time. So here we are."

I decided to test my weight, and he came to my side to take my elbow as I balanced there by the bed. Words seemed to tangle in my throat, and it was difficult to look at him, for it felt so strange to be . . . appreciated for this.

But I did understand one thing now. I knew what lay behind his frantic flood of tasks every hour of every day since his coronation, and that relentless drive to pursue his goals. He'd always meant to vindicate his very survival to this point by what he did once in power, and a tenderness swelled in my heart because he shouldn't feel that need merely for staying alive. Sidonia would have known what to say here.

But all I could manage was, "Stop lying to me, and I will stop giving you reason to lie."

"Deal," said Tyrus with a smile.

It was then that my gaze settled on the window. I jerked with surprise to see we were in hyperspace. "Where are we going?"

Tyrus looked at the void, a shadow falling over his face. "While you were unconscious, Pasus moved to circumvent me and petition the Senate directly for Devineé's hand. So I tried to stall that—by offering to negotiate the match between them myself. We are meeting him on Lumina." At the stunned shock on my face, he added, "It's as good a pretense as any to go there and fulfill my end of the bargain with the Luminars, anyway. I owe them technology and I promised them independence, and this is a chance to come through if I play it correctly."

I grabbed his tunic, bunched up some of the fabric in my hand. "You can't. Tyrus, you can't agree to this or let this happen. He will wed her and then he will most certainly find a way to kill you."

"I know," he said. His larger hand covered my tense fist. "He honestly believes me so young and untried, I do not see his clear aims. I must seem to bend for now or I will be made to do so."

I released him. "I know this was another reason you didn't tell me you'd spared Anguish and Hazard. You knew I'd want them dead because they're a threat to you. Pasus is a threat to us both. You can't possibly expect me to stand by and let him place a noose about your neck."

"I do expect you to stand by," Tyrus said, a hard edge creeping into his voice, "because I will handle this, Nemesis. You wish me to stop lying, and I wish you to stop giving me reason to lie. Don't act unilaterally on this."

"I lost Sidonia. If I let you die too . . ."

He gathered me into his arms. "My love, I am extraordinarily difficult to kill. I have no intention of letting this happen. I mean to stall him. And . . . and there is a way I can ensure my cousin never poses a threat to us."

"Short of killing her, I don't see it."

"It is short of killing her. But just barely."

# 8

TYRUS KNEW our ship couldn't go alone to Pasus's space, so he'd mobilized all the Domitrian ships but one to accompany us. The Grandiloquy followed him, as they always did. Tyrus knew not to outright insult them by ordering them away from him for the trip. Instead, he'd stocked and staffed all the other starships, except the *Tigris*, so Grandiloquy vying to accompany him hedged their bets and sought places on all but the *Tigris*, hoping to end up with the Emperor. Then Tyrus moved me to the *Tigris*. Because of its skeleton crew, none had gambled on our presence. That was how he'd secured us an interlude alone in hyperspace. We were alone but for Devineé, who was not going to disturb us. As I recovered from the spinal fracture, Tyrus did something quite rare—he slept most of the first day away to recover after the first weeks in charge of a galaxy.

Then it was just the two of us.

Free of the eyes at the Chrysanthemum, there was no need for formality. Tyrus had given me the finest guest quarters on the *Tigris* and taken a chamber just down the hall from mine. It spared me the curious mixture of terror and anticipation I felt when I considered the prospect of sleeping in the same bed together.

The next time I awoke, Servitors soundlessly came forward, holding an array of clothes for the day. I picked quite at random, then found Tyrus, already in the room overlooking the salt baths, service bots prepping the six-egg omelet he always ate for breakfast.

In his hand, a glowing phial of a narcotic.

"You're starting early," I noted. Perhaps he was more stressed than I realized.

Tyrus's brows jumped, and it seemed to take him a moment to understand what I referred to. "What, this? Oh, no. This isn't for pleasure."

"Of course."

He smiled. "I'm serious." He accessed the ship's database, and a projection bloomed to life in the center of the table. It was a schedule. Narcotics of varying sorts. Planned for the next three months like an exercise routine, complete with dosages. Today's was obviously a psychedelic.

"It's called mithridatism," he explained. "Ancient Emperors on Earth used to expose themselves to small amounts of poison daily to gain an immunity to them. Essentially, I try to do this to gain some resistance to intoxication—what you come by naturally."

"Recreational intoxicants are not poisons."

"That could be debated," he noted wryly. "At the very least, an assassin's blade could never threaten me so much as a foggy head might around my grandmother. Since I am not blessed with a Diabolic's metabolism, this is how I prepare my chemical receptors. When I use a narcotic socially, I've already practiced in private at a much higher dose, so I can keep a clear head, and merely pretend to feel what I don't."

I glanced down at his schedule for today. "Are you hallucinating as we speak?"

"Not much . . . apart from your antlers," he noted. "I am certain those aren't usually there."

"They aren't," I agreed gravely, reaching up to feel my scalp.

"And banana fingers," he noted, staring at my hands in an abstracted way.

On a strange whim, I wiggled them in his face. Tyrus leaned forward and playfully nipped at them. Yet not so hard that he broke skin. He was quite in control.

"Do I look strange?" I wondered, for I could never experience what he was feeling.

"Draw a bit closer. I'll tell you."

So I did, and his arms swept about me. There was a sweet liquid ripple inside me as I settled against the warmth of his body. His thumb traced the line of my jaw, down to the tender skin of my neck, his soft breath skimming the shell of my ear.

"You look as you always do. Beautiful."

Without thought, my fingers slid to the underside of his chin, and I pressed my lips to his. It was tentative, soft, testing the ground where I hadn't ventured since the coronation. His arms slid about me, gently, almost reverently, and then he drew me closer and deepened the kiss, until what had seemed almost frightening felt so natural, felt so right.

"Two weeks," I murmured against his mouth. "Just us."

His lips curved. "Just us."

I kissed him again.

From without, the *Tigris* took the shape of an arched claw, yet within, the labyrinth of decks yielded an endless series of surprises.

Our favorite level held an artificial forest teeming with plant and animal life. Toward the end of our journey, Tyrus suggested a jaunt ancient Earth humans might have taken. No machines. We swam in a river as the birds engineered with the sweetest voices sang overhead. Afterward, we dried off by a real fire.

At least, that was the intention. Tyrus had read of lighting a fire with the use of sticks alone. He began quite gamely, and then after several frustrating minutes and a great number of splinters, I began to feel true amusement.

"You are bad at this," I marveled.

His lips crooked. "Thank you."

"Truly bad."

"You are so supportive of me."

"I am merely surprised. You are bad at something."

He slumped back, befuddled. "The most primitive human beings could master this art. I live in space, surrounded by unimaginably advanced technology—and I cannot light a fire. Or can I?" Then he disappeared. Minutes later, he returned with a lighter—and flicked it on. He cast me a forbidding look as he cheated, as though daring me to say anything.

A rare impulse came over me, and I heard myself laugh. Flames sparked against the pale gaze fixed on me with wonder and amazement. "You laughed," he marveled.

"I did not." My cheeks flushed, but I found myself smiling nevertheless like some silly, foolish young girl.

"I heard it. I know what I heard." His grin was crafty. "I will make it happen again."

"Try to start another fire and I'm sure it will."

Tyrus pulled me to him, his lips hot and intent, parting mine. His hand cupped the back of my neck. The stroke of his thumb at my nape sent delightful chills skittering down my spine.

His hand slid downward, and his eyes met mine before his touch traced up the expanse of my leg. He searched my face, and I realized he was gauging my response. Wanting to force him out of his head, I shoved him onto his back. Tyrus gave a startled sound, but his lips blazed into a grin as I tasted the skin of his throat. . . . And then his legs were tangled with mine, rolling us over again, his face flickering in the warm glow of the firelight.

"I love you," he told me simply.

I pressed my hand over the hot skin beneath his tunic, and he closed his eyes as I stroked the indentations of his abdomen. His larger hand captured mine, and our lips met, his kiss insistent, searing me to the core. . . .

The vessel began to jostle about us, harder and harder.

Tyrus pulled back, dread on his face. He looked to be cursing inwardly, as I was.

Then the stars began to reappear through the sky dome overhead, and I knew we had just dropped out of hyperspace. Regret sank through me. Our eyes met. I ran my fingers through his coppery hair as the heaviness of our task settled back over us.

We both moved to the window without agreeing to do so. Then out we gazed at that bright point against the dark of space that grew larger as we neared it—the patch of malignant space just outside Lumina's star system.

The brilliant white-and-purple death zone was like a gash through the void, eerily beautiful. I wondered how many had perished on the vessel that had ruptured entering hyperspace, leaving this tombstone behind.

"It's grown since we last saw it," I remarked, puzzled by that. It grew faster than I would have expected. "What feeds the growth?"

"It doesn't need fuel to expand, it just does it." He gave a vague wave of his hand, staring transfixed at the brightness. He leaned against the window, his face suddenly remote. "The first time I ever saw malignant space, I was living on a planet."

"I didn't know you'd lived on a planet."

"Almost ten months," he said distantly. "I wasn't suited for it. The gravity was so heavy. The humidity seemed to strangle me. I was allergic to everything, and constantly sunburned. Bloodsucking insects loved me far too much, and . . . and it was probably the happiest year of my life." He admitted that softly as though it were something shameful. "All it took was one accident at the edge of the star system to wipe it all away."

"A ship ruptured. And then . . ." I nodded toward the sight in front of us, figuring it out.

"It's frightening and beautiful to see from here—but it's indescribable from a planet. The atmosphere shifts what light filters through or amplifies it. At the beginning it was a small slash, and then in mere weeks, it grew so large. You could see it in the day, but at night, it filled the sky. These clouds of orange and scarlet and gold . . . I wasn't on the planet by the time it was gone. Some evacuated early, but so many were debating or wrangling over what to do. They thought they'd find a way to fix it. They delayed. And I am very sure many were in denial until it was too late to escape, and that malignancy had filled their skies. Can you imagine the horror of that?"

I gazed at the whip of light, knowing we did so at a safe distance, knowing we could leave. I tried to imagine seeing it from under a planet's sky, but my mind couldn't wrap around the idea.

"Was it dreadful?" As soon as I said it, I regretted it. Of course it was a dreadful thing, dwelling somewhere, and then knowing it had been wiped away.

"It was important," Tyrus said. "Up to that point, I would have ripped off my very skin if I could have disowned my family. My mother was dead, and I could never escape who I was. But that planet showed me what it really meant to be a Domitrian: I wasn't ever going to be a victim of circumstance. I was going to shape the circumstances, if I just survived long enough to do so. One day, I'd have it in my power to do what that entire planet of Excess could not, and I would fix that sky."

He drew and released a breath, the light of malignant space harsh on his features. In that moment, I felt as though I saw the nineteen-year-old boy slip away, and in his place, the Emperor turned from the window and said, "Now here we are. Let's get started."

# 9

**THERE WERE TWO** branches of the Domitrian family, and both sides had been virtually decimated by Cygna Domitrian during her quest to secure the throne for her favored child.

The six-star sigil belonged to the royal Domitrians. They all descended from the Empress Acindra von Domitrian. The other side was Cygna's branch of the family, the nonroyal Domitrians, with the black hole sigil. They descended from Acindra's uncle, the Emperor Amon von Domitrian.

During his reign, Amon grew frustrated by his Senate and devised a most cunning scheme to control them: he slipped all the Senators an obscure poison called Vigilant's Bane. Only he held the counteragent, one that had to be taken to keep the poison's death spiral at bay. The Senators spent years voting and acting as he wished to keep earning their counteragent.

Then came Amon's fatal misfortune.

A freak accident with a shipment, and the counteragent dried up. The Senators began dying one after another. Amon tried to flee, but he didn't escape. He was torn from power, and his entire line of descendants was expelled from the succession.

Now here was Tyrus, descendant of both the black hole and six-star Domitrians, contemplating the very toxin that had been Amon's downfall.

"It's called Vigilant's Bane. I wasn't supposed to know my grandmother even had this, but I watched her too closely to miss it," he noted, his tone dispassionate, though I knew there had to be distress raging beneath that calm surface. He despised the very idea of killing his own family as his grandmother had. "The counteragent is easier to come by. If Pasus doesn't know he needs it, he'll never obtain it in time if we decide . . . if we decide it's time for Devineé to perish. Until then, I can keep getting her the counteragent as long as she's close, as long as he's cooperative. Then, if Pasus turns, if he seeks to rebel in her name and usurp me . . ." He didn't need to say more.

He would let Devineé die.

"It's a fine compromise, Tyrus," I assured him, closing my hand around his—and around the poison as well. "It's not murder."

"Yes, it is," he said, looking at me.

"No, it isn't. You are sparing her to the extent that you possibly can. It will be up to Pasus, and only if he turns on you will she pay a price."

"He will turn on me, Nemesis. You know he will. Think: he has informed me that he is willing to put aside a vendetta against you just to be the husband of the Successor Primus. What does that tell you?"

"That he is a liar willing to wait for revenge?"

"Or that his ambition burns so brightly, he can forgive where otherwise he would not. And that sort of ambition will not be slaked by the second most powerful position in this Empire."

"I know she's family," I said to him, "but it's just one life."

"One life. And tomorrow, one more life. And one more, and so many single lives . . . At what point will it be too many lives?"

"If I were to guess, I'd say it's the day you kill without wondering that." Then I took the poison from his hand and waited while Tyrus ordered his cousin to be brought to us.

I mixed it right in with a glass of wine, and sip by sip, I watched it disappear into Devineé Domitrian, knowing this would eventually be the cause of her death.

Of our salvation.

Her fate would be ours, and I would never feel remorse or regret to know we'd taken her life in hand. As for Tyrus's conscience . . . Perhaps it would pain him, but if it desensitized him in the slightest so he could more readily strike a lethal blow to his next enemy, all the better.

There was no communication between ships in hyperspace, and close to malignant space, communications failed as well. We were encased in silence until we were far enough from that ribbon of terrible light, and then transmissions bombarded us in a great blast.

Dozens, then hundreds of them . . . all from various personages who were on the *Hera*, or Senator von Aton's *Atlas*, or Tyrus's own ship, the *Alexandria*, all ships that had dropped out of hyperspace before us. Then a fresh onslaught when the other ships cleared malignant space.

Mostly, the inane messages were ones of greeting, hoping the Emperor had a good journey through space. Tyrus had a team of Excess employees sorting through them to find the messages of substance. A few status reports from the Chrysanthemum, a few reports of happenings in the Senate.

The vessels from the Chrysanthemum joined together in a smaller version of the Chrysanthemum, and then Tyrus and I were garbed and prepared for a public appearance by Shaezar nan Domitrian. The *Tigris* landed within a short distance of Central Square.

Then, the crowds.

The last time I came to this planet, the numbers of people shocked me. Space dwellers tended to have one or two children at most, and vast areas to rove without such dense humanity packing the walls. Our last visit to Lumina, I had been stunned by the size of the crowd. This time the numbers overwhelmed me.

Tyrus was Emperor now, not Successor Primus.

The dizzying array of faces, so much more varied than on the Chrysanthemum, rendered me mute and almost disoriented. They were all ages, not like the Grandiloquy, who kept the young out of sight unless they used a bot to make them suitably aged so as not to stick out. The Grandiloquy also tended not to age unless due to an eccentricity or strategic choice, but so many of these Excess were *old*.

My friend Neveni Sagnau met Tyrus in front of the onlookers. She had been acting as Lumina's Viceroy on an order of the last Emperor's, so she ceremonially surrendered the office to her elected successor. He then introduced Tyrus to the Excess, and the thundering clamor of shouts and applause—even some boos—seemed to vibrate my very bones.

Tyrus mounted the podium before this great square, shielded by an invisible barrier, and offered for the Luminars a variation of his Convocation speech. I half listened, too busy surveying for threats. I saw it the moment a gap appeared in the masses because it was so odd, and then out of their midst (ringed in a protective force field that had driven the crowd apart), Senator von Pasus emerged. He was trailed by a retinue of servants, employees, and Servitors and utterly heedless of the blistering glares from the Excess of the planet he owned.

I'd already been tense. Now my every muscle was a knot.

Tyrus saw him too. Not a flicker of reaction on his face. Nor did he hesitate at the next part of his speech: "As a gesture of my affection for this fair province, I would like to gift the museums of Lumina with some imperial artifacts. . . ."

My gaze shot to Pasus's face to see his reaction to these "gifts."

For Tyrus wasn't giving artifacts. And everyone knew it.

A floating container holding pieces of technology, blueprints, schematics, disassembled machines was being floated out of the *Tigris* and given to the Luminars. Tyrus was giving them technology and scientific knowledge, whatever he could find. It was a blasphemy that would offend a good Helionic.

An act like this had destroyed Senator von Impyrean.

And Tyrus did it casually, so offhandedly he gave all a cue about just how to treat this offering.

All took the cue—but for Pasus.

He was gazing narrowly up at Tyrus, an incredulous smile at his lips as though he couldn't quite fathom what Tyrus was trying to pull off. After all, Lumina was within his territory, and he was a Helionic. He could simply take that technology away.

I fought a smile of my own, for I knew what came next.

"In addition," Tyrus went on, "I would like to leave with you a number of my Grandilóquy friends for an extended visit to this fair planet. I know you will all enjoy each other's company and encourage relations between Luminars and Grandiloquy."

Pasus's smile froze on his lips.

His shocked eyes skipped over the faces of those Grandes and Grandeés being escorted forward, with all honors and ceremonies, like they were, indeed, vacationing guests. In truth, they were all Helionics, the prisoners Tyrus had taken at his coronation, and he was leaving them here in the keeping of the Luminars to serve as human shields in case Pasus *did* try to strip away the new technology of the Luminars.

One hostage was familiar to me, with his usual golden wraps about his dark hair, and those wide green eyes: Gladdic Aton. He was the son of Pasus's closest ally, Senator von Aton. His life alone would have been a bulwark against attack, even without the dozen others joining him here.

My gaze found Pasus again as understanding settled cold and hard over his face. Whatever slightly amused condescension he'd been wearing until now had melted away, and he assessed Tyrus with the icy eyes of a sniper regarding a distant foe. He saw, at last, that he wasn't dealing with an overwhelmed boy so easy to manipulate.

Tyrus and I had discussed how he should present himself, and settled upon this. He couldn't project artificial weakness with Pasus unless he meant to do so consistently. Although the predatory instinct of honing in on the weak might have misled Pasus into dropping his guard, we both agreed strength would be the more effective means of giving him pause.

These thoughts passed through my mind as I gazed down at him. Then Pasus's eyes lifted and met mine. All about me seemed to drain into a silent stillness as I regarded him and he regarded me. . . . I'd killed his daughter, and now I would wed his Emperor, entering the very same family he was clawing and striving to join.

The truth was, I wasn't sorry about what I'd done to Elantra. She'd deserved every moment of pain and fear I'd given her before ripping her heart from her chest. She took away Sidonia from me, and if I'd had the chance to kill her father, too, I'd have done so already.

I knew as our eyes held that the feeling of cold enmity was mutual.

Tyrus's speech concluded, and Pasus drew his hands together in applause, never looking away from me. That was when I knew it in my heart: we would destroy him, or he would destroy us.

And I would not let us be destroyed.

# 10

THE DIPLOMATIC compound was secure. Pasus could not strike down Tyrus while he was here, nor vice versa. The building itself defused all projectile weapons within its walls.

The negotiation chamber had no surveillance; it was shielded from any electronic eavesdropping equipment. I'd even ventured just outside the room to press my ear to the door, hoping my superhuman hearing would make out some words.

The walls, alas, were soundproof.

So I was left in an agony of suspense, waiting for Tyrus to emerge from his meeting with Pasus. My gaze darted toward every stray sound, and I could not keep still.

I was just trying to eavesdrop again when I heard something. . . . A faint *thump*, then a reverberating echo above me. My mind instantly sharpened. I was in the atrium outside the meeting chamber, so the sound was suspicious. I trained my gaze on the ceiling, heard it again, and I knew it: someone was in the ceiling.

I waited for the next thump—and then I jumped up and drove my fist through the ceiling. A shout, and I'd clamped my hand upon someone's leg, my full weight hanging from it. "Who are you?" I bellowed up at its owner.

"Stop! Nemesis, it's me!"

Neveni.

I released my grip and dropped to the floor.

Then a panel in the ceiling tilted down on a hinge, and Neveni peeked her head out, dark hair dangling down about her. "What do you want?"

"What are you doing?" My voice was quiet, deadly.

"I am going to listen to them while they decide the fate of my planet," Neveni said, her eyes glittering. "Are you going to punch me like last time, or are you going to let me go?"

I tilted my head, considering it. "I barely punched you, Neveni. If I had truly punched you, you would have died from the head impact. I've also refrained from killing you a great many times when it would have been very convenient for me to do so," I told her.

"That's so humanitarian of you. I suppose I owe you thanks for sparing my life."

"You're welcome."

"I was sarcastic, Nemesis! God. No one should thank people for *not murdering* them."

I pointed upward. "You'll take me, too?"

"If you'll stay quiet," she said.

I nodded.

"I have no idea how you can even get up here. I climbed up a bookshelf—"

"I don't need help." I leaped up and caught the edge of the vent.

Then I easily hoisted myself up into the vent with her. Neveni's eyes were wide and dark on mine as I reached down to pull the door closed behind us.

"You're so strong," she said.

A rush of pride, despite myself. "I know. Now lead the way." My voice reverberated in the darkness.

A flick, and a faint light glowed between us. She had something on her wrist to illuminate the darkness. "Stay quiet."

Then she crawled forward on her hands and knees. I was too tall to do the same, so I eased myself after her flat on my stomach, dragging myself with my elbows. Neveni mouthed something to herself as we reached a junction in the wall, then raised her wrist to illuminate her face so I'd see her finger pressed to her lips. She quietly eased up a panel of the duct between us, just a crack, to allow voices to float up to our ears.

". . . ask a great deal of me." Pasus sounded amused. "I may wed your cousin, but I may not have intercourse with her. I must not only accept as family the beast that killed my daughter, but I must throw my full-throated support behind the match *and* urge the vicars to authorize you to use the scepter. Then, this province. You want it as well."

"Does it seem a great deal to ask, Senator? I am giving you my consent to wed the *heir to the throne*. Your child will rule this galaxy. I could have demanded more. Randevald made any wedding to him conditional on paying down the Domitrian debts—"

"Yes, and so he remained unwed. His Forenight disasters did not help, either."

"I don't set such an onerous condition. With my cousin, she cannot consent in her state of mind. You wish to father an heir with her DNA? Use an incubator. And Nemesis is a given. You knew that coming into this."

"How decisively you make your will known! Such a contrast to a year ago, when you were speaking to walls and raving about being a deity."

"I was keeping myself alive a year ago, Senator. As for your support, your weight behind the vicars . . . That is the reason I've even considered this union."

"Truly? And here I believed it was my bypassing you and petitioning the Senate that forced your hand."

Pasus had a point there, and I hated knowing that. . . . But Tyrus's voice evinced no sign of defeat: "Believe that if you wish, Senator. Whatever you may perceive of my current position, I can make life immensely difficult for you. The marriage will not happen unless *I* allow it, and I can swear that to you right now." There was quiet vehemence in Tyrus's voice.

That, too, was the truth. A private satisfaction rippled through me. The Vigilant's Bane meant Pasus would never have Devineé without our consent.

Maybe Pasus sensed Tyrus's certainty, because he forged on. "And you demand Lumina."

"This province is beset with malignant space. Soon it will be worthless as a trading outpost. I cannot be seen to accept the disrespect of being accorded nothing, so I ask for this piece of your depreciating property. It's a symbolic gesture."

Neveni drew a sharp, angry breath, and I just pinned her with my eyes. *He is playing indifferent,* I thought to her, willing her to understand. It wasn't his true regard for Lumina.

"Lumina will not be lost anytime soon," Pasus said. "You overstate the threat."

"I am compelled to remind you that mere months ago," Tyrus said, "this planet would have violently freed itself of your dominion if I hadn't intervened."

"But you did intervene. You did so most effectively. Curiously effectively." An odd note in Pasus's voice, "And then—then they aided you at the coronation." A sharp, indrawn breath—and then laughter. "Ah. I comprehend you. You cut a deal. Didn't you?"

"I did not," Tyrus said, and it was a weak rejoinder. He hadn't expected Pasus to figure that out.

"You made a deal and now you mean to fulfill your end of it. My. That rather elevates Lumina's worth in this situation, does it not?"

Neveni's hands balled into fists, and she was glaring down toward the sound of their voices like she wished to rip the vent apart and crush Pasus's skull.

Tyrus gave it a moment's thought. Then, "I will offer you Gorgon's Arm for Lumina."

A murmur from Pasus that must have escaped without his intending it. Gorgon's Arm was a most valuable mineral outpost.

But his voice grew sly: "What was the deal? Actually, no, let me guess. There is only one thing the Luminars ask for. Independence. You promised them liberty, didn't you? Oh, don't deny it, I know this planet; it crawls with partisans and delusions of self-sufficiency. Of course you made that deal! Oh, dear young Tyrus . . ."

"We are not on such informal terms, Senator," Tyrus reminded him coldly.

"Very well—*Your Supreme Reverence.* Think ahead to the dangerous precedent you'd be setting by freeing this planet. Liberate one, and all the other Excess get dangerous ideas. More will want to leave the Empire. The ones of value who support the ones without will rip away first, and soon you are presiding over a worthless six-star system with no inherent worth of its own."

I looked up at Neveni's hard face. Yes, the Luminars knew that.

"You're seeing this from the wrong angle, Senator," Tyrus said, his voice softening, growing persuasive. "There is another solution entirely to such a situation: we ensure living conditions are such that these Excess wish to remain in a *voluntary* union! Surely that is preferable to an Empire bound by force."

A long silence. Then, "You are very young and idealistic."

"I strive for more. I wish to improve life for us all. Shouldn't everyone wish for that?"

"Look about us, Your Supremacy. This capital city alone has more people than the entirety of the Grandiloquy. There are four billion people on this planet. Four billion! If a fraction of those minds are inclined toward study, and a fraction still of those understand what they are looking at that, it's still a staggering degree of intellect all bent toward one purpose: making use of the blasphemies you so blithely handed over to them today."

"*Technology schematics* are not necessarily blasphemies. I've been studying the Interdict's original proclamation at length, and there is a very good case to be argued that we're interpreting his words too literally. If the Luminars have such intellectual might at their command, shouldn't we be relieved to have those minds working to solve the issue of malignant space?"

"I did hear your Convocation speech on that, and the . . . the new era you spoke of. Scientific pursuits. Hmm. Your blasphemies are on your soul alone, so I will not play vicar with you."

"Much appreciated," said Tyrus darkly.

"Instead I will speak to you as a Senator to my Emperor: this Empire is maintained by a very precarious balance between the Grandiloquy who rule, and the Excess who are ruled by us. We have a vast array of destructive technologies, yet these devices are in the hands of our small number of people—and that is why the rulers and ruled live in accord. Today you give the Excess databases, and I will give you the benefit of the doubt and assume they are harmless things. That is all well and good, but tomorrow? Tomorrow they will want weapons. Starships. And if you do not provide them, they will build upon the knowledge you have given them and develop weapons themselves. Then they will use them. On us."

"Which brings me right back to living conditions! Senator, they will develop those weapons because that's what human beings do when they see so much in the hands of others, and they feel they are being robbed of it. We live in a universe with literally *infinite* frontiers. There is no reason for anyone in this Empire to know scarcity. Remove the reason for them to turn those weapons on us, and it will not happen."

Pasus laughed. An inappropriate bout of true laughter that made *me* wish to drop down into the chamber and punch him. But he said, almost jeeringly, "And here I was marveling at your cleverness, yet now I am reminded that I am dealing with a mere child. They will turn those weapons upon us because they *hate* us, and they always have. Their descendants will hate our descendants, as their ancestors hated our ancestors, because even if we sink so far below them that we are being crushed by their feet, they will remember how we were once superior. What you propose, Tyrus, will lead to our sort, we Grandiloquy—and bastard of an Excess you may be, but Grandiloquy you are—being crushed by them. All in the name of tackling an existential threat that is only 'existential' to planet dwellers who cannot fly around it."

Strange, how Pasus gave no thought to those planet dwellers. He had no pity for those who, as Tyrus had described to me, would be trapped under a sky watching their doom grow and grow.

"There is no reasoning with you on this," Tyrus said, his tone odd. "Our views will never come to accord."

"Ah, do not be so quick to jump to conclusions. Perhaps a break is in order. Tyrus, I must admit, I'm impressed with you. Not just these . . . dreams and ideals you somehow held in your heart in secret, but how effectively you blinded all our eyes to you. Had fate taken a different turn, your children with my Elantra might have conquered this universe."

"For whatever it's worth," Tyrus said softly, "I am sorry for your loss."

"From the man who wed her murderer," Pasus returned, "it is not worth much, but I thank you anyway."

## 11

NEVENI AND I remained in the darkened shaft until the silence had lasted for a good minute, and then we crawled back along the slippery metal surface, heading the way we came.

"Do you . . . ," I began, then fell silent.

"What is it?"

"I just . . . You know more than I do about such things. Do you think that went well?"

She didn't reply for a long moment. "I think if the marriage goes through, Tyrus had better test all his food for poison."

"Of course."

"I don't know, Nemesis." She gave a faint laugh. "I've never dealt with galactic politics. I'm glad I'll never have to. You passed the exit."

I eased back around, saw her feeling about the metal shaft, finding a hinge. Then light spilled up into the metal enclosure, and she peered downward. "I think it's too far to jump here."

"No, it's not," I said, and thrust myself down, landing neatly on the ground. I held out my arms. "Trust me?"

"Um. You're sure you can catch me?"

"Yes." When she still hesitated, "I won't let you break your legs. I promise. You don't seem to realize how strong I am."

"One way to find out." Neveni dropped down, and I caught her easily, then set her on her feet.

For a moment, we just looked at each other, and then she said, "Are you hungry at all?"

Startled, I nodded.

"Come on. I'll introduce you to roasted snake. It's disgusting."

"Then why eat it?"

"It's a very good kind of disgusting."

She turned to leave, just assuming I'd follow, as we always had ventured together to new places on the Chrysanthemum. The ripple of happiness that moved through me was unexpected. . . . And so I followed her.

The roasted snake *was* disgusting. Until it was not.

I described it to Tyrus as we were led to our sleeping chamber for the evening. "You eat the venom pouch first," I explained to him as we stepped inside. "I tried it without, and it tastes like rubber. Then the venom is worse, but the rest of it transforms once you've eaten it."

Tyrus was a finicky eater. He'd try things to be diplomatic, but every morning he had the exact same breakfast, and generally one of the three same lunches. He had several such benign neuroses, like his need to always sit with his back to the wall, or to complete an even number of kilometers whenever he ran. Weights had to be lifted in sets divisible by ten, and if he fell a few short due to an interruption, he would always find his way back to the exercise chamber just to get in the final few he'd missed or it would "vex him all day." That sort of thing.

Knowing he'd never try it, I described the snake as well as I could. He listened to my account with a morbid fascination.

"After the venom, the snake tasted almost like . . . chicken."

Tyrus laughed as we passed through the doorway, bidding good-bye to our escort. Outside the windows, Lumina's proto-night had fallen as it often did in the planet's winter—a bright moon still lit the sky almost as brightly as most suns, but the sun itself was not in sight.

"Strange how wherever you go in the galaxy, you will encounter the taste of chicken," Tyrus murmured. "That's an oddity of . . ." He trailed off as he turned about, surveying the room.

One bed.

Tyrus stared a moment. So did I.

Of course, we were publicly engaged. And this was . . . this was normal.

A heat stole under my skin, and I darted a quick glance at Tyrus, caught him doing the same to me. We hadn't yet shared a bed.

"There looks to be an exquisitely comfortable couch . . . ," he said.

"You wish me to take it?" I said.

"No, I'd take it, of course."

"There's no 'of course' to that, Tyrus. You're the Emperor of the galaxy."

"I will take it," he repeated.

He stepped away—but I grabbed his arm. His bicep felt tense, and his eyes immediately shot to mine. He was nervous too, and the realization made a warmth surge through my heart.

"There's no need."

He smiled tentatively, a slight flush to his face. It was so rare to see him nervous in this manner that I couldn't help a giddy smile. Then he caught my lips in a fervent kiss, and my back hit the wall, and I found myself smiling again like some dazed, silly thing, but he was too.

A chirping. Transmissions. Always something to call to him. I eased him away and watched him walk—my gaze clinging to that exact posture, the easy grace honed by that same self-discipline that drove him to craft his own muscles. He called for an audio feed, and I turned away and stepped into the washroom.

A strange, dancing nervousness fluttered inside me, and it only mounted. I'd be alarmed and make assumptions about that roasted snake from earlier if there weren't something so thrilling about the sensation. Even my hands seemed to be tingling with a strange, pleasant fear.

I met my eyes in the mirror, two currently dark irises glittering with an intensity that made me start. I traced my finger over the bridge of my crooked nose. I'd never fixed it because Donia had loved it this way. . . . And I did too. It was always the reminder I needed, even now, even this day: *Here I am. And I am still me.*

I washed up, and when I returned to the bedchamber, I could hear Tyrus in the other washroom doing the same. Restless, I roved back and forth, trailing my fingers over the dresser. When I heard him switch off the water, my breath caught. I cast my gaze down, hoping I appeared perfectly calm, standing before the mirror.

Tyrus appeared behind me, and I felt his gaze like a hot, searing touch . . . tracing the bare skin of my back, my arms, my legs bared by the sheath nightgown I'd chosen.

Then he closed the distance, and how strange to see him reflected back at me, for I saw now that he was taller than I sometimes realized, that his shoulders were broad, his arms heavy with muscle. So often all I could see was how easily broken he would be compared to me.

He traced a finger down my back. My heart thumped wildly. Then his arms, muscular, strong, pulled me back onto the warmth of his body and his lips brushed over the tender skin of my neck.

"You are so utterly beautiful."

"I know," I agreed.

He smiled against my skin and then his lips laid the softest of kisses on my skin, finger brushing aside the strap of my gown, and the hot kisses trailed up the arch of my neck. There was something that made a tingling sensation spring through me, and a sound escaped my lips. One I hadn't meant to utter.

I looked at his reflection, saw a secretive smile on his face, like he was pleased to have figured out something. Then I turned, draped my arms about his neck, and gave in to the need to have him closer to me. His mouth met mine and his tongue probed between my lips, tasting me, and we made our way across the chamber.

My leg touched the bed, and my heart gave a frightened spasm. I asked him, "So do we begin the sex now?"

Unfortunately, that seemed to break the mood, because Tyrus began to laugh. Then I began to scowl. And I no longer wished to begin the sex.

He smothered his mouth with his hand, his cheeks pink, flushed. "I've just never heard it put that way. I think we should . . . begin the sex at a time that feels right."

"Not now?"

"Not now."

Every centimeter of me, from the tips of my toes to my hairline, seemed alive with awareness of him as I reclined in the bed. My gaze lingered on his back as he stripped off his shirt, neatly folded it, and then unlooped his belt, with the sheath holding the scepter. It settled on the table with a clank. Then his trousers, which he also took great care to fold.

His face was too rough to be pretty or handsome, his hair perpetually somewhat tumbled, whether by his hand, or something else, but every centimeter of him was lean, taut, disciplined. He sprawled onto the bed beside me, and we both looked each other over.

"I notice you haven't asked me about today. Did you manage to eavesdrop?"

A denial rose to my lips. Then at his teasing smile, I could not help but curve my lips.

"I did. Neveni and I crawled into the ceiling. I believe we may be friends again."

"That's great. What did she say?"

"You want to know?"

"I'm not demanding answers to questions," he said lightly, "but I'm interested. She's your friend. You don't tell me about friends every day."

"Because I don't have other friends." I pressed my cheek to his shoulder and his arm swept me closer still, to rest my weight over his chest.

"You can invite her to come back with us. She can visit as long as she wants. I'm sure she'd love to see the *Hera*."

"I don't think Neveni will care for that. The truth is that she—"

Then I heard a humming. A strange hum. I pressed a finger to his lips, for he hadn't heard it yet. Then it grew louder, and he heard it too. About us, the chamber began to vibrate, then rattle.

Only for a moment were we both frozen there. He launched himself to his feet and rushed across the chamber to look out the window.

"Something's about to happen," he shouted to me over the noise. "I think it's overhead!"

A dim thought flickered forward in my mind about strange phenomena that took place on planets like this—hurricanes, tsunamis, and earthquakes. . . . But I didn't believe for a second in coincidences. My mind flew over the exits I'd noticed, and the building's design. We were on the top floor. Three stories. Then the humming mounted to a clamor that resounded through my bones, and I knew the sound: a starship.

I launched myself at Tyrus, seized him, and dragged him under the heavy brass desk just as a great blast of light tore open the roof above us.

An onrush of searing heat. There, a starship loomed overhead, blotting out the stars, and Tyrus and I were already moving through the chamber, which looked now like a mountain of flaming, ashen debris. I urged Tyrus with me, counting on my superior strength if he resisted. He didn't. He stumbled along to keep up with me, but another blast didn't follow. Through the stinging in my eyes I saw the starship's bottom door opening, spilling people in respirators and rubber suits into the flaming structure. . . .

They had flashlights and scanners, and I could tell they were looking for something.

*Someone.*

I knew who it was they sought.

Pasus had been clever to attack this way. He couldn't have slipped armed people into this building designed to neutralize weapons. Instead he'd brought a ship down right from space to blast open the roof and take what he wished. We ducked down low and stumbled through the burning corridor. Tyrus tugged my arm so we swerved into a busted room.

There I saw her: the Successor Primus of the Empire crouched on the ground, hands over her head, screaming mindlessly.

Tyrus and I exchanged a glance. He moved to grab her, but I shouldered him aside and did it instead. I was stronger. I could move faster. I seized Devineé and hauled her up. She was the only one of us Pasus wouldn't kill. The closer we kept her, the better.

Choking black flames rose in the air, and Tyrus kept his hand on my shoulder so we wouldn't lose each other as we scrambled forward. A man in a respirator appeared amid the smoke, blade in hand. He aimed a slash at me and I shoved Devineé into his path. He averted his blow, only to receive my fist across his face.

Tyrus caught Devineé before she could fall, but more flames sprouted nearby and silhouettes of Pasus's people darted toward us.

We couldn't do this. We had to escape.

They wanted her?

She'd swallowed the Vigilant's Bane. Let them have her.

I kicked her away from us deliberately, where they could see her fall, and then grabbed Tyrus and fled.

He resisted only a second before survival trumped his misgivings about abandoning her.

We made it out of the building just as the great black shadow of the starship rose over the roof, and then it fired its cannon to finish off the compound.

The noise swelled, impossibly loud now, like a mallet striking my bones as I sprawled over Tyrus. I couldn't hear my own cry of pain as agony lanced through my ears, rattling my skull until it threatened to crack.

A hot, invisible wall slammed into us, and the ground disappeared, my vision going dark with the dust and debris that choked my lungs, my skin nipped by the tiny bites of shattered glass. Then we crashed to the ground, our bodies crammed together as the building collapsed above us. I covered Tyrus as best as I could, my eyes squeezed shut, rancid air scorching my lungs.

On all sides, all sides, we were trapped.

And Tyrus wasn't moving at all.

## 12

**MY HEAD CLEARED,** though it spun with every movement. I tried to rise, couldn't. Chunks of granite, something crushing my leg. With a scream of rage, I twisted, I arched my torso, shifting the weight above us until it rolled off, and then with a great heave with all my strength, freed us. A lance of a bright searchlight from rescue drones soared in toward us. One of the moons was rising.

I knelt over Tyrus, shook him. "Tyrus!" I couldn't hear my own voice.

His eyes opened, unfocused, and then locked on me. He was alive.

My ears buzzed. Tyrus and I just clutched hands as bots filled the sky. The Luminar disaster force cleared aside the rest of the debris and tangled wiring, clearing a path for us to escape.

A medical bot soared in and tended to Tyrus and then me—and the great buzzing in my ears receded. Then, still ragged and stunned by our escape, we were lifted together by one of the rescue drones, deposited out into safety. The sky had gathered a purple light.

Tyrus and I surveyed each other. He was coated with dust, a dark gash leaking blood from his cheek. His blue eyes struggled to focus, and then they did, and his thumb traced the line of my jaw.

"Are you all right?" he said.

I nodded, thinking of Devineé.

She was dead, or Pasus had her. Either way, he would not have a bride very soon.

"I know you didn't want it to go this way," I told Tyrus. "But I had to give her to them. They wouldn't have left." And it was a price I was willing to pay. For our lives, I'd throw her away gladly. Let her die if it would save us.

"I have to try to get her back."

"I know."

He could try. I didn't stop him when he lurched to his feet, stumbling a bit with the movement.

"I didn't see this coming," he admitted to me raggedly. "Well. No. I did expect it—but not this soon. Not nearly this soon." The realization seemed to shake him.

"We will survive it. Go do what you must. I'm all right."

He jerked an unsteady nod, and Domitrian servants and employees were about us now. As Tyrus departed, I waved away those tending to me, trying to wipe the dirt from my face, my hands. My gaze lifted to the vibrant purple sky, bright enough to bite my eyes now. Could I have seen this coming? Had Pasus's negotiations always been disingenuous, or . . .

I'd never anticipated he would strike so soon, so decisively. I should have seen this coming too.

Tyrus had a little over eight hundred minutes to recover Devineé. That, according to the Luminars, was the length of time required for a vessel to move from the planet to a safe hyperspace transition point. To save her, she had to be seized before then—or she was gone.

Pasus hadn't acted alone. He'd rounded up staunch Helionics to act in tandem with him. Senator von Locklaite, who'd accompanied us to Lumina in the *Ironheart*, turned her vessel on the other ships and fired wildly upon every Domitrian starship in orbit before zipping out of range of their weapons.

And Senator von Aton clearly decided he could have other children, for he did the same—and left a trail of automated mines in his wake that latched themselves onto any pursuing ships.

As a consequence, all vessels but the sturdy, powerful asteroid ship, the *Hera*, were in need of maintenance.

An outside observer might think Tyrus was drugged with something calming, as the news trickled in. Bit by bit, his Empire was slipping away from him, with a faction forming around Pasus and his soon-to-be wife, Devineé Domitrian. That outsider wouldn't know there was already a ticking clock counting down the hours of her life, ready to extinguish Pasus's civil war in its birth pangs.

I said not a word to Tyrus of what I knew must follow.

The petite, blond woman, Senator von Wallstrom, did. "What of the Aton boy?"

"Gladdic?" Tyrus said. "No. We're not executing him. Not . . . yet."

I gazed at Tyrus's back, since he was counting on time to solve the problem. Yet I knew something: Gladdic had to be killed, and killed now, as a direct response to his father's defection. To do anything else meant presenting Tyrus as a paper tiger for the rest of his reign. No one would fear his threats.

Instead I contacted Neveni. "Where is Gladdic being kept?"

She hesitated before answering me. "Right here with me, Nemesis. I . . ." She glanced back over her shoulder. Gladdic had to be in the house with her. She dropped her voice to a whisper. "I think he understands the situation. He knows what has to follow." Anger flashed over her face. "His father just threw him away."

Apparently.

But it fell to me to make certain of it.

While Tyrus saw remotely to a pursuit of Senator von Pasus's vessel, the *Colossus*, I quietly slipped away from the Luminar handlers assigned to me.

There weren't a great many Helionics on this planet, so the single heliosphere was just outside the capital city, a small, sad thing on stilts to approximate the expansive view one might obtain from a heliosphere in space. The moon's orbit was swift, and it had set—and the sun hadn't risen, nor had the second moon. It was true night.

Neveni was sprawled on the steps of the staircase leading up to the heliosphere.

I threw an urgent look around. "Neveni, are you the only one guarding him?"

"It's Gladdic," Neveni said, as though that was an explanation. I felt the weight of her gaze in the dimness. "So you're really going to do it. You're going to just kill him."

"You have a dozen more hostages who aren't related to Grandiloquy who just betrayed us. You can forfeit one."

"I know. It's just . . . You know Gladdic." She was searching my face, this girl who'd known only my facade, who'd only begun to see me as I actually was.

I withdrew a blade, one sharp enough to make this swift. "It's necessary to send a message. His father defected to Pasus. He chose this. I didn't." She was silent a moment. There was a smell drifting on the air, something sweet and fragrant that I picked up over the acrid scent of Luminar streets.

"It's strange how easy it is to forget you aren't the person I knew," she murmured. "I think that's why I felt most angry with you afterward. Because I missed what was right before my eyes. I missed more than anyone else did."

That smell, the sweet smell, some sort of flower . . . It nagged at me. "I'm not cruel, Neveni. This isn't something I'll enjoy. If we don't kill him, not only will Tyrus be known as a weakling unable to follow through on his own threats, but *your* people lose any leverage they've gained from the lives of the hostages because you will be doubted as well. You should thank me. Not condemn me for this."

"I'm not condemning," she said tonelessly. "I know what's happened today. Pasus has openly moved on the Emperor. He's a traitor. His holdings are forfeit. Including Lumina."

I nodded. Including Lumina.

"Which Tyrus will free."

"I'm sure he already has. He won't be your enemy. That doesn't mean other powerful people won't plot against your planet. They will fight your independence." I held up the blade. "And this is how you'll need to keep it."

She met my eyes. "Would you rather I killed him, then?"

The words surprised me, but searching her face, I grew certain she'd do it if I asked her. For Lumina, she'd commit a murder. I shook my head. "I'm very good at this."

I started up the stairs, the blade in hand. When I reached the top, I found Gladdic Aton sitting on the floor in the farthest reaches of the dull glass chamber. He'd lit a chalice of oil to lend him a flickering golden light, and he didn't move even though his ears had to pick up my entrance. His hair was coming out of its usual golden wraps, and he looked delicate against the view sweeping before him: those crowded Luminar buildings, and beyond, the bare countryside leading up to black mounds of hills.

No, not hills. Those were small things.

Mountains.

"I know what you're here to do," Gladdic said in a wavering voice. "Can we please . . . If you don't mind, can we wait for twenty minutes?"

"Why twenty minutes?"

He whipped around, surprised that it was *my* voice. "Sidon . . . Nemesis?"

I nodded. He'd been infatuated with me once, because he'd believed I was Sidonia. I'd attempted to feign interest in him when I posed as her. Then I saw him for the sniveling weakling he was and cast him away. He hadn't been worthy of her.

Now I walked toward him, and his eyes latched onto my crooked nose—as though my stature weren't enough to give away who I was. There weren't many natural-born women as tall as I was. He darted one quick glance at the blade in my hand, swallowed hard and averted his gaze.

"In twenty minutes, the sun will begin to rise. Even at night here, the atmosphere is too thick to see the stars. But I can gaze upon one star when you . . . when I die."

"I'll wait."

And so I settled just behind Gladdic, blade in hand, to wait out the twenty minutes until I killed him.

# 13

THE ONLY SOUND was the frantic, quick rasp of Gladdic's breathing in the heliosphere. He didn't move, but he was in terror. He'd seemed calm upon my arrival, but as we ticked down to the last minutes, his breathing rasped, his body trembled visibly. I sat behind him ready to spring if he panicked, if he fled. My idle gaze roved the heliosphere and determined all the weapons he could seize and deploy on me. The best was that chalice of burning oil.

I would overcome him and kill him, whatever he did, but I expected him to fight.

Yet he did not.

"Aren't you at least going to try to run away?" I wondered. "Or fight me?"

"There'd be no point."

"Of course not, but you're dead one way or another. I'd try."

He let out a shuddering sigh, and I saw his chalice was burning the last of its oil. "I know this is how it works. My father always found me disappointing. He wouldn't mourn long. I . . . I don't blame you. Or the Emperor. Don't feel guilty."

"I won't," I said, perplexed.

Before us, the midnight black sky lightened to a deep purple. A brilliant orange line snaked across the horizon. My gaze had been fixed on Gladdic's back, but the sight captured my attention. The dark purple grew to a brilliant purple edged with clouds of brightest pink and orange, and the golden orange over the mountains grew larger, burnishing the mountains gold.

A star as those ancient humans must have seen it. All the trees between us and the horizon, all those peaks, seemed to gleam, and the mountains grew dimension and form wherever the brilliant starlight set them alight.

Planets were stifling and dirty and crawling with viruses and micro-organisms; the skies were open to any true threat from space, and their inhabitants were so vulnerable without realizing it. I reminded myself of this, and yet there was some very primitive part of me, per-haps something of the humanity that had never been removed from my genetic code, that made my skin prickle in a wondrous way to see this star through atmosphere. This was a sight that should remain in Gladdic's eyes as I killed him. This was the time to strike.

My muscles wouldn't seem to move.

If he didn't die now, Tyrus would seem weak. His bluff had been called, and all his bluffs would be called from now on, so better to kill Gladdic than to stay my hand and face more opponents later.

Gladdic had begun to tremble. He knew any moment, any moment . . . The goblet at his side had burned out.

He accepted what I had to do. This was our universe, the way it worked. This was our Empire, the system, the order. Tyrus sought to change so much of it, but the fundamentals of life and death were always going to remain. The bonds of lovers, of parent and child, and those were such potent weapons that had to be used at times like now. Aton had allied with Pasus in full knowledge we held his son. He knew he'd forfeited Gladdic. He must not be spared this consequence.

"By the stars, what are you waiting for?" Gladdic said, suddenly breaking into tears. He buried his head in his hands.

I rose to my feet soundlessly, twined my hand in his hair, and yanked his head back to expose his throat. One quick slash. One I'd delivered so many times.

Yet I found myself looking outward again, for it was difficult when enshrouded in endless darkness, the stars such distant things, to comprehend it all . . . to understand what tiny beings we all were. There was an odd melancholy washing over me, as though for a second I'd stepped back from behind my eyes to glimpse something I'd never once noticed. How fleeting our lives were, not even a blink to the universe. I'd believed an atmosphere confining, but I saw now the richness of it, the oddity of having taken for granted that this perspective was totally insignificant.

All I'd seen the first years of my life had been the force field about me, the walls of the corrals, never the sky, and perhaps that had all been deliberate. That honed one's focus into a blade, narrowed one's perception until all that mattered was the heartbeat in my chest, which required ending the heartbeat in theirs. . . .

Then my thoughts stilled.

I was more than that now. Was I not? Was this death truly necessary? Did I *truly* have no alternative to this?

*You wish me to stop lying,* Tyrus had said, *and I wish you to stop giving me reason to lie.*

Reason to lie. Like seeking out Gladdic to do what must be

done—for fear Tyrus might not wish me to do this. And the truth was, *I* didn't wish to do this either. Not to this harmless boy I had no reason to despise. Tyrus wasn't a fool. He would preserve himself if it became necessary. I knew he would. All I'd been driven by since losing Donia was the terror of feeling that pain again. It had blinded me to the reality that Tyrus had survived years before I arrived, and he *had* killed in his own defense.

I didn't need to be his blade and I did not wish to be his Diabolic.

Instead, I would be an Empress.

I released my grip on Gladdic's dark hair and stroked my thumb over the scalp I'd been tearing at—all the reassurance I could give him.

"I'm not going to kill you. Go away."

Gladdic swiveled his wide green eyes toward me.

"Go," I repeated.

He opened and closed his mouth, and Gladdic took the first tentative steps like he was waiting for me to change my mind, to reveal this as a cruel joke. Then his courage failed and he ran, and his footsteps thumped down the stairs like someone tripping in his haste.

Seconds later, another pair of footsteps pounded up the stairs. Neveni peeked in, and I met her confused glance.

"Um, just checking. I thought . . ."

He'd come out, I hadn't. A smile touched my lips. "You thought perhaps Gladdic Aton got the best of me?"

"Yeah, that's kind of ridiculous."

"Donia was so gentle and sweet, and she'd never harmed an insect, yet even if I were her, I'd be more than a match for Gladdic. Take him somewhere to be a human shield for this planet. I don't need him."

"No problem." She turned to leave, and that was the moment it dawned on me that she'd actually thought to *check* to see whether I was all right.

As a friend would.

"One last thing," I called after her.

She turned back, and my tongue seemed heavy in my throat.

"Thank you for checking," I said.

She seemed puzzled, but just gave a smile. She would think it foolish, that this mattered to me at all, but I knew she had a great many friends. I did not.


I emerged from the heliosphere and smelled that floral scent once more, and knew it for jasmine. Sidonia's favorite. The scent still lingered after I was escorted to Tyrus's hasty assembly of those Senators with us who hadn't defected.

They'd been up all night, conducting the remote effort to retrieve Devineé.

It had failed.

Pasus had her, and soon she would be dead.

"If they're aiming for the Chrysanthemum, they have a head start on us," Tyrus murmured, gazing at a map of all imperial territory, which from the side formed a shallow U-shape of stars. As it twisted, the expanse of space jutted out in several irregular points, mostly from the central focal point of that U. "So we hold position here. We use our service bots, repair the ships one by one. Lumina is a stalwart ally, and a powerful planet with extensive defenses. We're too easy to ambush with the entry corridors to the six-star system. And I want a message sent to our allies at the Chrysanthemum: if other Helionics or even opportunists mean to defect—let them."

Murmurs of objection.

"Let them," Tyrus repeated. He leaned against the window, gazing out at Lumina's purple-hazed surface. "I want to see who flocks to

Pasus's side. What are those words? 'Let all the poisons that lurk in the mud hatch out.' So let's hatch all of them. Now."

His advisers looked to one another uncertainly, perhaps wondering if they'd backed a madman after all.

Tyrus missed nothing. He told them, "I am not at liberty to explain my . . . confidence to you, but I am certain this is a short-lived fracture. And you will all reap substantial rewards at its conclusion."

The promise of a bribe made them smile, pleased at the prospect. After all, trust was worth far too little on its own.

Tyrus waited until they were gone to gaze thoughtfully at that shallowly curved U-shape of stars. At Lumina, we were closer to the point that spiked from the center of that U, and Tyrus zoomed in to examine the systems nearest us. Great spots of gray indicated zones of malignant space, and purple shading covered those vast swathes of space that simply could not be traversed due to gravity, radiation, debris. There was a very narrow corridor of habitable space amid these zones.

I tore my gaze from it, looked at him.

"You should sleep," I suggested.

His fingers were pressed to his lips. "Not quite yet." He flicked his hand and zoomed out, and more of those purple zones swam past, more, and then that U receded into invisibility amid a vast spiraling swirl of stardust.

He'd once told me the term "galactic Empire" was a bit of an exaggeration. Now my stomach gave a curious jump. I stared in dumb shock, because . . . because that was *it*? The great, seemingly endless expanse of space under Tyrus's control fit into that tiny sector of the map, like a string amid those patches of intense radiation and heat and hazard?

Suddenly this Empire, so great, felt small. . . . And the intense vulnerability of our position registered in my mind. "It will take weeks, maybe longer, for her to die, and then . . ."

"And then there will still be a fracture. Yes, I am aware," Tyrus said, threading his fingers together, just watching that galaxy swirl. "That's why I'm keeping my hands off. As soon as I lift a finger in retaliation, I inspire true enmity. Vendettas. Holding strong, as though we are totally invulnerable—which we are if we stay here—and then offering a chance for his allies to win my forgiveness is the best possible course I can take. . . . I don't want any of them to feel they've entrenched themselves and their backs are to the wall once she dies. I will take bribes to forget this—and stars know the treasury needs the funds."

"And Pasus?"

"He's the exception. They will all know it."

Then he zoomed in on our position again, and with his brow furrowed, he began to turn the image about as though to examine the space around us on all sides. A twist of his hands, and he shifted the image toward a zone of white that appeared as a cluster of hundreds of stars all joined together. They formed the nearest border of dead space separating the Empire and whatever else there was.

"I've always found it interesting," Tyrus murmured, "how Lumina, the greatest holdout of the old faiths, could be the one closest to the Transaturnine System, the prize of the Helionics."

The star system of the Sacred City. Where the Interdict dwelled.

"Do you think he really exists?" Tyrus said. "The Interdict, I mean."

I didn't answer. Just on instinct. It was something one didn't say aloud. One didn't question that.

"The first thing I did when I ascended," Tyrus told me, "was look at our classified files. I wanted to know whether the Interdict is real. And whether sentient aliens are out there, of course. You hear such rumors."

"Surely not," I said. There were plenty of plant and animal life forms that hadn't evolved on Earth, and far more simple ones. "Nothing like us."

"I found that we are in a habitable zone of this galaxy virtually ringed by places that would fry our ships and kill us in an instant if we left. If there is anything out there, we're essentially cut off from it." He gave a rueful smile, as though sheepish to even discuss that. "But Amon was taken prisoner along with his children to the Sacred City, and those children returned claiming the Interdict did, in fact, exist. Yet . . . yet were they just perpetuating the myth? If he were real, why do we see so little of him? A vicar emerges out of nowhere every few decades with a command or a demand for some tribute or other. The vicars would have us believe that same Interdict, Orthanion, is still living there in the Sacred City. It's literally impossible for someone to exist so long. Even with med bots. Why so coy? Why not come in person?"

"You sound like you have a theory."

"I think Amon's children were terrified of meeting their father's fate, and so they lied. I think the vicars have invented this man and enforced that belief in him by tarring doubters with the word 'blasphemy.'"

"I wouldn't put that beneath them."

Tyrus abruptly turned off the image. "Nemesis, I think we need to go there."

I stared at him, flabbergasted. Then, "Go there? To—to the Transaturnine System?"

"Yes," said Tyrus, flashing a daring smile. "We're but a few days in hyperspace away from it. We still have the most powerful starship in our arsenal—the *Hera*—and it's in perfect shape to travel."

"So many pilgrims try to go there and never come back."

"Two possibilities," Tyrus said. "One: they found the Interdict and stayed. Two: they didn't find the Interdict, and someone didn't want them to come back and admit it."

The second possibility . . . It was malevolent. But oh, it made so much sense.

"The *Hera* is not a weak starship easily destroyed by an ambushing force," Tyrus said, his eyes burning. "And if anyone makes an attempt . . . All they will do is give us more evidence we can then use. If the Interdict is, as I suspect, a fabrication of these vicars, then the threat of exposure will make them most amenable to doing as we wish, won't it?"

I stepped behind him and laid my hands on his shoulders, looking at that projection of the galaxy. It would cost us a few days at most, and yes—yes, the rewards of this visit would be great.

"When do we leave?"

## 14

EVERYONE knew the origin of the Helionic faith. Sarolvana was an ardent follower of an old religion, and she chose to seek out Earth on a pilgrimage. Most who made the attempt did not return.

Sarolvana did, but she hadn't found Earth.

Instead she happened upon the Transaturnine System and a place like no other, a wondrous starlight realm. Her devotion to the old faith shifted as the Living Cosmos itself instructed her anew in her time of solitude, and she returned to the young colonies from where she'd come—only to find that all she'd left behind were long dead, and she'd become ageless. She was over three hundred years old, yet appeared all of twenty-five.

She spoke of the Living Cosmos and at first gathered only a few followers. So Sarolvana sought to prove herself, and vowed to her followers that she would leave them and return when they were of great age. In the decades that passed after Sarolvana again disappeared into the starlight realm, many lost faith.

Then she returned, as young as she'd been upon her departure. . . . And they were all old.

It was not false-youth. It was true youth. She'd been blessed by the divine Cosmos, and her followers grew in number as they saw with their own eyes how she'd been made immortal. But some asked questions that Sarolvana could not answer in a way they understood, so she began to share chemicals with them to open their minds, to give them the insight bestowed on her by the starlight realm. Coupled with her beautiful, resonant voice, a chemically influenced mind could be enlightened.

Contemporaries sneered at this "cult of the stars." They wrote it off as a pretense for young people to use drugs; they devised "scientific" explanations for Sarolvana's immortality. Laws were created just to limit this cult's spread, so Sarolvana gathered the most devoted of her followers and took them to the starlight realm. Then, blessed with her immortality, disciples returned still young to find themselves the same age as their great-grandchildren. They spread the faith even further.

Still, there were doubters. So many doubters that upon Sarolvana's final, fateful visit to the colonies, an angry group seized her, this speaker for the Living Cosmos. They proclaimed that a true ally of a thinking, conscious, feeling Cosmos would surely never be killed by it. They launched her into a star to burn to death.

Yet Sarolvana did not die—not truly. The man who became the first Interdict roused from his despair and heard her speaking to him, for she had joined the pulse of the Living Cosmos with her death as all good Helionics must do, and in her name, this Interdict moved to dwell full-time at the Sacred City, training more and more vicars to send to all corners of the galaxy and spread the true faith. The Helionics had an advantage no others did: immortality, the ability to exist over lifetimes when others aged and died. And so Sarolvana's truth spread, and now the faith of the stars truly dominated the stars.

Centuries passed before that Interdict met a star himself, but his successor followed, and then her successor. Now it was Orthanion whose massive crystalline statue had towered over my head in the *Penumbra*, and if it was to be believed, he'd presided over the Helionics for a half an eon from within the Sacred City.

It wasn't humanly possible.

And yet—Tyrus and I would soon see the truth for ourselves. One way or the other.

Since there was a chance this gamble could backfire spectacularly, Tyrus and I considered our options. There was only one person who had no involvement in the Chrysanthemum's politics, who had enough personal enmity toward Pasus to serve as an objective observer.

"What is it?" Neveni said when I gave her the electronic document.

"It's just insurance. If a month passes and we haven't returned," I told her, "it will unlock itself so you may see what it says about where Tyrus and I have gone, what we've meant to do. I can't tell you more than that."

She would only see it if something went spectacularly wrong and we perished. In that case, the Luminars would have the knowledge to use to their advantage first.

In the meantime, the rest of the galaxy wouldn't miss Tyrus and me the fleeting few days we were gone, and the closest advisers would just think he was taking an inappropriate interlude in the serene wilderness of Lumina, far too casual about the developing firestorm in the Empire.

He was hardly the first Domitrian Emperor prone to such eccentricities. "Such is the consequence of rule by bloodline rather than merit," Tyrus sometimes said. If all went to plan, we would return well before

Devineé perished, holding just the trump card we needed to force the vicars to give us the scepter. Then it wouldn't matter if Devineé died and Pasus's back was to the wall, and he lashed out wildly, desperately. Tyrus would have overwhelming force supporting him.

If all did not go to plan, Devineé would still perish. We would be lost in the Transaturnine System, as so many pilgrims had been before us, and there would no longer be a Domitrian to claim the scepter—forcing an entire systemic change in the Empire that might or might not work out for the best.

And of course, there was also that doubtful third possibility: that we'd end up the first people outside the body of vicars to encounter the Sacred City and the Interdict in centuries.

It remained to be seen.

There was no blissful time basking in the five days of hyperspace to the Transaturnine System. We gathered up tribute for the Interdict—just in case Tyrus was wrong and we did somehow end up in the Sacred City. It was paltry. Spices, jewels (some broken right off the wall of the *Hera*), artwork, and even some of Tyrus's books.

As we soared through hyperspace, I kept noticing Tyrus's face. He had that expression like he was questioning, questioning himself, over and over.

"Stop that," I ordered him.

His brow furrowed. "I'm not doing anything."

"You are thinking too hard," I said. "I can tell. Stop. We made our decision. Let's see it through and worry later."

"Worry later? You ask something quite impossible there," he said. Then he reached out and drew me onto his lap, leaned his chin on my shoulder. "Distract me."

I'd never spoken just for the sake of speaking, but with the Interdict on my mind, I shared Sidonia's old words about how we were all stardust formed into conscious beings. And then, as soon as I spoke of her, so many things poured out, all in a great torrent, and Tyrus just listened.

"The vicar told her I didn't have a divine spark, but she believed him in everything else, yet not that. She never accepted it. I told her I wasn't like her. So many times, I told her."

Tyrus leaned over to press his lips to my bared shoulder. "She was a remarkable person."

My vision blurred. A knot lodged in my throat. She had been.

"I think I will seek a higher price from the vicars than just the scepter," Tyrus decided. "I want you granted personhood."

The words took my breath. I stared at him, astounded. "That can be done?"

"It's a legal and spiritual status. I am the law, so we need only fix the latter. I've no doubt you are a person, Sidonia had no doubt of it, and you must know the truth of yourself." He reached over tenderly, smoothed my hair from my eyes. "At least, you should. We'll do this."

It didn't seem possible to me. It didn't.

Yet everything about us had been impossible, had always been impossible—and who knew what else there was to come?


When we dropped out of hyperspace, Tyrus took a place by the window in the *Hera*'s command nexus. We saw it in the distance, a great mass of pure blinding light—stars gathered so close to each other as though something more powerful than even a hypergiant star tugged them together.

Then space changed about us, and rather than darkness, we were drawing toward bright, vibrant light strewn in currents that almost resembled raging rivers flowing through space. Then the *Hera*'s steady shaking turned to violent jolts as the gravity ripped at us.

Tyrus rushed over to the navigation panel. The *Hera* was designed to steer itself, but the gravity here . . . It felt wrong. "What are those stringy lights?" I said.

"I . . . I have no idea. Let's pause here a moment."

I nodded, but he'd already ordered the *Hera* to a stop. . . .

The ship continued forward, shaking harder. Tyrus ordered the ship to pull back . . . and it still didn't stop. He surged to his feet, stepped toward the window, rubbing his hand over his chin, thinking quickly, pondering those glowing ribbons of light.

Then he froze.

"Nova blast me," he breathed. "Stars. Nemesis, these are stars!"

"What? Stars . . . ?"

"They've been torn apart. These are burning streams of hydrogen. It's this gravity. The gravity . . . And we're going right into this. We have to turn around!" He threw himself back to the navigation console, faster than I'd ever seen him move, even at full sprint. My heart thumped wildly as he pounded at the console, ordering the *Hera* to apply its full power to driving us backward.

But the starship wasn't responding as it should. The jolting mounted until I could hear it, could hear the strain of stone tempted to fissure.

Ice filled my stomach.

*Tearing away from this will kill us*, came a cold and terrible voice in my head.

Tyrus had taken navigational control from the ship now. And I fought for my balance as I stared at his back where he was leaning over the console. The ship hadn't done as he ordered it on his own, so he was circumventing it. . . . Those commands written into the computer long before many of his ancestors had been born, by people with more understanding of space and technology and science than anyone alive.

Tyrus was so incredibly sharp and inventive and perhaps that was also his weakness—because he had too much faith in his own competence at times. Like right now. And through the rattling, straining chaos about us as the ship hurtled forward and he tried to steer us back, I knew we were about to be destroyed. He couldn't drag us out of this, but this ship was a magnificently clever machine and we had to trust it.

So I didn't think on it further. I didn't explain myself.

I charged forward, seized him, and ripped him away from the console, knocking him back. I slammed my hand on the autonavigation, then whipped around and blocked him when he shot back toward the panel. A jostle of the ship and we both plunged to the floor, and I couldn't hear what he was shouting at me, but I pinned him there in the heaving, dimming light. . . .

Outside the window a brilliant twine of burning light was whipping toward us, and just as it was about to hit, Tyrus abruptly stopped struggling and suddenly rolled himself atop me. . . . Then the deafening roaring about us receded and the jostling became vibration, and his blue eyes opened, fixed upon mine.

*See?* I thought, reaching up to stroke his cheek, seeing the beads of sweat on his forehead.

All we could do was leave this to fate and technology. There'd been no time to explain, and I knew it would be anathema to Tyrus to do such a thing . . . to take a backseat. Then he would have killed us both.

For a while, we remained there gripping each other and waiting for the moment my decision backfired terribly. But the *Hera* adjusted itself as the currents of the gravity buffeted us this way, weaving among the ribbons of obliterated stars, but never straight into the heart of the vast clouds of burning hydrogen, stringing the system like entrails.

"This must be what happens," Tyrus murmured. "This is why so many don't return. A weaker ship than this one, manned by one less decisive than you are . . ."

It would already be in pieces. The *Tigris* in all its beauty, opulence, would be fragments of debris in this system.

"How did you think to do that?" he said to me.

"You don't tense your muscles to receive a punch," I said. "You roll with the momentum."

A strangeness settled between us. We gazed at each other amid the rattling starship. There were certain things I'd come to understand about Tyrus without ever consciously thinking on it, and one was this: he needed a sense of power over a situation. I knew it could be termed a neurosis—only natural in someone inclined to be a control freak, trapped in a life where survival depended upon adjusting to the whims of his dangerous relatives.

That was simply Tyrus.

I was far and away his physical superior and capable of taking decisions out of his hands at will. . . . It was something that only grew glaringly obvious when we were in danger, and usually we didn't have a quiet moment immediately afterward. But I'd just made this decision for him, and now the moment was over. He pulled himself up, gripping the back of a chair.

"There was no time to explain," I said. "I'm sorry."

"You saved our lives, Nemesis. Excellent thinking."

And like that, any potential strangeness was simply gone. We turned our attention to the window and gazed out at space for the hours as we buffeted through the hydrogen currents. Then at last we were delivered beyond the currents of light. We saw what was so ferociously causing those gravity eddies in the Transaturnine System:

a curve of pitch black. The light all about it was made of stars, or the remains of stars, and they were being twisted into an unending darkness.

A deep shiver from within my soul. I knew what I was seeing.

"It's a black hole," said Tyrus.

A chill raced down my spine. A black hole had such intense gravity, light could not even escape its event horizon. That's what accounted for the stars all so close to one another. The black hole was drawing them in.

Tyrus splayed his palm over the window. The rounded, unfathomable black grew larger and larger.

"Tyrus, are we being pulled into it?"

"We're nowhere near the event horizon. We seem to be entering a wide orbit." His gaze flickered toward me. "That's where Amon died."

I looked at his profile. "After his excommunication?"

Tyrus nodded. "That's the penalty. One is cast alive into a black hole to be torn apart."

A proper Helionic death meant disposal in a star. The dead were thus reunited with the pulse of the Living Cosmos and would assume a new form as the Cosmos willed it. A black hole, though, was very different.

Tyrus drummed his fingers one-by-one on the window. "If Amon was launched into this black hole, then someone launched him. The Interdict. I think we have found our answer. The Sacred City is real."

A flash drew my eye. A bright, vibrant light pulsed over our view, and again. Tyrus leaned against the window to stare with some wonder as it illuminated his pale lashes, his burnished red hair, and then he leaned back so I could see. "I think . . . I think that's called a pulsar? One of the stars being drawn into the black hole is giving it off. . . ." He fell silent.

For the pulsar's light caught upon an asteroid, which then cast lights all about it like netting, and the closer we drew, the more we saw that it formed a vast webbing through space, an artificial webbing. And the asteroids were not pure asteroids, but shards of glittering diamond, and on them perched machines like scorpions poised to sting.

I grew rigid, and Tyrus drew a sharp breath. . . . Yet no weapons were unleashed on us.

"We must be close," he managed, as we moved through the gauntlet of so many weapons, they outnumbered the Chrysanthemum's, that webbing of light continually flaring between them. . . . A power source, I realized.

Suddenly, a sharp lurch.

My heart bounded into a frantic beat, but Tyrus just stroked my arm, gazing upward. "Towing cables?"

I listened, heard the familiar thump of them, and smiled at him. "Yes.'"

Excitement, terror leaped into his eyes, and he gripped my shoulders soundlessly, just staring at me intently as though to say, *We made it!* And I reached up and squeezed his hands so tightly in my excitement that he winced, and then I loosened my grip.

"So we're not going to be able to blackmail the vicars with this."

"No. We can do something better," Tyrus said, his gaze snapping with anticipation. "We can go over their heads and appeal directly to the Interdict."

I grinned at him.

And in that moment, I knew we were about to forge our destinies. Tyrus hauled me up and pulled me into a searing kiss, like a man who'd just surfaced from drowning, drawing in life. I returned it with the same frantic energy, for in that moment, I was certain: nothing lay beyond our reach.

# 15

I FELT as though I'd passed into a dream as the towing cables drew us toward the body that had to be the Sacred City: a massive, moon-size gathering of pure diamond interspersed with the marks of deliberate crafting where the formation had been transformed into a habitat. Through the glazed crystalline surface, we saw swirls of different self-contained atmospheres, enclosures for plants and livestock. Water and other liquids seethed in veins through the diamond's natural fissures. . . . Some windows were opaque, and in some, I could see silhouettes moving against the light.

The pulsar flared again and again, and the receiving rods of the Sacred City absorbed the energy. Fragmented rainbows pulsed off the rods into the halo of stardust all about this system.

The *Hera* was pulled down toward a gleaming bay of jagged purple gems. A door of granite slid closed behind us.

Minutes passed in agonized suspense as we waited for the exterior bay to pressurize. Then, a shrill beep outside the ship that we could hear inside—telling us it was safe to exit.

For a moment, we both hesitated. We'd prepped space sheaths just in case. Inwardly, I debated whether I'd be safer bringing a weapon, or whether it would be a dangerous provocation of people who outnumbered me, people whose goodwill I wished to win. . . .

But then an alarm chirped, warning of external airlock access. Tyrus and I exchanged a glance, then hurried down the corridor to meet the intruder.

A jovial voice rang down the hallway. "Hullo there, friends."

Tyrus and I rounded a corner to see a short, stocky man who was examining the walls about him with interest. He was bald like an Excess.

"Are you . . . the Interdict?" Tyrus said uncertainly.

The man laughed. "Of course not. No. And I know, I know quarantine protocols, but I haven't seen a ship like this one before. Thought I'd look inside, but . . ." He glanced about as we just stared at him. "Looks like it's a standard brigadier ship just enclosed in an asteroid. Lovely build, though. Very impressive."

Tyrus and I looked at each other.

"I am standing next to the Emperor of your galaxy," I told the man.

Tyrus belatedly remembered to fish the scepter out of its sheath at his waist, and flashed it up for the guy to see. Then he shot me a look that told me I needn't be indignant on his behalf. The man gave a start.

"You're the Domitrian? Oh. Forgive me. I thought—she—"

Yes, I did have the symmetrical look of someone who made use of beauty bots; Tyrus did not. "I'm Tyrus von Domitrian," Tyrus said. "Our tribute is waiting just within our cargo bay."

"It will be collected, I assure you. I'm a vicar, so I can guide your way." He looked us over again. "Well, come on, Your Supremacy."

115

We followed him in a daze, passing Exalteds who waited outside.

"They have tribute," said the vicar, pointing behind him.

The Exalteds scrambled past us. Then Tyrus's hand clutched mine tightly as we reached a circlet of metal spanning the corridor leading to the rest of the Sacred City. A green light bloomed from the circlet, subjecting us to a pathogen scan.

The vicar was squirming, fidgeting, and finally his self-control broke. "Now, I am sure you are here on serious business. The last time, when it was Amon, well, I used a bit of tact. I can't resist."

"What?" Tyrus said.

He broke into a grin. "How are the Gorgon's Arm Wayfarers doing? Just a rundown. Any idea you have."

Tyrus stared at him.

"I don't need a year-by-year account. That would take ages."

"The . . . Wayfarers?" Tyrus echoed.

The vicar's smile faded. "In Astroclash. Surely there's still a team for Gorgon's Arm?"

Tyrus sputtered a moment.

"There's no Gorgon's Arm team?"

"There's no league," Tyrus said. "There hasn't been an Astroclash league since Gannex ordered the losing team put to death after every match. Vicar, we've not had a sports league of that scale in three hundred years."

The vicar's face fell. He grew somber suddenly, as though he'd just been told his home world had been obliterated. "That's . . . that's so disappointing to hear. I was looking forward to catching up on that someday."

The scan ceased, and doors parted to give us access to the general environment.

"Off you go now," said the vicar.

He touched a button, and the floor beneath us rose, a panel detaching and soaring up into air. Tyrus and I caught each other as we began to sail through corridors that gleamed and winked with flashes of the outside pulsar.

"Nemesis," Tyrus said to me quietly, "that man is over three hundred years old."

"How is that possible?" I wondered.

He bore no trace of false-youth. Even with total organ replacement and regrowth, no one lived that long. People simply expired at some point.

Tyrus shook his head. His gaze was trained now on the floor panel beneath us, intent and careful, because the drop beneath us was far enough, our speed fast enough, that we might both break our necks if we somehow did tumble.

But instead, the panel alighted outside a door, and Tyrus stepped off on shaky legs, though he was reaching back to help balance me. I was steadier, but I let him make the gesture. I also made sure to step through the door before he did just in case some danger awaited us. It was a viewing box. It overlooked a vast crystal-and-diamond chamber that resembled a ball dome.

There was perfect gravity in the box, but when I experimentally stuck my hand out, my fingers felt light, as though they were floating upward. I snatched my hand back. "That's zero gravity."

"We aren't here for entertainment," Tyrus said, looking about us.

But a low *zzz* sound filled the air, and a long, flat, disc-shaped service bot soared into our box. *"Please state your refreshment preference."*

"We wish to speak with the Interdict," Tyrus answered it.

*"I do not understand that request. Please state your refreshment preference."*

"Water," Tyrus snapped.

"We've come this far," I told him. "We can sit through a performance."

He sighed. Nodded. Then he flung himself down into a seat.

There was no ease in his posture as I took the other. The bot returned with water and a surprisingly sparse selection of fruits. At least, that was what I assumed, until Tyrus bit into his apple, then pulled his head back.

"It's infused with something. I don't recognize the narcotic," he said.

I held out my palm. It wouldn't be polite to toss it away, but I knew he wanted a clear head. It would pass right through my system. Tyrus smiled at me lovingly and let me take it. So I ate the apple myself. In the meanwhile, one of the boxes across from ours bloomed with light. It was like a screen of starlight behind the silhouette of a single man.

I could see no details, but I sensed he was watching us.

"That must be him," Tyrus murmured.

We ignored the other service bots buzzing in with us, carrying various substances, elaborate dishes, and more drugged fruits, no longer willing to trust any of them.

Tyrus looked at the Interdict, and I knew the Interdict was gazing back at us, and then performers glided into the center of the ball dome. They were decked in ultraviolet feathers, and the lights dimmed to bring out the sharp glow. The feathered men and women launched into their dance, a classic fable set on old Earth.

"Are those vicars? Exalteds?" I whispered.

"Devout Helionics devote their lives to this dance," Tyrus said, clearly recognizing the first strains of music. "This is the King's Immolate."

I recognized the name. It was a performance that used to be showcased at every coronation. Tyrus banned it over the objections of his grandmother. It was a tale of the importance of obedience to authority, for it featured birds learning that the king was going to hold a feast, and then flying to the castle to offer themselves for his pie.

All but one bird, a rebellious, sulky one that escapes. Of course, the twist is that the king is so moved that the birds offer themselves to him that he rewards them with crumbs from the feast, rather than killing them.

The rebellious bird, on the other hand, is hunted by predators in the forest, and at last killed by them—in an actual sacrifice where the dancer playing the Immolate is butchered for the pleasure of the Emperor. Condemned prisoners sometimes served as the Immolate, with automated gravity rings strapped to their limbs to manipulate them through the dance. Oftentimes, though, a very pious Helionic willingly served as the sacrifice after years of training for the part.

"I banned this for a reason. I won't watch it now," Tyrus said quietly. His gaze fixed on the screen of sunlight where the Interdict himself was sitting. "Shall we go introduce ourselves?"

He rose to his feet, and when I understood his intention, I followed. We climbed onto the ledge of our box and hurled ourselves forward. The sense of gravity disappearing made my every cell feel like it was light. We soared right past the astonished dancers.

The music halted, and the dancers were so shocked, they stopped frolicking. That was the last I saw of them before we slammed through the screen of warm sunlight, into a chamber with standard gravity, and hit the ground.

A man was already on his feet, a vicar by the reflective garb he wore, and then my eyes caught his and I realized I was looking at the Interdict.

*The* Interdict—as in the very man depicted in that crystalline statue.

And the shock of it froze me, and Tyrus recovered first, pulling me to my knees with him.

"Most Ascendant One." He kept looking up at the Interdict, though

S. J. KINCAID

he should have been looking at the floor, for he clearly saw it, too. The resemblance.

That vicar had to be over three hundred years old.

This man? This was Orthanion. He was over five hundred. Five. Hundred. Years. Old.

How could it possibly be? Was he a clone? A hologram?

For a long moment, the Interdict Orthanion gazed down at us with what I swore was amusement.

And he spoke in a wry, gravelly voice: "Well, Emperor Tyrus, you know how to make a first impression. Were you too bored to sit through the performance?"

"N-no," stuttered Tyrus. Stuttered! I'd never heard that from him. "I'm just— You're—"

The door to the box slid open and a group of indignant vicars rushed in, but Orthanion waved them back with the careless ease of a man who'd long held total power over his domain.

"I am quite safe," Orthanion said. "The young Emperor was over-eager to meet me. Leave us."

Tyrus watched them dip out, then said, "Forgive my insolence, Most Ascendant One." He swiftly lowered his head, drew the hand the Interdict offered to one cheek, then the other. He licked his lips. "But I . . . I have seen the King's Immolate before, and I wish to decline any sacrifice in my honor."

"Ah, I see." He took Tyrus's chin to tilt his head up. He smiled. "My child, don't trouble yourself over this sacrifice. It's not even in your honor. It's in *mine*." He gave a negligent wave of his hand. "End it."

The dancers in the ball dome descended upon the Immolate, and their blades arced down, sending great bubbles of blood sailing up into the air like a rose in bloom.

# 16

TYRUS AND I followed him with some stunned shock, because we were both trying to figure out how he could be so old. And that vicar, the one who'd first met us . . . Whatever false-youth or . . . or technology kept the Interdict young must function with that one as well.

"The last Domitrian I met was Amon," remarked the Interdict, his gaze dropping to the scepter at Tyrus's waist. "I removed that from his hands, and then I stripped him of the power he held over it. I am glad to see another Domitrian under better circumstances."

His voice echoed as we entered a reception chamber with walls of hollowed diamond. Inside seethed liquid artwork, trickling like blood through the veins of our surroundings. With the aid of gravity, a river was flowing on each of the walls, but not composed of water—rather gushing with substances that didn't appear to mix. They moved over one another like oiled tentacles or ribbons. Every time the pulsar flashed, the whole room seemed cast in light, playing under the Interdict's very skin.

Orthanion turned to us and went on, "The Domitrians have such an arrogant self-love, I feared Amon's descendants might reunite with Acindra's in an overhasty manner. My machines checked your genetic code, and I see you are a product of a reunion—but due to a marriage of third cousins. Sooner than I would have liked, but that's acceptable. What's unacceptable is a certain finding from your database."

"What finding?" Tyrus said.

"I gave the Emperor Lotharias a private decree. The last vicar to come with news informed me there were a mere four royal Domitrians, and that was unacceptable. I sent him instructions to increase that number immediately. He failed me. Your databases say there are now but two of you."

Tyrus gave a grim smile. "My grandfather fulfilled your decree, Most Ascendant One. Against my grandmother's wishes. She only wished to have one child, so he harvested her ovaries and acted without her consent. He had a great many children. Grandmother went on to kill a great many children. She set out to rectify his mistake after he perished. So there are two of us."

"Domitrians," said the Interdict, shaking his head, amused. "You never change. I wonder how differently our history might have been, had the scepter been wielded by a family less inclined to war with itself." Then, looking at me, "But she—she is not a Domitrian. She is a change. What do I call you, young lady?"

"This is Nemesis," Tyrus said.

"Nemesis dan . . . what?"

So he knew. He knew I wasn't a person. "I'm Nemesis dan Impyrean."

"You've a very interesting configuration," murmured the Interdict. "Just since entering these halls, your heartbeat has ranged from thirty-eight beats per minute to over three hundred. Twice a standard blood volume, and those kidneys and that liver . . . I imagine you've never been drunk in your life."

I shook my head.

"And I must say, that hypothalamus of yours—a very acute fight or flight reflex. Tell me, can you hibernate?"

"Hibernate?" I repeated.

"A very deep sleep in icy conditions. Alas, I will take that as a no, but do let me know if that changes. I consider myself somewhat of a scholar, and anything intriguing to stimulate my mind, I welcome. I do hope my questions haven't made you feel uncomfortable."

"Not at all."

"Most excellent." Then, to Tyrus, "And you needn't remind me I am wasting your gravital window, my child. You can tell me your purpose in being here."

"Gravital window?" Tyrus echoed.

The Interdict's brows flew together. "Yes. You . . ." He looked between us. "You timed your entry into my system, surely. You didn't simply . . ." He trailed off, and then he gave a low, rasping chuckle. "You flew straight to me without checking whether it would be safe in advance. . . . Did you really?"

"Why?"

The Interdict reached over and patted his cheek. "My, fate truly does protect children. The gravital forces around a black hole are shocking. There are years, even decades at a time that one cannot safely reach the Sacred City. It's why I send my vicars back and forth so irregularly. Why, if you'd come mere days ago, you'd be in pieces now!"

I said, "Our ship is very strong."

"The strongest ship cannot survive this system at the wrong moment. You two do not comprehend your good fortune! Astonishing. Our divine Cosmos must have a great mission for you." He focused on Tyrus. "Do share why you are here. I listen breathlessly."

Tyrus dropped to his knees, reached out to draw the Interdict's knuckle to his cheek. "Most Ascendant One, I wouldn't seek the honor of your company in this stronghold if I didn't have a great need of you. I have taken the throne, yet your vicars have denied me power over the scepter."

"That's a grave thing for them to do. Why do they object to you?" said the Interdict.

"Because of the one I love." Tyrus lifted his eyes to the Interdict's. "The woman who stands before you."

"And you seek me in hopes I will override my vicars?"

"More than that," Tyrus said. "Nemesis has saved my life so many times. She is a woman with more courage and integrity than anyone I've ever known. I want her to be my Empress. And I wish you to imbue her with personhood so I may do so."

"And then the scepter issue should resolve itself, you think," said Orthanion knowingly. "I see. You must love her, to risk so much for this meeting. Yet surely you knew my vicars enforce only the edicts I gave them."

"That," Tyrus said, voice strained, "is why I do not appeal to them, but to you. I would never ask them to disobey you, Most Ascendant One. You are the one who must decide this."

"Indeed I am. And clearly, you are very attached to this"—his gaze traveled over me—"this girl. Let's discuss this girl, Emperor Tyrus."

"This girl is right in front of you," I couldn't help saying.

The Interdict's lips flickered in a smile. "I apologize for being rude. I am too accustomed to Exalteds, and they never take offense at anything. So . . . Nemesis. We will discuss you, Nemesis. You exist because someone in possession of a synthesizer told it to make a humanoid. They also told it to imbue you with certain properties. . . . Looking at your scans, I'd say they wanted a very fast and powerful being. Am I right?"

"Yes," I admitted.

The Interdict began circling about me, examining me with a clinical interest. "So your mere existence took place because someone told a synthesizer to make a strong and fast creature with an outwardly human appearance. The synthesizer had samples of DNA and RNA from all different organisms, and it pieced those bits that gave strength, those bits that gave speed, those other bits with other qualities, and pasted them all together until it formed a single cell: an embryo. That embryo was placed into an incubator and grown into a being that could exist outside an incubator. Not into a baby, but into a toddler. Only then was it removed."

"Forgive me if I do not see your point," Tyrus said.

"My point is, *this* is the process that created the very first creature like Nemesis. That toddler was watched, monitored, tested, and evaluated for how useful it would be for the function it had been built to perform. When that toddler was fully grown, and deemed viable, the same pattern of DNA and RNA crafted by that first synthesizer was used over and over again. There were tweaks . . . a male version, a female version, a taller version, a brown-skinned version, a pink-skinned version . . . one version that became this lovely young woman standing before me. Nemesis, as with all living beings, you are wondrous and a miracle, but I cannot call you a human being. You are not."

"Most Ascendant One," Tyrus said, stepping toward him, "I think if you familiarize yourself with her—"

"I am sure she is most winning and will impress me immensely, my Emperor, but that still does not make her just like us, who are a result of millions of years of natural selection," the Interdict said patiently. "She is only outwardly similar to you. Take a thousand different materials and craft them together, and you may create a visual duplicate of your asteroid starship, but inside, is it a starship? Your Nemesis looks human because we like the look of beautiful humans, but inside, she is made of amino acids and DNA sequences chosen by that synthesizer in an arbitrary fashion. Is your heart strong, Nemesis? If so, thank the kangaroo."

"The what?" I'd never heard of such a creature.

"A hopping animal with a very efficient heart. Most popular cardiac material for a variety of creatures. And judging by those efficient kidneys, I'd guess feline. The musculature . . . That can be any number of things, for humans are quite weak. Bear? Tiger? Chimpanzee? Who knows. Not human. Our muscle mass is not primed to accumulate so rapidly."

The words disturbed me, but Tyrus's hand tightened on mine. "What does this matter? All you are saying is, she's an . . . an Earthling. As am I. That's what matters. Most Ascendant One, I will wed her one way or another. Whether I do so presiding over a united Empire, or one divided by a ruinous civil war, is up to you."

"Oh, you attempt to do that with me, do you?" said the Interdict, but he merely looked amused. "Tell me, truly: how old are you, Emperor Tyrus?"

Tyrus narrowed his eyes. "Why does that matter?"

"If it doesn't matter, then answer me."

"I am twenty. Almost."

"So you are nineteen. A teenager. By any reckoning, you are essentially still a child."

"That's not—"

"Eight more years of brain development and I will say otherwise. At twenty-seven, your mind will be fully formed. I've received word you've included books with your tribute. I'm not inclined to fiction myself, but I will be glad to pass on fascinating works of philosophy, of scholarly thought to aid in the last years of that development. You will not always be a child. When that day comes, you will care about things you are indifferent to at the moment. . . . Such as Nemesis's inability to have children with you."

"I have thought of that," Tyrus said. "And I know husbands and husbands use incubators. My ancestor Gannex—"

"Was a human being, as was his husband. As was their issue. The young woman at your side may combine her DNA with yours, but there is no guessing what will result!"

"If it's merely a problem of children," Tyrus said incredulously, "then it's really not a problem. I am not having them. Do you want them, Nemesis?"

I didn't have to think about that. "No."

The Interdict gazed at Tyrus a long moment. "You were unaware, I take it, that you needed the consent of the faith to control your scepter. This may be another thing you don't realize: the choice of whether you have children isn't yours. You will not be allowed to remain childless."

Tyrus sputtered a laugh. "Of course that's my choice."

The Interdict shook his head. "Not when it comes to a Domitrian. Certainly not one of the last two."

I looked at Tyrus. Not the last two. He was the last *one*.

There was a flash of anger in Tyrus's eyes now, but the Interdict held up his hand. "Having said that, I am inclined to favor you for your boldness in seeking me out. I've met many Domitrians, and you are certainly most unique, Tyrus. So I am inclined to grant your request to offer your beloved personhood, on one condition."

Tyrus caught his breath. So did I. I had not dared hope for such an easy agreement.

Orthanion smiled. "Come back to me and ask again in twenty years."

# 17

"TWENTY YEARS." Tyrus repeated the words, stunned.

But Orthanion didn't even look the slightest bit abashed at the ridiculous, impossible condition he'd just laid upon us. "In twenty years, I will grant you this request."

Tyrus looked down at the ground, a vein in his temple pulsing. "Why not just say no?"

"Because I'm not refusing you," the Interdict said, and he spoke as though he earnestly believed it—as absurd as his condition was. "When you return to me twenty years older, I will know a seasoned Emperor is asking this of me. I will do as that Emperor Tyrus requests. I'll know *he* fully understands the implications of his request. I will also know that the love between you is long and enduring enough that I make the proper choice for you both."

With a short, curt nod, Tyrus said, "In that case, I must return to the matter of—"

"The scepter. Yes. Which my vicars rightly object to granting to you. At this time devote your energies to winning their goodwill, and perhaps they will think otherwise. Or again, you can wait but twenty years. . . ."

Tyrus let out an incredulous laugh. "Wait, so in twenty years, again, you'll grant me power over the scepter—just in case I've not won the vicars by then? Most Ascendant One, do you realize how you are imperiling this Empire? If I must mobilize thousands of ships for an evacuation or a relief effort, I will not be able to do so. The Chrysanthemum will begin shutting down ship by ship without service bots, and with no security. . . ."

"It is challenging. Such is the life of an Emperor. I know this well."

"Do you."

"I am not idle here. I am likely the most learned of scholars you will ever encounter. I speak from a position of informed knowledge."

"How can you possibly?" Tyrus said. "You are completely detached from the rest of this Empire. In any possible sense."

"It's a position that gives me objectivity you do not have. Clarity of thought you do not even realize you lack. I assure you, twenty years is a short time to wait. You see two decades as a great stretch because you are very young. Too young to even realize how young you are, and far too inexperienced to make such a drastic request of me. Tell me." He jerked his head toward the side. "What do you see out of that window?"

Tyrus didn't look. A muscle in his cheek ticked. "The black hole. Why?"

"You should look a while longer," said Orthanion. "There isn't just the black hole there. There is a stream of energy emitted by it every so often. A quasar. Now, the pulsar is a star being torn apart by the black hole, but the quasar—it is what emerges from the black hole. It's most breathtaking. I know it's there because I spend a great deal of time gazing upon that black hole, so I've seen the brilliance of that quasar. . . . But time is required. Time and care, and then it may be glimpsed. In such a way, my experience grants me insights you lack, for no reason other than your youth. I have simply been around longer, so I have seen more than you have."

"That is the problem for everyone at some point," Tyrus said with an edge in his voice. "The way to overcome inexperience is to learn, to read, to discuss. Tell me what you think I am overlooking and give me a chance to make my case about whether I am missing it or not."

The Interdict pursed his lips in thought. "Very well. My primary issue is, you ask me to give personhood to a creature. This entire Empire was *founded* upon a belief in the purity of humanity as it was crafted by nature. You are the Emperor and you are asking for something that challenges that fundamental value at the core of our existence. Do you know why we are nowhere near Earth right now?"

"Our ancestors left for more pristine frontiers. Earth was a ruin."

"Ah, so the propaganda has become so effective, even the Emperor believes it," said Orthanion, with some satisfaction in his voice.

Tyrus just stared at him, as bewildered as I was.

"Here is the true story, one that my predecessor as Interdict believed was best left behind: Earth is very much habitable. Our home planet is intact and human beings still live there. May live there still, if they haven't decided to go elsewhere."

I felt a wash of shock, trying to understand that. And Tyrus opened and closed his mouth. Then he said, "They're . . . they're all still about? Out there, alive—they are there?"

"Yes, the mother species never left Earth. We branched off. The reason we separated and are now nowhere near Earth is because those we abandoned had rejected the sanctity of humanity."

Tyrus rocked back a step. Then, for lack of a chair, he lowered himself onto the ledge by the window. "So there are two entirely separate civilizations of humans," he said.

"Oh, two at the very least," the Interdict said. "Likely more. I wouldn't necessarily call them 'human,' however. Not anymore."

"What did they do?" Tyrus asked quietly, fascinated despite himself. "What was so bad?"

"They did what we do with beauty bots. What we do with study, with any number of activities undertaken for enhancement of self: they improved. Not through genetic manipulation, as with your Nemesis— for oddly, they always had a taboo about genetically engineering humans. No, they undertook a much more extreme form of self-improvement: they hybridized themselves with machines."

"Hybridized? What—I don't—" Tyrus said.

The Interdict pointed to his temple. "They started off installing computers in their brains to make themselves smarter. Then more. Bionic eyes, limbs, tiny machines to supplement their immune system. They embraced the *artificial*. And I don't mean they did so the way we would use a med bot, or a beauty bot. They did the equivalent of implanting a beauty bot under their skin, a med bot in place of an arm. They removed the natural and inserted the unnatural. Tell me, if you replace one neuron—a single cell in your brain—with a mechanized duplicate, are you still you?"

Tyrus didn't answer.

I spoke instead: "Obviously, you are."

"Ah, then if you replace five?" said the Interdict. "Ten? A hundred? A thousand? One million? If you take every bit of your brain and you duplicate it electronically, and replace yourself with that duplicate . . . Tell me, at what point are you no longer you? At what point are you something else entirely?"

Neither Tyrus nor I spoke. There was no answer to such a question.

The Interdict spread his palms. "And there you have the reason we are out here, and Humanity Prime—as you might call them—remains on Earth. They became something that was no longer human. Our ancestors were but twenty thousand people in the beginning, and they chose to be done with those unnatural improvements. They ventured out here and devoted themselves to returning to their natural state. Now, without those machine minds, some things certainly became more difficult. Technology such as this"—he gestured about us—"is virtually impossible to duplicate or figure out with a standard human mind. You need the machine men to create such things."

Tyrus gaped at him a moment. Then, soberly, "You are saying that we didn't make any of this."

"It was all crafted before departing Earth, or by the first generation to settle here. They were cleverly built. You are looking at ancient machines that have repaired and sustained each other for thousands of years. The first generation knew their descendants wouldn't have their same intellectual capabilities. There are limits to human intelligence in a natural state."

A dimness came over Tyrus's face. He seemed to look inward, and I knew what had just occurred to him. So much of what he'd planned for the future when it came to repairing malignant space and restoring the sciences depended on the assumption we could *learn* once again what our ancestors knew.

The Interdict had just suggested otherwise.

"Our ancestors knew they were giving up those staggering minds," said Orthanion, "and they did it willingly—to save their souls. That is why we must honor the legacy of those twenty thousand founding mothers and fathers and act as they would have wished. The Empire's body is in your hands, but its soul is in mine. Today, I will protect it.

In twenty years, if you return and have the same request, I will abide by it. Now go and catch your gravital window. This is a short one."

Tyrus was speechless. This wasn't one of the responses we'd prepared for.

But the Interdict was walking away, and I didn't know what to do. I just knew this couldn't stand, it couldn't. . . .

So I slammed the flat of my fist over the back of the Interdict's head, knocking him unconscious before he could leave us.

"Nemesis!" exclaimed Tyrus as the Interdict collapsed.

"What?" I said. "He wasn't cooperating. Think of it: he's been living here in this beautiful place removed from everything for so long. Let's take him onboard the *Hera* and make him see the state of the galaxy."

Tyrus opened and closed his mouth several times. I'd already knocked the man out; it was too late to take that back.

"Maybe we are not machine men," Tyrus said, speaking almost to himself, "but we can try. He won't stop us from trying to recover what we've lost." He darted a glance out the window, and a wicked gleam came into his eyes. "We'll take him on the *Hera*, but . . . but I've a different destination in mind. One that will speak to our Most Ascendant One in a way he'll never forget."

Then he strode over and drew me into a hard, reckless kiss. We grinned savagely at each other, and possibility electrified me.

Then we kidnapped the holiest man in the Empire together.

# 18

WHATEVER ELSE the Interdict was, he served as an excellent distraction and human shield for our trip back through the Sacred City to the *Hera*. Indeed, the vicars, and the armed vicars who served as Inquisitors, didn't truly know what to do with us, or to us, as we carried him away.

We shut our ears to the cries of grave sin, and threats of excommunication, and we shuffled the limp, old—very, very old—man onto our ship. Then we tore away from the towing cables and launched into space.

Tyrus flipped on a med bot, then paced back and forth briskly next to the unconscious Interdict. His heartbeat was so frantic, I could see it in his neck. "This is the most insane thing I've ever done."

He'd played the madman for half his life, so that was saying a lot.

"If it doesn't work," I said evenly, "then we follow my plan. Turn around and take him sightseeing."

Tyrus jerked his head in a nod.

Then . . .

A moan.

The med bot was rousing him.

I hastened to Tyrus's side so we could present a united front in this mad tactic. When Orthanion sat up, he froze at the sight of us.

"Most Ascendant One," Tyrus said coolly. "Welcome to outer space."

The Interdict launched to his feet, took in his surroundings, and sputtered with disbelief. "What in the . . . Are you . . . are you utterly mad?" he demanded.

Tyrus gave a crooked smile. "I've been called that once or twice."

"You are kidnapping *me*? This won't get you what you want! This is a crime against the Living Cosmos! Every Helionic in the galaxy will turn upon you for this!"

"Not with you right in reach of us," I said coldly.

"And they won't have a chance," Tyrus affirmed. Under pressure, he showed only a cool, unshakable demeanor, as though we were passing a pleasant interlude, not committing a terrible crime. "We are not kidnapping you with the intention of continuing our lives as they are. You seem to think I am mercurial and young, that something will change if I am accorded another twenty years. Well, I won't wait that long. If Nemesis and I cannot be together as people, then . . . Then we are going to seek oblivion together. Along with you."

The Interdict paled. "What are you doing?"

"My cousin is doomed. I am the last Domitrian. And you—you may be the last Interdict. We disappear together." Tyrus shrugged. "Or whatever you call it. What *does* happen to people thrown into a black hole?"

All color disappeared from Orthanion's face. He whirled about and dashed faster than I would have thought he could move. He reached the window and saw the curvature of unfathomable black we were aimed at.

Tyrus and I exchanged a tense look behind his back. Our hope was to terrify him into giving me personhood, and therefore his tacit consent to Tyrus holding his scepter. We would record it, and then leave here—and broadcast it to the galaxy. My personhood would obliterate the grounds for the vicars to object to Tyrus holding the scepter. By the time a vicar came out of the Sacred City with the Interdict's decree in hand saying he'd been coerced, well, a vicar could be intercepted easily enough. We would keep the truth a secret until the scepter was Tyrus's to command, and then the truth would not matter.

Nothing terrified a Helionic more than the ultimate death.

Flying into a black hole.

Orthanion's strangled gasp gratified me, as did the raw terror on his face when he said to us, "Turn us around. You have to turn us around."

"Not going to happen," Tyrus said, unmoved. He had to notice, as I had, the way the jostling of the *Hera* grew increasingly violent all about us. We knew there was a point of no return, a point where even light could not escape.

We hoped to terrify the Interdict into submission long before that point.

"I have to admit, I'm rather curious about what will happen when we reach it," Tyrus said to me conversationally.

"It will be so interesting," I agreed.

"FOOLS!" shouted the Interdict, rushing over to us. "You don't know what you're doing!"

"I know exactly what I'm doing!" roared Tyrus. "I am not waiting twenty years! It is a short time to you, but the rest of us do not live five centuries!"

"You think . . . you think I am so old?" sputtered Orthanion, looking between us with disbelief. "I am but ninety-one."

"Nonsense," I said. "There's a statue of you, of your exact likeness, and it bears your name. It is half an eon old. We have both seen it at the Chrysanthemum."

"Yes," he snapped out, "I posed for it. Five hundred years ago—for you. For me, it was mere decades ago."

I looked at Tyrus, trying to see if this made sense to him. He was looking at me, doing the same thing.

Orthanion surged toward the window looking onto the ominous curve of black and activated the magnifiers, amplifying the view again and again and again. "Look. Just look here. Do you see it? Do you see anything there?"

"No," I said sharply, for I had excellent eyesight.

"That is lucky," rasped the Interdict, "for if we get closer and closer to that black hole, you *will* see something: the tomb of the Emperor Amon von Domitrian."

Tyrus made an incredulous, sputtering sound.

"That's not even possible," I cried. "He was excommunicated *centuries* ago."

"Yes. For *you*, centuries have passed." The Interdict trained his gaze on Tyrus's face. "For Amon, close as he is to that singularity? He's passed mere *minutes*. A thousand years from now, if an onlooker glimpses Amon falling into the black hole, Amon will have passed another second. Time is not *constant*. Do you understand? *Gravity bends time.* The closer we get to the black hole, the slower we creep through existence!"

I saw Tyrus go deathly pale as it all fell into place for him, just as it was forming coherence for me. The ageless vicars, the ancient Interdict, the sheer remove of the Sacred City from the rest of us. . . .

They literally existed in a slower time frame.

And we were in it now, too.

"Oh stars no," Tyrus breathed. He leaped over to the navigation panel. The *Hera* gave a ferocious jolt as it turned about, but I couldn't make sense of it.

"He's making this up," I said uncertainly to Tyrus. "Time is time. It doesn't . . . It can't just change. It makes no sense."

The Interdict stared at me.

"Are you just making it up?" Tyrus said to the Interdict hopefully. "Be honest. I will take us back either way, I swear—"

"*I* am not inventing the theory of relativity!" the Interdict roared. "I am not *Albert Einstein*. Are you telling me that you, Tyrus—the Emperor—do not know the basic laws of physics?"

"How would I know them?" cried Tyrus. "You made such things blasphemy. Where would I learn of this?"

"My reforms weren't meant for the likes of you! And they weren't aimed at destroying all understanding of basic sciences! I meant only to eliminate those destructive technologies that . . ." The Interdict fell deathly silent, his face blanching.

*He didn't realize this.* The thought crept over me. *He never intended us to become so ignorant.*

Strange.

It had been infuriating to think the Interdict had meant to change the galaxy, meant to render everyone so ignorant.

But to realize he'd been as shortsighted and blundering as the rest of us . . .

That was vastly more frightening.

# 19

**GRAVITY ALTERED TIME.** It was something I had not known, and Tyrus had not known. Now we did. At a painful cost.

On the Chrysanthemum, in standard space, there was a regular flow of time everyone else in the Empire was living. The Sacred City, near the black hole, shifted constantly between slower and much slower time differentials. Sometimes a day outside was a month within. Sometimes a year.

And in aiming directly for the black hole, we'd merely traversed into slower and slower time. The Interdict himself could not tell us how long we'd been gone, not without the database at the Sacred City, which could calculate this down to a millisecond. The knowledge left Tyrus standing stock-still in the middle of the command nexus, just staring at space, his face ashen.

The Interdict was the only one of us with the presence of mind to act: he settled by one of the *Hera*'s computers and began typing in search terms in the database. I glimpsed a few of them: *entropy, causality, diffraction, negative refraction.* He must not have found them, for he started jabbing in the words faster and faster, the pinch of aggravation on his face mounting.

Then, with a great expulsion of breath, he shoved away from the console, looking as sick as Tyrus did.

"This cannot stand." He caught me staring and said, "Tell me, Nemesis, has this computer been through a catastrophic accident? Has it been wiped or . . ."

I shook my head.

"I wished to discover the extent of your ignorance. I began searching your computer for complex terms, and then moved to the simplest ones, hoping every time my worst fears would not be confirmed. They were. I have never been in opposition to learning. On the contrary, had I not found this calling, I would have been pleased to pass my life in a university, teaching, learning, sharing. But it was the supernova that necessitated the blasphemy decree. I aimed it at those who couldn't be trusted with our technology. It was a pretense to disarm those who didn't understand the implications of their actions. Not everyone should have the power we'd gained through science."

Tyrus dragged his gaze over to his. "You just decided others weren't responsible enough to hold technology? I suppose the Grandiloquy were?"

"It wasn't only my opinion, Tyrus. Our ancestors didn't leave Earth of their own volition," said Orthanion. "Humanity Prime forced them to go. They believed natural human beings were too destructive to handle the technological progress the species had made with mechanized brains. They gave our ancestors—the twenty thousand of faith—a choice: if they became fully organic, they had to give up all advanced technology and live on a nature preserve. The alternative was to return to an organic state, keep that technology, but go very far away from Earth."

"Far away?" Tyrus said.

"Here. To this region. Somewhere we would inflict harm upon none but ourselves. So here we are, in this fragile corridor of habitable space, surrounded by natural barriers of radiation and gravity and cosmic rays. We spread out as humans do and occupied all of the territory in reach, and then half an eon ago, we did just what was predicted of us. Some of us mere organic human beings ignited an artificial supernova and wiped out half the Empire."

"That was intentional?" I breathed. "Why would anyone do that?"

The Interdict shrugged. "We are all descended from zealots. Faith can inspire greatness, but it can be used to justify breathtaking cruelties."

I couldn't understand that. Someone had done that on purpose.

"That's when your ancestor Tarantis von Domitrian and I realized there'd been some wisdom to Humanity Prime's warnings," Orthanion said. "So much knowledge had been lost after the supernova, so we ensured it remained lost—by instituting the decree forbidding the sciences. Machines were concentrated among those responsible enough to use them wisely."

He looked between us, and for the first time, his perfect, calm arrogance had wavered, his eyes those of a fallible man who'd lived too long, who'd made a most dreadful mistake.

"It was meant only to walk back progress a few steps. To prevent such destructive devices from ever being wielded again. I would not have suggested it without having studied history and made myself an authority in human affairs. I never anticipated the basic laws of physics disappearing from public knowledge—eluding even an *Emperor*."

"Perhaps," Tyrus said with a bite in his voice, "you should get out more."

"I have most certainly been too complacent, counting on my vicars to keep me apprised when they arrive so infrequently. . . . This is the Living Cosmos rebuking me for my arrogance."

I stared at him, for there was a staggering egotism in his assumption that everything was aimed at teaching a lesson to him.

"I believed I saw our divine Cosmos's aims so clearly, and yet now I must think of it anew. I must think of an Emperor—a Domitrian Emperor—falling in such obsessive, unwavering love with a creature that he would seek me out. . . . For of course it would be me, I am the only one who can imbue her with personhood. . . ."

He was almost mumbling to himself now, trying to puzzle out why this was all about him.

A strange urge to smack him came over me. I balled up my fists to restrain it, and when I looked at Tyrus, his shoulders were sagging. He seemed in a state of stunned shock.

"I see now the will of our Living Cosmos," said the Interdict, straightening up. "The Emperor fell in love with one only *I* could gift with personhood, all so you could come to me, so you would show me the error of my ways. . . . Yes. Yes, it is all so clear."

Tyrus looked at him wearily. He was clearly still thinking of the time lost, of the time we were still losing.

"Miracles hide within tragedies," the Interdict said. "And the path we must take has opened itself before me as vividly as a sunrise. My young Emperor, you must undertake the most difficult of missions on behalf of your Living Cosmos."

Yes, the urge to hit him truly made my palm tingle. Tyrus couldn't muster any expression of eagerness for him.

"You will be the Domitrian who restores the study of scientific learning," announced the Interdict.

And Tyrus's mouth fell open, my head reeled, for . . . for was this really happening? Now? After this?

"You want . . . restoration of the sciences. After all this time," Tyrus said.

"I do, my child. This is your purpose. And I command you to do it. I will impart to you everything on our system, on our computers, all the knowledge lost, so it may be rediscovered with your help. Will you undertake this mission?"

Incredulous, Tyrus dropped to his knees before the Interdict, torn between hope and total bewilderment. "You are asking me to do this for you, Most Ascendant One."

"Yes. You've been an agent of this Living Cosmos, and you will be one again, on this much more daunting of tasks. And you, you—the creature Nemesis. To your knees. Let me touch you."

Baffled, I practically stumbled down to kneel at Tyrus's side as the Interdict offered us each a hand and let us both draw them to our cheeks.

"The divine light of this Cosmos brought you to me, brought you both to me." His eyes burned with conviction. "And now it will shine a path forward, because you ask me to grant her personhood, my young Emperor. I will not only do that, I will confer on her my holy mark of blessing. She's been my agent as much as you have, and I don't believe you were put in my path without design." He drew us both to our feet. "We are all three of us agents of that which is greater than us all, and isn't this a glorious purpose indeed?"

The ceremony was conducted right in the heliosphere of the *Hera* in those fleeting minutes before we reached the Sacred City.

The Interdict adjusted the reflective mirrors about him, and

at space as though he could will the vessel to hurry up with just his mind.

For someone who had planned every step and the next ten ahead of it the entirety of his life—including backup plans for any scenario his mind could concoct—this unexpected setback had to horrify him.

"Eleven months," he said to himself, as though trying to wrap his head around it. "We left for the Transaturnine System . . . and stayed away for almost a year. Children have been conceived and then born in the time we have been away, and we left right on the cusp of a conflict. Stars help us."

"Whatever awaits us," I said, "we'll make do." And I believed those airy words as I spoke them.

Tyrus pressed his forehead to the window, squeezed his eyes shut. "We can't jump to hyperspace until we're clear of this gravity. That means . . . eight hours. We have eight hours to wait, and then weeks in hyperspace. Time we can't afford to lose, if it makes a difference at this point. Eleven months . . ."

"We can't change it now. It could have been far longer."

"Maybe it should have been. Ten years. One hundred. If we'd returned then, we'd have come back to something so drastically different, it wouldn't make a difference one way or another." He spoke with rapid-fire, clipped words. "But we were gone just long enough . . . My cousin is dead, and I wasn't there to frame it. Pasus armed himself and united allies, and I . . . I just left mine. They probably thought I was dead. Every spy I've cultivated has long since found a new master. Helios devoured, we have nothing."

"Tyrus." I gripped his face, and he blinked at me sluggishly like he'd just seen me. "We still have one person we can rely on." At his blank look: "Neveni. She knew."

"She'll have told them where we went," Tyrus said. "That's what we instructed her to do if we hadn't returned in a month."

"Yes. And now she will tell us what we've missed. Pasus had her mother killed. Believe me, Tyrus—she can be trusted."

"It's hearsay from an Excess who isn't even at court."

"Yes, and she has links with many Luminars who *are*, Tyrus."

"True," he said.

"Then we will find someone you trust at court, depending on what she says. And we will ask them. Who do you trust?"

He stared at me a moment. His lips curved. "You."

"Who else?" I said, patting his cheek lightly, in a mock slap.

But my levity didn't reach him. He leaned back against the window, his reflection shifting with him. "Nemesis, I paid for loyalty. Anyone I paid is being paid by someone else now. It is utterly impossible to form deep and intense personal relationships while playing a madman and refusing to trust any of them. I set up a system of loyalty with one party watching another, but none of it works without me there to oversee it."

"We are going to have to change that when we're back," I murmured. "We need to figure out a way to win support."

"We have to ensure we survive that long. They may have an entirely new government by now. We'll . . . we'll count upon Mistress Sagnau's animosity toward Pasus. And beyond that . . ." He looked about us. "Would that we had a different ship."

"The *Hera* is why we are alive."

"Yes, it was most excellent. Now it's our liability. It's too recognizable. If we had another vessel on hand, I'd say we aim for somewhere visible, as visible as possible. Eurydice, perhaps."

I knew that planet. It was the wealthiest province for the Excess. It was center of the galactic media.

He rubbed his temples. "But we won't get there in this ship. There

will be too much advance warning, too much opportunity to stop us."

"So why not head directly to the Chrysanthemum without warning?"

He looked at me, turning it over in his mind.

"Think of it, Tyrus. We are both quick on our feet. The entry and exit corridor is too narrow for any alert foes to chase us in. We will be there and at the palace before anyone can muster a decent ambush."

"Once we are there, we are virtually trapped," he said.

"It's been almost a year, as you said. Who will expect us? It's the best of many poor options."

He leaned his forehead against the window again. Released a jagged breath. "I suppose we have eight hours to think of an alternative."

Though he was strung like a tight wire, I felt almost like I was floating freely in an exquisite ocean. I stepped up behind him, ran my hands over the tense muscles of his back, felt him relaxing despite himself. My gaze kept straying to my bared arms, for there was something within me that had stirred with the starlight bathing me. I was a real person. It had happened. A strange peace hummed in my veins, and I wondered if I looked different somehow.

Tyrus glanced back at me with heavy-lidded eyes, and a smile tugged at his lips. "You're glowing."

"I'm a person now."

He turned. His broad hands settled on my waist, and he nuzzled his lips over the curve of my cheek. "Don't tell the Interdict," he said gently, "but I think you always have been."

"Blasphemer," I teased him.

There was a shift, so subtle, like a charge on the air. A buzz, and I melted into his arms and he guided my lips to his. I parted his mouth, and stroked my tongue over his, and he responded with a sudden fervor that rippled down to my core. I looped my leg about him to draw

him closer, ever closer to me, and there was a low sound in his throat that made me smile against his lips.

Then it was all still about me, the ship, the galaxy, this Empire, and everything was his heat, the taste of his mouth, his skin, and I dipped my mouth to the hollow of his throat.

Now.

My fingers threaded through his reddish hair and my lips touched the shell of his ear. "I'm ready."

Tyrus's blue-eyed gaze shot to mine, electric with his need for me. "You are certain?"

"Yes. I love you. I'm sure."

"I love you, too, Nemesis. More than you can know."

The broad, deep kisses accompanied us as we made our way through the ship, a rapturous sense of possibility, of beauty seeming to unspool in this moment I wished I could capture and relive at will. I was his equal and a child of the Living Cosmos, and all I wanted now was to show him how I loved him. I aimed us for my own chamber, but he slipped his arms around me and steered us into the nearest one we came across. I recalled with a soft laugh that these were *all* my chambers now. . . . In the haze of glorious happiness, I couldn't touch him, feel him, taste him enough, his feverish, hungry kisses drawing an exquisite fire to my surface. Then he was over me, balanced on those limbs corded with muscle, and we looked into each other's eyes. The silken sheets were cool against my back, his body radiating heat into mine. . .

He took that moment, that breathless moment, to just gaze at me as though he saw the most wondrous of mysteries in this Cosmos.

"I can't believe it," he remarked, "that you and I are here. That we found each other."

And I understood what he meant. I knew, and the miracle of it

seemed to pulse through my very being as I wrapped my legs about him and drew him closer to me.

Our bright figures formed ghostly reflections rippling across the brilliant, vibrant light of the star system. He was mine and I was his, and for a fleeting moment as we joined together again within the endless void all about us, there were no prying eyes, there wasn't another soul, just the two of us, and the universe ignited golden and complete.

I awoke thrumming with expansive joy to find Tyrus watching me, his thumb trailing circles over my bared hip. His lips curled as our eyes met, and we shared that moment of hazy, sweet contentment under the ivory sheets.

My voice was bleary. "What time is it?"

"Does it matter?"

"Mmm. No." We just smiled at each other in a ridiculous way like we were any other pair of young lovers.

But we were not.

We never had been.

I needed to protect this. To protect us.

That cleared my thoughts.

I eased myself up. "How long until we can enter hyperspace? We should contact Neveni as soon as we're in standard time."

Silence rested heavily on the air. Then, in an odd tone, Tyrus said, "We cleared the Transaturnine System about a half hour ago."

His face was remote now—his eyes trained on the ceiling.

"Did you contact her already?"

"I . . ." His pale lashes flickered. "Not yet." He looked at me. "I thought we'd talk about it first."

"What is there to discuss?"

"Well, we were gone a long time. We didn't time our entrance with the gravity window—a short delay, and we might have missed it and been destroyed. They may think we're dead."

"Yes. We'll have the element of surprise on our side when we return."

I gathered the smooth sheets about me, noting the way his gaze automatically traced down the bare expanse of my leg where it had slipped out of the covers. Tyrus was so self-disciplined, so controlled, that there was something gratifying in these small moments of his where he reminded me that beneath it all, he was a nineteen-year-old boy who was entranced by me.

Tyrus cupped my cheek with his broad palm, stroked my skin with his thumb. "I was caught up in just . . . just looking at you. And then I remembered—I have fallen behind on whatever narcotic I'd planned to use today to keep myself accustomed, and then a thought came to me: What if I didn't bother?"

I gazed at him blankly. If he didn't wish to do it, he didn't have to. He imposed that regimen on himself. No one else did.

He gave a soft laugh and drew me closer, my weight resting entirely on him, the heat of his skin soaking into mine. "What," he said hoarsely, "if I never bothered doing that again because I never *needed* to do so again, because . . . because a year ago, the Emperor Tyrus von Domitrian vanished with his wife-to-be, and . . . and never returned."

I smiled at the absurdity of the idea, but his eyes remained deadly serious.

"They think we are dead, Nemesis. If we want to, we can stay that way." His fingers stroked my skin, his gaze distant. "I did it once before. Years ago. After my mother was slain, and I'd escaped her killers . . . I decided that I was sick of being a Domitrian so I tore out my identity chip. *Bit* it out, right then and there, and smashed it.

Then I stowed away on a ship and just meant to disappear."

"You've never told me about this."

"I've never told anyone about this." He spoke quietly. "You see, I had a father. 'Father' in the loosest definition, of course, since he was an Excess who hadn't even known my mother chose his DNA for her offspring. I found him and I showed up at his door and finally met this red-haired man with a huge beard and freckled skin and he was just so . . . astoundingly *ugly*."

I laughed. "I can't believe that."

"It's true. He was dreadfully ugly," insisted Tyrus with a grin. "I hadn't seen enough of people without beauty bots. And Arion—that was his name—lived with too much sun, too much chemical exposure, too many fights." He touched my own crooked nose lovingly, that relic of my own history of such skirmishes. "I meant to get him to claim me as a son so I could secure a new identity chip, but my very clever plan failed. Arion had a husband. He'd never been interested in women, so I couldn't sell myself as a one-off of a forgotten lover. He learned who I was, because my Excess accent was terrible, and I slipped into the speech tones I have now, and he was spectacularly clever."

"That's no surprise," I said.

"He learned I was a Domitrian. My family—if they found me there—would most likely kill the entirety of his family just for the crime of concealing me."

I rested my chin on his chest, knowing there could be no good outcome of this story, or I'd have heard him speak of Arion sooner.

"Despite all of that," Tyrus murmured, "Arion ended up letting me stay. I was there almost a year. I might've passed my life there."

My breath caught. "The malignant space?"

He closed his eyes. "The Excess on that planet honestly believed they could . . . just solve it themselves. They wouldn't evacuate. They embargoed information from the planet, and that meant they risked delaying a proper evacuation force until it was too late for anyone to reach them. It was ludicrous and they didn't understand it. And how could I explain to them that they were making a mistake? I was a kid. The Grandiloquy looked at me as a Domitrian above all, but to the Excess, age matters. A child is insignificant, a creature to be reassured by meaningless words and sweet candy and hugs. They were all going to die and I couldn't get them to see otherwise."

"They truly believed *they* would solve a problem the entirety of the Empire had not?"

"They had no perspective," Tyrus said. "Most hadn't even left the atmosphere of that planet. The scale of this Empire can't be understood unless one has seen it. I knew how much effort had disappeared into studying and fixing that monster in their sky, but they didn't. And when it became absolutely clear there was no convincing them to see it my way, I had to . . . I had to call my uncle and tell him I was alive."

"Oh."

And that's what he'd done. Tyrus had told his Domitrian family where to find him. The Empire then had to have learned of that planet's situation, and evacuated it.

"And your father?" I said.

He shook his head.

Of course Arion hadn't survived. Randevald and Cygna would have no mercy with Excess who dared to hide a Domitrian from them.

"Maybe we've done enough," Tyrus said quietly. "The Interdict is training his vicars. He will make certain his decree is widely known. Maybe this is the solution I vowed to pursue. Perhaps we are done."

I slipped out of the covers and sifted through his clothing and the lump beneath it all: the box with the Interdict's decree. The restoration of the sciences. The goal Tyrus had sought his entire life, the justification for outliving so many others.

There were a great many ways we could get this out there and known to the galaxy without returning.

"Where would we go?" I asked him.

He was staring at the box. "We wait for the next gravital window and then we aim for the black hole. It wouldn't take long for us. A few months. The key is, we stay somewhere we won't end up torn apart."

A few months outside of time and we could leave it all behind us. What a strange thought.

*I* could do it. All I'd leave was Neveni, but she likely believed me dead, and had moved on already. I could shed this present with ease. This starship had value. We could sell it, or use it, and live quite well, I assumed. . . .

Then I regarded Tyrus, and grew very certain he couldn't do this. Not the way I could.

I tightened my grip about the box with the decree. He'd secured it. The first step toward vindication. But this was a decree, and it needed an enforcer. The Interdict was a well-learned man of theories, not one who oversaw their application. If we abandoned this galaxy and entered the future, only to find no one had solved this . . . Tyrus would never be at peace again.

Even if malignant space *was* fixed, he wouldn't live with his own defection. No. Not Tyrus. I knew him too well. Everything we saw that was wrong—for there was always something wrong—he would see as his own failing. He would see it as something he'd allowed when he'd washed his hands of this responsibility.

The conviction welled up within me, because I knew this, even if he didn't realize it.

So I would refuse this, and take the burden of refusal out of his hands.

He was afraid of what awaited us. The unknown we would soon confront. I would be his strength.

"No, we can't leave," I said, crossing back over to him, letting him draw me down into his arms. "Not because it isn't tempting"—my hand stroked over the plane of his cheek—"but because this isn't you. What of the imbalance between the Excess and the Grandiloquy? What of the stagnation of this Empire?"

"Someone else will fix it. Someone always does."

"Yes, someone like you comes and fixes it. So that is what you'll do. We go back, we do whatever we must to survive, and then we do exactly what we planned. Whatever happens, we'll face it."

He was silent a long moment, my words sinking in. Then his lips grazed my bare shoulder. "One condition, then. We contact Sagnau— but only after you tell me what it is you want from this."

"What I want?"

He reached over for the scepter, left lying across the bedside table. "This," he said to me, "is a lifelong commitment. It's more final than any marriage. You will exist as public property, with demands that never cease even when you are tired, even when you grow old, and there is no getting away from it once it begins. Tell me what you want to do as this galaxy's Empress. Give it thought before you get trapped in this role for good."

I plucked the scepter from his hands and considered it. The device was a warm weight, resting in my hand, the jewels winking in the starlight.

This should have been an easier question to answer: what did I wish to do as Empress of this galaxy? I'd always wrapped my thoughts in his own visions. And before him, in Donia's. Had I given thought to my own desires?

Yet . . . I did have one dream. There was something I wanted. The realization ripped through my mind.

"I want to ban Servitors."

The words were in the air, and then I knew this was something I could do that was profoundly right. Excitement drove me upright. "Tyrus, they do nothing that can't be done by a service bot. They can't even save their own lives. We saw your uncle order one to skin herself alive, and she . . . that pitiful girl did it. How can Grandiloquy ever see creatures as anything but worthless when they have Servitors about them their entire lives?"

Tyrus looked inward. "They learn to devalue others from them."

"Yes."

"The Excess despise them too."

"Yes." I gripped his chin. "That's what you can do for me." Then, I realized, "No, it's what *I* can do. That's what I want to do. For everyone. And not just Servitors. Harmonids. Creatures, Tyrus. Humanoid creatures. We put a stop to them all."

"I swear that we will," Tyrus vowed. His mouth found mine, and I met him with an insistent, eager kiss, the heady anticipation of what lay ahead for us blinding me to any lingering fears.

And only then, only then, did we let Neveni know we were still alive.

# 21

"NEMESIS, *I am so glad to hear from you.*

"*The major news first: the Successor Primus died. It happened two weeks after you left. I don't know the details, but obviously I've been weeping off and on ever since. . . .*"

"Sarcasm, clearly," I said to Tyrus, since Devineé and her husband had assaulted Neveni.

"*Pasus is gone. No news of him, and from what I hear, no one has seen him in the Chrysanthemum.*

"*I waited a month, and then I finally let Tyrus's allies know what your destination was. They sent a couple of ships after you into the Transaturnine System, but they just lost contact . . .*"

I glanced at Tyrus. "Must have missed the gravital window," I murmured.

He nodded. We were listening to the computerized voice narrate the encrypted text transmission Neveni had sent. I'd had no idea how the cipher Tyrus left her worked, but Neveni had clearly figured it out.

We listened to the rest. Lumina's governing officials were still going back and forth with the Empire over the precise terms of their exit. There'd been a blackout in the galactic press on news from the planet for the last five months.

Tyrus was visibly relieved to hear it was still happening without him. "They have to frame the departure carefully. This is entirely expected."

Without Pasus, the mutinous coalition of Senators had fallen apart. Locklaite, Aton, and the others had slinked back to the Chrysanthemum, but they were shut out of power by Tyrus's allies.

Transmissions had been fabricated once a month of Tyrus addressing the galaxy to maintain the fiction that he and I were about. The entirety of the Empire was ignorant about our disappearance, and still believed he was secluded in deep mourning after losing his cousin, his last family.

*"On a last note, I'm going to the Chrysanthemum to meet you when you get back. I'll probably beat you there by a few days. There's a lot going on with Lumina's independence, and it will be useful to bring you up to speed. Have a safe trip home!*

*"Your friend, Neveni."*

Silence fell.

I cast a sidelong glance at Tyrus, where he sat with his arms crossed, gazing up at the speaker on the ceiling, rigid.

"What's wrong? I think that's the best we could have hoped for."

He rubbed his palm over his mouth. "Yes," he dragged out after a moment. "I just . . . That worries me. It's too perfect."

"I trust Neveni," I said. "I know I can't ask you to trust her too, Tyrus—but can you trust my judgment?"

"Yes. I trust you," he said. But he remained like a tight string as we finally aimed for the six-star system and leaped into hyperspace. The journey back to the Chrysanthemum was devoid of the pleasure we'd taken heading out to Lumina.

Tyrus had archived all the news transmissions he could gather from a mix of respectable news outlets and the sensationalist ones. Both were equally fictional. The respected gave a public narrative of current events as the Chrysanthemum wished the Excess to perceive them. . . . The "consensus" opinion, so to speak. Though factually questionable, Tyrus watched them first for an idea of what the larger Empire believed. Had the transmissions focused negatively on him, it would have warned him of danger awaiting us at the Chrysanthemum.

Nothing to put us on guard.

"Whoever rules at the Chrysanthemum, they've commanded the media not to assassinate my character. That's what they'd do if they anticipated our return but meant to prepare grounds for my destruction," Tyrus said. "But they've maintained the public image."

Then he passed hours sifting through the other transmissions, the ludicrous ones fed by heresay and rumor. Some were sensationalist shows, some were those underground self-styled purveyors of information who operated independently. . . . The very sort Randevald von Domitrian had occasionally ordered assassinated for airing something too close to the truth.

Mostly the truth was lost in the swamp of ridiculous conjecture and outright lies and fabrications, but the points of alignment helped us verify elements of veracity in the official consensus.

The evening before we were due to arrive, I walked into Tyrus's chamber to find him asleep. Snoring, even—and Tyrus never snored. One of the silly transmissions piped in the air, earnestly discussing the alien brain parasites controlling the Grandiloquy.

". . . claim they use narcotics for recreation or spiritual reasons, but

160

it's a lie. Those narcotics are the primary food source of the Screekuth Symbionts. . . ."

A smile crept over my lips. Tyrus's mouth was hanging open, and his head was resting on a pile of electronic displays. I tugged one out from his sprawled hand and my gaze passed over the text.

". . . *chemical potential of strange quark mass . . .*"

He raised his head. "S'from the Sacred City." Tyrus's voice was bleary. He had the misfortune of being a light sleeper. I was one, as well, but I didn't need nearly so much sleep as a regular person.

"Strange quark mass?" I said. "What is that?"

"Blast me if I know. I've been trying to make sense of it and . . ." He threw his hand up in the air.

"Off," I called to the screen, and the absurd segment about Screekuth Symbionts disappeared. "That probably does not help."

He rubbed his eyes. "Even without the noise, I don't think I can make sense of this stuff, Nemesis. It references mathematical theorems I have never even heard of. I looked it up and I have no idea what the symbols even represent. I just can't decipher what I'm reading."

"Maybe you don't have a scientific mind."

He lolled his head back to look at me. "Are you saying I'm stupid, my love?"

He'd probably never been deemed that in all his life. But I wished to tease him, to distract him, so I made a great show of thinking it over.

"You are taking far too long to answer that," Tyrus exclaimed, mock indignant.

"Forgive me, Your Supremacy. I was just recalling your talent for setting fires by hand. A caveman on ancient Earth would have believed you quite stupid."

"I would like to see that caveman become supreme ruler of the galaxy." He shook his head ruefully. "Although that caveman might be better prepared for the job than I am when it comes to these documents."

I snared his hand, tugged him to his feet—where he swayed a bit with weariness. "I just learned the Grandiloquy all have alien brain parasites."

"Do we?"

"Hmm. Yes."

"Was that from the same reputable program that said you're a sentient sex android?"

"I had not watched that far." I looped his arm in mine as he fought back a smile. "To learn you're infested by a brain parasite—well, it explains a great deal about you."

"You just had to find out the truth," he said, and then I was in his arms and his lips were on mine, and everything we would face tomorrow, everything—it was momentarily forgotten.

Our reprieve lasted until the next morning, when we dropped out of hyperspace in the six-star system. After what must have been a shocked twenty seconds as every vessel nearby noticed us on their sensors, a sudden bombardment of transmissions hit. Greetings. So many greetings. Amador was so glad we had returned and he needed to complain about the grasping Wallstrom woman. . . . Wallstrom had a most cursory hello and she was very put out with Amador and Fordyce, and . . .

On and on it went as the *Hera* navigated the gravity of the six-star system. Greetings, expressions of how thrilled they were that the Emperor was back! How they, and they alone, had been certain of his return, and how ill the conduct of this political rival or that political rival had been while Tyrus was away.

"Helios save us," Tyrus said, rubbing his hands over his face. "They are exactly as they were when we left."

But when he rolled his eyes and set about answering the most vital of the transmissions, there was ease in his posture for the first time since we'd learned of the theory of relativity. We docked with the *Valor Novus* and emerged into a bustling crowd of Grandiloquy favor-seekers already eager to speak to the Emperor, and Tyrus drew me closer to whisper in my ear, "First thing we do, the very first, is gather the primary Grandiloquy in the presence chamber."

"You have the decree in hand?"

"That's not all I wish them to see." His finger brushed over my collarbone, and I smiled at the thought of the mark.

"Nemesis!"

There were many voices calling my name as we made our way through the jostling crowd, but that voice—Neveni's—drew my notice. I saw her at the edge, just near a doorway, and when our eyes met, she beckoned me over.

Tyrus saw her too.

He tapped his ear briefly, reminding me to stay in contact at the first sign of trouble. Then I headed through the unusually bustling crowd toward Neveni. She was facing away from me by the time I reached her, looking down at the ground.

A tingle of uneasiness washed all over me.

"Neveni, what it is?"

Her voice was a whisper. "I'm sorry."

And then a strange noise arose in the air at the same time that someone seized me from behind, driving me down to the ground. My hand flew up to my ear, but someone else had already torn away the transmitter I'd clipped to my lobe so I might stay in communication with Tyrus. My gaze sliced to the side as I tried to heave myself upright, as I found my arms unable to budge the weight on me. I couldn't shake off the hand clamped over my mouth. . . .

And Neveni stared down at me with haunted eyes, the crowd

strategically arranged—I saw now—to hide me from Tyrus's sight. Then a projection glowed up from an imaging ring. A duplicate of me. She threw a wave to Tyrus. And then another man entered my line of sight.

My blood ran to ice.

It was Pasus.

One of his servants handed him the ear node. A circlet—a voice modifier—was clipped to his throat.

"Eyes on me," Pasus spoke. "Go on, it's fine. Tyrus, trust me. I'll be along shortly."

And my holographic double moved her lips with the words!

*Don't, don't believe this!* I thought, my alarm mounting at the strange weakness of my limbs. Then a large Pasus servant stepped forward and drove his boot down onto my head.

## 22

**I NEEDED OXYGEN.** I was suffocating.

A low, droning sound filled the air.

My consciousness returned slowly, and I leaned my head back to escape the pressure on my throat, only to smack it against the wall, and then I was wide awake. A cold shaft of metal was looped about my throat, magnetically trapping me against the surface behind me. . . . My hand flew up, felt the contours of the clamp. A mobile restraint, the sort that was always handy on a starship.

My hands tugged at it.

It didn't give. The ugly shock of realization registered in my mind just as the memory of how I'd gotten here spiraled back.

Neveni.

It was a trap.

We'd been trapped.

"Hello, Nemesis."

My eyes shot toward the voice, and there he was: Senator von Pasus. Alive and on the Chrysanthemum, and that's the moment the knowledge made my stomach plummet. Neveni had been compromised. He'd forced her to send me false information, or he'd done it himself, and . . . And he tilted his head with his blue eyes glittering maliciously.

"Are you weak in the knees at the sight of me?" Pasus said.

That's when I realized why this magnetic clamp wasn't giving. Why I felt strange and slow and swampy. Why there was a . . . noise on the air. Just below the buzz of lights, the churning of engines, the roar of oxygen vents . . . Something new. Something that didn't belong.

*The neural suppressor*, I realized with an electric prickle of horror. It was there, embedded in my lower back, too dangerously placed to remove.

"Your fellow Diabolics told me of that suppressor," remarked Pasus. "Remarkable instrument. That enormous one, Anguish, could be felled with one punch." He shrugged his shoulders. "It's been a great amusement for some Grandes to test themselves against a weakened Diabolic. I've made a tidy profit from it. And now . . . Here we are."

Pasus. Here. Gazing down at me with icy blue eyes, his black hair to his chin now, grown with time. I tried to pull free again, though I knew now it would not happen.

"What do you want? Where's Tyrus?" I knew this corridor. It was just outside the Emperor's presence chamber. I'd fought Enmity to the death here.

"The Emperor is very close. Entirely unaware of my presence, if those fools have followed their instructions and occupied him with their silly complaints," Pasus said, nodding toward the presence chamber.

"What are you going to do to him?" I demanded.

"Perhaps you should be more concerned for yourself."

"Answer me!"

"I've been waiting for you a long time now. I was all set to exile myself when Devineé perished, and how furious I was to realize you had poisoned her. Yet you didn't return. Nothing. So I waited. And waited a while more still. That Excess girl surfaced with news of what had happened and I could have laughed for an age to hear it. I had her abducted right off the planet, taken here so we could learn everything. Do you know how many people in this Empire know the truth of the Sacred City? I could count them on one, no, two hands."

Sickness churned up within me.

"Luckily, I was one of them. So I claimed the Chrysanthemum." He knelt down before me, and oh, if he'd just draw closer, so I could kick him . . . "How cleverly he played it, only to lose it all on one devastating mistake. My, I would pay a fortune to have seen the look on his face when he learned of the time dilation factor. I imagine he'll wear a similar expression when I walk in there."

I stared up at him, my heart slamming my rib cage, my focus narrowed upon his face. What did he plan? What would he do to Tyrus? To me? Why was I here, a prisoner, weakened, not dead?

"You don't intend to kill me," I realized.

Pasus straightened. "I would love nothing more than to strip the skin from your bones, Nemesis dan Impyrean. I doubt I could have resisted a year ago, but I have had time to think. You will be useful to me." And then an odd look came over his face. He suddenly knelt down again, moved aside the collar of my tunic.

He'd glimpsed it, then. The Interdict's mark. Just the top, but now he saw the concentric suns and his face paled with the realization the "beast" who killed his daughter was now blessed by the Interdict.

"It's Nemesis Impyrean now," I told him, my voice soft and deadly.

Pasus recoiled from me. "He can't have," he said.

"He did. I am beloved by your faith, Senator. Release me."

Rage flared on his face. "You think that means anything? Do you, *monster*?"

"Your Interdict does."

He stared at the mark with revulsion, betrayal, almost.

"Senator, release me. And whatever you've planned for Tyrus, abort the plan. The Interdict himself has—"

"Has desecrated the Living Cosmos," spat Pasus. "As our last Domitrian has tried to desecrate our Empire. Not any longer. It stops here."

My heart plunged. I gave a frantic tug at the clamp, but couldn't free myself. "What are you planning, Pasus?"

He feasted his eyes upon my face, relishing my distress. "I entertained so many ideas about what I'd do to you to avenge Elantra. So many, Nemesis. And when your fellow Diabolics ended up in my hands, I set out to see what terrified them. What hurt them. What degraded and broke them. And do you know what I found?"

I didn't venture a guess, just remained mulishly silent.

"They never feared anything. They never broke. All they did was stare at me with the same cold, dead eyes I see in your face, and that's when I realized they were invulnerable. Vulnerability is too human. So I cannot hurt you." Then he smiled. "But you do have one weakness. One you will never overcome. You are invulnerable to me, but that young Emperor in there? *He* is not. I can hurt him. And anything I do to him, you will feel five-fold. So live, Nemesis. And watch."

I stared up at him in mute horror. He swiped his hand over the wall opposite me to flip on a viewing screen . . . a feed from the presence chamber.

And then he moved to leave me.

"No. Wait," I said sharply, realizing he was trapping me here. Trapping me here to witness whatever was about to happen, and Tyrus on that screen was giving an impatient nod, and a move-along gesture as Wallstrom kept inserting herself back in front of him . . . babbling about something or other.

Helping Pasus. They were all helping Pasus.

"Pasus. PASUS!" I shouted at him, desperate not to be left here. . . . But he stepped through the door and there I was, helpless. Useless.

On the screen, I saw Pasus enter the chamber. The Grandiloquy about him fell silent. Tyrus noticed their fixed attention and turned with a smile—perhaps expecting me.

His smile disappeared as he saw Pasus too.

# 23

"YOUR SUPREME REVERENCE," Pasus said. He did the full courtier's gait, three steps forward, dipping to his knees with his hands to his heart, then three steps more.

And thus he approached the thunderstruck Tyrus in the presence chamber, and other various privy councilors backed away to cede authority to him.

"Senator von Pasus," Tyrus said, looking and sounding unshaken, though I knew he was anything but. "An unexpected pleasure. *Very* unexpected."

Senator von Pasus reached out, captured Tyrus's hands. "How excellent to see you once more." He drew Tyrus's knuckles to his cheeks in a slow, mock-reverent way.

Tyrus snatched his hands back as soon as they were released, folded his arms to keep them from being grabbed again. More Grandiloquy streamed into the presence chamber from other entrances. . . . And

Tyrus froze. His gaze lingered on Credenza Fordyce, a strange expression washing over his face just for an instant.

I knew why. Credenza was one of the hostages who'd been left on Lumina.

And another . . . Tyrus spotted Gladdic at the edge of the crowd. Both here. Free.

Pasus had abducted Neveni. Had he demanded the dozen Grandiloquy released in exchange for her life? How had he managed to retain Neveni after that? Why would the Luminars fall for such a paltry bargain—twelve and all the advantages they conferred for just one?

Tyrus looked to be thinking quickly. He now realized his Grandiloquy mobilized against him during our absence, and they'd also freed the hostages he'd left on Lumina—which meant the Luminars had cut a deal.

Pasus spoke: "As you can see from the assembled company, I am here to lodge a formal protest on behalf of my family and others. We believe Your Supremacy should heed the will of your foremost Grandiloquy. In fact, we demand it."

There it was, the naked force he'd artfully concealed until now. He had Tyrus at knifepoint, and they both knew it.

Tyrus's gaze broke from the Senator's and roved over the crowd in a long, slow sweep. A smile crossed his lips, his eyes chilly as night. "I see my allies are behind you," he said bitingly. "How long did it take the lot of you to scurry to the nearest strongman?"

A few such as Amador and Wallstrom stirred uneasily, those "allies" with Pasus now.

"What does it matter?" Pasus spread his hands. "You fled the consequences of a most terrible crime—the murder of your own cousin."

Tyrus's gaze jolted up. He looked so genuinely surprised, he could almost fool me. "My cousin? What . . . Wait. She's dead?"

"Do not pretend to be ignorant."

"Did my cousin perish?" thundered Tyrus, looking at all the faces about him. Then, to Pasus, "You monster. What did you do to her?"

"What did *I* do?" echoed Pasus.

"Did she refuse to cooperate in your treason?" Tyrus said disparagingly. How furious he looked! "You abducted and murdered a helpless woman; now you dare to stand before me with her blood on your hands—"

"You accuse *me* of her murder? You think anyone will believe these lies after you actively distributed heresies to the Excess?"

Tyrus shook his head. "No. Not heresies. I'd say 'no longer,' but they never were heresies. The Interdict's decree was misinterpreted. According to the Interdict himself." He reached into his pocket, and many of those about him tensed as though preparing to draw weapons. He unveiled the wooden box holding the electronic decree the Interdict had given us. "Perhaps some of you own one of these from centuries long past. Look your fill."

A few muted gasps. They knew what they were seeing.

"Within it is a decree," Tyrus said. "From the Interdict Orthanion. With whom I passed many hours . . . Many months, you might say, in conversation."

With a snarl, Pasus charged forward and snatched the box, ripping it right from Tyrus's hands.

Tyrus let him seize it, a cool, triumphant smile on his face. "Feel free to examine it, Senator. My long absence was necessary. I had questions over the wording of our Most Ascendant One's decree on the sciences, so I did as a person of faith must—and sought the man himself to clarify with his own lips."

Murmurs of amazement rippled about him.

"I stood face to face with him," Tyrus said, "as he *personally* ordered me to foster an intellectual rebirth. He has learned the state of the

Empire and he is aghast. He has charged me with restoring the sciences. To help me in this great task, he has given Nemesis personhood. This very night I will share this news with the Excess and exhibit the Interdict's mark over her heart—so all might see. I've been mindful of those vicars who have required persuasion on her account, and have gone to great lengths to satisfy their concerns, as they will all see. This matter is settled. You have your next Empress, and I trust the matter of the scepter will be resolved in short order."

Stunned silence met his words.

"This document is very clearly a forgery," Pasus declared. "This is a laughable deception, Your Supremacy."

If my eyes could have burned a hole into his image on the screen, they would have.

"Do not lie to your peers," Tyrus said, "for you know it is genuine. Your family has always championed our faith. How tragic to see a crooked branch of such a noble tree."

"This. Is. Heresy."

"You accuse *the Interdict* of heresy?" Tyrus said, soft danger in his voice. "You dare?"

"I do no such thing!" cried Pasus. "Do not twist my words. Whatever deception you employed to manipulate him into honoring that creature, to manipulate him into desecrating his office . . ."

"Now you accuse the Interdict of being *feeble-minded*?"

Shocked gasps.

"Don't you dare," Pasus said.

"You dig your grave deeper with each utterance, Senator."

"This is not *legitimate*," Pasus insisted. "This is what I think of it!" He dashed the document to the floor and stomped on it.

But the reaction Pasus must have hoped for wasn't there. Instead, there were cries, gasps, and the tiny ripple of glee over Tyrus's face, quickly buried. "I am outraged, Senator. Outraged. You have insulted the intelligence of our Interdict, as good as called him a heretic, and now—now you destroy his decree? No more!" And before Pasus could argue, Tyrus went in for the kill, thundering to the chamber: "I look about me and I see a room of fine men and women, misled by a *viper*. His sin is unpardonable but not yours—not if you denounce him now."

My heart rejoiced and anticipation crackled within me, because yes. *Yes*. Tyrus had turned this around, and I could have danced for the delight of it if I'd been free to move. . . .

"Let's be absolutely clear about the stakes here," said Tyrus, pressing his advantage. He spread his arms, and I saw then that he'd drawn the scepter to hold lightly in his hand, a symbolic reminder of the power he would inevitably hold, of the importance of winning his favor now.

He could have commanded them without it. He wore none of an Emperor's regalia, and he was younger than every Senator among them, yet he held them in thrall. A casual glance would pinpoint him as their leader.

"Ally with this man today, and you are not just a traitor to your Emperor and your galaxy. You are declaring yourself an open and avowed foe of the Living Cosmos *itself*. The Interdict *himself*." Tyrus let that sink in, let it settle in their minds like a tangible weight, before he said, "I was absent, and any actions taken in that situation are understandable and excusable. I do not condemn honest mistakes. All is forgiven and excused if you join your voices to mine now. All of you, denounce Pasus."

They swayed as a body, and the physical space about Pasus grew as though he radiated poison. I saw the moment of deathly terror on the Senator's face as his isolation grew, stranding him alone and exiled. His allies were melting way in every sense and leaving him alone. . . .

And then his face shifted. He tilted his chin up, some secretive knowledge settling in his mind. "Denounce me. But it does not change the past. We were united five months ago. In this very room, we made a decision together. And it will bind us all unto death."

And those words, those words . . .

They rang over the chamber, and a total silence fell in their wake. Those who'd been withdrawing from Pasus froze. Those muttering, stirring as though ready to turn on their new master first . . . they closed their mouths. Those whose chests had swollen, whose faces had lit, who'd been just on the cusp of shouting their support for the Emperor (likely all eager to do it first) . . .

Like a light, that impulse was extinguished. One by one, shoulders wilted, heads bowed, and whatever influence Tyrus had seized over the Grandiloquy vanished.

Now Tyrus appeared alone among them, and from the way he looked from face to face—he didn't understand what had happened here any more than I did.

"You were very clever, Your Supremacy." Pasus's voice rang out. Tyrus turned sharply toward him. "Very clever, indeed. But you see, all of us in here took an action to mitigate damage you yourself had done. We all worked in concert. All of us, but for the few who were hostages still on that planet. We meant to address the heresies you seeded on Lumina. And do not tell me again that they are not heresies. Perhaps you did twist the Interdict's arm, but I've seen no such decree and, in fact, must question it from a man who also gave a Diabolic personhood."

Tyrus opened and closed his mouth. He looked around incredulously, for the words were a shocking, open, blatant challenge to the *Interdict's* authority.

There should have been outrage.

There was silence.

Then Tyrus's face took on that total absence of expression, the telltale sign he was growing afraid so he'd switched off some part of himself that felt it. Fear crawled into my heart too.

"Gladdic." Tyrus spoke very softly. "Approach me."

If I could just get free, I could make it through the door and . . . and what? What? I couldn't help. I wasn't even strong enough to hurt Pasus.

Frustration raged through me as I watched Gladdic drop to his knees before Tyrus.

"I've known you for a very long time," Tyrus said, slicing his gaze down toward him. "You will answer me honestly." Then something spasmed across Tyrus's face, a crack of true emotion. "Is she still alive?"

*Me.* He meant me.

Pain burned in my chest. That was his first thought. He feared they'd killed me.

"Yes," Gladdic said quickly. "Nemesis is alive."

Tyrus's expression twisted a moment before he schooled it back into impassivity, and I felt like I'd been dealt a blow that stole my breath. How I weakened him. He was so controlled in the face of every setback—except for the prospect of my destruction. I was his weakness just as he was mine, and if anything could override his good sense, it was his fear for me.

Pasus stepped between them. "Your abomination lives. Because I chose to keep her alive—as a favor to you. You must be made to understand the situation you have returned to. Look over there."

He pointed to an imaging ring planted on the floor. A holographic projection fizzled to life above the ring, and I knew what it was showing. The Central Square on Lumina.

"You gave them technology," Pasus said as Tyrus, confused, watched the image of Luminars roving about their capitol city. "You gave them independence. Neither were yours to give. You were clever to leave them human shields of our ranks to protect them. We couldn't possibly save all twelve from their different locations on the planet. So instead, we visited each in turn and inoculated them."

"Inoculated?" Tyrus echoed.

And then I saw what the dozen Grandiloquy hostages had been inoculated against.

Brownish-yellow clouds swelled amid the mass of people. And the crowds in that image began to run, but it was too late and the cloud expanded, expanded. My breath caught in my throat when a suspicion came over me about just what I was seeing.

There was no sound, but the mouths of those we could see opened in screams as the cloudy wave began to consume Central Square.

I had never seen it myself, but I knew what I was looking at: a bio-weapon in action. The most potent bioweapon in the Empire.

Resolvent Mist.

Understanding crashed over me: the hostages hadn't been rescued.

They'd been shielded. Then everyone else around them had been killed. Every Senator in the presence chamber had been in on it.

Tyrus took a reflexive step back from the imaging ring as those people in the square began to boil about with panic. They scrambled to escape the very air, piling atop one another in their desperation, clawing at the ground, at one another, at themselves. . . .

So this was their covenant. This was the bond too powerful to be broken: they'd committed an act of mass murder together. As I stared at the image of Lumina, where dying Luminars glowed at me, a deep certainty welled in my heart: Tyrus and I were doomed. The Lumi-nars had been his most stalwart allies, and Pasus had done this to them. They were ordinary people and he had done this. How cruelly and cleverly he'd struck this blow, and implicated every last one of the power players in the Empire in his scheme to ensure they would never betray him for Tyrus.

Because Tyrus could not let this stand.

Tyrus would avenge this, if he had the power. They all shared this guilt. They all merited punishment.

No decree from the Interdict, no appeal to reason, no clever maneuvering could overcome this.

A buzzing sound filled my ears as I watched the victims on Lumina expelling the blood they were hemorrhaging inside by coughing, vomiting, then collapsing. . . . And so swiftly it struck, and so swiftly it receded. In less than a minute, all had gone still.

I stared at the feed in the presence chamber—where Tyrus was transfixed by unvarnished horror at the sight before him. Tyrus spoke, his voice strangled: "That wasn't real. Surely that . . . You didn't . . . That didn't happen." But he cast a look about, waiting for someone to reveal the jest, and he paled as no one confirmed that his fears were empty.

In Tyrus's shock, Pasus asserted mastery. He strode up right behind Tyrus and clapped his hands on his shoulders. He drew him back toward him in an overly familiar manner that reeked of disrespect.

"What you saw is what happened," he said quietly, speaking right near Tyrus's ear. "It was a dreadful and doleful event, and it was done *because of you.*"

Tyrus couldn't seem to muster a word. All that careful self-control, all that self-discipline was extinguished by shock, and had I been in there . . . I could have offered nothing. Now I just stared in mute bewilderment, for none of it felt quite real.

"I have assumed the regency in your absence with a very heavy heart, Tyrus, fearing you would never return . . . Preparing in case you did. Concealing my hand, even cloaking all news of Lumina from the rest of the galaxy under the guise of protecting those precarious independence negotiations . . ."

The words seemed to snap Tyrus out of some paralysis. He ripped forward out of Pasus's grasp. "How many?" he demanded.

When no answer came, he whipped around, staring with a ghastly look on his face at those Grandiloquy all about him. "HOW MANY? Someone must know. How many people did you murder on that planet? How far did that weapon spread?"

When there was still no answer, he raised his hands, clutching at his hair, the frozen reflection of the holograph casting a sickly light on his face. "There are billions on Lumina. Someone tell me. *How many died?*"

Pasus finally answered.

"All of them."

*All of them.*

*All.* The words resounded through my head.

The world swayed. I had to get into the next chamber. I had to get there now. But the magnetized clamp trapping me against the wall wouldn't give, however I pulled on it. With a roar of frustration, I pulled with both hands, then even pushed with my neck. . . . That wasn't a good idea.

I gasped for breath, as trapped as before.

Voices floated from the feed of the presence chamber. . . .

"Your Supremacy surely sees now the position you are in. I will list our terms for you." There was no answer for a beat, and Pasus took that as a reason to go on: "We require an Emperor. That much was clear before you disappeared for a long interval. In fact, we do want to see you wielding the scepter once more, but only—"

"Are you mad?" Tyrus rasped.

I angled myself to the side so it wasn't my esophagus pressing

S. J. KINCAID

against the clamp. I bent my legs so I could push with all four limbs, and . . . and the slightest give! It pulled away, but then fastened back against the wall.

I was on the right track. I just needed to recover my breath—and then use all the force I could muster.

"Are you utterly mad?" roared Tyrus again, and I twisted about to see him encircled by them in the presence chamber. "What . . . what kind of . . . What . . ." He stumbled over his words as though he could find none for this. . . . And then he howled at them: "How can you see that and live with yourselves? How can any of you? You have terms? *TERMS?* You honestly believe I will turn away from genocide?"

He surged toward Pasus but bodies blocked his way, and Tyrus seemed afire with fury, madness.

"You think I will consent to be your puppet, and rule as you say, as you wish, when you have murdered all those people? I would sooner fall into a black hole! The lot of you deserve to burn for this!"

With a gritting of teeth, I threw myself back and yelled out as this time, the magnet was driven from the wall, and with a twist of my body, it whipped away from my neck and reconnected to the wall with a clang.

I collapsed to the ground, gasping for air, bathed in sweat. I surged to my feet, and how heavy, how *wrong* my legs felt even now with the neural suppressor humming in the air, but I shoved my way through the door as Pasus purred, "You seem to think we are asking you to behave as we wish. You're mistaken."

Bodies blocked my way. I raged at the strength I'd lost, for normally I could fling them aside like so many puppets, or hurl myself onto their shoulders.

"We anticipated your resistance, Your Supremacy," said Pasus. "And that's why I had the foresight to spare your abomination. She will even be permitted to sit at your side as Empress, provided you cooperate."

180

My steps paused, for that was why I was alive. He meant to use me against Tyrus.

"I don't believe you," Tyrus said scornfully. "You will kill her one way or another. I won't even give you that chance."

Through the gap in the bodies, I saw him pull something from his sleeve—an energy weapon. Shouts and cries sounded about me, and Pasus's servants and lackeys formed a human shield before him. Behind the shelter of their bodies, he called to Tyrus, "What does Your Supremacy think you will gain?" There was amusement—damn him—in his voice as he spoke. "You cannot hope to kill all of us with that!"

Tyrus took one deliberate step back after another. "You're right." His voice was quiet, resolved. "I only get one shot. Best make it count."

Then Tyrus angled his weapon toward that thin sheen of diamond protecting the chamber from the unforgiving void beyond.

So he could blow out the window. And vent every last person in this chamber to space.

# 24

THERE WAS only one person in this room I cared about, and he was closest to the window. The words ripped out of me:

"Tyrus, NO!"

And the sound of my voice made his eyes widen with a fresh terror, and he roared, "Get out of here!" at me, but I shook my head frantically. . . . Then arms seized me from behind, and with my strength dampened, I couldn't break the hold. Pasus saw me, waved the man holding me forward, then clasped my arm and yanked me toward Tyrus.

"Vent the room and she dies too," Pasus said, breathless. His fingers dug in so hard, my skin throbbed.

And I didn't fight him now, because I wanted him to succeed. I wanted Tyrus talked down, and Tyrus had an indecisive moment to just look at us like he was strangling on thin air. . . . Then bodies bowled him over, piled on top of him, shouting, "Disarm him!"

"Get the Emperor!"

"Keep him down!"

At my side, Pasus's harsh whisper. "Well done."

Our eyes met like bared blades. If I'd been able to rip him to shreds with just a glare, he would be in slices. Then he hauled me forward with him, shouting at Tyrus's captors not to suffocate him, to stand him up.

And then Tyrus was trapped, two arms around each of his, by men straining to contain him, others grappling his legs, and a hand at my back shoved me forward hard enough to unbalance me. I didn't care that Pasus meant me to do this, that he was sending me over for this. I just blasted forward and hurtled into Tyrus, throwing my arms about him. He must've been released, because he clasped me fiercely in return.

"You're all right," he said, his voice choked.

"Stay alive, Tyrus. Don't do that again. Don't."

And I was only dimly aware of those who'd tackled him being waved away, of Pasus circling us at a careful distance, his sharp eyes taking in our embrace. I knew we were displaying our hideous weakness for each other before hostile eyes, that it was unavoidable, but Tyrus's heart beat against mine, and his ragged breathing fluttered my hair, and we would get out of this somehow, I knew we would.

Then the chamber was mostly empty, and Pasus was sitting languidly on a windowsill, Tyrus's energy weapon held casually over his lap, and I pressed my lips to Tyrus's ear and whispered that entreaty, "Stay alive. Just stay alive."

Tyrus's eyes sought mine, and for the first time I saw raw terror there, unconcealed by so many years of training, for what was there to do against an enemy who could murder billions of people?

"Shall we talk now?"

Pasus's voice floated over to us, and Tyrus and I held eyes a last moment. Then his face became a granite mask, and my heart turned to cold black stone. And then we shifted our focus to Pasus.

Pasus's lips twisted. "After losing my Elantra," he said, "I could think only of avenging her. But for you, Tyrus, I will put that aside."

"To keep your leverage against me," Tyrus said, clutching me closer. "Do not pretend this is generosity."

"Well. You and I would be corpses floating outside that window if not for your love of her, so yes, there is no generosity. Her preservation is clearly a necessity." Pasus's eyes glittered. "And what a tragedy it would have been, had you fired on that window. I don't speak of losing my life, or those of all the personages in this chamber. . . . But losing the last Domitrian. There is no returning from that."

Tyrus stared at him incredulously. "You have your boot on my throat, Senator. Don't feign reverence now."

"I am pretending nothing," Pasus said. "I knew Randevald as a youth. Always, I thought—this man is no more remarkable than I am. And then I saw him claim his scepter and awaken the Chrysanthemum. That boot is there by necessity, not choice. All I've ever wished is to join with your family! To unite my bloodline with the greatness of the Domitrians. . . . You are as close as we mere humans will ever be to the deities of old. I planned for you to wed my daughter." With a chill glance toward me, "And we know why that did not happen. Then I sought to wed your cousin, but she perished. Again, we know why."

"We do," I snapped. "Because you tried to murder him."

"I am your greatest advocate," Pasus insisted. "Some believed we should lobotomize you on your return, and reign through you that way. . . . But the idea was distasteful to me. Your cousin lacked her wits and I saw firsthand how difficult she was to manage. So now we are left with option three, and I think all of us will find this one acceptable."

Pasus reached into his pocket and withdrew a jeweled case. "Give me a reason to trust you."

A vein in Tyrus's temple flickered. I took the box from Pasus, popped it open. A phial rested inside. It was merely a narcotic. Tyrus spared it a contemptuous look. "What is it?"

"It's how we will establish our trust. This is a drug by the name of Venalox," Pasus said. "You'll take it."

"Venalox?" said Tyrus. "I've never even heard of it."

"Nor had I, until recently. You yourself are the reason I found its chemical configuration. I searched for obscure substances, hoping for something that would preserve your cousin's life. Then—I saw this. It is ideal for us. I tested it on the Excess to ensure it was safe. I am going to provide it every day."

"Why? What does it do?"

"It fosters a powerful addiction that confounds med-bot detox subroutines," Pasus said. "This is how we will operate: I will give you this substance, and you will take it. Because you'll need it, and only I will have it, and in this way, my life will be protected from you, and we will be assured allies."

"If you wanted trust, if you sought an ally," Tyrus said, "you could simply have approached me in good faith in the first place."

"No. That was never possible. I couldn't have trusted any mere assurances of yours," Pasus responded. "You see, I earnestly believed you, Tyrus. I believed you were mad along with all the others. You were so very convincing, and now, this is the price for it—because I am not even sure who you truly are. There is only one way I can feel certain of you, and it's if we establish that certainty on *my* terms. With the Venalox. Now, in injected form, it hits quite hard. Rather like a sedative that leaves one awake enough to follow basic suggestions. But I'd only have it injected for the first stretch, just to be entirely certain it's in your system. Then we'll transition."

"To what?" Tyrus ground out.

"An inhalable powder. You'll be able to administer it to yourself—after I provide it, naturally."

"You think I will agree to be an addict," said Tyrus.

"Your Supremacy, addiction devastates those who lose their health, their status, their finances. All three of those will be in my control. You will be entirely safe, and you will have your chosen Empress. This is not an offer you can refuse. Make your decision."

"Give him time to think," I cut in. "Can he not have a minute of thought?"

"There is nothing for him to think about," Pasus said, his eyes narrowing. "He is not in a position to refuse me. But as a courtesy, I will give you both an interlude to reassure each other. I must oversee the docking of the *Colossus*. . . . I couldn't leave it in the inner ring until you had returned."

Of course he'd kept it obscured among the mass of distant ships. Senator von Pasus's vessel in the dead center of the Chrysanthemum would have told us with a glance that he was here. Tyrus closed his eyes until he was gone.

Then his gaze snapped back open, and there wasn't a trace of defeat in the pale blue depths. He snatched the phial from its box and shook his head, determination crackling on his face. "He will make this easy."

"Easy?"

"In the past I always had to contrive some weakness to put my enemies at ease, and selling that weakness was every bit so difficult as taking advantage of the moment they underestimated me. . . . But he's created the perfect situation for me."

"You have a plan."

He nodded. His hand cupped the back of my neck to draw me

forward as though for a kiss, but really so he could whisper as softly as possible, "He's already laid it out for us. He means to turn me into a dependent addict. I will play along with it. I will give him an addict. This will lull him and then we strike back."

Misgivings churned within me. I had never been intoxicated, but I had seen Tyrus's mind at work. It was the most powerful weapon in his arsenal and there was no knowing what this Venalox might do to it. "No. Tyrus, no. Let's find the nearest ship and hijack it. I don't have my strength, but we'll have surprise on our side. We can return to the Interdict."

He let out a breath. "We'd have to get there and back within this same gravital window, Nemesis, or else we are truly undone. You saw the schedule. The next one lasts three years. We can't lose three more years. This keeps us in the center of things. We can't risk it."

"But . . ." I pulled back, searching his face. "You've never used this . . . this Venalox. What if you can't master it?"

"I will." Tyrus stroked his thumb over the back of my neck in circles. "This is just a chemical like any other. Mithridatism. Remember?"

Mithridatism. His practice of exposing himself to small doses of substances to master them.

"Mind over matter. The very worst-case scenario is, I truly do get addicted—in which case it will be a matter of willpower, and I have plenty. I will endure the pains of breaking free." He drew me into a kiss, and then spoke against my ear, "Whatever I do and whatever you see, *don't* be worried. Trust me."

I would trust him. I had to trust him.

"Once he closes his eyes," Tyrus whispered, "I promise you, we will destroy him for this."

# 25

**WITH THE** *Colossus* docked, Senator von Pasus strolled back into the presence chamber, looking between us expectantly. Tyrus now had uncertainty and anxiety on his face; he'd plastered on the expression as soon as we knew Pasus was in the room.

"You win," Tyrus said. "All right? I'll—I'll take the Venalox. As long as Nemesis is safe, I'll do it."

"How wonderful," Pasus said. He stepped over to Tyrus and clasped his shoulders. "This is the beginning of a new era for us all. It's not my victory. A day will come when you see it's *our* victory."

Then, releasing him, he retreated.

"One last small request," Pasus said. "I am still grieving my daughter. I would like to see as little of your intended as possible. Nemesis dan . . . Nemesis Impyrean, you are never to step foot on the *Colossus* without my explicit invitation."

Bewildered, I assured him, "I have no desire to see your ship."

Pasus smiled. "How pleased I am to find you both so reasonable."

"Do we begin this now?" Tyrus said, lifting the phial.

"Yes, that would be most excellent. Six milliliters, directly to the blood-stream." He waved over a med bot, and Tyrus let the machine take the phial with its metal claw and liquefy its contents with a flash of light.

Tyrus met my eyes with steely determination. *Trust me*, he mouthed out of sight of Pasus.

And then the bot drove its injector into his forearm. Tyrus winced and told Pasus, "In the future, I'm perfectly able to find my own veins—" He stopped talking.

For a moment, he stared into space. Then, "Oh, that's . . ." And he plunged toward the ground.

I hadn't been ready for that.

Pasus had. He caught Tyrus immediately and nodded for a pair of his people to rush over. He stroked Tyrus's hair back from his face so he could examine it. "Hmm. Not what you expected, was it?" He smiled. "It never seems to be."

I stared at Tyrus. His eyes were rolled back, his pale lashes fluttering. I'd seen this happen to people who overdosed on opiates or other sedating substances. "Are you sure he's . . ."

"He is quite well." He shook Tyrus. "Your Supremacy. Your Supremacy!"

"Tyrus!" I said.

Those eyes pulled open sluggishly, unfocused, pupils dilated. A tangle of anxiety within me.

"Satisfied?" Pasus said, and then he reached down and withdrew the scepter from the sheath at Tyrus's waist. "Your Supremacy will feel the weight of this in your hand one day. But only after you've learned that art so alien to you Domitrians. I would have introduced it to Devineé, had she retained the wits to speak, but I think I prefer to show you." He grazed the scepter over Tyrus's cheek. "You will learn to say 'please.'"

He tucked the scepter under his arm and snapped his fingers. Two Pasus servants hiked Tyrus up between them, one with his arms, one with his legs. They began to carry him out of the presence chamber, and Tyrus's head flopped back toward the ground, exposing his column of throat.

That roused me out of my spell, and I jerked forward to follow.

Pasus's hand shot out and seized my arm.

"No," he said, holding up a forbidding finger.

My fist had risen on instinct, ready to punch him—though I still felt like every movement was dragging, heavy, the low drone of the neural suppressor just in my hearing range.

"You agreed never to board my ship," Pasus said.

I threw a surprised glance toward Tyrus, saw the men disappearing into the corridor leading to the *Colossus*. "Wait. No. Then bring him . . ."

*Back.*

That last word never left me. I understood now why, specifically, Pasus had demanded I never board his ship. He was going to keep Tyrus there.

Hatred seethed between us.

"When will I see him?" I said.

"If he asks for you, I'll arrange it," Pasus said, his voice dripping with condescension.

Only after he'd left me did I realize how vaguely he'd answered me. If he drugged Tyrus heavily enough, he would never ask for me.


After Tyrus disappeared into that ship, I didn't see him for a solid week. At first I paced in the *Valor Novus*, eyes on the corridor leading to the *Colossus*. As my anxiety mounted, I began accosting anyone going in or out, but the Grandiloquy guests just smiled with contempt or awkward refusal, and Pasus's servants and employees did not even speak to me or acknowledge my questions about Tyrus's well-being. I didn't have the physical power to obtain answers the way I most wished.

Then the news bounced from ear to ear, and I heard it: the Emperor was throwing a gala of celebration to honor the reconciliation of all the Grandiloquy.

I would see him there.

Shaezar nan Domitrian dutifully presented me with a selection of attire, but he hadn't been allowed on the *Colossus* either.

"I hear only the most trusted Pasus servants are given access to him," Shaezar said. "They don't speak to the rest of us."

Disgruntled, I chose the first outfit and color scheme he showed me. The only specification I had was that a V neckline needed to show the concentric sun mark of the Interdict over my heart. He fitted me with golden steering rings, the magnetized loops clasping my limbs so I could direct my momentum in zero gravity.

Then to the ball dome, where I felt like I was crawling out of my skin. We detached from the rest of the Chrysanthemum. The gravity disappeared as we floated a short distance away from the superstructure. I leaned out of the viewing box, batting aside my purple-blue halo of hair when it kept drifting into my way.

No one was in the Emperor's box yet.

I waited, on edge, my eyes idly picking over the decorations: algae plants wavering in the air, a scattering of animals engineered just for this occasion. I found myself watching the swirling limbs of a creature with eight slippery legs. When the first strains of music sounded, and I still didn't see Tyrus, dread welled in me.

Yet as Empress-to-be, I had to dive out first, so I thrust myself down, hoping to have a wider view from outside my box. Maybe Tyrus was elsewhere. Maybe he'd join me.

But it was Senator von Aton who rippled down next to me, his garb floating in the weightlessness like some sea anemone. With his false-youth, he resembled his son Gladdic—if Gladdic were not so pretty.

"I am partnering you first tonight," said Aton, offering a palm.

I was aware of all the eyes about me, all these ridiculous Grandiloquy looking on with their own costumes, their vivid, multi-hued scales, a Grande laughing with his friends where he'd snared the eight-legged animal as it floated by and was mock-dancing with it in his box. The music was playing but I didn't even take Aton's hand.

"Where is the Emperor?"

"I am the one here." Since I didn't take his hand, Aton took mine, and he smiled pleasantly. "I've been so curious about you."

But if he wished me to play along, to dance, to make a show of acting like everything was fine, he would be disappointed. I didn't move a muscle, so anyone looking down at us saw an extravagant Grande twisting and turning about a woman who was at a total standstill.

"Is the Emperor even coming?"

"Yes," said Aton. "On another subject, did you know I had a Diabolic?" He hooked me under the arm to spin me about, though I did nothing to aid him, as though he hadn't even noticed my intransigence. "His name was Rancor. Great big creature with brilliant red hair."

"How interesting," I sneered.

"He was more loyal than a dog," said Aton sadly. "I did hate to crush him in my gravity chamber, but it was an Imperial decree. I meant to watch him out of respect, but I simply could not abide it. When I heard Gladdic had been deceived by you, I wondered how I'd fathered such an astounding idiot."

I looked at Aton, malice seething through me. I knew when I was being toyed with. And in one abrupt movement, I tore him toward me, and clamped my knees about his head. "Surely Rancor showed you that even with minimal strength, Diabolics are deadly. I can break your neck with ease. Where is the Emperor?"

Aton's hands settled on my thighs, and it took me a moment to realize he wasn't trying to break my hold on him. . . . He was roving his hands over them. "The Emperor is with Alectar von Pasus." There was something cheeky, too revoltingly pleased in his grin.

"Fine. So *where* is Alectar von Pasus?"

"He is with the Emperor." His hands squeezed. "I may need more incentive to say more."

Oh . . . Ohh, I was so hideously tempted to damage him. I gritted my teeth and stamped my leg to knock him away from me, and ignored the gasps of those who'd noticed my uncouth, uncivilized conduct. Shaking with anger and frustration. I thrust myself into the viewing box directly opposite the Emperor's. I fastened my eyes on those empty seats. I waited. I passed the gala that way, ignoring the silly people romping about like sea creatures. Outside the ball dome, great explosions of vibrant lights flared against the void, and at first I ignored them. . . .

Then I found myself looking at them, for who was paying for these?

Between dances, celebrants began to call out cheers for the good fortune they'd received recently. Incredulous, I called up the transactions registry of the Chrysanthemum. The computer screen in the box dutifully listed each of the gifts these Grandes and Grandeés had received recently, the gifts they were giving thanks for.

The *Hyperion*. That was a Domitrian vessel, inactive since the death of one of Randevald's sisters. Now it belonged to Senator von Amador. The *Tigris* went to Aton. The *Farthingale* was used for Domitrian servants. Now it was Senator von Wallstrom's. Worst of all, the *Alexandria*, Tyrus's own vessel, was for Senator von Locklaite, the first to defect to Pasus.

On and on the list went, and a sickening realization crept over me that Pasus had divided up every asset of Tyrus's, of the Domitrians', of the Chrysanthemum in general, and had given them away.

Pasus even had the gall to give himself Gorgon's Arm, which Tyrus had offered him for Lumina. He had both now.

And an eighty-year lease on the *Valor Novus*.

Tyrus was now a guest on the vessel of the Domitrian royals.

All that was left was the *Hera*.

For now.

I'd never really understood money, having never controlled it, never earned it, but I knew this was a devastating blow. Near the end of the night, the dance Hades and Persephone began, and applause swept over the ball dome. Then—across from me he appeared. A silhouette in the box, and another behind him that had to be Pasus.

I shoved myself out of my box and angled the steering rings toward him so I could see how he was faring, what toll the Venalox was taking, or . . .

Or . . .

Abruptly, my magnetized steering rings jerked me to a stop, someone remotely barring me from flying in Tyrus's direction. I floundered there amid applause, like swimming in sludge, while Tyrus was shown to them, to give a sign of the Emperor's approval of the event.

Fine. I couldn't fly directly to him. I would still get closer, I would see his face. I had to.

I aimed myself first at a wall, then ripped off my steering rings just before I met it. Then I kicked off as hard as I could. Startled cries as Grandes and Grandeés quickly steered out of my way, but Senator von

Wallstrom didn't move in time, and she and I collided and knocked each other off course. She had steering rings; I'd cast mine aside. In anguish, I flipped end over end, unable to control my momentum. I caught a glimpse of the box holding Tyrus, but Pasus was all I saw now, and he caught my eyes a moment before his lips twisted into a hateful smile. . . .

And an opacity screen rose to block my view.

Couples swirled all about me, and then trios for the dance called the Triumvirate, and still I spun with little forward momentum. A flash of stenciled scales, and then someone caught me, and I dragged my gaze up bleakly to meet Gladdic's eyes. In my thunderous mood, I couldn't say thanks. Just, "Steer me to the side."

"If that's what you want. Should I help you find your rings?"

My head pulsed. A wild thought came over me that those were probably too valuable to lose, now that all that remained of Domitrian wealth was the *Hera*. Abruptly, I felt like I was going to be sick.

I barely noticed as Gladdic steered me back toward the box opposite the Emperor's. His voice was like an afterthought in my ears: "I apologize for my father. I don't know what he said to you, but you looked angry and I don't blame you. Father is . . . He's constantly bored. He treats everyone like—"

"Gladdic, I don't care. Stop talking."

"Of course." He lapsed into silence. And then he couldn't resist: " I knew nothing about the Resolvent Mist. I didn't know."

"Your inoculation against Resolvent Mist didn't tip you off that Resolvent Mist might be deployed?" I said, pitiless. I had no sympathy to offer.

"I didn't know what it was," Gladdic said gravely. "I thought it was a tracking diode, maybe. But . . . but I was there when it happened." His face crumpled. A tear streaked down his face, drawing black kohl with it. "They didn't deserve that. The Luminars—they treated me well. I was a prisoner, but they didn't treat me that way."

He looked in need of a hug. I was the wrong person. "What's your point?"

"I asked my father to help Neveni."

Neveni. My hands curled, and I thought of her waiting for me to walk into an ambush. That had not been a hologram. It was actually her. "I don't care. She aided Pasus. He destroyed her world and she *still* sided with him."

"Nemesis, she didn't know about Lumina."

I dragged my gaze over to him. "She didn't?"

"She passed along your information after you'd been gone a month. Then . . . then she just disappeared. I was still with her family. Her father grew worried, and I was even getting ready for a trip back here. They trusted me to make inquiries, to search for her. . . . Then you know what happened."

The words stole my breath. "The Resolvent Mist."

"Pasus kept her in isolation for months. He convinced her he had her family, that their lives hinged on whether she cooperated with you. After . . . after you were here, I finally had a chance to see her. I told her I was so sorry about Lumina, and that's . . ." His face fell. "That's when I realized no one had told her."

"Oh. Oh no."

"Before that, though, she told me . . . she was frustrated. She'd tried to tell you without Pasus realizing it that she'd been compromised. She said it was in the message. Something about Devineé."

The breath seemed to have been stolen from me.

*"The major news first: the Successor Primus died. It happened two weeks after you left. I don't know the details, but obviously I've been weeping off and on ever since. . . ."*

I thought it was sarcasm.

She'd tried to tell me something. She knew that I knew she'd never mourn that woman. My vision blurred out of focus. I'd assumed Neveni was a traitor, deceived into making some deal on behalf of Lumina. I hadn't given thought to her since learning of her planet's destruction. There'd been too much to worry about when it came to me, to Tyrus. My anger at her melted away.

"The other two Diabolics are still alive, also. They're not scheduled to be killed. If you're wondering."

I couldn't care less about the fate of those two, but Neveni—she tried to warn me. She had to be saved. "Gladdic, I need you to do something. Find out when she's due to die. Tell me as soon as you know. If you have any influence, urge explosive decompression, not gravital crushing. If it is crushing, let me know soon enough so I can sabotage the gravity chamber. I just . . . I might be able to do something for her."

He nodded and looked at me with those wide green eyes like he wanted to ask, but he thought better of it. And despite everything, as I gazed down at the dancers, a tiny bloom of hope opened within me. I didn't know if I could save Tyrus. Or myself.

But Neveni was my friend.

I would save her.

# 26

I WAS summoned for the first meeting of court since our return. I knew what it meant: Tyrus would be in our midst. I could finally see if he was well. I chose a gown that deliberately angled down in a V to display the Interdict's mark on my heart, and then I plunged out into the sea of hostile eyes in the presence chamber.

There was a throne lower than Tyrus's, yet positioned at the top of the chamber . . . meant for his future Empress. I took it, and it gave me a grim satisfaction to see the resentment and bitterness on the faces of the onlookers as they beheld me in the Empress's place. That was the single pleasure I could take from Pasus's bargain.

And then—at last.

Pasus stepped into the presence chamber, and I saw with a rush of fury that the scepter was in a sheath at *his* waist. He was followed by two of his servants, steering Tyrus forward by the arms. I rose to my feet, gazing at him intently, waiting for his eyes to meet mine, but they didn't seek me. Tyrus's face was cloudy.

That was why he hadn't waved back to me, or done anything at the gala. *Trust me*, he'd said.

I trusted Tyrus. But trust also implied something: it implied he'd be in a position to act in a way that might disappoint or please me, and when his eyes drifted past me, a cold, crawling realization sank over me that the Venalox was stronger than he'd realized.

He would give me an indication if he was faking this. Some tiny, tiny hint.

But his head slumped back without anyone holding it as he was placed on his throne. He never turned toward me, his fingers dangling toward the ground.

*Tyrus, look at me*, I thought, staring hard at him.

Then I said it: "Tyrus. *Tyrus*."

His head moved toward the sound of my voice, his eyes unfocused. I reached out to touch his arm, and his gaze dropped to my hand with a naked, open, lost look that belonged on a child—not on *Tyrus*.

I felt like the breath had been driven out of me. We needed a new plan.

"You've helped him," Pasus's voice came to me. "Now remove your hand."

I tightened my grip. "You expect me never to touch my fiancé."

Pasus prowled toward me. He said in a furious undertone: "Sensory input confuses him. You will agitate him."

"How much of this drug have you given him?"

"Enough. Let go, or I will say you have taken ill and must be removed."

And as I was, I couldn't fight back. I lifted my hand from Tyrus, and it shook in the air with my rage. How glorious it would be to feel Pasus's heart thrum in my hand as Elantra's had, to watch his life seep out beneath me. . . .

I pressed myself back in the seat, knowing what those thoughts were.

The malice of a Diabolic.

I traced my finger over my concentric suns mark, reminding myself: *I am a person.*

Even if people, I mused as I watched Pasus, did most malevolent things too.

"Shall we begin?" spoke Senator von Pasus, to the hearty assent of those about. He linked his hands behind his back in a masterful gesture, surveying those present, then turned gracefully as if doing a pirouette and began walking in a reverent Grandiloquy gait to the seat of Tyrus's throne—three steps, dip, hands to his heart, three steps, dip.

Why even bother? The strange bits of formality he clung to bewildered me. He knew Tyrus was in no state to notice his presence or absence. Everyone watching here knew just what the situation was. But Pasus reached the foot of the throne, and Tyrus wasn't looking at him. He was staring at an overhead crystalline chandelier as though he, new to this universe, was viewing such a thing for the first time.

Pasus snapped his fingers. Twice. The second time, those glazed eyes looked toward the sound. "Your Supremacy, tell me to rise. As we practiced," he said quietly. "Remember? Rise. *Rise.*"

Tyrus's brows pressed together. He blinked sluggishly.

"Rise?" Tyrus said.

Pleased, Senator von Pasus straightened—and that was the last involvement of Tyrus for a good while as Pasus turned to address the gathered Grandiloquy like he was their Emperor. He might as well have been, though he recalled himself at one point, removed the scepter from its sheath, and then slung it across Tyrus's lap.

Tyrus gazed at it with puzzlement, and then his head flopped back again.

"I don't know how much of what I say you can understand," I told

Tyrus quietly, and surveillance equipment might be recording this, but I didn't care. "But this is not what we had in mind. Tyrus, please, if this is for show . . ."

Nothing.

"No." I swallowed. There was a mass in my throat, it felt like. A great panic clawed at my chest.

I didn't know what to do.

". . . been coordinating with media outlets on Eurydice," Pasus was telling the other Grandes and Grandeés. "In case our primary narrative does not come across as we wish, we're preparing a secondary story. A backup."

My gaze fastened on him, a laser focus to my thoughts.

"Our Emperor is very young, and of course, it was well known before he took the throne that he was not entirely stable. He is in love with . . . a woman of, shall we say, violent tendencies, who influenced him. If our story is doubted, we will cast it as an attempt to shield this story: that the Luminars attempted to take advantage and stir up trouble, and this boy so new to his power overreacted to it. This will also quash any speculation about my remaining here—"

I surged out of my seat, swelling with outrage. "No. No! You will not cast us in that light!"

They all looked to me, to the woman by Tyrus's side, the one who dared to talk over them, but I felt as though I sizzled like lightning with this raw fury.

"You will *not* say Tyrus is responsible for what *you* did on Lumina!" I bellowed. "That wasn't him. It was you. How dare you say that!"

Many sought to reply, but Pasus waved them silent. His lips were a jaded twist. "We will not say anything. We mean the public to believe the Luminars—always a fractious sort—were secretly experimenting with bioweapons and had an unfortunate accident. This is merely a contingency plan in case that story is not accepted."

"You did it. And you will not say it was Tyrus's doing."

"He is a *Domitrian*," Pasus said. "He is the *last* Domitrian. He is the only one who can shoulder blame for this without dying for it. And our Emperor himself will agree to make that gesture for his Grandiloquy. Right now. Today."

That was when I realized why Tyrus was so drugged. They were going to use him as their safety net—with his complicity.

"I won't let you," I vowed, and what I wouldn't have given for my strength.

"Retire her for the day," Pasus said to his servants. "She's disrupting the proceedings."

I leaned over and swiped the scepter from where it still lay on Tyrus's lap. As the first servant reached me, I swung around and crashed it into his head—as Tyrus had done to Hazard. Then I raised it overhead, but the second man caught it, and the rare feeling of someone struggling with me, overpowering me, made me grit my teeth and drive my heel into his shin.

Then—a fist across the face.

Normally I could absorb this. Today bright lights flashed behind my eyes and I found myself on the floor, close to Tyrus's feet. And his hazy eyes were directed my way, his brows flickering down.

Hands were already grabbing me, so I implored him, "Say nothing. Say nothing, Tyrus—SAY NOTHING!"

But irresistible forces dragged me back, and Tyrus was looking my way, but did he see anything? I fought every step toward the exit as Pasus stepped up to Tyrus, as he clasped his face to turn it right toward him so all Tyrus saw was him.

"You ordered the Resolvent Mist deployed on Lumina."

"No, you didn't!" I shouted, and then a hand jammed over my mouth.

I sank teeth in, and my heels skidded over the floor as Pasus spread his palms to block me from Tyrus's sight.

"Just say yes. Agree that it was you. Say yes. As we practiced."

My teeth dug in deeper, but the hand remained.

"Say yes. Say *yes!*" Pasus shouted now.

And the entire chamber—all these smug perpetrators of mass murder—they were watching intently, hopeful! Hopeful as though their own crimes would be forgiven by another wrongly, dazedly accepting blame!

"Yes. As we practiced. *Yes.*"

Tyrus keeled forward, and delight made me almost laugh—because it was clear he was trying to walk away. Pasus caught him in a bear hug to keep him there, to keep him on his throne, and they were both crammed between the armrests now, and how ridiculous it looked.

"Say it! *Say. Yes.*"

Tyrus's head swayed about, to fix him with a confused look. ". . . Yes?"

Applause followed, and he sent a bewildered look over the Grandiloquy giving cries of relief, bringing their hands together, and Pasus smiled broadly, and that was all I saw before I was out of the presence chamber. But Pasus's noxious voice poisoned the air:

"All of you heard it. The Emperor's word is sacred, and it was spoken with all of us as witness. It may be said with total honesty that we heard this—all of us. No drug and no lie detector will ever say we deceive. Let's congratulate our young Emperor for ensuring peace! Very well done, Tyrus. We are so proud of you."

The fight had left me. It was done. If the Excess refused to believe the Luminars had destroyed themselves, then Tyrus and I were to be blamed for the deaths of four billion people.

When a Servitor appeared with a discreet-sheet, I almost crumpled it up, in no mood for intrigue. But I looked, and it was from Gladdic.

*Explosive decompression tonight. 2000 from the Justice Hall.*

I crumpled the paper to powder.

I could do this much.

I'd never worn a space-sheath before, but I knew it was prudent to check it for leaks before using it. I didn't. There was no time. I sorted through the formfitting silver-and-black sheaths already on the *Hera* and found a size that would fit. The material felt rubbery and resisted as I tugged it over my legs and zipped it up over my breasts, but then after I'd secured the gloves and helmet, the material inflated and pressurized. The in-built steering rings shrank as well, and then the sheath's material hardened into a rigid shell.

Oxygen pumped through the helmet, and my focus narrowed as I approached the *Hera*'s air lock. One flick of my hand, and the meager air propelled me out into space.

With the momentum at my back, I plunged into the still and deathly silence. For a moment, I drifted that way, the absence of gravity somehow more jarring and unnatural out here, somewhere a human body could not exist, could not survive.

Then I played a mental game with myself: this was a ball dome with a very clear exterior. The vessels, these massive metallic and granite structures I drifted through, they were just walls. Obstacles. It was a game.

And so I moved my legs to steer my momentum as I would in any ball dome, drifting soundlessly past the empty windows of the *Hera*, and how very hard and imposing Cygna's starship looked from just outside. At the final airlock I passed, I yanked the door open, left it that way. Then I aimed myself toward the *Valor Novus*, which the *Hera* attached to by a corridor that appeared a spindly arm out here, though I'd walked through its sturdy interior hundreds of times.

I kept my eyes fastened on the windows, but the void was great and dark. Even had someone stood near the windows of the *Valor Novus*, they'd never spot my black-and-silver suit drifting past against the background of starships. I peered in window after window, trying to orient myself from outside a ship I knew so well from the inside.

Then I found it. The Justice Hall.

I'd just have to hope Neveni had the foresight to exhale before she was vented. If she held her breath, her lungs would rupture immediately, and she would die. It all depended on her.

I positioned myself just above the air lock, hearing my own breathing within the narrowed helmet, my own heartbeat. . . . Such total silence out here in space. Gleaming metal starships shrank in all directions. So still out here.

A thought crawled into my mind: no sound waves traveled through a void, which meant the neural suppressor could not be sonically triggered out here. I had my full strength right now, and though the lack of gravity meant I couldn't feel it, it was there.

My gaze traveled about, searching for the *Colossus*, for this was a possibility. I could rescue Tyrus from the outside. Who would see it coming?

A burst of light, and out came Neveni, totally exposed with no space suit, cast to her death in this void.

And so I launched myself forward to save her.

# 27

HER BODY was like a doll tumbling into the darkness. She must have passed out quickly, because I met no resistance when I grabbed her, when I hauled her with me toward the *Hera*.

Precious seconds dragged by as I neared the awaiting air lock and thrust her inside. I caught her before she could bounce back out, and sealed the door shut behind me. The repressurization sequence kicked in.

I knew when oxygen returned, because Neveni drew a huge gasp of air. I sagged back against the wall, my heart drumming in my chest. It wasn't until the door opened between the air lock and the rest of the *Hera* that I ripped off my helmet. A nearby med bot, responding to her vital signs, soared into the chamber with us.

"Neveni," I called to her as it hummed about her. "Neveni, can you hear me?"

She made a sound.

"Are you brain-dead?" I asked her.

She obviously couldn't answer this if she were, but I could tell she wasn't because her face grimaced with distinct vexation. I assumed that a brain-dead Neveni couldn't manage that.

Sure enough, she spoke as soon as she could manage: "Why didn't you just let me die?"

Her voice was a dry rasp. I thought I'd misunderstood her.

Then, "I wouldn't let you die. I'm not holding a grudge over the transmission you sent me. I know Pasus forced you, and he would have trapped us without it. So . . . so if you think I was angry, I wasn't. That didn't merit letting you be killed."

"This isn't about you, Nemesis. Why didn't you let me die for *my* sake?" she cried raggedly. "I wanted to be dead. I was glad it was over. I should be with my family. I want to be with them."

"Space is still out there," I told her. "It's not going anywhere. One touch of a button and I could vent you back out into the vacuum if you prefer."

Neveni gave a sob. "Do it, then."

"No," I said, indignant. "I just went to a great deal of trouble saving you. Vent yourself to space if you want."

I turned around to leave her, then thought better of it. She might take me up on that suggestion.

"I'd rather you didn't do that," I told her quickly. "I prefer you weren't dead. You surely realize that even if you've just lost everyone you know and love, everything will be better soon."

She made a choked sound and covered her face with her hands. Even the brief vacuum exposure had blistered her skin with the cosmic rays of the stars, so the med bot turned its attention to that next.

I didn't know what else to say, so I left her. The noises she made, which followed me down the corridor, could have been sobs or laughter.

I made sure to dispatch a service bot her way with recreational narcotics. Venalox was a dreadful narcotic, but I still had faith in other sorts. Drugs were a most excellent means of coping with grief.

For the first time, Pasus summoned me to his vessel, the *Colossus*. Once I boarded the ship, I found Tyrus seated across from Senator von Pasus at a long table amid a garden. Servitors placed an array of freshly sliced breakfast fruits before them. In the great light of three suns beaming through the sky dome, Tyrus's skin looked wan, sallow. He'd lost a great deal of weight.

"Ah, Nemesis," said Senator von Pasus. "Sit. Eat breakfast."

I would sooner drink poison. I eyed Pasus, wondering what his game was. He sat with Tyrus's scepter positioned on the table in a short stand . . . closer to him than to its true owner.

"Your Supreme Reverence, look who has joined us!" Pasus said loudly.

Tyrus stirred, met my eyes just for a moment.

"He is not eating," Pasus told me. "Withdrawal will do that."

Withdrawal!

My gaze flitted hopefully to Tyrus. He clearly knew what uses he'd been put to while under, because there was a bitter cynicism on his face.

"Are you all right?" I asked him quietly, knowing there was no way to speak without Pasus hearing us.

"Just queasy," Tyrus said hoarsely.

"Do you . . ." I looked at Pasus, watching us with a smug satisfaction that made me want to break his skull open. "Tyrus, do you remember everything?"

"I remember signing away every possession I have," he said, his voice a rasp. "And then accepting responsibility for a mass murder I didn't commit. I remember enough to deem that the worst drug trip of my life. Now my mind is clear. Why?" He looked up at Pasus. "Do you have all the plunder you meant to take?"

"I'm satisfied we're off to the right start. We no longer need the injections. From now on, you will simply need to ask me for doses when you feel you need them, and I'll give them to you so you may inhale them at leisure."

Tyrus closed his eyes. "I have no ships, no colonies, no resources . . . just my vaunted bloodline. Tell me, how am I to pay my oxygen allowance? Food. Water. Now that you have the deed to the *Valor Novus*, shall I go elsewhere, or do I rent from you? And that brings me back to money. I would vacate the premises, but I suspect you would not allow that. You see my difficulty."

"You're right. You won't be able to shoulder those expenses. Especially when Your Supremacy has ruled out the prospect of marrying for wealth," Pasus agreed. "Fortunately, I'm willing to lend you what you need."

"Which again brings us back to the issue of money. One can't simply borrow without end."

"Your ancestors certainly had no issues with running a deficit. I will take care of all the arrangements for you to make payments toward your debts to me through taxes. Tariffs. Fines. You have the mechanisms of the state at your command. Your uncle was liberal with his use of them."

"I am not," snapped Tyrus.

"Not yet." Pasus's eyes gleamed.

Tyrus had no choice here. They both knew it.

Tyrus leaned back, gazed up at the ceiling, and gave a fatalistic laugh. "Between genocide and extorting the Excess, you mean me to be a very popular Emperor. Why even bother with Venalox? A borrower is already slave to a lender."

"You wish to stop using the Venalox, then?" Pasus said.

Tyrus didn't answer. He knew there was a catch.

I cut in, "Why even ask that?"

"He can stop now if he wishes. He can stop today," Pasus said.

Did the man truly imagine Tyrus so addicted already, he'd make another choice?

"Withdrawal is most unpleasant," said Pasus. "But if you want to stop using the Venalox, you can endure it. It will torment you for about two days, gauging from the Excess who tested it."

"I don't believe you for a second," Tyrus said. "You wouldn't allow me to stop."

"I would. Of course . . ." He picked up his glass, weighed it in his hand. "I cannot guarantee I won't wait out the two days, then force another injection upon you again so you may get addicted once more. We'll repeat again and again until you understand the utter futility of your predicament."

"Fine." Tyrus raised a palm, his eyes hard. "Consider it understood. Will you give me the other form of the drug now?"

"That question was not posed in the manner I'd like." Pasus considered it carefully. "What I want is for you to use my title, a respectful tone, and the word please. I want you on your knees. We'll do this in the presence chamber."

"Are you utterly mad?" Tyrus said.

"Why subject him to that?" I demanded. "Does it please you to humiliate him?"

"This has nothing to do with his feelings," Pasus said. "It's about how we will be perceived. I need the Grandiloquy to see me in a position of mastery over the Emperor so they will understand how it is to be. And it will also be for your sake, Tyrus."

"My sake?" Tyrus said with a nasty smile. "This will be an interesting explanation."

"You will remember this. Always," Pasus said. "Shall we go to the presence chamber now?"

Tyrus threaded his fingers together, just considering them, as though he wished to inspect his nails. They were dirty. I noticed that abruptly. Tyrus, so meticulous, and there was dirt under his nails. I couldn't seem to look away from them.

"This is entirely too gratifying for you," Tyrus said.

Pasus considered the words a moment, then smiled. "But of course it is, Tyrus. Why wouldn't it be? I'll admit it. I enjoy this. The Senate was in my grasp while you were still wearing diapers, and but for a stroke of luck, you might have cut my legs out from under me at the height of my power. This—after scorning my daughter for the creature who murdered her. I have been insulted by you in myriad ways, so I will not pretend there is nothing . . . pleasurable about this."

"I wouldn't have guessed you were so sensitive, Senator," I told him. "Have you been tallying up his slights all this time?"

"It's human nature, which I wouldn't expect a Diabolic to understand," Pasus said, his eyes on Tyrus. "It may be inevitable: the youth are the downfall of the aged, but it will not be you, and it will not be today. A hundred years from now, when you are a much older Emperor and some insolent chit of a boy marches in and sets himself to destroying everything you have fought so hard to build . . . Perhaps then you'll understand the need to crush that young person in your fist. For now, I am content for all to see you kneel before me."

# 28

I'D NEVER been ill. I'd never seen Sidonia suffer anything worse than a cold. The most dreadful illness I'd glimpsed was Tyrus after that first visit to Lumina, and I'd mostly avoided him during that time. Now, I saw signs of fever in the bright eyes, the waxen cast to his face.

Tyrus dragged his gaze to mine, and said raggedly, "Nemesis, before this, when we discussed my plan . . ."

I knew what plan he meant. His suggestion he'd handle this substance. "Yes?"

"I may have overestimated myself," Tyrus said. "Just a bit."

More than a bit, and we both knew it, but I managed a smile. "I know, Tyrus."

His smile was loving, hopeless. Then he keeled over and threw up.

My first instinct even now was to recoil from the sight of sickness, though this time, I knew it wasn't a virus. It was just a human body that had accustomed itself to a poison, now feeling a lack of what it had grown to expect.

A most dreadful lack.

Soon he couldn't hold down so much as water without it coming back up. A constant tremor rocked his arms and legs, and I had to help him move to keep the cramps at bay. He wasn't at liberty to leave the *Colossus,* so we roved the expanse of the garden within.

Tyrus stumbled over his words as he tried to explain the narcotic to me. "It's like I'm submerged in a swamp. Everything is still there, but there's this thick sludge blocking my every sense. . . ."

"Go on," I said, clutching Tyrus's arm with both of mine to keep him walking.

This was the first occasion I'd *truly* noticed the problem of the neural suppressor, because stars, he was so *heavy.* Normally I could outright carry him, and today he was only leaning some of his weight on me, yet it made me stagger.

"Then it clears, just a bit," Tyrus murmured, "and I hear myself talking and see myself eating or moving and I realize—I've been doing this all along. And I'm still doing it. I am asked to sign this, or affirm that, and this person I am not quite inhabiting is so pleased to be able to accommodate any request. Then I surface entirely and stare aghast at what I've just handed over, but before I can voice my doubts, I am lost. The agreement about Lumina . . . You did something. I wasn't sure—but I knew you were in danger, and I surfaced. . . ."

"You tried to walk away rather than surrender. I saw it."

"And then nothing," Tyrus whispered. "Like that, everything disappears again."

"Pasus claims the inhaled form is milder."

"I should hope so," he muttered. "I haven't anything else to give."

"Titles. Perhaps the *Hera.*"

He closed his eyes a moment. "I assure you, he hasn't forgotten that one. I've given him the title to it."

"It's mine. You can't do that."

"It becomes communal property when we wed, and . . . and on the bright side, the Senator now has an incentive to wish our union to happen soon."

"There's no end to his avarice," I muttered.

"I'm sorry, Nemesis."

This wasn't his fault; the apology was foolish.

Though I still thought of the ship as Cygna's, a surge of unexpected possessiveness swept over me at the idea of giving it up. Pasus would not have it.

Somehow, I had to preserve it.

Despair chased that thought. How? I couldn't preserve anything else. Tyrus's whole body shook now as though hit with an electric current, and his misery blared from his face, though he was still trying to hide it.

"Tyrus, you'll need to beg him for the powdered dose. Just get it done. Look at the alternative: he will let you suffer through two days of misery, inject you with another dose, and then you'll repeat it again. Put aside your pride."

He let out a slow, shaky breath. "It's not pride. I've always done this, and if I must be a pathetic, hopeless, abject beggar before all the great in this realm, I will do so. I can go to him on bended knee and show them all an Emperor in total subjugation. He means the Grandiloquy to understand he is their new master by exhibiting himself as mine, and I can endure it. It's just . . ."

"It's just what?" I stroked his forehead, the skin so hot against my hand.

"This feeling, the . . . the need to end it . . ." His eyes were haunted. "I can pretend, but some part of this won't be pretending. I'm ready to kneel and beg for it. And next time? The next?"

I nodded. "Then . . . then perhaps we should think of my suggestion."

He looked at me.

"Shall we return to that?" I said.

Not just to the suggestion—but to the Sacred City. He'd been confident enough to dismiss my idea of returning to the Interdict before, yet now . . . Now he was turning it over in his mind.

The Interdict was the only ally we had left. He was the only person whose voice was too powerful to drown out. We just had to get back to him, and then take him out here with us.

Then Tyrus began to laugh. I frowned at him.

"Do you remember suggesting that originally?" he murmured, smiling oddly. "Think. You wished him to see the Empire. I chose to scare him with the black hole. And the reason I opted for that is . . ." He started laughing again. "It's because I thought your idea would take far too much time." Then he had tears of laughter in his eyes, and I remained silent.

At the look on my face, his smile slipped away.

"Nemesis, I . . . I've completely lost track of the days. Do you know . . . The timing . . . We were lucky the first time."

"I know the windows," I said, barely moving my lips.

"Say no more," Tyrus said.

Everything we said, every syllable spoken within the walls of the *Colossus*, was likely being overheard.

But yes, I knew the gravital windows. It was a twenty-three-day journey straight there, a day in and out of the system, and from the schedule of gravital windows, we had a little over two weeks to leave here if we meant to escape in time.

"For how long does it close next?" Tyrus said, keeping it vague enough for only my understanding. "Remind me. I'm still hazy."

"Three years."

He cursed softly. "This one or never, then." He swallowed, and I knew he was fighting down the nausea again. "I don't know how I will . . . think after I am dosed again. Even if I can, I am watched and I am overheard everywhere."

I nodded.

"It's why I won't be allowed on the *Hera*." He looked at me. "The very walls of that vessel repel distant eyes and ears."

My ship was safe from surveillance, then. Good. "You gave me the best."

"Always," he said.

"I will make do." I gripped his hand. "Trust in me."

He nodded. Gratitude washed over his countenance, though that terror he was too raw to hide from me remained.

I stroked his face, the only relief I could offer. He leaned his forehead against mine, and my mind raced. Such a great promise I'd made to him. I'd do the thinking and planning for us. I hadn't the slightest idea of how to start.

There were murky tendrils of ideas, but I didn't know where they led, or what I'd find on the other end. But the fact was, Tyrus could not act, and my mind was perfectly clear. It had to be me. I had to save us or we would not be saved.

So I would do it.

I would save us.

When he keeled over, sick yet again, I made my first decision as the one of us who had to plan. "Now. I am taking you to the presence chamber to speak to Pasus exactly as he wished. I won't allow you to suffer for no reason."

He rubbed at his face miserably. "Do me . . . one favor."

"Anything."

He spoke softly: "Don't watch."

I smoothed my hand through his hair and nodded. I wouldn't.

My eyes wouldn't glimpse his public humiliation. At least, any more of it.

Pasus had indeed been eavesdropping and had manufactured reasons to summon as many as possible to the presence chamber. He waited as a petitioner might before the thrones, but his hands were linked behind his back in a calm, masterful stance. As Tyrus approached him, I trained my eyes out the window, gazing toward the *Hera*, that beautiful and powerful asteroid ship I'd vowed never to surrender.

"Senator von Pasus, please give me the Venalox."

"Wait a moment," Pasus said, then he withdrew Tyrus's scepter, and handed it to him. "Now, repeat that."

Tyrus bristled. He looked down at the scepter, the mockery of having to hold it and say this. "Please, Senator von Pasus, I would like the Venalox."

"Oh, but you were so resistant before," Pasus said, his voice loud.

Tyrus had to do better than that. He dropped to his knees, and out they poured, the pleading, the begging, just what Pasus wanted to see. I couldn't put my hands over my ears, so I made myself focus on the *Hera* with all its power. Even a sneak attack and an onslaught of automated mines hadn't dented her. The gravital forces in the Transaturnine System were nothing to her. She would be our liberation.

". . . so gracious and kind of you to do this . . . ," Tyrus was saying.

No, this ship was mine. I would not give her up. I would use her and I would fix all of this.

Murmurs were sounding about me, and I shifted my gaze to see the sheer pleasure radiating from Pasus's face as everyone—all who had the slightest bit of power in this Empire—beheld the Emperor debased at his feet.

"Oh, you dear boy. I hate to see you in pain. But of course, you may have this, Your Supremacy," purred Pasus, uncorking the phial.

Tyrus began to rise, but Pasus's hand fell on his shoulder, telling him to stay right where he was. Tyrus reached for the phial, but Pasus said a sharp, "No."

And I'd told him I wouldn't watch, and I hadn't meant to, but now I saw the tremor of raw hatred pass through Tyrus's body as Pasus maintained his hold on the phial.

"Go ahead," Pasus said.

Tyrus leaned forward, just his head, and inhaled from the phial right in Pasus's hand. I watched his face, trying to gauge how strong this was, how coherent he would be. The narcotic set in and a haze washed over his features.

He sagged forward, and Pasus balanced him with a hand, then said to the watchers, "It's safe to say the Emperor and I are reconciled at last."

Laughter. It seared my ears, and perhaps it was polite laughter, perhaps it was the sycophantic sort one offered to a Senator who now ruled over all in this room. . . . But I did not forgive it. My hands twitched to rip out the vocal cords of everyone I saw. I wanted nothing more than to ram the *Hera* through this ship and . . .

Then my gaze shot to that beautiful asteroid ship, my very blood electrified with the thrill of the idea. This one was more than a tendril; it cut right through the murky darkness until I could see a way forward. Hope blazd within me. I clutched it like a shield about my heart as Pasus reminded Tyrus to scoop up the scepter he'd dropped . . . then paraded his Emperor about here and there, like a tiger trained to jump through a burning loop.

Tyrus and I were in a bind, but we would not be for long, and when we turned on Pasus, nothing in this galaxy would save him. I would make sure of it.

# 29

IN THE Great Heliosphere, Pasus stood in the next ring outward. He held the scepter in his hands idly—bearing it "for the Emperor," as he always said. He was staring fixedly at my chest. Another man, and I'd have assumed it was lust. With him, it was the concentric suns of the Interdict that trapped his gaze. My mark of personhood by the leader of the faith he wholeheartedly believed, and yet had willfully disregarded for his own convenience.

How did he justify it to himself? Truly?

In any case, Fustian nan Domitrian stopped before Tyrus, who hadn't had a dose of Venalox since the night before and looked like he hadn't slept in his entire life. There was one dose in the morning, which meant he began to look miserable by evening—before he received the other. By the time morning came about, he was already sick and uncomfortable again. It was a wretched torment that waxed and waned without stopping. He rubbed his arms as the vicar drizzled oil over his head, then Fustian stopped by me.

I waited, my chin lifted.

Fustian paused a moment, then blessed me.

The Interdict had decided for him, and it seemed that was enough. As the lights were extinguished to adjourn the service, Pasus swept forward, clasped Tyrus by the shoulder, and almost took mine, then thought better of it and settled his other hand on Tyrus's other shoulder.

"Vicar Primus, the Emperor and his future Empress should wed soon."

Fustian nan Domitrian nodded thoughtfully. "The issue of personhood is no longer. What of heirs? There is still the . . . genetic difficulty. Obviously, any child will have to be . . . entirely human."

Until this, Tyrus hadn't paid the slightest bit of attention to anything. He'd been staring at Pasus with bloodshot eyes, waiting for his morning dose. Now his gaze snapped to the vicar. "I'm not having children."

"Of course he is," Pasus said smoothly. "And we will take whatever is human of Nemesis, for surely there is something or other, then the Emperor's DNA. . . ."

"I would sooner castrate myself than produce an heir to this situation!" Tyrus roared.

"The Emperor does not know what he is saying," Pasus said. "As for . . . Nemesis, whatever is inhuman in her genome can simply be substituted with parts of mine."

Tyrus broke into laughter. A strange, high sort that made him double over, and I just glared at Pasus, who seemed unappreciative of the laughter.

"This is precious," Tyrus said, wiping away tears. Or maybe sweat. He looked ragged. "The three of us will have a baby together. All the Senator's dreams will come true."

"Does the idea of my DNA repulse you? That's insulting, Your Supremacy." Pasus withdrew Tyrus's next phial of Venalox and considered it. "I would like an apology. Or perhaps I will smash this next dosage."

Tyrus's eyes were feverish with hatred, but the need overtook him and I had to look away. He wouldn't want me to see this; I didn't want to see it.

Craving had a will all its own, and it seemed to colonize his mind, driving out whatever else had once been in its place. I was sure of it, because Tyrus would never willingly place his lips on Pasus's boots, or endure the hand that stroked through his hair as he was rewarded for it.

"In any case," Pasus said, gesturing with the scepter (Tyrus was out of the conversation, sitting on the floor, propped up against Pasus's leg and totally lost to the Venalox), "We are arranging a great spectacle on short notice, but I do want His Supremacy's new bride exhibited for all the vicars in the Empire now that she has the Most Ascendant One's approval. The vicars will likely feel more flexible when the time comes and I wish to revisit the matter of the scepter."

"When will that time be?" said the vicar.

Pasus's gaze dropped to the young man below him, and he seemed to be weighing something in his mind. "Not more than a year, I should think. The wedding we can do now. There will be a most magnificent view of the stars in four days. Shall we do it then?"

"Very well," said the vicar.

My heart felt like it was jolted.

Four . . . four days?

"Excellent," Pasus said with a smile. "It's decided." To Tyrus, "How wonderful for you!"

Tyrus gave a low sound in his throat that might've been agreement or objection, and I stared down at him, aghast. Four days. I had only four days, and then I would lose the *Hera*. Pasus would claim it as soon as it passed into Tyrus's co-possession.

I couldn't envision any possible escape without that ship!

Whatever I did, I had to act as soon as possible.

My thoughts were urgent, darting things, racing this way, that. I'd hatched a tentative plan to don a space-sheath, rescue Tyrus from the outside of the ship, and then we'd simply use the *Hera* to plow straight through anything in our way.

It was a fine plan—except for the fact that he could no longer be found on the *Colossus*, somewhere predictable I could plot to reach beforehand.

Where he stayed now shifted from night to night.

Tyrus had been wrong about having nothing left to sell. Pasus could offer one very valuable asset on behalf of the Emperor—and it was the Emperor himself. The Domitrians were the foremost family in the Empire, and just by virtue of who he was, Tyrus was a status symbol with a variety of uses.

His mere presence in a chamber meant there had to be ceremony at his entrance. Tyrus never stuck to that formality unless it was an important occasion, but now that Pasus had assumed the role of proxy Emperor, he insisted that such honors be paid to Tyrus—and Pasus was always there to drink them in as though they were meant only for him.

Images of Tyrus taken while wearing certain fashions could be distributed to help sell them. Any food, drink, or narcotic he enjoyed could be publicized to market that product as "so fine, the Emperor himself partakes of it." And of course, any chamber on any starship where Tyrus passed the night soon fell into the annals of that family's history. Their future guests could luxuriate in the knowledge that they were sleeping in a chamber deemed fit for a galactic Emperor.

I suspected Pasus shared custody of Tyrus partly to mitigate concerns that he had too much influence over him. He always wore a most uneasy look, passing the next dose of Venalox onto one or the other of the Grandiloquy so they could preside over the Emperor for an evening.

Arguments began. Then a session of court was even called to hash out the ground rules of these arrangements, as Tyrus just clutched his temples, ignoring whatever they were saying. I listened, shaking with rage as the cloying, false-youth-abusing Wallstrom said, "But what if *he* visits and *he* wishes to have sex?"

"With you?" said Pasus skeptically.

"With anyone!"

Boiling inside, I couldn't sit here and just watch this. I ripped to my feet . . . and Tyrus's hand caught my arm. I threw him a furious look where he'd just been sitting, eyes closed, almost as though asleep.

"This isn't theirs to decide," I snarled.

Tyrus shook his head. "Don't. Just sit."

My heart thudded with blinding rage as Pasus reproved the company. "Domitrian DNA is a matter of *state*. It may not be slung about carelessly. When an heir is born, it will happen *after* we have all made a decision that it's the appropriate time. No sooner."

I wanted to break them all apart. But Tyrus just seemed to want to sleep.

It was horrifying to realize he'd accepted such a fundamental decision was out of his control.

*We will leave here*, sizzled my thoughts. *Tyrus, this will not last much longer—one way or another.*

I couldn't say the words. Anything I spoke to him would be overheard. I could only speak to Neveni in the shelter of the *Hera*.

The rest of the galaxy believed she was dead, so I had her at my total disposal. I bombarded her with everything I couldn't say to anyone else, but it was rather like talking to a wall.

In fact, she spent most of her time staring at walls, or worse, scraping her arms and legs with a diamond she'd found on the ship, drawing small lines of blood over her skin. She seemed to prefer that to even the most euphoric substances. The only time I saw any emotion from her was when I mistakenly left a screen on, a broadcast from Eurydice—an account of the Luminar tragedy. They'd been experimenting with bioweapons and accidentally triggered one.

That was the official story.

She broke the screen. Then she lapsed back into silence.

I spoke to her despite the sullen silence. I'd never been particularly verbose, but it was better than the empty void that settled about me when I was alone, when every doubt and fear would seep into me.

I was in the middle of rambling to her: ". . . of course, we can't truly fix any of this until we reach the Interdict again. The time is growing short—"

"The Interdict?"

Neveni's voice startled me. It was rasping, dry, crackling with not having been used. Now she looked at me flatly.

"That's your plan? Go to the Interdict?"

"He's a man with a conscience."

"He's an arrogant old coward who's hidden away from the galaxy for five hundred years."

"He's that, too, but he'll help us," I insisted. "If he knew of the Resolvent Mist, of this situation . . . Don't you see? Every single Helionic professes total obedience to him. He is the single person in this galaxy who is totally untouchable. Even Senator von Pasus's faction won't dare to question him. A few words from him, and we'd solve this."

Neveni was really looking at me now, and I realized I'd gotten through to her. She said, almost to herself, "You're right. The Interdict matters to them. They all revere him. He's valuable to them." Life kindled in her dark eyes. "I'll help you get there."

"Yes?"

"Yes." Her voice was a whiplash of determination. Then she was on her feet, shooting past me. "Let me shower. I smell horrible. Then— then we figure this out."

# 30

TYRUS WOULD PASS the evening on Senator von Vander-fuld's starship, the *Zeppelin*, and the plan was simple: I would enter the vessel from the outside, bringing a space-sheath for him with me. At my signal, Neveni would tear the *Hera* straight from its moorings, we'd use the space-sheaths to board the ship, and then we would flee.

Neveni was skeptical: "I really wish we could have more time to plan."

"We don't," I said flatly.

Tomorrow was the eve of our wedding. I was desperate.

This had to work.

My careful glide through the void toward the *Zeppelin* took nearly an hour. I held my breath every time a shadow stirred in a window near me, fearing the wrong pair of eyes might glimpse me. But I made it.

No one thought to lock their ship from the exterior. I tugged open the *Zeppelin*'s air lock, thrust myself inside, and then the trickiest part proved prying open the space-sheath with the strength of a regular girl.

I stepped out into the corridor just as one of the *Zeppelin*'s service bots hummed past. Yet—no alarm. Why would it react to the sight of me? I was just another person. Another bot swept past with a tray of narcotics, and I followed it down the corridor until doors parted for it, revealing a glimpse of laughing, chattering Grandiloquy. I plastered myself against the wall, out of sight, until those doors slid shut again.

All were still awake and about. I had to wait them out . . . assuming Tyrus was among them.

But of course he was. One didn't bribe Pasus for the Emperor and then fail to exhibit him at a party. So I needed a position where I could wait without attracting attention, where I could hide and keep an eye on him until the party concluded.

My gaze strayed upward toward the ventilation shaft. If I could get up there . . . Indecision gripped me until a Servitor wandered toward me, heading in the direction of the same chamber.

I stopped him. His glassy eyes both aimed at me and did not focus, in that swampy, empty way Servitors always seemed to look at you.

"Hold this position," I ordered him. I arranged his hands together, stepped onto them, and then climbed up onto his shoulders. My balance, at least, was still as good as a Diabolic's.

I shoved open the panel, then gripped the edge of the shaft and . . . and I couldn't do a single pull-up to get myself into it. This was ridiculous! Were people truly this weak?

To the Servitor, I said breathlessly, "Put your hands straight into the air."

He raised them both, and with that boost, I shoved myself into the shaft. I began to ease the panel back down, but the creature was still standing there with his hands straight up.

*Ban Servitors*, I'd told Tyrus.

If only we'd done that much.

"Now go where you were going," I told him. He began to walk, and I hissed, "And put your hands to your sides!"

The hands fell back at his sides, and I closed the shaft at last.

Once I'd made it to the grate above the reception chamber I'd glimpsed from outside, the voices reached me. Inane chatter. Eight people. The scent of a narcotic crystal, something sweet. The slightest glimpse that way, and I could see the flash of the Servitor who'd come in before me, now being manhandled, enduring it with the empty expression he'd worn with his arms in the air.

A lone, clumsy thump of footprints, and then there was Tyrus, moving through the corridor into the chamber just below me. My heart raced, but I dared not ease myself down.

*Wait until he has retired for the night. It must happen.*

A voice: "Your Supremacy."

"I'm ill," Tyrus responded. "Leave me in peace."

"I'll fetch a med bot." Following him into the chamber was a disheveled Senator von Vanderfuld. Tyrus threw off the hand his host had settled on his arm.

"Leave me be for a few minutes," Tyrus snapped. "Can I not have a minute away from your lot?"

Vanderfuld stepped back, and then I saw Senator von Aton join him. The two men inclined their heads toward each other. Aton murmured for Vanderfuld's hearing—and unwittingly, for mine, "Alectar did tell us all to be mindful: he is an Emperor, but he is also newly twenty. Some moodiness is expected."

"But my guests will get restless," Vanderfuld said to Aton. "Should I use the Venalox . . . my son is the same age."

"No. Hold off on the dose. Leave me to speak with him," Aton said.

Vanderfuld retreated. My gaze focused sharply between the lines of the grate as Aton considered Tyrus, and then cleared his throat loudly to announce his presence.

I angled myself to try to catch a glimpse and saw Tyrus leaning both hands against a podium holding a bust. In fact, the chamber was filled with them, bronze heads of . . . of dead Domitrian royalty.

I stared at the empty bronze eyes of Randevald as Aton said, "A fine likeness, isn't it?" He nodded to the podium.

Tyrus sighed, weighed it in his hand. "I knew her well, Horatio."

"Excuse me?"

Tyrus just shook his head, setting the bust back down. I glimpsed whose head it was.

The realization made me start. His grandmother. The Grandeé Cygna.

"It feels as though she is in here with us, watching us," Aton said.

"Oh, you'd know if she could see through these eyes," Tyrus said bitterly. "We would never hear the end of her laughter."

"I was very fond of your grandmother. She was most clever— though not so generous as Your Supremacy. I never did thank you for the *Tigris*. Such a bountiful gift," Aton was murmuring.

"Yes," Tyrus said shortly. "I am continually astonished to discover my own expansive generosity."

"I have considered renaming it in your honor."

"The *Ozymandias*, then. A fine name."

"Ah, I fear I do not know the reference. I am not so inclined toward perusing those old books as you are. I know you quite enjoy them. The most interesting feature of the *Tigris*," Aton said, a sly note in his voice, "is surely the surveillance archives."

Silence.

From where I observed them, suspicion stirred within me. I'd never liked Gladdic's father. What was he up to? For his part, Tyrus did not move for a long moment. Then, "Senator, I vastly prefer you delete the logs."

"Your Supremacy, I assure you that I am discreet. I've no intention of exhibiting them. Such insights I have gleaned from them! I understand you better, Tyrus. I know just how vexing this entire situation must be."

"Do you."

"No time to yourself. Always used as the entertainment. So many powerful men seek to invert that in their private lives, but not you. I respect that."

"What," Tyrus said, rigid, "is it you want from me, Senator?"

"I am offering to help you." And Aton produced a phial. Tyrus's posture grew rigid. He couldn't know the raw, unquenched need for it all over his face—because he would have been desperate to hide it. "We might keep this between us: I have obtained the chemical recipe. You needn't rely only on Alectar. Won't that be a relief? An occasional reprieve from scraping and pleading when he wishes to withhold from you?"

Tyrus's face twisted. "What's the price for this?"

Aton took a step back, another, and Tyrus trailed him with sharp, watchful eyes that never left the phial. "I want to invite you to my starship. Once, twice a week, perhaps, if it can be contrived. And when you are there, I will have *nothing* to do with you. Would you have any use for such a thing?"

Tyrus didn't answer. He knew—and I knew—that Aton was still angling for something. This was a hard sell and he had yet to demand his price. But something passed over Tyrus, and he pressed his hands over his face. "I just wish I could sleep."

"Sleep?"

"I am so tired. All the time, I am tired. It may be the Venalox, or it may not be. I am never at liberty to sleep when I wish, or so long as I wish and I just . . . Senator, name your price. You've drawn it out long enough that I am growing certain it is dreadful. If all you desired was my presence on your ship, you'd speak to Pasus."

"No, you don't understand. My price is not dreadful by any means. All I seek is what I've asked for: visits to the *Tigris*. And I would like you to bring your . . . future wife with you."

Silence.

Tyrus's hands dropped from his face. He just stared at him.

"I have watched her in your surveillance archives, and in the ball dome, and I am entirely bewitched. If you tell her to accompany you."

"Are. You. Insane?" Tyrus's voice seemed calm. But there was a deadly rage in the words. "You must be. You must be utterly *mad*. You think I would ever . . ." Tyrus stopped. Then, "No. A thousand times, no! Delete those archives and put those thoughts from your head!"

Aton had abandoned any shade of deference, his tone sour. "Surely Your Supremacy realizes denial only strengthens one's ardor. Now I must insist. I came to you as a courtesy, but you are correct—I have the means to circumvent you entirely. I needn't ask you, or even ask *her*. . . ."

Tyrus swept up Cygna's bronze bust and slammed it into Aton's skull. The movement was so abrupt, even I didn't understand what I was watching for a moment as the next and the next plunge of Tyrus's arm and the sickening thuds that followed split Aton's head open. . . .

Voices from the next chamber, partygoers pouring in, then screams.

My mind snapped back to action and I gripped the edges of the shaft. It was all I could do not to tear it open and fling myself down there.

But I couldn't. I couldn't. My hands felt like claws as I forced them to open, as I forced myself back. Below me, Tyrus pummeled Aton's head long after it had been reduced to a mass of blood and pulp. There were horrified onlookers ringing them, but none dared approach. When Tyrus finally took notice of them, his tunic was smeared with blood in a surreal pattern.

He straightened, rubbed clean his grandmother's bloodied bust, and set her back on her podium. Then he swiped up the fallen phial of Venalox and settled by the window to use it like nothing had happened.

Deathly silence descended. He'd ended the party.

I closed my eyes in the ventilation shaft. All I could hear now was my own breath in the air as my plans for rescue died away. I had no choice but to wait it out as people swarmed the ship, and then Pasus himself came, sending the others away with a gruff voice.

"Well, now you've done it, Tyrus."

"Have I?"

"That man and I have shared a half century of friendship. You know the consequences." Then, in a louder voice—so a servant lurking near the door could hear him—"Fetch Nemesis. Bring her here."

My heart gave a lurch. They'd go to the *Hera*. I wasn't there. Neveni was.

I debated throwing fate to the wind, plunging down there . . . But Tyrus just chuckled. "Alectar, you won't hurt her." His voice was slightly thick with intoxication, but his words were clearer than they usually were immediately after use of the substance.

"I've told you any violence on your part will be met with violence against her!" thundered Pasus. "She will lose a limb. I am tempted to take two. . . ."

"Aton was not your friend," Tyrus said. "Would a true ally give me this?"

Silence. I peeked down to see Pasus had taken the empty phial of Venalox, the one Aton had gone behind his back to slip to his

Emperor. "I trust this buys immunity from consequences."

Silence. Then, "Yes." And after another second, "This time."

"A half century of friendship. You were truly fond of him, weren't you?" Tyrus's whisper was mock sympathetic, filled with poison. "Such treachery. How cruel the universe can be."

*Indeed.*

The universe was cruel. Tyrus had secured me a reprieve from paying the price for his violence, but he'd also ended any chance I had of removing us from this cage altogether. He'd be too closely watched tonight for me to sneak him away.

My eyes sank closed. My head throbbed.

One more day of liberty, and then the next day, that liberty ended. We would be married, Pasus would have the *Hera*, and I saw no way out.

# 31

NEVENI KNEW with one look at my face upon my return that the plan had failed. She didn't seem surprised. Maybe she'd grown accustomed to accepting the worst.

I hadn't.

"I'm not surprised. I'm a bit relieved, actually."

"Relieved?"

Neveni helped me pry off the half-stiffened space-sheath. "I kept running it over in my head. Even if you'd gotten the Emperor, signaled me, and then gotten him onto the *Hera*, well . . . Think about it. Every single Grandiloquy starship would have chased us the entire way out of the system. I think they could've stopped us."

My head pulsed. "I'm pleased you're satisfied. You do realize that we've just lost any chance of escape."

"No, actually—we have one more chance. A good one. I thought of it too late to stop you from going out, but now . . . I think I figured out the perfect time for your plan."

I looked at her sharply. "Did you?"

Neveni smiled.

It was the day before the wedding, and Tyrus and I would receive the Laudatory, and begin our Forenight. A contingent of Senators' spouses were to be my anointers. They bustled onto the *Hera* to pretend to awaken me and I let them go through the ritual.

I'd been Elantra's anointer before her Laudatory, and that had been . . . It had been the most devastating day of my existence.

The smell of the oil the Grandeé von Canternella opened to apply to my back stirred images of Donia's dying eyes in my mind, and the look on my face must have reflected my anguish. The husband of Senator von Wallstrom made a choked noise where he happened to be directly in my line of sight, and he stumbled back and tripped over the low table behind him.

And despite myself, I smiled, and uneasy chuckles sounded about me. He didn't know it, but he'd diverted my mind. They eased on my robe of white liquisilk, and I told them: "Go ahead and anoint each other. I'll be in the washroom."

I left them occupied with that and shut the door behind me. "I'm alone," I said.

Neveni emerged from the bathing chamber. "This is the best I could find," she said, showing me a length of rope. "It's sturdier than it looks. I'd use the synthesizers and make more, but . . ."

I shook my head. Pasus had confiscated all but one of the *Hera*'s synthesizers, and I was fairly certain he was monitoring that to make sure I wasn't trying to get my hands on a Venalox substitute or an explosive.

I yanked on the rope to test it. It didn't break when I pulled it, but that meant very little at my present strength. "This is enough for me to tie Tyrus to me."

Neveni's gaze flickered. "You should use that knot I showed you and tie yourself to the wall. Let him hang on to you."

"No," I said. "I don't know if he's strong enough."

"You don't know if you're strong enough," she pointed out, an edge in her voice.

"I'll find out soon enough," I told her.

"I, uh, I think you need to run this whole thing by him. In advance. If you get a chance."

"Of course." But that was a big "if."

I'd begun tying the knot to hold the rope about my thigh, but Neveni waved my hands away, then set about doing that elaborate tie of her own that left one end of the rope flopping out, ready to give with a light pull.

"Thank you," I told her sincerely, and eased my robe back into place.

We just considered each other for several heartbeats. She'd been crackling with determination ever since she'd broken out of her stupor, but Neveni still appeared a shadow of herself. Too thin, like she'd been hollowed out on the inside. She put on a brief smile that I knew was entirely for my benefit.

"Are you nervous at all?" she said.

"No point to nerves. This succeeds and we are free, or it fails and I will die." I considered her thoughtfully. "And you . . ."

"I'm not nervous. Worst-case scenario, this fails, I'm discovered, and I die, and I don't care about that."

"I won't apologize for saving your life."

I turned to leave, but Neveni said, "Nemesis, for whatever it's worth, thank you for saving me. You're a better friend to me than I think I can ever be to you."

I'd saved her life, I'd only struck her once in the grand total of our acquaintance, and I'd been fairly patient with her. "Yes. I am an excellent friend, aren't I? Strange that you're the only one I have."

Neveni laughed. "Very strange." She leaned forward, kissed me on the cheek, and said, "See you on the other side."

The Laudatory generally took place well before the Forenight.

The Laudatory was the beginning of a formal engagement. It often bound two Grandiloquy who'd never met each other, much less had sex. The vicar would begin the thirty days by administering hormonal stimulants to sync the pair's bodies. Each morning, the engaged would formally meet under the influence of mood-elevating narcotics so they might associate each other with pleasant feelings.

In the evenings, they undertook other bonding experiences: shared psychedelics to nurture spiritual bonds, shared amphetamines to complete a detailed task together (generally, a thorough preparing of their future bedchamber). Stimulants so they might have extensive discussions into the small hours of the nights, sedatives so they might experience their first shared slumber. Then, Forenight: when the vicar gave them the powerful aphrodisiac Fireskiss.

This was when they consummated their relationship.

Many marriages had been canceled after disappointing Forenights. If a couple could not satisfy each other at the very height of their physical and emotional desire for each other, then they never would. Since Forenights were generally a witnessed event, family and friends often weighed in on the couple's sexual chemistry as well.

Since Tyrus and I had already had sex, we were going straight from the Laudatory to Forenight. Unfortunately, even though we were already certain of our chemistry, we would also have surveillance for those who'd like to critique us or offer their input.

My anointers did not realize I could hear them as they quietly speculated about it during the walk to the Great Heliosphere.

". . . bet she's a brute with him."

"Wouldn't she injure him?"

"No, I hear she's harmless right now."

"She wouldn't harm him. Diabolics are very skilled at handling such things . . ."

I lost interest in their whispers as we headed into the Great Heliosphere, and the positive crowd of anointers for Tyrus fell into silence. I saw Tyrus, dressed in the same robe of white liquisilk that I had. I was painfully aware of the press of the rope bound about my leg. . . . The plan I needed to share with him. Somehow.

We took our place before Fustian nan Domitrian, and he began his Laudatory. "Normally I would receive contributions from both your families discussing great sexual deeds, but Your Supremacy has no living relatives, and the bride . . . She has a most complicated situation. . . ."

A snide whisper from Senator von Wallstrom to a companion, "He should go on about the prowess of a synthesizer. . . ."

Faint giggles that Fustian did not hear. ". . . so instead I will laud the sexual feats of our Domitrian sovereigns, your predecessors, Tyrus. Our first Emperor Sephias was a humble man, bewildered with the power thrust upon him. He treated copulating as a friendly sport to be undertaken with great cheer and vigor . . ."

Then, Sephias's daughter. Tyrus's face bloomed with the same horrified realization I had just reached: Fustian meant to talk about the Domitrian ancestors one-by-one.

Our anointers swiftly realized it too, because they began to stealthily and then not-so-stealthily escape the room.

By the time Fustian reached Randevald (having praised many,

many Domitrians for "vigor" and described many with the ambiguous word "unconventional"), the Great Heliosphere had hemorrhaged most of the anointers. Including Senator von Pasus.

". . . I presided over three Forenights for Randevald in this very heliosphere . . ."

And with those words, Fustian fell silent, realizing three Forenights and zero marriages could not be cast in anything but a supremely negative light, and it was never a wise idea for someone who was not Domitrian to insult one who was.

Not only that, but everyone was looking at one of the few anointers still here with us, the Grandeé von Canternella—the late Emperor's mistress. Her cheeks flushed. "He was creative," she mumbled.

Awkward shuffling. Fustian quickly concluded: "And now it is Tyrus von Domitrian's turn, and we are all eager to exalt in the prowess we'll witness from these two young lovers."

Fustian turned away to retrieve the Fireskiss, and I glanced behind us. "We've lost most of our audience," I told Tyrus. "However will we know if we have sexual chemistry?"

But Tyrus did not smile. There was nothing but a dark anger to his face. "They'll return. They won't miss the event." His gaze dropped. "But we'll disappoint them."

He tilted his forearm so I could see it, and after a moment, I picked out the slight difference in skin tone from the rest of his arm. I wouldn't have noticed had he not pointed it out to me. . . . Fake skin to shield him from the Fireskiss.

It was such a small, unimportant thing, yet his eyes gleamed with an ashen triumph. My chest seemed to grow hollow. Had we truly come back here intending to ban Servitors, to bring back the sciences, to fix this galaxy? And now—reduced to this. To enjoying only victories so small as not being watched on Forenight without our consent.

Tyrus made a show of succumbing to the Fireskiss. Fustian rubbed it into our wrists, and Tyrus began to breathe harshly, he swayed in place. His gaze riveted to me heatedly.

He aimed himself for me as though desperate to reach my side as our anointers led us from the Great Heliosphere back to the Emperor's chamber of the *Valor Novus*. The anointers did their job and held him back from me.

We nearly made it.

Then a few of the anointers who'd stepped out caught up with us. One who returned was a man who had taken to watching Tyrus so closely, he was the only person who could read him so well as I could.

"Your Supremacy's Venalox is within," Pasus said, and took advantage of the turn of Tyrus's head toward him to seize his chin, keep it there.

"Don't," Tyrus said, jerking back from his grip.

Fustian nan Domitrian tugged at Pasus's sleeve, and whispered, "Best not to touch him with the Fireskiss in his system . . ."

"He's faking," Pasus said. "Are you blind?"

"What are you . . . You're imagining things," Tyrus tried hazily. He reached for me . . . but Pasus's hands fell to his shoulders, pulled him back.

"Did you bribe someone to adulterate it?"

"Best not touch me right now," Tyrus said between his teeth.

"My touch is much the same as always because you . . . What? Took an anxiolytic to nullify it in advance? What?"

Tyrus glared back at him. "Let. Me. Go."

Pasus lifted his hands, but dropped his voice to a dangerous whisper: "You know exactly how much I value your personal dignity. Do you really want me to check in front of everyone—in front of *her*— whether you are lying to me?"

Her. Me.

Tyrus's eyes closed. Then he viciously dragged his nails over his forearm, scoured a gash in the fake skin.

"Clever boy," Pasus said. He beckoned over Fustian and administered the Fireskiss to Tyrus himself, rubbing it directly into the veins of his neck.

And so even this small victory—even this tiniest of them—was taken away from him.


I awaited him in the bedroom, not wishing to see him succumb as I'd witnessed far too many times with Venalox.

I unwound the rope from my leg, slid it under the bedsheets. No one would bother looking through the surveillance while I was alone in here. But once we were together . . .

The door slid open and raucous voices washed in. Tyrus stood there gripping the doorway, his face hazy. Desire scorched him, but all I could think of was his determination in the Great Heliosphere not to give our watchers what they wanted. I made up my mind.

I bolted forward, yanked him inside and shut the door to block those eyes. Tyrus swept me up in his arms. "Nem . . ."

Then his lips were on mine, insistent, hard.

"Tyrus, the . . . ," I said, pulling back.

"Mmm?" His arms banded about me, hauled me against him. There was a roughness and urgency to it all. The warmth of his body pressed up against mine made my blood race. If I still vastly overpowered him, this wouldn't make me uneasy. With a forceful push, I escaped his grip.

"This way," I said, trying to move us toward the attached washroom.

His eyes were fever bright, hands tugging me back as I dragged us forward, but I bundled him into the next room as he sought anything close to him with his lips, with his touch. We stumbled against the sink, and he swept me up onto it, hooking my legs about him.

"Tyrus, you didn't want . . ."

"Love you," he said breathlessly, kissing me desperately.

I evaded his kiss, shoving his head to the side. He was unbalanced, so I made it past him into the bathing unit. He caught up to me as I stood there looking about, confused.

"Where's a tub? A shower?" I said to Tyrus. This chamber appeared filled with rocks.

"So beautiful . . . ," he replied, not very helpfully, drawing me back into his arms.

"Turn on the water!" I called to the air, trying the standard command.

That did the trick. Water gushed from the walls, streaming over the rocks in foaming torrents, pooling in the basin that resembled a small pond. The walls shifted from dull gray to an image of stormy skies. The ceiling shed rain droplets upon us, and they sizzled in the steaming water.

So this was meant to seem like the outdoors. "That accounts for the rocks," I told Tyrus.

"Rocks . . . ," he moaned as though I'd said something intensely provocative. Anything I spoke right now likely sounded that way.

I changed to cold-water mode. A shimmering wall of heat bloomed up from the water, and the walls shifted their image from storm clouds to clear blue skies. I twisted about, since Tyrus had his arms around me, and pressed him up against the edge of the water. "Tell me if it's cold." I had to repeat it a few times before he dangled his fingers into the water, the other one roving over my skin wherever he could reach.

"Too cold. Like ice."

"That works." I shoved him headlong into it.

He surfaced with a shout, but the icy water had awoken him like a well-delivered slap. He blinked at me, hair plastered to his head, eyes wide.

"Better?" I said.

His face flushed. "Better." He dipped down into the water, emerged, soaked all over, and said, "Much better."

"How long will this Fireskiss last?"

"Give me ten minutes. I'll be able to keep myself in check then. Nemesis, did I . . . did I do anything untoward?"

"You told a Diabolic you loved her and that she was beautiful. Most of the galaxy would deem that untoward."

He didn't smile. Intently, almost angrily: "Did. I. Hurt. You?"

"You did nothing wrong, Tyrus."

"I despise every aspect of this," he said hollowly. "Some days I feel I am going to lose my sanity."

I cast my gaze about us. Pasus would be most vexed I'd thwarted the evening's entertainment, yet now that I surveyed this bathing unit with its gushing water, its fizzing waterfall . . . "Tyrus, I have something to tell you as soon as you can trust yourself closer to me."

I could see that interested him. He said, "Just . . . just stay out of the water, I'll . . ." He drew a jagged breath when I leaned down toward him, but didn't grab me.

So I whispered it in his ear:

"Tomorrow we escape."

# 32

NEVENI AND I had worked it out. It was a long shot, but it was our last hope.

Tomorrow morning, Tyrus and I would usher in our wedding day with a standard blood sacrifice. This would take place on the *Tigris*, in the arena. The sacrifice Pasus had arranged was meant to be an insult to me: we would preside over a battle to the death between Anguish and Hazard.

Pasus meant to rub it in my face, their subhuman status—watching them die for sport like any other animal.

But I'd figured out something about that blood sacrifice. The Grandiloquy would not crowd forward in hopes of seeing two ordinary men battle to the death. They wanted to see two full-strength Diabolics.

That meant their neural suppressors would need to be off.

And mine as well.

We would be on the weakest of the Domitrian starships, surrounded

by the masters who commanded all the other vessels of the Chrysanthemum, and for a few hours more, I still had control of the most
powerful Domitrian ship.

We would escape.

Or we would die.


Shaezar nan Domitrian was due to arrive with his servants at 0800.
Tyrus and I rose from bed. We'd continued to vex anyone watching
by simply passing the night in the sleep that I knew Tyrus desperately
needed. . . . Yet whenever my eyes opened, I found him just watching
me with a strange peace on his face.

"Please tell me you've gotten some sleep," I said.

"I've gotten some sleep."

"Tell me you're not just telling me that."

He laughed. It was a genuine, pure sound, and I curled up against
him, never wishing to let him go. He wouldn't even have taken the
Venalox, he was so invigorated by our plan. I convinced him to do so.
We didn't need him in withdrawal during the event ahead.

As he garbed us, Shaezar nan Domitrian made polite conversation,
"How was Forenight?"

"Terrible," Tyrus said briskly.

"Yes. We mean to call it all off." We both kept very severe faces, but
then our eyes met, and we were both smiling. Shaezar had grown very
tense, and now he realized—and gave us a polite laugh.

Metal was a social taboo in the arena, so we were both clad in black
leather. Tyrus's was a sweeping tailcoat, and mine formed one seam-
less bodysuit that dipped into a deep V to expose my mark of personhood. Effervescent essence was carefully applied to give my features a
striking glow, and my hair was stripped down to a platinum shade not
too much darker than my true one.

Tyrus, by his own choice, appeared much as always. His coppery hair was combed back, his garb obsidian like mine, to contrast with the scepter Pasus would bring for him to wield before the crowd. That meaningless instrument of power was almost a mockery of us at this point. I hoped for that to change.

"Any doubts?" Tyrus said to me intently.

An observer would mistake this for a talk about the wedding. "None. You?"

"None whatsoever," he said, his face hard. He took my hand, and then we strode out to meet our fates.

The arena of the *Tigris* was jam-packed today. The blood sacrifice for a royal wedding was a major event. So many of these decorated, foppish Grandiloquy had battled one another for the finest seats around the animal-fighting arena. The second most desired area was the one that allowed a full view of my reaction to the sight. What a humiliation they were hoping to see!

Tyrus's expression was unpleasant as he observed the highly ranked Grandiloquy who'd made the unusual seating choice of viewing us more closely than the animals. He told me, very quietly, "Don't tell Anguish and Hazard what we planned."

"But if we don't . . ."

"There will be no warning." His eyes were hard. "They deserve none."

It was the same thing Neveni had suggested, when I'd figured out the part the Diabolics would play in this plan. I'd refused her, too. "We have to warn them."

Tyrus drew a breath, released it. He clearly wished to argue, but then the crowds about us grew dense, and the path cleared on either side of us narrowed. We were surrounded by Grandiloquy, all too close to us. I was only vaguely aware of imperial processional music, of recording bots buzzing overhead.

I spotted a single person in the crowd who did not look excited for the sacrifice.

I slowed.

"One minute," I said to Tyrus, and I felt him stare after me as I crossed the distance to the boy whose father he'd killed.

Gladdic jumped to his feet as I approached, and reached out to draw my hand to his cheek.

"It's all right," I said. ". . . Senator von Aton." He closed his eyes. Yes. That was his title now. "I heard. I'm sorry for your loss." Senator von Aton had deserved it, but that didn't mean Gladdic should feel this pain. And I didn't want to take the slightest risk he'd be harmed. There were many who deserved what lay ahead. He did not. "Gladdic. Go grieve in private."

"I wanted to be here to support you."

I shook my head. "Don't be here." I drew closer to him, suddenly intent. "If you are truly my friend, don't watch this."

He looked about us urgently, and then leaned in very close: "I have to tell you something. I'm the new Aton Senator. So . . . so I was told something, but you need to know it. It's about the Venalox."

It wouldn't matter after today. I pressed my hands to his shoulders to tell him to simply go, but his whisper lashed out: "It's neurotoxic. Pasus, Locklaite, Fordyce . . . They all know it. It's poisoning his brain, and it's a cumulative effect. They said it's why the Emperor . . . why he killed my father."

I stared at Gladdic, the blood roaring up in my ears. "He . . . he doesn't seem slower of wit."

"It's not his intellect being damaged. It's . . . I don't know the names."

He gestured vaguely toward his forehead. "It's empathy. Conscience. That's the whole reason they had to reduce him to a pauper—he can't pose a threat without autonomy or wealth of his own. . . ."

Blinding fury swelled inside me. Of course. Of course that was their plan. It didn't matter if a foe wished to strangle you if you chopped off his arms before he could do it.

"But the real reason," Gladdic said in the softest whisper, and I knew he'd noticed—as I had—that people were beginning to look our way. Soon they would seek to overhear us. ". . . is they hope the Venalox will nullify you."

"Me."

"The parts of the brain . . . they're interconnected. Wipe away empathy, wipe away a conscience, and they think they'll wipe away . . . you."

His attachment to me.

An icy hand clutched my heart, for I could see exactly what their aim was. Hadn't I once felt no empathy, no qualms of guilt—no love? Until I was bonded to Sidonia, I was totally incapable of any such feelings.

When I broke away from Gladdic's side and walked back toward Tyrus—watching me with those pale, clever eyes amid the crowd of our foes—I felt cold flutters all through me. An image blared in my mind. The day Pasus had arranged our wedding in the Great Heliosphere, Fustian mentioned the scepter.

And Pasus had cast a long, careful look at Tyrus.

Gauging how rapidly he'd progressed toward the aim. That aim was indifference to me. Did Pasus think he would be able to kill me when a day came and Tyrus had no love for me? Or did Pasus hope Tyrus himself would wish to be rid of me?

When I reached his side, and Tyrus slid his hand down my arm to link our hands, there was a reassuring softness to his eyes.

It wasn't too late.

"You didn't tell him," he said, an edge of warning to his voice.

He didn't care if Gladdic died. Gladdic, who had done nothing to us. And it wasn't just anger at our situation accounting for that now. I banished the thought. "I ordered him to go grieve in private. No one wants to see his tears."

Tyrus's face grew shadowed. *Yes, I know what you did to his father,* I thought.

"I had very excellent reason," he said.

"I know."

I was not such a hypocrite I'd condemn him for a murder. There were things I expected of myself, though, and actions I expected of Tyrus. This wasn't like him. Now I knew why.

Tyrus and I made our first political stance against the animal fights. Pasus had thus decided we would celebrate our wedding by reinstituting them. I waited until the warm-up animals were raised out of the floor of the arena and unleashed to rouse the crowd, ready them for the blood sacrifice they'd all come to see. One was Randevald's old manticore, the other a bear hybrid.

The bear looked dazed by its sudden freedom. The manticore was not; it gave a deafening screech and pounced. The first blood spilled and the crowd roared.

I took advantage of the moment to lean over and kiss my way to Tyrus's ear. Anyone looking at us would have believed I was inappropriately nibbling on his ear in public.

I was telling him about the Venalox.

Tyrus listened without expression. At first, I wondered if he'd misunderstood me, but then I saw his fingers thread together to stop their shaking.

"So there's a reason. There's a reason I've felt . . ." His voice caught.

The bear was already dead, and it hadn't put up a decent battle. Groans of disappointment pervaded the air. The manticore licked at the blood on its lips, and then its next challenger rose into the arena: a curious mixture of lion and shark. Hands flashed down to tap in frantic bets.

"You see why I can't accept it," I said quietly, "when you say you don't wish to use Anguish and Hazard."

"You think . . . that I should care more," he said.

I nodded.

The lion smelled the blood and was already on guard. When the manticore pounced, the lion hybrid was ready, and this fight had more vigor. The manticore, overpowered, resorted to slashing with its poisonous tail, a cheat Randevald had engineered into it. Grandiloquy privately muttered about the paralyzing venom "ruining every match."

And then a shadow slid over us, and Pasus approached us with a poisonous smile all his own. "Your Supremacy. Nemesis. I trust you two slept well. There were a great many disappointed people last night."

Tyrus spread his arms over the backs of the chairs. He didn't bother to conceal his abject loathing for Pasus. "I suppose you will have to refund whatever they paid for viewing privileges."

"What a low opinion you have of me," chided Pasus. "I wouldn't monetize such a sacred event. I was paid entirely in goodwill and favors." He placed the scepter on the pedestal.

"Don't venture far from us," Tyrus said mildly. "We will have to discuss the fight."

Pasus speared him with a questioning look. Then, "I am never far."

Tyrus's lips spread in a smile. Pasus took a seat just below us.

I trained my gaze on the arena where service bots were cleaning the blood and entrails of the lion hybrid, and electricity guns subdued the manticore so other bots could drag it into a cage, draw it under the floor.

The betting screen for the match between the Diabolics raised out of the floor, and neither Tyrus nor I touched it. Pasus, I saw, had tapped in a bet on Anguish's victory.

Then my neural suppressor turned off. I knew it, because my muscles suddenly prickled as though they'd awoken from a slumber, and the air itself felt lighter about me.

I flexed my arm, and Tyrus's lips flickered. "Let's see," he said, offering his hand.

I clasped his, we both propped our elbows on the armrests, and then—his strength strained against me as he tried to force my arm down. I allowed it for a few seconds, then slammed his hand down. He grinned and so did I.

I was back at full power.

"Will you need any help?" I said, nodding toward Pasus.

"Oh no, I won't," he vowed softly. Sinister anticipation glinted in his eyes. He'd kill Pasus all on his own.

"This is not the Venalox. I want him dead."

"No. Not the Venalox."

Hopefully, in the tumult, I'd have a chance to watch.

Then the cheering swelled as the pair of Diabolics were lifted up into the arena. They were buck naked, exhibiting their great swells of muscles. A rack of weapons had already been placed in the arena with them. Hazard and Anguish disdainfully ignored their audience as though they were not the subhumans but the superior beings.

"Time to go." Tyrus offered me his free hand. "My love?"

I put my hand in his and we walked forward to make our sacrifice.

It just wasn't the sacrifice anyone expected us to make. The crowd cheered now.

Soon they would scream.

# 33

THE FLOATING CATWALK circled the arena once so all might look upon the Emperor and his bride. Tyrus and I stood in the center of it, and our gazes were locked on each other. No one else mattered.

When we came to a halt in the dead center, Tyrus kept his gaze fixed on me and spoke—to the Diabolics below us who could hear every word.

"You are not about to be sacrificed. Do not kill each other."

I chimed in: "Anguish, Hazard—the force-field surrounding the arena is only ten meters high. It's generated thirty degrees to the right of you, Hazard. If you don't wish to kill each other, then wait for the third shock. Start slaying the crowd as you wish. Do this and you will escape."

They both peered up at us suspiciously. "Why would you save us?" Anguish said. "Do you think you will secure our goodwill?"

I cared nothing for their goodwill. I knew they'd kill Tyrus at first opportunity, so it was vitally important they die today. I repeated the words to Tyrus because I knew he didn't have our hearing.

Tyrus's reply was unexpected: "Yes. I want goodwill. Not for myself. I am not such a fool. But for Nemesis, who has done you no wrong—yes. Look to her. When this vessel begins to shake, do as she does. Hold tight to something."

My hand, clasping his, began to squeeze. I saw him wince with the force, and belatedly recalled that I had more strength to command now than I'd had in ages.

But I didn't understand him. Why had he said that? What was he *doing*?

We needed Anguish and Hazard, but not after this. If they survived, why . . . If they lived, I'd need to fight them off! We promised escape, but I didn't mean for them to truly flee with us. They'd kill Tyrus.

What was he thinking?

But Tyrus turned his attention to the crowd and raised his hands, and a deep and penetrating silence lapsed over this vast chamber. His pale-eyed gaze roved over the faces of those watching us, the territory-holders of the Empire and their hangers-on. Those who fell over themselves to exalt him for his bloodline when he acted exactly according to his wishes, those who cut his legs out from under him as soon as he raised his voice for those outside their ranks.

"I am delighted to see so many of you," Tyrus told them. "I will enjoy this."

They were atypical words for an Emperor, but the Grandiloquy cheered anyway. Tyrus smiled and pressed a hand to his heart, then watched the crowd pressing hands to their hearts and kneeling down, back up.

I tried to puzzle it out as the catwalk floated back to our viewing box, as Tyrus took my hand and I stepped out, and we settled in the chairs.

The force fields about Anguish and Hazard dropped, and the crowd screamed in excitement. We were forgotten. I reached under my skirt, undid the knot holding the rope about my thigh.

Even Pasus was not looking back at us as I fastened it hastily about my waist. . . . But Tyrus laid his hand on my wrist when I moved to tie the other end about him.

"Don't," he said.

"We should do this well ahead of time."

"Don't bind me to you at all," he said.

Hazard and Anguish hadn't moved, so a shock of electricity jolted out to goad them both.

"You have to be tied to me," I said. "You don't seem to understand how hard this is going to be—"

"No, *you* don't," he said insistently. "Look at the size of this room. Nemesis, you're going to struggle to hold on as it is. I won't tie myself to you and risk both of us dying. You have better odds without me."

I opened and closed my mouth, and below us, the crowd screamed with impatience as a second electrical spike sizzled the two Diabolics, trying to increase the discomfort until they were goaded into battling.

He was being . . . He was being irrational. This made no sense.

"If it will be hard for me, then it will be . . ." *Impossible* for you, I almost said.

And then I realized it. Then I knew: it would be. It would be utterly impossible for Tyrus to survive unbound to me. The sick, terrible understanding gripped me, and I knew then that he'd already decided it would be impossible to survive *at all.*

"Stars ignite, you think you're doomed," I breathed. Below us, the third shock had spiraled, and finally Anguish and Hazard responded. Everyone in the crowd surged to their feet to see it as Hazard stepped over to the rack of weapons. He grabbed a sword in one hand, an ax in the other. Anguish threw a contemptuous glance about.

"Tyrus, you can't give up," I said frantically.

"I am not giving up," he said. There was a sinister, unsettling peace to his face, and that just terrified me more. "I'm being realistic."

Below us, Hazard charged Anguish, ax raised, and the crowd roared with approval—and then Hazard leaped up onto Anguish's shoulders, and hurtled himself over the force field above them.

I seized Tyrus's arm, ready to shake him apart. "That's why you told them! You don't think you'll be there afterward!"

"Nemesis . . . ," he said thickly, his eyes shining. He stroked his hand over my face, and there was such tenderness in his voice: "This has to happen. Let it happen. I will do what I can for myself. I swear it to you."

Hazard landed amid the crowd as he spun around and hurled his ax at the force-field generator to knock it out. The ax thunked into place in a shower of sparks.

"No," I said, aghast. "Are you mad? No! We abort."

"It's too late."

"I won't let this—" I surged to my feet.

He pulled me back down beside him. The screams of the crowd had changed pitch—because Hazard turned on the nearest Grandiloquy and began to kill them. Anguish, freed, stalked out of the arena with a terrible grin.

Pasus had clearly realized something was going very wrong with the Diabolics and was now shouting instructions for his people to come to the *Tigris*. "Turn the suppressors back on!"

But the screams would drown them out long enough that it wouldn't matter.

Anguish raised an enormous, spiked mace, and I could see him in the distance smashing open a Grande's head. Panicked Grandiloquy fled the two Diabolics, streaming toward the exits.

"This *isn't* just about us!" Tyrus told me vehemently. "You know that!"

Tyrus took the end of the rope and began to tie the scepter to me.

"The shaking will begin. Then I have my pound of flesh," Tyrus said quietly, a malevolent anticipation gleaming in his eyes. "After that, I will do everything I can to hold on—but not at cost to your hold. As for this . . . this device, if I don't make it . . . If I don't . . . Throw it into a star. Douse it with thermite. Just be rid of it. If there's a Domitrian bastard out there, I can do this much for them."

I shook my head wildly, no, no . . . And chaos gripped the entire *Tigris* as people rushed out of the many exits, and I was aware of Pasus looking up toward us now, comprehension dawning on his face—he knew we'd played a part. It was too late for him to change it now. Tyrus seized me and pressed his lips harshly to mine and said to me over the roar of the crowd as the ship began to shake . . .

"You've been the joy of this sun-scorned existence," he rasped in my ears. "Every moment of unhappiness I've had, I'd relive a thousand times just for the heartbeats I've passed with you. Now by the light of all the stars, *save yourself*."

The vessel was jostling violently and I loved him more than anything and Pasus was shoving through the crowd up toward us. He had to know I was at full strength, yet he moved for us because . . .

Because his first impulse was to grab the Emperor.

Because he had more stake in Tyrus's life than anyone.

It was a dreadful thing to realize. He was the one who'd been horrorstruck on Tyrus's behalf when he'd pointed his weapon at the window, when he'd nearly cast the last Domitrian out to space, and the shaking was so hard now, I had to think quickly and this was a revolting solution.

Tyrus saw Pasus approaching too. He stepped forward to meet him, looking delighted to see him—because he was about to take out every last bit of frustration and anger upon his tormentor.

My hand locked on Tyrus's shoulder.

He looked back at me in question.

I rammed my fist into his face.

Down he tumbled, sailing to the ground, stunned by the blow. Pasus jerked to a stop where he'd been clambering toward us, and I didn't want him to leave. I lanced down and seized his shoulders. . . . And oh, what pleasure I could take in grinding his bones to powder! But there was no time.

I dragged him to Tyrus. "Get him and *go*! *Get off this ship! GO!*"

Pasus paled, but he immediately dragged Tyrus's limp body up and slung him over his shoulder. He'd die before fleeing without him. The Domitrian Emperor was his most valuable possession in this galaxy, and how it boiled my blood to think of letting him go. I knocked aside Grandiloquy to clear Pasus's path and didn't focus upon anything else until I was certain they were gone. The rumbling filled the air, rattling my bones.

Now to save myself.

I turned and aimed myself down the vibrating stairs. There were very few Grandiloquy left to obstruct my path. At the edge of the arena, my rubbery hands settled upon the railing, my fingers tightened.

A whimper.

My gaze darted back . . . to Senator von Wallstrom, who'd opted to hide, not run, who now was on her hands and knees under a bench in full view of me.

Wallstrom's voice trembled. "Are you—are you going to kill me?"

"No," I told her, and pointed up. "But that will."

Then the *Hera* smashed through the ceiling.

# 34

THE EFFECT was instantaneous and bone-rattling. Overhead, the *Tigris* crumpled in, fire bursting and sparking from its walls as the massive asteroid starship plunged through it, the noise so deafening it felt as though my eardrums had ruptured.

And the flames sprouted with a great furnace of heat before the atmosphere blew up, roaring out of the *Tigris* and into space, carrying with it those screaming, flailing Grandiloquy. Senator von Wallstrom met my eyes for a brief moment of shocked horror before she was carried up into the endless void.

I held to the railing as the atmosphere buffeted me on its way into space, and I knew then that Tyrus had been right, we could not have done this tied together. My muscles, my fingers, my very shoulders were being torn, and any normal person would be dead. If we'd tied ourselves together, he'd be a weight jerking at me, and my whole body strained to fight the outward force right now. . . . I squinted against the ripping wind as the *Tigris* kept emptying out, and soon the force wasn't so overpowering, but that meant the air would diminish quickly. . . . Where was the hatch? Where was it?

Then . . . a small circlet of light glowed against the stony exterior of the *Hera*. There!

Already I was exhaling without intending to, my breath being forced out of my lungs, which meant the clock had begun ticking before I lost consciousness, so I couldn't wait. I squinted at the air currents, gauged their direction, aimed my legs—and released my grip. Then I careened up, sailing helplessly on the current, and slammed into the stone edifice of the starship. The escaping atmosphere, littered with fragments and flames, buffeted past me, dragged at me. My fingers dug into the rocky surface, but slipped, and then I was sliding across the starship. I groped outward frantically, clawing desperately for something, anything, any small handhold to seize. Then I snared one. The entire force of my body jerked against the tips of my fingers, but I held on.

I wasn't alone. Through the currents of debris pounding out of the *Tigris*, I saw Anguish clinging to the *Hera*'s rocky wall, and then Hazard hit the vessel next and clung on to it as well.

Then one of the arena's benches hurtled out, plowing into Hazard and breaking his hold.

In an instant, he was gone.

I saw him sailing off into the black.

*Move. Move!* My lungs were exhaling with my volition, oxygen driven from my blood to the nearest escape from my body. Darkness crept into the edges of my vision, and I clawed my way across the rock toward that elusive circlet of light. I had to reach it before I passed out, I had to!

The weakness of my limbs crept in, and still the gases from the

*Tigris* were hitting at me. . . . And my suddenly feeble handhold loosened without my meaning it to. . . .

The air lock jostled past me. . . .

A clamp of a hand on my leg, tearing me back into the cave of light. I rebounded off the far wall, and then the door to the air lock slammed shut just before I collided with it. Chugging in the air of repressurization . . .

Then . . . then I was gasping in greedy breaths, and I craned my head to the side to see Anguish collapsed against the wall, gasping as well. . . .

Then he twisted up his face and screamed with frustration, rage. . . .

The thought of Hazard flickered through my mind.

He was dead. A full-strength Diabolic, and he'd been lost to this plan. None of the people still in the *Tigris* upon impact had escaped with us. . . .

Tyrus had made it out in time.

With Pasus.

Pasus. Pasus—*PASUS*! Who had *lived*! I rammed my fist into the wall at the very thought of it and the pain gave me no relief. He was alive, and he had Tyrus, and if I simply could have killed him . . .

I ripped to my feet. Tyrus should have made it clear from the start he expected to die. He should have made it totally clear and then I could have . . . could have . . .

With a growl, I forced myself to move. I slapped open the doors to charge into the main body of the *Hera*. My legs carried me through the starship as it rocked about me. The impact of the *Hera* against the *Tigris* had jostled this vessel, though it remained powerful and intact. When I tore into the command nexus, I saw Neveni sitting on the floor, her hand clamped over her head.

"Sorry. Hit it. Just need to . . . ," she said blearily, blood trickling through her fingers.

"It's fine," I rasped.

The *Hera* awaited my command to set up a course out of this system. My eyes fixed on the remains of the *Tigris* outside the window . . . and the ship nestled beyond it.

We had to escape, but first I wanted to do something.

I used the autonavigation—and the *Hera* plowed right into the proud *Colossus.*

Neveni gave a choked laugh as Pasus's prized starship busted apart around us, and my heart rejoiced with the malicious pleasure of knowing I'd taken something—*something*—from him. Since most every master of the starships about me had been on the *Tigris*, only a few starships managed to take potshots at us as we navigated the gravity corridor to the edge of the star system.

Then . . .

Then I needed only touch one button. Just one.

My hands went cold. I stared down at the panel.

I was leaving Tyrus. I wasn't just leaving him behind, at the mercy of his enemies. . . . I'd also killed many of those enemies in the process.

*What am I doing? WHAT AM I DOING?* I thought, horror rocking me.

Then Neveni pressed up behind me, and one strike of her hand sent us hurtling into the starless void of hyperspace, the Chrysanthemum disappearing far behind us.

My legs sank out from under me, and now I sat on the floor.

It was done.

I'd left Tyrus behind with our enemies.

# 35

FORTY-SIX DAYS. At a minimum. Forty-six days.

As the adrenaline of escape seeped out of me, I clutched my temples in my hands and just sat there on the floor of the command nexus. It took me several minutes to notice the press of the scepter digging into me. I untied it from my waist and stared at it, my vision blurred out of focus.

What would two more months of Venalox do to him?

Then a much worse thought occurred to me.

"Black hole take me, *what if he was on the Colossus?*" I cried, jolting to my feet, horrified to the depths of my soul.

A med bot tending to Neveni's head. "What?" she said.

"Tyrus." My lips felt numb. "I sent him out. I sent him with Pasus. If they went to the *Colossus* . . ."

"Wait. Wait . . . ," Neveni said.

"I told Pasus to take him and what if Pasus took him . . . No. No, there was no time for that. . . ."

"Wait, what are you saying?" Neveni demanded.

I blinked at her, as though a swamp filled my skull ear to ear.

"You cannot seriously be telling me you let. Pasus. Live."

"I did."

"Are you kidding? Are you serious?"

"I had no choice, Neveni. Tyrus would have died, and he was the only one I knew would get him out—"

"WHAT IS THE MATTER WITH YOU?" screamed Neveni. "You let him LIVE? The entire point of this was to *KILL HIM*!"

"Not at cost to Tyrus—"

"Tyrus isn't an idiot!" bellowed Neveni. "Do you really think he went into the plan without realizing he was going to die?"

I stared at her, my mouth dry. "You knew he'd perish."

"Yes." Her face was wild. "I knew. No one could survive that! I wasn't sure if *you* could survive it! And Pasus shouldn't have survived it! Why do you think I told you to explain it all to him beforehand? It was so he would know! *HE* KNEW! He knew it was death, he chose it, and you threw that away?"

"How dare you hide this from me," I breathed.

"You wouldn't have done it if you'd known! And obviously Tyrus hid it from you too!" Venom made her voice shake. Her black eyes sparkled with tears. "Tyrus got the choice. Unlike everyone on my planet who was murdered by the man whose life you spared, he got to choose his fate! And now... Now what was the point of it? How could you?"

She let out a scream and whipped away from me, hands clutching her head.

"I didn't get a choice," I snarled at her. "I won't apologize for saving Tyrus."

Vibrating with malice, Neveni turned back to me. "I'm glad you're happy. You know who won't be? Tyrus. What do you think is going to happen to him, stuck there without you? All you care about is life and death. It's all that simple to you. You know Pasus will watch him now. Tyrus played a part in this and meant to die, and he's too useful to them for that to happen. Now they'll be on guard. They'll watch him. They won't let him escape them however awful it gets."

"Good! I don't want him dead."

"Thank God you never fell in love with me," Neveni snarled.

At that moment, Anguish stalked into the command nexus with us, and Neveni gave a startled cry . . . then made a choked noise when she realized something.

He was still totally naked.

"H-hi," said Neveni.

Whatever they said to each other, I ignored it. I just walked away with the scepter I'd salvaged and retreated into the cold depths of my starship.

I spent hours just gazing at this symbol of power. In my hand, it felt cold and worthless.


Neveni's irritation with me mounted when I dropped us out of hyperspace solely to collect news transmissions that might indicate whether or not Tyrus had survived. Just as before, the news made things seem murkier, and my hours were consumed with sifting through it trying to find some small grain of truth.

She nearly pounced on me the third time I ordered us to stop.

"No, we are not stopping again," she cried.

"My ship, and I am deciding this," I returned.

She charged toward me, and Anguish abruptly swept forward, caught her in his arms.

"Do not attack those who are stronger than you," he counseled her, steering her firmly but gently away from me.

She screamed at me, *"Do you want to get to the Sacred City or NOT?"*

But I just collected every transmission I could, then launched us back into hyperspace. This third time, I found what I sought amid the news broadcasts.

Every one of them had the same thing: woeful news from the Chrysanthemum. There'd been a dreadful tragedy, a blow directly at the heart of the Empire. Excess radicals had murdered many of the Grandiloquy, along with the bride of the Emperor on the morning of their wedding.

Fustian nan Domitrian gave a long speech with a heavy heart, and then the image focused upon the figure behind him, sprawled in a chair like he was boneless, face drawn, eyes empty. His faithful adviser, Senator von Pasus, hovered at his side, and the bereft young Emperor "understandably" was too grief stricken to do more than appear in public.

He'd survived.

And I knew it was Tyrus. I knew it, because they wouldn't make him look that defeated and hollowed out if they were faking it. They'd present a robust young Emperor, as they'd done those months we were absent.

My heart flooded with the sweet relief of the realization, even though watching the transmission over and over made me notice new details. The heaviness to his lids . . . The slump to his shoulders . . . He'd been injected with Venalox again. He must have been. Pasus couldn't risk any unpredictable actions from Tyrus on a live broadcast.

I was rewatching it yet again, and my thoughts spiraled away as the news report carried onward discussing the culprits: the Luminar radicals who weren't content with destroying their own planet with their hubris. . . . They had gone on and murdered the Emperor's bride. . . .

Usually I flipped off the transmission before now, but today Neveni happened into the command nexus while it was replaying, and snapped at me when I tried to stop it.

S. J. KINCAID

"I know that guy," she said, narrowing her eyes when the so-called radicals behind the attack appeared on the screen. "Is he being charged with a crime?"

I drew a bracing breath. "For the *Tigris*." I was too wrung dry, too raw, to sit here while she learned her people were being blamed again. I didn't want to see the pain on her face when she realized those names were familiar because they were Luminars who'd been on the Chrysanthemum as employees. They'd been executed for the *Tigris*, taking the blame for it.

"You knew they'd lie about this . . . ," I said, turning to her.

But as she stared at the screen, a grin suddenly flashed over her lips. Startled, I peered back at the segment I'd never reached, watching this on my own.

"*. . . ringleader. Her parents had radical leanings, and it's believed . . .*"

It was Neveni.

Whether Pasus forced the information from Tyrus, or whether my doings had been retraced, they'd discovered her role in it all. It seemed she was the Luminar villain to take all the blame for the deaths on the *Tigris*. For my death.

Neveni broke into peals of cackling laughter. And for some reason, learning she was the new most wanted terrorist in the galaxy cheered her up as nothing else could have done.

After we dropped out of hyperspace, Neveni and Anguish joined me in the command nexus to watch the approach to the Sacred City.

That's when it began to dawn on me that I was traveling with two people who'd lost everything they loved. We'd reached the Transaturnine System during a gravital window—but waiting two days would have been safer. The currents were stronger than the last time. The gravital currents

266

that made me tense up, wince, seemed to entertain Neveni. Anguish just sprawled on his back, hands linked behind his head, observing the burning currents of hydrogen whipping toward us as though he saw them from a great distance.

Neither of them were over concerned with survival.

They even carried on idle conversation.

". . . two different moons. One was larger, and it had an atmosphere, and it was a nature preserve. The other had a habitat dome because it was settled before Lumina was terraformed. I guess they're both still there"—Neveni's voice grew very quiet—"orbiting a dead world."

"I dislike planets," Anguish said. "There are always insects."

The *Hera* gave a great jolt that made me suck in a breath. How could they think about *insects?*

Neveni caught her balance and said, "You're a big, scary Diabolic and you're afraid of *bugs?*"

"I do not fear them," said Anguish. "I dislike them. They are too numerous and they are everywhere. If they attacked in great numbers, there is no defense I could employ to hold them at bay."

"Can you two stop talking?" I said, staring out the window. We *were* within the gravital window, weren't we? I was sure I'd had the dates memorized.

"Nemesis, he's afraid of an insect uprising," Neveni said.

"He is joking," I snapped. "And why are you in such a good mood? Are you drunk?"

"That's a good idea. I could use some booze."

"I do not joke," said Anguish belatedly.

"Nemesis never jokes, either," Neveni said. "Don't worry, Anguish. I'll smash your spiders for you. Especially if you know where I can find a drink here while we ride this out."

Then they mercifully left me to stumble through the jostling ship, in search of the alcohol Neveni wanted. They'd both gone utterly insane.

She smelled of a brewery when we arrived at the Sacred City, since she'd clearly spilled whatever she'd found all over herself. Yet there was that eerie good humor about her as the pathogen ring scanned us. I waved away the startled vicars who had seen me off a short while ago.

The Interdict secluded himself with the feed from Lumina. We'd smuggled out images of the Revolvent Mist being deployed. I'd seen Neveni watching them over and over again.

Neveni sobered up quickly from whatever had made it down her gullet rather than spilling in the turbulence. "This place . . . They are completely on their own here." She paced in circles, looking about us.

"The Interdict is meant to be immortal and infallible," said Anguish.

"Oh, very infallible. We see how well his decrees have worked out. Can you imagine the egotism of existing in this coddled little shelter removed from the rest of us, and telling everyone what they should think, how they should live?"

"Speak more softly," I urged her, though we seemed to be alone.

"He's surrounded by people who worship him here. The only insights he gets come from people he teaches to parrot his own words back to him. It's unbelievable. He *should* hear this," she said.

"Not from you," I snapped. "And not right now."

When Orthanion at last emerged, he was ashen, more shaken even than when he'd realized Tyrus's ignorance of black holes.

"This was done in my name," he said hollowly. "They meant to enforce my decree."

"They destroyed the new one. Most Ascendant One, we can't wait three years for you to train vicars to deploy. You are needed. You are the only one who can fix this," I said.

"My child, I will do whatever I must." He drew toward me, took my hands. "What is it you wish me to do?"

"I need you to leave with us." I leaned closer to him and stared intently into those stunned, sorrowful eyes, knowing this was the only path, the only salvation, and it all depended on winning his support. "We need to save . . ." Save Tyrus. My love. My heart.

*This is bigger than us*, I knew. It was so much greater than two people.

"Join us," I said, "and we'll go save the galaxy."

# 36

THE INTERDICT'S body shook, and I didn't know if it was anxiety or anticipation at the prospect of leaving, of following his calling and rescuing the galaxy of his faithful. I didn't hear his argument with his vicars, but I did see their distrusting, worried looks as they regarded me. They probably recalled all too well that I'd kidnapped the Interdict the last time I was here.

Of course, after they looked at me, they looked at Anguish—and one glance at him dissuaded them from saying another word of objection.

The Interdict beckoned me to follow him. I stayed by the Interdict's side as Neveni and Anguish trailed us.

Orthanion spoke rapidly to me. Nervously. "This starship is called the *Arbiter*. It's the only vessel in my possession that can move of its own power. My inquisitors are selecting some among their number to accompany us. As for the *Hera*, I mean it to follow us with more of my vicars to reinforce us. In the meantime, your ship will be safe."

Certainly safer than it would have been in Pasus's hands. We floated up in a lift to reach the access plank. I found myself gazing down at the starship, which had appeared as just a curved wall from the ground. From above, it was six concentric circles braided together.

"My immune system is out of date," noted the Interdict.

"Yes. We can harvest antibodies from my blood."

I sent Neveni and Anguish about to explore the ship, check for any visible repairs needed before we left. In the medical bay, the med bots examined my blood. I'd been exposed to a few pathogens, but not a great many.

"Neveni would be the ideal donor, but . . ." I fell silent.

"That girl is Luminar, is she not? I recognize the accent."

"She is."

His lips twisted. "I can understand if she'd refuse."

She'd more than refused. She'd informed me she'd sooner bleed out than donate a single drop of her blood to the Interdict. "We'll find other volunteers once we leave this system. It's a good thing you do."

The med bot finished isolating my immune cells, and then it was only a matter of waiting for a synthesizer to duplicate them for Orthanion's immune system "The first thing we must do is announce my return," said the Interdict. "I will need as visible a platform as possible. I can also command my vicars to end their stalling with regards to that scepter. . . . Though if the situation is as dire as you said, perhaps we should wait until the Emperor is freed from the hands of his foes."

"No need." I unzipped my coat, drew the scepter from within. "It's right here."

"May I?"

I let him take it, turn it in his hands.

"The last time I held this," he mused, "the Emperor Amon had just been revived from his artificial coma. The Domitrians vary widely in their ability to command this device, and Amon was not one of the more skilled wielders, but even casual use of this makes one a threat. He was sedated his entire trip to my doorstep, and the entire process of draining and reinfusing his blood, over and over. Shocking his body, over and over. I only had a vague idea about how to loosen his power over this. Finally, we tried stopping his heart. The third artificial cardiac arrest, and this machine readied itself for his successor. His mind was terribly damaged by the entire process, but he was still aware enough to panic when he realized he could not command this any longer." His dark brows furrowed. "It was quite pitiful truly."

"So much effort to defuse the threat of that machine," I said.

"It should never have come from Earth with us, Nemesis. It doesn't belong here. Our ancestors abandoned a great deal of technology when they left Earth—and this should have been abandoned as well. This is a machine that can only be commanded by one who is colonized by . . . *machines*."

I looked at him sharply. "Colonized?"

The Interdict considered me for a long moment as though weighing something in his mind. Then he seemed to come to a decision. "What I tell you must remain between us."

I dared not say a word. All I did was nod.

"All of the humans we left on Earth had these internal machines. They were one of the initial steps of human and artificial hybridization. They infested an entire body from birth. They were in one's sperm, one's eggs, in the new embryo they formed. They adapted to the DNA of each successive child born, multiplied as that child grew, and then when numerous enough, they formed a network within that child's body. Our ancestors strove to be rid of those internal machines, and any technology that necessitated such a network of machines to control. One man thwarted them. Domitri Orlov."

Domitri. Was this the ancestor of the royal line?

"Domitri realized that in this new world, all other humans would be natural ones, so if he retained a technological edge over them, he could position himself as their king."

"That was surely a Domitrian."

"Actually, no. Domitri had no children. I am fairly certain he died in prison after he was found out. His blood was purged against his will and this device was placed in a vault. The thing was, Domitri wasn't the only one who had that idea. Quite a few sought to keep an advantage, and soon they earned a pejorative—the Domitrians. The day came at long last when a single child was born infested with these microbots, and it was only a matter of awaiting the day she was old enough to be purged of them."

I understood it. "And yet—that Domitrian instead became the first of the royal line."

He touched his nose. "The new colonies broke into their first proper war, and someone thought of this device and that girl who could use it—and the potential to seize control over all enemy ships at will. It so effectively ended that conflict that the girl was kept as she was, and then her child was also preserved. The entire Empire sprang of that one family line."

He slid his nails over the metal surface until they caught on something. A press of his fingers and it unlatched . . . Revealing its empty insides. Empty at first glance, at least . . .

The Interdict withdrew a sliver of metal. It was as thin as a human hair and as long as a pinky finger.

"This is a the royal scepter. A supercomputer. The outside is just decoration. I suggest you carry that casing, I carry this supercomputer, until it's safe for us to give them both to your Tyrus."

I nodded. "How will you . . ."

The Interdict poked the tiny, sharp end of that metal filament through the top layer of skin on his forearm and threaded it under his skin. That didn't look comfortable to me, but he just pulled his sleeve down over it. "We should begin by—"

And then it happened.

A loud shriek of metal scraping metal drove into my ears. The *Arbiter* jolted around us, sending the Interdict tumbling. I hoisted him back to his feet, and said, "What's happening?"

"I don't know," he answered.

"Where's the command nexus?" I said.

"This way," he said.

We charged into the chamber to see Neveni there, all by herself, and out the windows, we saw the rear of the ship straining against the docking clamps holding it to the Sacred City. Anguish rushed into the nexus as well and cast me a suspicious look.

Neveni greeted our entrance with a smile. "Right in time."

"Neveni, what's happening?" I demanded.

"Looks like we're busting out of our moorings," she said.

"What?" I cried.

Then the *Arbiter* ripped right out of the Sacred City's docking tethers, hurtling us into space. I hurled myself toward the navigation panel, saw that it was locked.

Which meant someone had locked it.

I looked at her over my shoulder. Her black eyes were fixed on the window. "Orthanion. Look closely."

"Pardon me?" said the Interdict.

"Blink and you might miss it." Neveni's voice dripped with poison.

The *Hera* veered into view, and my heart gave a spasm at the realization it had also torn out of its dock, but it was swerving itself around, hurtling back toward the Sacred City. *The Arbiter* glided farther and farther back as the fearsome asteroid ship accelerated toward the massive habitat of diamond.

And then—impact.

The *Hera* met the Sacred City at full speed and this was no starship to be torn through, but a celestial body of equal mass that erupted in a blinding swell of light.

"Neveni!" My scream at her was lost in the erupting roar of the shock striking us.

Outside: splintering diamond and graphite and fire, and about us a feeble starship bucking, straining, the wave of heat driving us into a crazed spin. The burning, shattered remains of the holiest place in the Empire whirled in and out of sight, and my head smashed back into the wall. The weight of our spin pressed me to the floor, but a small, determined figure clawed across the floor toward the fallen Interdict. I shouted as another blast hit us, but my warning went unheard.

And Neveni reached the Interdict. The blade in her hand glinted as she screamed: "How do you like watching your entire world get destroyed?" Then she plunged the blade into his chest.

"NO!" I screamed.

But the blade plunged again, again, into his heart, his stomach, his throat. He raised his hands, but the skin of his arms shredded to the kiss of metal. . . .

"*NO!*" I heaved myself over to them, clasped her fragile body, and ripped her away from him. I paid no mind to where I'd tossed her as the ship rocked around us, and flung myself over the Interdict.

Blood. So much blood. Too much. No med bot would save this, but I pressed my hands to his hot, seeping chest, desperate to contain all that fountained from his aorta. "Don't die. Don't die! *DON'T DIE!*" I screamed, and then I saw Anguish hauling Neveni to the navigation panel, and she grinned madly as she jerked us to a sudden halt.

And fell into silence.

Neveni looked at the bloodied man beneath me and laughed as she had seeing her face on that screen, the new greatest terrorist in the Empire. In substance, not just name now. Blood saturated her, but Anguish's strong grip held her steady—looking more about comfort than restraint.

My mind ground to a strange halt. The Interdict's blood was already crusting on my hands. This man was the only salvation. I peeled back his eyes and saw the sludgy absence of life.

It was done.

And then Neveni whispered to the Interdict, but it might as well have been to me:

"Where's your Living Cosmos now?"

# 37

OUR SHIP floated listlessly away from the ravaged Sacred City. Then I turned slowly, dangerously, toward the girl responsible for ruining everything.

"Why?" I looked at the Interdict's blood on my hands, the dead man on the floor beneath us. "You . . . I told you . . . You knew . . . Neveni, why?"

"How can you even ask?" she screamed. "The Grandiloquy killed my planet, so I killed their god! I destroyed their Sacred City and their glorious Living Cosmos did nothing to stop it, and I've never been so happy in my life." Rage made her entire body quake. "Let them all see now that their faith is a grand joke! Let them drown in the blood of Luminars just like their Interdict." With those triumphant, angry words, Neveni crumpled to the ground and descended into frantic tears, belying her claim to happiness.

Numbly, I gazed down at her, thinking of the contradiction of tears

I still didn't understand. She raged with fury, and yet tears flowed. She'd murdered, and destroyed everything, and yet—tears.

"Why do you think I wanted to help you?" she sobbed. "Why do you think?"

Sickened, I recalled our conversation when I'd spoken of going to the Interdict. Only then—only then had she taken interest. She'd meant to murder him all along. She'd meant to wreak this destruction. That's why she'd grown so cheerful the closer we grew to the Sacred City. Her goal was in sight.

She never meant to help me.

She meant to eradicate any hope Tyrus and I had left.

Some of the Sacred City had been propelled toward the event horizon of the black hole. Those sections I could still see as they descended into a slower and slower frame of time. I could never venture there. Not without risk of losing years I could not afford to squander.

I moved through the ship feeling as though I'd entered a strange and surreal dream. Near a window, I came to a stop, seeing what was left. There were great chunks of the Sacred City intact, spinning about through the void . . . insides exposed to space. The pastures. The plants. Those Exalteds and the dancers and that vicar who loved the Gorgon's Arm Wayfarers . . .

And my *Hera*. That proud and beautiful starship. Obliterated.

My gaze shifted between that terrible destruction to the dull reflection against the clear pane. For an odd moment, I did not recognize myself, this woman who was too small to be me. The one with finery that had never belonged on her, but I'd worn it to impress the Interdict. I couldn't make out distinct features. My hand raised, touched my crooked nose. Mine. Me. This was me.

A presence entered the room with me. Anguish.

"Tearing out of the dock damaged the ship. We also took a hit from a part of the city itself. I don't believe it can enter hyperspace safely."

I spread my hand on the window. Wouldn't that be ironic, to go through all of this only to die from a failed hyperspace jump . . . from malignant space.

We had to repair the ship or take that risk. Without a hyperspace drive, it would take several million years to return to the Chrysanthemum. I pressed my forehead to the cool window and closed my eyes, my head pulsing. "I've no technical knowledge. Unless you do, the only one of us who might be able to fix it is *her*."

"You believe an Excess could fix a hyperspace drive."

"I believe Neveni could fix a service bot that can fix other service bots. They'll tend to the drive. Her mother was the Viceroy of Lumina, one who tried to restore the sciences. Neveni is . . . I am sure Neveni has more understanding than you'd expect."

"She is a girl of many surprises," remarked Anguish.

I looked at him. "Did you know she'd do that?"

"The little girl told me nothing."

Little.

Little. A strange word. Neveni was "little" only in the physical sense, and only compared to *us*. I couldn't call anyone "little" who'd just altered our destinies and likely irrevocably shifted the course of galactic history.

My eyes met their ghostly reflection in the glass, which rendered them hollow, empty-looking black pits.

The Interdict could not fix this. That meant someone had to.

Someone always did. It would have to be me.

"We need to see what's left of the Sacred City. I'm going to steer us closer. Can you see if there are any space-sheaths we can use?" My voice sounded cold. Granite firm.

"I will check."

Minutes later I'd navigated us closer to the largest chunk that remained of the habitat, and Anguish wordlessly returned with the space-sheaths. None would fit his broad, muscular body, but I could don mine.

"Lumina's atmosphere will be long clear of the Resolvent Mist," noted Anguish. "I suggest we see about going there. . . ."

"No." I shook my head. "We have to go back."

"Back?"

"To Tyrus."

"You wish to return to the Chrysanthemum?"

"We are returning."

"Are you mad?" said Anguish. "We will be killed on sight."

"We are Diabolics," I said to him coldly. "Don't tell me you're afraid."

"If I ever return to the Chrysanthemum," said Anguish, "it will be to execute your young Emperor. I will not risk the little girl."

"I will," I snarled. "Her welfare stopped being my concern when she ruined everything."

"You believe," he said contemptuously, "that she will fix this ship for you when that's your plan?"

"I believe she must fix the ship. If you wish to be the slightest bit useful, *you* will make her fix it while I'm gone."

His eyes snapped with warning. "If you are hinting at me torturing her into obedience—"

"Hinting? No. I am telling you to do it. Or I will."

"No pain we could inflict upon her will exceed her grief."

"That remains to be seen." I moved to jam my helmet over my head, but Anguish's large palm swiped out, sent it careening into the far wall, and my heart felt as though an electric prong had spiked through it.

I rushed over to it, my throat clenched, and examined the precious helmet. No cracks. Good. Oh, I could destroy him. I could murder him. . . . He leaned toward me, eyes afire with rage of his own.

"If you lay a finger on her, Nemesis dan Impyrean, I will return the pain to you fivefold."

The words, the words . . . The challenge, the hostility in them stirred some long-buried chord deep in my being, and the surge of beautiful malice that swept over me propelled me toward him one step, another.

"Is that so?" My lips pulled into a smile, baring my teeth.

"It is," he promised, and there was a dangerous light in his eyes that told me his instincts were being stoked with the promise of violence just as mine were.

It didn't matter, then, that he significantly overpowered and outweighed me. How glorious it would feel to hurt him, to see him bleed, and from the way his great muscles shifted and he began prowling about me, as I circled him, I knew the sentiment was mutual.

"She," I said to him, my voice trembling with fury, "has doomed us all."

"She has doomed your young Emperor, you mean."

"And you despise him. How pleasurable you must find this."

His smile taunted me. "Yes."

That was it. I threw myself at him with a scream of rage, and he absorbed my weight, twisting me about to crash to the floor beneath him, his body crushing me. I raised my head and bit the nearest thing to me—sinking my teeth into his shoulder, blood welling up like copper in my mouth. The move surprised him long enough for me to raise my leg and drive my knee into that weakness of male Diabolics. At the same time his fist slammed my side hard enough to send acid boiling up my throat. . . .

"STOP!"

Icy cold water splashed us, drenching us, and Anguish stumbled up to his feet, and I shoved my way up to mine, my garb plastered to me, hair soaked, and Neveni stood there, the upended basin in her hands spattering a few last drops on the floor of the ship.

"Stop," she repeated, her voice a croak. "I am going to repair the ship."

Neveni dropped the empty basin with a clang. She held herself like every bone, every cell in her body hurt her, impossibly fragile and breakable.

"I don't want to be stranded here until we die," she said. "So I'll do what I can. If that's what you're fighting over, don't bother. You two just stay away from each other. I mean it."

And with that, she left us. Anguish and I exchanged a last heated glare, then I stalked out of his sight.

The docking bay was gone, so I struggled to orient myself as I entered the segment of the Sacred City nearest us. It took me some time to seal the doors, to switch back on the artificial atmosphere, but soon I could pull off my helmet and breathe in the chill air. In the days that followed, I went back and forth. I retrieved any freeze-dried rations I could find, any bots I could recover—functional or no—while Neveni worked on repairing a single bot to enable her to repair others.

Four days. That was what it took. Four days of Neveni trying to figure out what did what, flitting through the *Arbiter*'s database when she came across something perplexing to her. Yet once she repaired a single bot, it repaired the others, and then they were all working on the hyperspace drive. I repressed the horrified, frantic thoughts that licked at my mind, telling me the time that was truly passing was so much longer than I knew.

Then Neveni called us into the command nexus. "I think we can get out of here. Or we'll explode. Either way, let's find out." Silence settled about us, thick, tense. She looked to Anguish. Nodded. They both turned to me, and I knew they were about to let me know how we would proceed from here. "Nemesis, we're not going to the Chrysanthemum."

"Fine."

My agreement surprised Neveni. Anguish narrowed his eyes, not trusting me.

"Fine," I repeated, looking at him now. "I've given it thought, and we can fly from here to the colony of Caladrail. It won't cost us too much time. I will drop you off, and then proceed without you."

"That won't work for us," Neveni said. "I'm a fugitive, remember? I can't just go on with my life."

"Oh, yes. Your wrongful label as a terrorist," I said dryly.

Her lips curled at one corner. "I know I sort of fulfilled that prophecy, but the fact is, my reputation's going to limit my options. I'd be caught in two seconds if we landed on Caladrale or any significant colonies, and we'd stick out too much somewhere smaller. We have to find a transient population . . . a frontier, maybe. And what about Anguish here? Can you imagine any reality where this guy would blend in with a crowd?"

"Yes," said Anguish. "I can."

"I was asking her, and I meant that to be rhetorical," Neveni told him. "I was making a point that you're enormous and terrifying."

I'd swear he looked flattered.

"Where do you suggest, then?" I asked her.

"I suggest we part ways," Neveni said. "You can get to the Chrysanthemum without the *Arbiter*."

"How?" I snarled. "By *floating*?"

"Turn yourself in. You'll get brought to the Chrysanthemum for your quiet execution. I'm sure of it. Face it: you're as good as dead if you return. So you might as well not drag the rest of us down with you. How does your corpse help out Tyrus, hmm?"

"What is my alternative?" I raged. "Just leave him?"

"Yes!" Neveni cried. "Leave him. You've already done it. You had to, and he wanted you to do it. You can't save him."

"Yes, and I have you to thank for that," I shot back.

"Fine, go die for him. Great. What good does that do either of you?" She threw up her hands. "People love. People die. People lose those they love with all their hearts, and it happens all the time, Nemesis, and people move on. Look at me. My planet is dead. I have no one. My one friend now plans to go to certain death for the *stupidest* possible reason. You told us what you learned about the Venalox. If that's true, he is not even going to care about you anymore."

"There is a chance if we stop wasting time and go right now," I retorted. "Can't we argue in hyperspace?"

"That's the real cruelty of making a Diabolic," Neveni said. "We exist in this enormous universe with endless frontiers and infinite possibilities, and you only see as far as the bounds of a single person. If you want to throw your life away, I can't stop you."

No. She could not.

She turned to Anguish. "*You* stop her."

"Wait. What?" I said. I snapped into a defensive position—just as his fist impacted my face.

Someone was drilling into my head. My eyes opened and I moaned as light pierced my eyes. . . . My voice was strange. It sounded wrong.

My gaze shot wide open, and I saw my space-sheath clad legs

floating above me. With a jolt, I realized I was wearing the suit, and I had no idea where I was. My hand lashed out, connected with . . . stone. With stone.

I dragged myself closer to the structure. An airlock door blurred in and out of my vision, and I shoved myself toward it, then forced my way inside. Long after the atmosphere repressurized, my brain seemed to jostle in my skull, and I groped for understanding.

Then I saw the Interdict's body on the floor where I'd placed him. Understanding came to me in a terrible jolt.

"No. NO!" I shouted, my voice ringing out, and I rushed toward the window—but the *Arbiter* was not there anymore.

Bright, surging ripples of hydrogen swam through the darkness of space, as far as I could see, and then the world dimmed about me and I felt like the air left my lungs. I knew what I was seeing. Gravity. Powerful gravity tearing at the Transaturnine System now that the gravital window had closed.

"Neveni, I will kill you. I will kill you for this." My words were flat, heard only by me.

They stranded me and took the ship.

They left me alone in the ruins of the Sacred City.

I sank down to the floor, my head pulsing with pain, and the hideous reality of what had just happened sank into me. The schedule I'd examined, again and again, to determine the timing of our return to the Sacred City . . .

I knew it by heart. I knew just what gravital window had closed, and when the next one would open. A scream seemed to build within me, but I choked on it.

They'd stranded me here for twelve days.

And on Tyrus's end, when I emerged . . .

Three years.

# 38

## THREE YEARS.

Three. Years.

On top of the full year I'd lost, that meant four years of Venalox. The realization beat through my brain long after I'd screamed my voice out, long after the wild fantasies of strangling Neveni to death had receded.

Four years of Venalox. I'd hoped to salvage something. I'd hoped to come back to whatever I could save after nearly a year away. . . .

Not this long.

It was too late.

She'd left me rations. She'd scratched arrows into the floor, and when I followed them, I found myself gazing at one of the vicars' travel pods. I might as well get into it now and let the gravity obliterate me. There was nothing I could do but wait here as time charged forward for everyone else. Yet I walked onward.

I looked out into the wavering tendrils of starlight, twisting and spasming with the gravital forces of the black hole. A chunk of debris spun past the window in lazy circles. I pursued it from one window to the next. And then the next. Light glinted off its contours, and then I knew I was seeing the bronzed trees from Cygna's metallic garden in the *Hera*.

She'd contrived, manipulated, and maneuvered so many of her children into their destruction. Somewhere in between, she'd also looked upon an asteroid and envisioned just how to reshape it about a ship, and then carve it without and within. She'd schemed and wrestled for control over the Empire and yet must have paused now and then to touch this beautiful work she'd made and feel the quiet satisfaction of having done it.

Half a lifetime of dedication, love, and effort, and it was demolished in a second.

The universe was so cruel.

What a fool I'd been to forget it.

Very little survived of the Sacred City. It was deathly cold with the environmental controls down, and some doors would not open, alarms flashing to indicate that bare space lay beyond them.

I sliced open the Interdict's forearm and extracted the sliver of metal . . . that supercomputer.

Neveni had taken the casing. If she still had it when I caught up to her, I would have to break her skull open with it.

"At least she grabbed the wrong thing. We beat her," I muttered to the dead Interdict. "Though I understand if you don't particularly appreciate that. By the way, it's cold enough here that I think I can answer your question. No, I do not hibernate."

And that began a very unhealthy habit. As I paced the confines of the Sacred City, exploring where I could, forcing open doors whenever there was air on the other side, I brought his stiff, dead body with me. There were no microorganisms to cause decay here, so it was like keeping the company of a very silent, asleep Orthanion.

"I know the *Arbiter*'s transponder frequency," I told him with dark satisfaction. "I know exactly how to track down the ship. I'll get out of here, and . . . and she'll pay for this." Oh, so many torments I could envision for Neveni. And Anguish, he just had to die, and . . .

It was easier to dwell on searing hatred for Neveni rather than my unfathomable horror at what had happened.

I found some waste reclaimers, and began kicking them open, one by one. I only cast a cursory glance inside at their contents. I didn't need anything. It simply passed the time.

My thoughts couldn't help returning to Tyrus. Four years for Tyrus meant he might already be married to another. He'd have an Empress. Some proper Grandeé. Pasus would select her. He probably would profit from the bribes of those seeking his support in such a union.

They'd have little Domitrians. The line could not die.

Would Tyrus be killed once he had a child? The thought paralyzed me for several heartbeats.

"No," I told the Interdict's corpse, lying nearby. "He wouldn't need a baby to hold more control over the Emperor. He *has* the Emperor. He can literally force him to do anything. A baby can't even talk, much less play puppet. Not for a few years, at least."

No reply from the Interdict, of course.

But I began to ponder what I'd said, and told Orthanion. "Or maybe . . . maybe he *wouldn't* want a child born simply because that entails a parent. Someone would need to be the other half of the DNA, and if that happens, Pasus has to allow that much of an inroad to someone else. He won't want that."

Then I laughed bitterly, because the realization came to me only now, too late to matter.

Pasus would have chosen me as Tyrus's consort in a heartbeat.

He would *not* share influence. The Grandiloquy tolerated one of their number having such undue power because he'd ensured that they all incriminated themselves alongside him. They put up with his virtual ownership of the Emperor—and, coupled with his control of the Senate, of the Empire as well—because he doled out favors here and there.

But there was one thing they would never tolerate from Pasus, and that's if he sought to partner the Emperor himself. The ultimate power grab. I had no doubt whatsoever he'd considered it, but the Grandiloquy wouldn't accept him as the Emperor consort. That was official power, naked and unmasked. Tyrus's personal preferences were too well known for the Excess to believe it was a true union, and the Grandiloquy would take advantage of the chance to angle for a deal. They'd seek a pardon from Tyrus, even for genocide, and hope for gratitude—in exchange for liberating him.

No. That would not happen. So truly, for Pasus, the ideal consort was *me*.

No friends, no wealth, no allies, no charm, and by my very nature, I repulsed the other Grandiloquy. . . . I'd filled that slot of Empress perfectly and blocked anyone else from taking it. After learning of the Venalox, I believed Pasus wanted to remove Tyrus's love of me so he could then kill me, or even convince Tyrus to do so.

But that wasn't the case.

He'd meant all along to keep me around, even after Tyrus lost any semblance of love for me, so I could pass decades of misery and unhappiness . . . And Pasus would enjoy knowing he'd caused that pain. That was his revenge. I was too convenient for him. He needed me alive.

If I'd simply known this sooner . . .

There was no use thinking on it. No one could reverse time, but oh, if I'd realized what was to come, I would have learned to be charming! I would have learned to forge friendships, win allies, even . . . even flirt with the lecherous ones like Aton. That's how influence was won, and that's how I could have been useful to Tyrus as an asset—not useful to Pasus as Tyrus's millstone.

The thought tormented me as I kicked open the last of the reclaimers, already sorry I had no excuse to open them all for the first time again. . . . Which likely was a testament to how bored I was.

Yet in this one, I picked out a distinct, rectangular form.

I reached inside and pulled out the book. There was a skittering down my spine as I looked at its cover, in a language with only some hints of familiarity.

My fingers traced the shapes of the letters. *H-A-M-L-E-T*

I'd brought this here, hadn't I? Tyrus and I had to scrape together tribute for the Interdict, just in case we encountered him. Tyrus had one thing on the *Alexandria* that couldn't be found many other places: his books. He hadn't believed there would be an Interdict, so he let me take a good number of them. He would have taken more care with it if he'd realized there truly was an Interdict and a Sacred City to receive his tribute. He'd loved those books.

Locklaite had the *Alexandria* and its bookshelf.

This might be the only one Tyrus had left.

Fury boiled up in me. "How could you?" I said to Orthanion. "We gave it to you and you just threw it away. Do you know what this means to him?" I struggled for the best words to capture how profane this act was—throwing this book away! "You have . . . you have *no* concept of value. None at all."

And that felt right, and then I realized I was talking to a corpse and this was ridiculous. This was something a crazy person would do. I turned and walked away from the corpse. I had a book now.

I couldn't read the old language, but I could see the wear of Tyrus's fingers upon the fragile paper. There were dimpled pages every so often, and Tyrus was not one who would drop it, or bend it to mark it. . . . I imagined him falling asleep while reading this, and then I grew so certain that had taken place, that I felt as though I'd been there and seen it happen.

It didn't matter that I couldn't understand this ancient language, but for a few small words here and there. A hollow place within me filled, and peace settled over me.

I would return this to him.

I'd failed utterly, but this much I could do.

On day twelve, I gazed out the windows until the turbulence began to wane, and then I boarded the vicar's pods. They had no propulsion of their own. They weren't meant for long-distance travel, but simply for sailing the gravital currents of the Transaturnine system to standard space, where they would be received by Helionics waiting.

I tucked the sliver of metal deep within the pages of the book, hugged it to my chest, and then launched myself into the grasp of those great, moving bodies bending space. Their gravity directed my momentum as a leaf might float in a river.

It took a full day to reach the edge of the system, where the pod jostled and startled me awake, and I looked up to see a small vessel drawing me up into its bay.

The chamber repressurized, and I glimpsed the eager faces of Excess waiting. They were Helionic converts and aspiring vicars, eager to show their zeal for the Living Cosmos by passing their lives among the stars, waiting for the rare decree from the Interdict.

So when I opened the door and they saw I was no vicar, their mouths dropped open.

"I can explain," I said.

"It's you!" gasped one of them.

*"Nemesis Impyrean,"* said another voice.

*"Nemisis is . . ."*

*"It's her! She's here!"*

I looked from face to face. They all knew me on sight. They all began to lower themselves down, to kneel, and my first impulse was to wave them up.

*No. Not yet. Use this*, I thought.

"I thank you," I said, allowing them to kneel a moment longer.

"You're truly alive," said the girl, closest to me.

"I am. And . . . and I cannot explain why just yet. Do rise. I would like to hear from all of you—what has transpired since my . . . death?"

Tyrus was not married.

There was no royal heir.

There were painful taxes, rumors of mounting debt. Pasus was widely known to be the Emperor's favorite, and the Emperor as a young man devastated by the violent death of his true love.

To my surprise and slight amusement, the official narrative about Luminars destroying the *Tigris* was in doubt.

Most believed it was an inside job. With a specific aim, by a specific person.

"Everyone knows . . . ," said one of the Excess, a young girl who couldn't hold the alcohol she'd been drinking off duty. Then she realized herself, and bit her lip.

"Go on. You have such insightful words. Speak." I smiled at her, hoping I could entreat her into blurting it all out. If she did not, I would resort to threats.

Her cheeks grew pink. "The Emperor loved you so. Oh, everyone knows how romantic it was! He defied everyone just because you meant so much to him, and then Pasus wouldn't have it. He tried to kill you, didn't he? He struck at you so he could remove your influence."

I quite liked this conspiracy theory. "I can say very little. The Senator was most desirous of my absence. He will not be pleased to see me return from death. Now, no more." I pressed an enigmatic finger to my lips, and she mimed zipping her mouth closed, her eyes shining with adoration.

They all looked at me this way. My every mundane quality had magnified into greatness after death. I could use this.

I had them keep quiet about my return until we were within the star system of Eurydice, and then I broadcast it on a general frequency to the planet. It was too late now for any Grandiloquy foes to descend and attack.

As we soared in to land in the capital, I found myself gazing down at the heaving . . . What was it? Water? What was I looking at, clogging those streets, in the square?

My stomach seemed to open up as the answer struck me: people.

Masses and masses of people had gathered to watch my arrival, even on this short notice. I'd passed the sterile days alone in the Sacred City furious with myself for never forming a power base, but it seemed one had spawned without me, and my lips pulled into a giddy smile as we touched down and the thunderous cheers from outside were piped into the vessel with us.

The Grandiloquy could not contend with this.

There would be no quiet assassination, no stealthy death. There was only one thing they could do now that I'd come here, now that I stepped out of the vessel and presented myself before people who vastly outnumbered the entirety of the Grandiloquy.

All the Grandiloquy could do—all they would dare to do—was cheer my deliverance.

# 39

I DID NOT WAIT long on Eurydice. When my summons came, along with an honor guard of starships, I boarded without fear. The public welcome had guaranteed my survival. Now I had to use it.

Those escorting me worked for Pasus. That, or they were on his payroll. Their eyes followed me everywhere, they questioned relentlessly but answered nothing in turn. So I stopped speaking to them.

By the time the eighteen day voyage ended and we jostled out of hyperspace, the Grandiloquy had all heard the news. I could tell, because we began passing docked vessels much farther out from the core of the Chrysanthemum than usual. There had to be another thousand here, converging upon the already massive superstructure.

The closer we drew, the more detail I picked out. The windows of several pylons had gone totally dim. Either they'd been rendered inactive to preserve power, or they'd fallen into disrepair without a centralized system.

Thousands of messages crowded for my attention, the standard, perfunctory greetings.

Then one came in that superseded all the others, and they blinked out of the system to allow it first priority.

My heart began to thud.

Tyrus.

Sweat pricked all over my body. Genuine terror began to gnaw at my gut. My hand shook when I activated the transmission.

Senator von Pasus appeared before me in holographic form. My heart hardened. I did not give him the pleasure of glimpsing my disappointment.

"Senator."

"Nemesis."

For a moment, he looked at me, and I at him.

"You are back at last," he said.

"I've been most welcomed," I said icily.

"Did you bring anything?"

"Anything?"

"A scepter." He leaned closer. "An Interdict."

"Your spies surely told you I did not." Of course he'd have heard by now that we meant to bring the Interdict back. He couldn't know what happened to the Interdict, though. . . . Unless Neveni had told people.

She'd had a head start on me.

"Have you lost the scepter?" Pasus said.

"No," I said.

He seemed to clench his teeth. "Do you intend to hand it over?"

"You will have to wait and see."

"Very well played, the public entrance. Tyrus and I were most impressed."

His casual use of his name, his first name, oh . . . And I slipped. "Is he all right?"

I'd lost the game.

Pasus smiled coolly and blinked away. I would have to learn for myself.


The Chrysanthemum looked much as it had when I'd left it. The interior was missing the *Hera*, the *Tigris*, the *Colossus*, but other ships crowded in their places. Windows were more consistently lit this close to the center, but Berneval Stretch had a great, gaping hole where something had collided with it and repair bots had not arrived to fix it in time. Three more years of malfunctions ill-repaired. The very formation of the ships looked clumsy, like a chaotic glob rather than a precise Chrysanthemum.

When I stepped out into the *Valor Novus*, silence met me. After the thunderous reception on Eurydice, the stark hush was deafening, but not surprising. A pair of Domitrian servants had been waiting.

"The Emperor requests your presence."

"Lead the way."

Despite what they'd said, when I arrived in the presence chamber through the main doors, it wasn't to an awaiting crowd. All in sight were crowded about some other diversion, and I waved the servants away. I could take it from here.

My heart began to jerk in my chest, though I had yet to spot Tyrus. Raucous voices met my ears.

"Try a watermelon next."

"What about a glass?"

". . . can have gravital crushing anywhere, Your Supremacy. No need for the Justice Hall. Don't you see how much potential this opens for entertainment?"

"There is a great deal of potential," agreed that voice I'd know anywhere.

Tyrus.

His voice. His voice . . . I stopped where I was, knowing it, and none in the crowd seemed aware of me.

"I've never seen one so portable before. It's the size of an imaging ring. Same weight? Impressive. What level is it at now?" Tyrus said.

I saw him.

He was Tyrus, but he looked subtly altered. His hair was lighter, a reddish gold, and the last hint of childish roundness had fled his face. The broad bones, the sharply angled brows, the light blue eyes all contrived to render him simultaneously harsher in appearance, and more classically handsome. In fact, there was a touch of vanity in the alteration, as though he'd lost some of that distaste for beauty bots and began using them.

His natural musculature had faded before my eyes under Pasus's regime, since the Venalox had not lent itself to rigorous exertion, even had Pasus allowed him to undertake it. Now, the artificial symmetry of beauty-bot-crafted muscles had taken their place, stretching the shoulders of the sweeping coat favored by fashionable Grandes.

Tyrus had yet to notice me, though those nearest me had. They had gone silent.

"I'd like to see what it can do at eight atmospheres," Tyrus noted.

A humming as the mechanism increased in power. I could see now it was a metal ring of sorts. "And now, let's see . . ." Tyrus cast his gaze about at the faces nearest him, searching for someone. Smiling like a jackal when he locked on target. "Gladdic. Put your hand in there."

Gladdic. I hadn't recognized him immediately, with the alterations he'd made to his hair—a platinum shade now to contrast with his light brown skin. I recognized only his signature feature, those unnaturally spring-green eyes.

"Your Supremacy, I think that might not be safe."

"That's the point. Put your hand in. You skulk about and ruin a good time. Do something to entertain us. Reach in," Tyrus said.

Gladdic cringed, stepped toward the ring—and raised his hand. He yowled out when a crackling sounded through the chamber, blood bursting from his skin, skin peeling from bone. . . . He yanked his hand back to the resounding laughter of the watching Grandiloquy, tears on his face, whimpering. Med bots soared in to tend to him, and Tyrus began to laugh.

The Grandiloquy all about Tyrus did exactly as the Grandiloquy do: they took their cue from Tyrus and began laughing as well.

"Look at your hand. Ah. That's disgusting. Why would anyone do that to himself? Helios devoured, Gladdic, surely you realized I was joking." He was still laughing as he turned away, called, "All right, kick it up to max and let's throw in a spare Servitor. . . ." Then he laid eyes on me.

"Your Supremacy," I managed, my mouth bone dry.

Tyrus grew very still. His face suddenly went blank. "Nemesis . . . You are come back, then."

I used to be attuned to the slightest ripple of feeling under that blank expression. Now it just seemed—blank.

"Yes." My voice sounded hollow.

"You took your time returning."

"Not by choice."

"Of course." Tyrus tilted his head. He studied me closely as I searched him for any slight trace of feeling—even just a memory of what he'd once felt.

None.

I was only half-aware of the Grandiloquy who'd been enjoying the spectacle. Some had already gripped a Servitor to offer up for the gravity ring. Tyrus had quite forgotten his request.

"Well. Only one thing to do." He turned to address the company. "Kick it up to twenty atm, and a delightful intoxicant to the one who chucks her into the gravity ring. Let's see it work!"

*What?*

Bodies swarmed toward me, hands hooking under my arms, and I was so shocked I did not react for a moment. . . . Then I was steered toward the gravity ring, which would crush me in an instant, and my survival instincts raged forth. I wrenched myself from the grasping hands and drove my fist into the nearest face, my legs into ribs. I snared a collar and hurled a Grande who'd manhandled me into the gravity ring so he might enjoy it, and he gave an abbreviated scream as he passed the metal barrier, then his lungs and skull flattened—

"ENOUGH."

The chamber went deathly still about me, and I whirled around to face Tyrus, furious, bewildered, yet there was something new on his face. His eyes seemed aglow with an electric intensity, belying the careful, cautious set of his polished features.

"It is you."

"Yes. As I said!" I roared at him.

"Now I'm certain of it." He pointed to the unfortunate Grande with the crushed head. "Someone clean up the Grande Falcaunt."

"It's Rutherfain."

Tyrus shook his head. He did not care.

Then a woman was before me, a young girl. "What of the Sacred City? We've heard dreadful rumors."

And all eyes were suddenly on me.

"Quiet."

It was one word, softly spoken, but Tyrus's voice made all those crowding about me step back, lowering their eyes.

"This is state business. I will discuss it with my . . . beloved in private."

I searched his face hopefully.

Tyrus nodded for me to accompany him to the privy chambers, then raised his palladium glove to his mouth and said, "Alectar, are you about?"

*Alectar,* I thought darkly.

"I'm in my chamber," answered Pasus.

"Excellent," said Tyrus.

Then, as we stepped into the privy chambers, Pasus emerged from one of the rooms, and shock rooted me in place.

He'd been in his chamber.

Here.

Inside the royal privy chambers.

Pasus should not be staying there. He had no right to it. How audacious of him, to force his way in. My jaw clenched.

There was new furniture. . . . Hangings and sculptures that were distinctly not Tyrus's style. A singed spot on a table told me these might've been salvaged remnants of the *Colossus.* So Pasus had gathered them up, then glommed onto Tyrus like a persistent parasite and installed himself here.

Now it fell to me to remove him for good.

# 40

WHEN I recounted what became of the Sacred City, Tyrus met the news with laughter. Pasus went gray.

"I fail to see humor," Pasus said. "This will lead to chaos."

"You have long abandoned piety. Don't pretend to be the aggrieved believer," Tyrus said disparagingly. "Chaos will only ensue if people learn of this. We won't let them."

"There have been rumors," Pasus said.

*Neveni,* I thought. It had to be.

"There are always rumors. There will be no official confirmation, Alectar. The Interdict lives, the Sacred City is intact, and if anyone doubts—let them seek the Interdict for themselves and ask him."

It disturbed me, seeing them discuss it, planning a course together like true allies. Now Tyrus turned his attention to me. Looked me over. "So I sent you to bring back the Interdict. Instead he is dead and the Sacred City is destroyed."

"Yes."

Tyrus began laughing again. "How do you not find this funny?" he said to Pasus. Then he raised his hand, and light glinted off a ring he wore. A flick of his finger popped open a gem atop it. "My mistake sending a Diabolic."

Tyrus nodded as he huffed in the Venalox from within the gem.

"Ask her," prompted Pasus in a low voice.

"My love, do you or do you not still have the scepter?" Tyrus said.

My eyes narrowed. It made me grind my teeth together, the way Tyrus just obeyed him.

"As I told the Senator, I have it. I've sent it into space with a transponder frequency only I know." It was a lie, but I was certain Pasus was having my ship ransacked, searching for that familiar casing Neveni had stolen. They wouldn't find it in the book—or so I hoped. "If anything happens to me, it will be lost forever. I'd rather have a reason to give it to you. I want my conditions met."

Tyrus grinned broadly. "Listen to her," he said to Pasus. "You'd think she was the one who'd had several years to sharpen her wits. Do tell me the conditions, Nemesis."

I looked between them. Was Pasus's power over him still total? I tested it: "I want him gone."

Tyrus arched his brows, pointed a questioning thumb toward Pasus.

"Yes. Him."

"It seems absence has not made the heart grow fonder," Tyrus remarked.

"Not for either of us," Pasus said. "It seems she imagines we've been in stasis while she has."

"Then some catch-up must needs be done," Tyrus said. He snatched a handkerchief from one of the Servitors, wiped away the Venalox residue from his nose, and let it drop to the floor. I stared at it. It was

303

the sort of decadent, wasteful, *Grandiloquy* gesture Tyrus never used to do. "My darling, we have passed a long while and you have not. The time of ugliness is far behind us. Alectar and I are reconciled."

"He has won the right to the first room?" I said.

Tyrus rolled his eyes. "Alectar, move to another chamber. Go get started. Now."

Pasus stirred. "Immediately? Perhaps I should . . ."

"Immediately."

The two men exchanged a long, silent glance. Then, "Of course." He dipped his head and left us.

Tyrus snared my limp hand, but made no move to draw me in closer. "I know this is difficult for you to understand. My existence became profoundly uncomfortable in the wake of the *Tigris*. There were still dozens of dead and it was known I had a role in it. Some Grandiloquy wished to have me lobotomized. There were proposals to remove my sex organs for the creation of new Domitrians so I might be executed." And though his lips twisted into a smile, a shadow passed over his face. "At the time, I was . . . I was far beyond caring. In fact, I may even have cultivated a small rumor that Alectar himself was responsible for the *Tigris* massacre. His reputation has never recovered from that suspicion. Yet still, he was my shield. He prevented anything too dire from happening."

That Excess girl's conspiracy theory . . . Tyrus had crafted it. I just had to shake my head. "There was no mercy in what he did, Tyrus. He needs you alive and in *his* power. And now he dwells in the first room, like a consort or . . ."

"A member of my family."

"Family." Family meant something very different to Tyrus than to most people. I wasn't sure if he intended to tell me they were close, or that Pasus was still his dread enemy, using that word. Maybe I was seeing a cold war between them, one masked in civility, the sort I had never mastered. He slung himself back onto a chair, legs wide. "He needed me alive. There are many states of existence, Nemesis, and I could have endured much more miserable ones."

"Than a life of involuntary addiction? Of constant humiliation?"

His eyes grew hard. "You made the decision for me. You decided I would remain here. So yes, that was a preferable alternative. I learned the value of having a single person I could rely upon in that situation, even him. . . . It was better than no one. Once I told him that you were a given in a marriage union, and now I must tell you that exact same thing about him. Do you still love me, Nemesis? If so, then that's grand. We should just go ahead and get married as we meant to. You do wish to make an exchange for the scepter, do you not? I find the idea most agreeable."

Agreeable. The word stung me.

"You're very sure Alectar approves?" I muttered.

"Wholeheartedly. He is your earnest champion now as well as mine."

I scoffed. No. Pasus knew I was exactly the wife he'd want for Tyrus. The unthreatening wife who would never detract from his power, and now—now that the Venalox had been in use for four years—one Tyrus could look at after three years apart with this detachment. There was no love for me in his gaze. Not now.

And I'd known it. I'd braced for it. I'd hardened myself against this possibility in advance. It still threatened to hurt me.

Dwelling upon my loss would split me apart.

"When?" I said.

"Alectar!" called Tyrus.

And then Pasus returned so abruptly, I knew he'd been listening, waiting for this. I shuddered with hatred to see him. This whole thing bewildered me. I'd known I'd return to a Tyrus who did not look at me the same way. There was an uncharacteristic detachment to him even when he smiled at me. I had never imagined he'd be a friend to Pasus, much less regard him fondly like a trusted friend.

"What about tomorrow?" Tyrus said.

"The wedding?" I blurted. "Tomorrow?"

"So soon?" Pasus said, startled as well.

Tyrus flashed a grin. "Why not? No one can argue we haven't covered the blood sacrifice. Let's jump right into it."

Pasus folded his arms. "And the arrangements . . . Still as we discussed?"

"Exactly as we discussed." Tyrus drew a huff of Venalox and used his sleeve this time to wipe his face. "It's over three years since we were engaged. No one can say it's sudden." Then with a laugh, he pointed to the window. "Look at all these ships gathered. Shouldn't we eagerly exhibit ourselves for so vast an audience?"

Pasus turned his gaze to me. "And when can the Emperor expect the coordinates of the scepter?" Pasus said.

Tyrus's eyes were now locked on my face, waiting for the answer too.

"Is there now support from the vicars?" I said, looking between them.

"I have been making many inroads in hopes you would return," Pasus said.

"I will do my part if he does," I said to Tyrus. Then, to Pasus, "And do not ask me questions on his behalf ever again or speak to me if it's unnecessary. I will hate you with all my heart until the day I die."

"As will I," agreed Pasus, "until the day you die."

Tyrus smothered a laugh, and drew another great breath of Venalox. "You see? Bickering and thinly veiled death threats. Add in some attempts on each other's lives, and we'll be a proper Domitrian family at last."

I chose Gladdic as my escort for the wedding ceremony, for he was the single person here I had any interest in seeing.

As soon as I walked onto his ship, I saw it resting there on a pedestal. The bronze bust of the Grandeé Cygna.

I stared at her sightless eyes, perched above me. What would compel a son to display the instrument of his father's murder like a prized possession? When Gladdic appeared in the doorway, he came to a stop.

"Nemesis! It's you. I'm so happy to—"

I waved off the courtesies and nodded toward the statue. "Why do you have this?"

He drew a jagged breath. "The Emperor gave it to me."

I looked at him, really looked at him. There was a hunted, nervous strain to him, like an animal pursued too long by a predator. His eyes looked too large for his face now.

"He . . . he gave it to me in exchange for this ship," Gladdic said. "What?"

"I sold him the *Atlas* for that bust. He immediately sold the *Atlas* to someone else. He gambles extravagantly when he gets the chance, so he's probably already squandered it all. . . . He's told me how kind he's being to let me stay onboard until its new owner collects it." Gladdic's face twisted. "I didn't exactly secure a bargain," he admitted.

"Why would you agree to that?" I exclaimed. Then I recalled him also agreeing to stick his hand into the gravity ring. "You're that afraid of him now."

"I'm one of his favorite amusements lately," Gladdic said bitterly. "He took to making me use Venalox with him, since it's not an enjoyable drug and no one else wants to try it. It was after you left. Daily for a while. Then he grew bored . . . until the day after the news reached

307

everyone that you were alive. . . . He wanted to celebrate. He made me use it, then convinced me to sell him my ship. This ship. For the price of that bust."

I was speechless.

"Venalox really does something to your mind," muttered Gladdic, rubbing his head. "It honestly seemed like such a great bargain when he suggested it."

"Yes, I recall how that works."

"It's a bit of a bind," Gladdic said, voice shaky. "This is what he used to kill my father. I . . . So you know how I feel looking at it. But it's also the bust of a Domitrian. I can't *not* display it. Not without insulting the Emperor. So I have to see it every single day. Every single one."

I recalled Gladdic sticking his hand in the gravity ring. Tyrus ordered it, and then laughed it off as a joke afterward. It was a cruelty. Very deliberately inflicted. A fraction of the cruelty he'd received himself, but a very clear indication of the damage wrought by the Venalox. The real Tyrus never would have done this sort of thing.

"I can't change anything that has already come to pass," I told him, looking into Cygna's sightless eyes, "but I can promise you, I'll intervene in such things in the future."

"Nemesis, you already saved my life once. With the *Tigris*. I would never ask you to risk yourself over anything so minor. . . ."

"Small things become great ones," I snapped back. "So I'll stop the minor offenses, too. And you needn't thank me for not murdering you."

He seemed to muster his courage, and then he met my eyes like it was difficult for him to hold them. "I . . . I consider myself . . . I like to think I am a friend to you. So please, listen to me. Things are not the same. He's not the person you think he is."

My eyes were on the bust. I had no illusion about Tyrus after four years on that toxin. I knew cruelty when I saw it. I knew there was no possibility the Tyrus I'd left could accept Pasus as a friend. As family. Not without something very essential within him being destroyed first, and the Venalox had certainly done that.

"Please be careful around him."

"I think," I told him, feeling a faint amusement, "that you've forgotten the sharpness of my teeth."

"I wish . . ." His voice grew wistful. "I truly wish you would escape while you can. We could go together. We could steal away, on this ship, another, somehow. . . ."

I scowled. "Gladdic, are you in love with me still?"

"I . . . I . . . no. No, I'm not."

"Good. Because if you were, I'd tell you to stop that. At once."

He fell silent, and then a reluctant smile broke over his lips. His eyes were still sad, like he was witness to a tragedy in motion. "I am glad to see you again."

"I came because I need an escort for tomorrow. You are the only person here I don't despise. Will you do it?"

"Of course I will."

I stepped away from him, then turned back. "And as your future Empress, I demand a wedding present from you. A bust of the late Grandeé Cygna would do."

I could take this torment from him at least.

The tears that brightened his eyes made me escape his presence as quickly as possible, for fear that he'd soon need a hug.

I'd made up my mind, and my course was clear: wed Tyrus. Get him alone. Gauge the truth of the situation I'd returned to, and then inspire him to seek revenge with me. And if I could not . . . if he was truly so loyal to Pasus . . .

Then I would devise something new. There had to be some way to salvage this. I would find it if it killed me.

# 41

THE COLONNADE was one of the largest pylons of the Chrysanthemum. The wedding was delayed twelve hours due to the unexpected time it took to repressurize this entire chamber. The Colonnade ate up so much power that even when there was a functioning scepter unifying the system and the superstructure was at peak functioning, it was used only for ceremonial occasions.

I stepped into the Colonnade and found myself in a long corridor that appeared to be a platform jutting straight out into space. There were force fields on all sides, protection from the void. A strange moment of disorientation gripped me, for I'd been here once before. Not in person, but . . . but as an avatar. I saw the platforms rising up about us, holding onlookers now; they appeared to be standing among the stars, though I knew otherwise.

I'd first encountered Tyrus in a virtual forum set in this very place. Using Sidonia's avatar, as he stood there naked, feigning disbelief when his lack of clothing was pointed out to him.

The rush of grief paralyzed me.

*Stop it. Don't think of it now.*

A gentle touch, and I looked back at Gladdic, who was decked in gleaming gold for the occasion. Distant Harmonid voices carried over the air, and the onlookers stirred, and I knew it was time to begin.

Walk. And bury the pain.

I crossed the last meters between us through a gauntlet of sound crystals, those gems resonating with the voices of the Harmonids, seeming to vibrate the very air about my skin. I passed the final one, the chamber stretching out on all sides of us, all six stars visible from here.

Tyrus held out a hand. He was facing away from me, as per custom, his hand extended at his side. Here a bride could choose not to take it, and he would never turn, would never see he had been refused. That was the thinking, at least.

His garments were gleaming crystal and ivory-white liquisilk, as mine were, and the light reflected off him into my eyes as I drew toward him and placed my hand on his. The Harmonid voices swelled in the air, and I trained my eyes straight ahead, as did Tyrus. The Vicar Fustian orbited us like a satellite, gently dousing us with the essence of starlight.

Then Tyrus and I stepped away from each other and the Harmonids fell silent, the onlookers who'd stood on the sides of the Colonnade—viewing us with eyes or with screens—hushed as well.

My steps brought me in a circle about the perimeter of the solarium, and it seemed endless and over too quickly, when Gladdic awaited me—and I knew Pasus was awaiting Tyrus.

Gladdic raised his palm, coated with the reactant. I raised my own and touched his, smearing my palm with it. Tyrus and I completed our orbit, and our eyes at last met.

None of the detached, eerie amusement on his face now. He was gazing at me with an odd mixture of pain and tenderness that fooled me for a terrible moment. Our hands touched our hearts.

The reactant on our palms set the starlight essence aglow over our bodies.

I could barely see as we both grew brighter, radiating light as a star might, but that glimpse of him scorched me from within and abruptly I felt as though I would fall open, as though I would combust, as though I would disintegrate. . . .

Because he was gone and this was not him and it should have been him. *Him.*

I couldn't do this. I could not.

He stepped forward, gleaming, and his hand took mine and I obeyed but could not seem to make myself stir of my own will. Hands clasped, he drew me into an orbit about him, or was he the one orbiting me? Two binary stars and then he closed the distance to meet me. We grew so blindingly bright I could only see him and he could only see me and his hands clasped my hips, and his lips claimed my own, hot and insistent, demanding, scorching me as the painless shroud of fire dissolved all about us.

We were no longer a glowing star but a pair of humans, and there was applause that seemed to float to my ears from another world. I just stared at this man who was now my husband, stricken because this should have been so joyous, and he lifted our joined hands together before them all. Now, the final act of this ceremony: the electrical bond. A dart of pain in my palm as Fustian penetrated our hands with the twin electrodes. I could feel the prickling where our palms met. My heart raced.

Then Fustian announced, "From the fusion within stars arises every trace of this Living Cosmos, and today two young lovers unite into one." He pulled our hands apart to reveal the electricity spiking between our palms.

Painless, as long as we remained close, and soon to dissipate—once we consummated this union. We strode together to the end of the solarium, which led into the starlight oubliette.

The thunder of applause and searing of so many eyes followed us until the door sealed behind us. Then the starlight oubliette detached, and I turned to see those faces watching us shrink away.

Silence fell between us.

Then it was just me, just Tyrus. Husband and wife, enclosed and alone amid the stars.

I looked at him and found him watching me, caressing me with his eyes, and a shiver passed through me at the realization we were here at last.

Tyrus regarded me in the dimness as the painless lightning flickered between our hands. Then he stepped away from me. The current between our palms sharpened, still not painful yet, as the distance between us grew.

"I've a gift for you," he said.

I traced my hand along the window. . . . Not a true window. I reminded myself of that. It was a screen that provided the illusion that we were encircled by a starscape so we might have a view, but now that we were away from the crowds, it would shift to full opacity if any voyeurs tried to glance in our direction with magnifiers.

Tyrus touched the wall, and out slid the platform holding the groom's offering. He lifted it gently, and the sharp edges of the rubies and sapphires caught my gaze. A jeweled hair clip.

But not just any hair clip.

My heart caught. I stared at it as he watched my face.

"You remember this," he said, watching me closely.

S. J. KINCAID

Of course I did. It was the very first gift he'd given me, back when our relationship was but a ruse between a Diabolic and an ambitious Successor Primus.

"How is it possible?" I wondered.

He'd torn it out of my hair and tossed into the nitrogen fountain on the *Hera* back when Elantra lived, and we were pretending not to love each other.

"I retrieved it."

"What? How? When?"

"As soon as no one was looking."

"Didn't it burn your hand?"

"It was worth it," he said.

Tyrus crooked his finger for me to tilt my head. I did so, and he gathered my long locks into his fingers, smoothing them back in a way that was almost reverent, before weaving the clip into my hair, pulling just enough back from my face. He straightened, his rough palm caressing my skin, his eyes tracing over me, soft, curious.

I shuddered and stepped back. How easily—how very easily—I could forget myself. And the pain of that felt like it bore straight into my heart.

"I have yours." My voice jerked out of me, stony, businesslike. A swipe of my hand, and I'd opened the other compartment.

To reveal the book. Tyrus's face transformed with surprise. "*Hamlet*," he breathed.

"So that's how you say it."

"Nemesis, where . . . ?"

"In the Sacred City. It survived. I knew . . . I knew it had to be yours. I couldn't understand it, though." I watched him intently, and that hideous part of me that insisted on hoping was desperate for any slight emotion, any reaction.

314

Tyrus brushed his palm over the cover, turned the book over, and opened its pages.

"It was yours," I said, sure of it now.

"It was . . ." Emotion shadowed his face, as though the memory of who he'd been when he last held this reared up within him. His voice caught. "It was a very important book when I was younger."

"I couldn't read it."

"It's an old language. It's complicated, but . . ." He looked at me, his eyes misty. "This is one part:

> *"'Doubt thou the stars are fire*
> *Doubt that the sun doth move,*
> *Doubt truth to be a liar*
> *But never doubt I love.'"*

Abruptly, something strong, something bracing, seemed to buckle under the weight of what I was doing. My eyes closed, and the emotion brimming in my chest swelled to the point of overflow. I sat on the floor, with the cold and distant stars below me.

I squeezed my fists until my fingers throbbed, until my nails cut into my skin, and then I felt Tyrus before me, his hands sliding up my arms.

"Are you hurt?"

I managed to look at him, where he sat gripping my arms, the current tingling down my forearm to join us. "It's nothing you can heal. I just . . . It's just that a short time ago, I had you. I had your love, and your heart, and for you, I'm a memory."

Tyrus leaned forward and removed the clip from my hair. For a moment, I stared at him, befuddled, certain he was taking it back, that he'd grown irritated.

Instead, his steady blue eyes on mine, he flicked his finger at the end, and the clip began to flash. My brow furrowed. He extracted a small device from amid the jewels, then wove the clip back into my hair.

"I smuggled this in with us," he said, showing the jamming node to me. "There is absolutely no privacy on the Chrysanthemum, but here is the one place I can ensure that we have it. I have just blocked any means that might be used to eavesdrop. Now there's no more need to lie."

I stared at him. "Lie?"

"Surely you knew back when I spoke to you before that I don't utter a private word. I know I was cold, but I had to be. Do you imagine for a moment the man who has been my captor for these last years would have agreed to this if he believed I was anything but indifferent to you?"

It couldn't be.

It was impossible.

I stumbled over my words: "The Venalox . . . four years of it . . . it's not possible . . . Don't do this. Please don't deceive me. Tyrus, don't say this if it's not true. I can't bear to hope. . . ."

The words escaped me, and I hated myself for speaking them . . . for putting them out there, for offering my neck to a blade. He reached out, and his fingers slid through my hair, his hand clutched the back of my neck, drew me closer, his breath playing over my lips.

"Look at me, Nemesis. Really look."

My eyes rose to his, and how warm they looked—but it was a lie. It had to be.

"You think I am indifferent to you? What about this?" And with that, his lips captured mine in an insistent kiss that I felt like a jolt of electricity down my back, like a flare of starlight in my heart. I gasped

316

against his mouth and then his tongue met mine, and I couldn't understand this wonderful, glorious, impossible moment. . . . I ripped back.

"This can't be."

"It is. Nemesis, I had to be careful, measured, when I spoke to you. Only a show of indifference could win me this moment with you. And now here you are." He gazed at my face as though I were a miracle. "I am afraid if I close my eyes, you will disappear."

"You . . ." I breathed. It was impossible. I was terrified by the hope that reeled through me, terrified it would be a mistake. . . . "You mean all that you say?"

"Everything I say," he told me, "everything I could never put into words. Sometimes, I almost believed I'd imagined you. No one could burn so brightly as you did in my memories, in my dreams. Then I would awaken and you were gone and all that remained was emptiness. Even the best days seem these hollow echoes of what I once had with you, and how much easier it might have been, had I forgotten you."

"How can this be possible? Tyrus, you've been poisoned for four years. I saw how it was changing you in so short a time. . . . How . . . how can . . ." I was desperate to believe him, desperate for it, yet I couldn't.

"This is how." Tyrus raised his hand, showed me the ring, the one he'd been drawing in the narcotic from. "Stylish, is it not? It's fashioned out of a metal alloy that neutralizes the effects of Venalox on contact."

I stared at him. I dared not even draw breath.

"Did you hear what I said? Did you understand?" Tyrus said. "It never destroyed me. I've been pretending for years. Playing his ally, waiting for your return. Waiting for the moment I could claim the scepter and destroy him. . . . My love, it's me."

And then he kissed me.

# 42

AS I'D KNOWN him before, Tyrus was a creature of total delib-
eration. His mind was always turning, working, even with his arms
about me, his lips warm and leisurely, tracing and stoking fire. But
Tyrus—my new husband—was feverish, burning for me. He was
not careful and calculated and deliberate as his mouth came down
over mine, as his sparking palm twined with mine, fingers braiding
between mine, hands locking about my waist with a suddenness that
might bruise any but me.

I met him with the same fervor, all the blood in my veins singing
with the exultant joy of this, that it was him and I had not lost him. It
was like being delivered from a nightmare into a miracle.

His lips scorched my skin, demanding, taking, the sparks of our
palms crackling together as he pressed me down. His grip before had
always been careful, though I was the one who could break him with a
flexure of muscle. Now he grasped as though he feared a wind might

rip me away, he sucked fierce kisses as though he sought to keep them forever. I could break him apart with a blow and yet he crushed down atop me, heavy with muscles, a feverish intensity to him that stoked a maddening fire from my skin . . . that left every part of me aching, full, thrilled.

And when we joined, I drew him as close as I could, reminding myself not to hurt him, reminding myself not to break those shoulders I grasped, that body I loved more than any other, that I never wanted to release.

After, I dared not take my eyes from him, nor did he look away from me. We drank in the sight of each other. He ran his hands over me reverently, stroking my skin as though he needed to memorize it, and I just touched that face . . . his face.

"Look," he said, raising our interlinked hands.

The electrodes had registered our consummation. We watched as the current flickered away, for we were joined in earnest now. He drew my hand to his lips and lovingly traced my skin with a kiss. "My wife."

"My husband." How strange it sounded. And it was real.

The great empty pit in my heart was gone, filled to swelling with the blinding white joy of this miracle, this deliverance. I could have passed an age trying to put words to the feeling within me, but there was only one way to preserve this. We had to think, and plan, and share everything we had to keep secret once we left this haven.

So I spoke rapidly, telling Tyrus what had become of the Interdict. And he never released me from his arms, as though he feared I might be torn away. In turn, he told me what had happened here. How he'd defeated the Venalox.

"I recalled something Pasus said on our Forenight. He believed I'd neutralized the Fireskiss with another substance, and so I realized— why not do exactly that with the Venalox? I began to test Venalox in combination with anything I could find. Then it occurred to me: I could force someone else to use it with me and find what I sought twice as quickly. So I used Gladdic as my test subject."

"Oh."

Tyrus looked at me. "Did he say something, then?"

"He told me you'd taken the *Atlas*. And sold it."

Tyrus let out a breath. "Yes. That. I needed the money and I'm barred from any other sources. I was desperate."

"I understand more than I did."

Tyrus smiled. "I've made his life quite miserable. I knew I couldn't just seek him out for Venalox use. It would inspire questions. I also knew that Alectar would feel threatened if I seemed to be forging a friendship and passing the time with another in companionship, so I became what the situation warranted: I was a bully, the terror of his life. I coerced him, tormented him, and all the while, he enabled me to experiment with neutralizers in half the time. I always had more Venalox than I needed after the *Tigris*. Those eager to diminish Alectar's influence began to sneak it to me. They were all my unwitting helpers. And once I had this"—he spread his fingers—"it was simply a matter of neutralizing more and more of the substance each day, until I was using none at all."

I threaded my fingers with his, and Tyrus pulled my hand to his lips.

"You've had time to plan. Tyrus, have you any idea what to do next? We might not get this chance to speak again."

"I do." He sought my gaze, intent. "I can't tell you details as of yet, but . . . but I can only ask you to trust me. Nemesis, I have people I've been paying in stealth, seeking out vicars for me. If you give me the scepter's transponder frequency—"

I smiled at him. "I have something better. Open to the marked page of the book."

Tyrus opened *Hamlet*, and the volume fell open to the page with the scepter tucked in the crease. He looked up at me, brow shadowed, and read, *"'I must be cruel only to be kind: Thus bad begins and worse remains behind'?"*

"It's not the text I'm asking you about. It's the bookmark. Look at it."

Tyrus picked up the scepter. His gaze focused on it, sharpened. "Nemesis," he said quietly, "what is this?"

"The scepter's casing was just there to hold it. That's the real scepter," I told him. "I never cast it into space, Tyrus. You're holding the supercomputer that makes the Domitrians . . . Domitrians."

That stunned him into utter silence. "You've . . . had this all along?"

"I just had to wait for the right moment. Whatever you are waiting to do, wait no longer. The Interdict pierced his skin with it to hide it."

Tyrus jabbed at his skin, and a bead of blood welled up. I took the scepter, leveled his arm, and threaded the sharp metal through the top layer as the Interdict had done. He just gazed at my face, and when I met his eyes, he seemed as though he was gazing into another world, caught in some thought.

"We can do this," I told him. I grabbed his shoulders, drew him into a last, urgent kiss, pulled back to whisper, "And do whatever you must, Tyrus. Be cruel, be indifferent, if you must. . . . Whatever it takes. Just get Pasus to win those vicars to your side so we might turn this around."

His lashes lifted and he studied my face as though seeing me for the first time. His hand reached up, calloused palm brushing my skin. "How wondrous it is," Tyrus said, "to find myself . . . pleasantly surprised. I hope to do the same for you very soon."

With those enigmatic words, he rose to his feet.

When we reattached to the Chrysanthemum, the door opened, air rushing in about us. Then Tyrus stepped away from me, and the transformation was immediate . . . a mask slapping back onto his face as he announced to the waiting Grandiloquy: "I am pleased to announce that your new Empress is magnificent in bed."

The crude words were spoken for effect, but they still caught me off-guard, as did Tyrus holding his palm aloft to exhibit the electricity that was no longer flaring. Bawdy voices gave calls of approval, and he grinned shamelessly. Then Pasus strode toward him.

"Well done, Tyrus," he said. "So well done."

Tyrus turned to him. "My performance? Thank you. I told you, I'd get it out of her."

Pasus grabbed him in a brisk hug.

Get . . . what out of me?

"Did you hear everything?" Tyrus said.

"Everything," Pasus affirmed, pulling back to regard him fondly.

Everything.

Wait.

What?

Pasus looked at me, and Tyrus glanced my way too, and there was an air of triumph about Pasus now as he marveled, "You had the scepter the entire time. Well done. We don't need you now."

My mouth sagged open.

That was when the neural suppressor hummed to life, and I realized I'd made a deadly mistake.

# 43

MY LEGS SANK out from under me, and Tyrus gave a tut of disapproval.

"A bit of overkill," he said to Pasus. "Surely you've realized I can talk her into most anything." He flicked open the gem on his ring and drew in a sniff of the Venalox with a shudder of relief. It didn't seem to be an inactive substance neutralized by the alloy.

"Even you could not talk her into this," Pasus said.

Tyrus laughed hoarsely. "I might have liked to try," he said, and the wash of calm over his face . . . like an addict getting his fix . . .

A sick feeling curled in my stomach.

*He's faking*, I thought. *Surely* . . .

Pasus caught his shoulder to steady him. "You endured well."

"It was not easy. Diabolics," he said, sending me a crooked grin, "do not use the bathroom very often. I kept giving her more wine . . ."

He *had* urged a good deal on me. . . .

". . . hoping she'd go relieve herself so I could sell the story of overcoming the Venalox, but . . . it's like dealing with a camel. Perhaps literally. My love, did the Interdict mention camel DNA in that talk about creatures? It's been so long."

Now I looked inward, and had he used Venalox in the washroom?

No. *No.* I shut the thought down, because we were in private, so he didn't have to. He didn't have to . . . No. This was a ruse. He'd told me . . . He'd said . . .

"Oh, I did learn some interesting things," Tyrus said, wheeling away. He punched in a transmission code and said to the voice on the other end, "There's a starship called the *Arbiter.* The fugitive Neveni Sagnau is on board. Send out a bulletin."

"Tyrus!" I said, aghast, because . . . because even if he was just playing a role (and I told myself—I *told myself* he was!), he actually might get her hunted down.

"My love, my dear heart," said Tyrus, "Sagnau is your friend—but she's not mine. There's something off-putting about that girl. And frankly, I think we're going to deal with this Sacred City issue by burying it, so I can't have her running around spreading rumors. I'm sorry, but I need to hunt your little friend down and kill her."

"But . . ." But I'd told him of Neveni just for him. For Tyrus. Because . . . because I trusted Tyrus.

*Tyrus,* I thought to him, *you are starting to terrify me. Please give me a hint this isn't real.*

"I see no reason we can't get started right away," Pasus told Tyrus. "I signaled all the interested parties. Many will just use screens throughout the Chrysanthemum, but quite a few agreed to your suggestion. Most creative. They're going to assemble in sight of the heliosphere."

"Why?" My voice was a whisper.

Tyrus ignored me and set about examining himself. "I do wish

I'd had time to change. White does not become me."

Pasus smiled. He withdrew from his pocket a folded green garment.

"I am touched," Tyrus said, shucking off his tunic right there, yanking on the close-fitting green shirt as I just gawked at them, trying to make sense of this. "You haven't spoken of the *Atlas*."

"The vessel you apparently obtained and then resold behind my back?" Pasus said.

Tyrus paused where he'd been smoothing down the shirt.

Pasus laughed. "Tyrus, you've earned it. You made a bargain, the profits are yours. You needn't hide this from me in the future."

A poisonous sensation spread through me at Tyrus's surprised delight, to realize Pasus wasn't going to wrest something from him that he'd stolen from someone else. "Did you make sure the ships out there obtained the best vantage points, Alectar? I really want to win back some favor with the Grandiloquy."

"This will do it. They will adore you for the gesture," purred Pasus.

Tyrus gave a satisfied nod. "Nemesis, come on."

I did not move as Tyrus started down the hallway. He swiveled around when he realized I wasn't following. I didn't like the enjoyment on Pasus's face. A terrible picture had formed in my mind, and my worst fears of all seemed to be true.

"You said what I wanted to hear." My voice was gravelly. "When you spoke in the oubliette, you planned every word with him."

"Not every word," said Tyrus. "But yes, I spoke what I thought you wanted, and you gave me what I wanted, my love. In more than one sense." His gaze trailed down me appreciatively. "Isn't that marriage? And now you will do me one more service yet." Then he jerked his head. Footsteps scuffled over to me and arms seized me, but I didn't fight.

I just . . . didn't.

Something dreadful was soon to take place. The knowledge was a death knell, thudding in my brain.

I had believed him.

And to offer me the hope I hadn't lost everything, only to withdraw it again . . .

If they meant to kill me, I couldn't imagine I'd even fight. I hadn't understood Gladdic in the heliosphere the day I'd come to slay him. For the first time ever I felt so hollowed out that it didn't matter.

It didn't even matter that Tyrus didn't care enough to linger, and Pasus had fallen back to delight in the look on my face as I was forced to walk the heliosphere.

"You did very well, heading to Eurydice straightaway," Pasus said. "I was very pleased you did that. Moreso even than the Emperor. I'm the one who sees the expedience of this union. He would have wed for wealth had I allowed it. He certainly would have cavorted with other women had I not kept an eye on him. I have become the chiefest advocate of your union."

If he was aiming for a response, I didn't give it to him.

I was out of words.

I was out of everything.

"The fact that you are popular with the Excess makes this march excellent all around. That leaves only the matter of the Grandiloquy," Pasus said. "Since you are now known to have survived the *Tigris*, that confirmed their suspicions you orchestrated it. Many died, or almost died, and they have one more reason to despise you. It is time to satisfy the Grandiloquy's need for revenge."

"Just get to the point," I said. "What do you want, for me to tell you that you won? It means nothing to me. Kill me. Slit my throat in the heliosphere, it won't matter."

"No. Alas, your death would inflame the Excess. We need you alive.

But we also need to appease the Grandiloquy. Your husband had a most inventive solution. I may have floated a variant of this idea by him a year or two ago—but he proposed it himself as soon as you returned. I want you know this is all his doing."

We entered the Great Heliosphere, and it surprised me only for a moment to see all the starships that had arrayed themselves out there, angled toward us. They'd taken up Tyrus on his suggestion to see whatever would occur in here with their own eyes, through the magnifiers of their windows.

Then Tyrus waited expectantly by Fustian, and my captors drove me forward, and Pasus called, "May I have the honor of telling her?"

Tyrus waved his hand negligently, his ring winking in the light. His gaze was fixed on those starships outside the window.

"You are here for a Ritual of Penance," Pasus spoke right in my ear.

A Ritual of Penance.

My mind ground to a halt.

I knew what that was.

The halfway, the compromise that was not execution, yet was not the insult of me as Empress presiding over Grandiloquy.

A Ritual of Penance was performed to remove one's capacity to engage in offensive conduct. It was just the punishment the Grandiloquy would deem fair to inflict upon me.

It could be done with Scorpion's Breath in high doses, or Fustian might drive a piercer up my nose and damage my brain directly. Either way, the result was a ritualized lobotomy.

I would never be capable of acting for myself again.

And there was no healing me. Not ever.

This wasn't possible.

This was awful beyond my comprehension.

And Tyrus was waiting with ill-concealed impatience before

Fustian. He seemed to look through me as Pasus waved forward a servant carrying . . . carrying a jeweled piercer.

To drive up my nose.

Into my brain.

In the holiest possible way.

"No," I blurted. I wrenched at the arms holding me, but I couldn't break away from them.

Tyrus was just glancing outside the window again. Then he raised his glove to speak into the transmitter. "Tell them to close formation. The ships in the back will miss it."

"Tyrus." My voice shook. "No. Don't do this. Don't!"

"Don't struggle," Tyrus said to me. Now he met my eyes, placid and indifferent. "This needn't be painful."

"You don't . . . Tyrus, please. Pasus is manipulating you. . . ."

Pasus laughed. "I told you, your husband decided this. Not me."

Tyrus didn't deny it. He didn't care enough to acknowledge me now that he had what he wanted. He just adjusted his green tunic, concerned with appearances—now of all times.

I shook my head. I kept shaking it. It couldn't be. This was a ruse, a trick, Tyrus wouldn't really do this to me. He wouldn't. Tyrus needed to tell me. He just needed to look at me, one glance to tell me this was going to plan . . .

Surely he would do it again, deliver me from this, prove himself my miracle, and yet as I was forced down onto my knees before Fustian nan Domitrian, and he began to pronounce a Liturgy of Misdeeds over me—centering primarily on the deaths from the *Tigris* massacre—I realized it.

No ruse.

It couldn't possibly be a game, a show, a charade, because we'd passed the event horizon of this black hole. There was no turning back. All those ships out that window were arrayed because the Grandiloquy wanted to see my downfall, and even without Tyrus spearheading this, they'd get it. They had overwhelming force. It was going to happen.

This was reality, and reality was cruel. It would only be ignored for so long, and then it would sink in its teeth with a sharper bite.

"Don't!" I shouted. "Tyrus, kill me first. DON'T DO THIS."

"The next time she speaks, slice out her tongue," Tyrus said to the men holding me. "Proceed, Vicar."

Fustian raised up a sealed container. Within would be the numbing vapor, and my face would be pressed over it so I would grow disoriented. I wouldn't feel it when the piercer drove up through my nose and ruptured my frontal lobe. I screamed out like an animal and began to fight with all the strength the suppressor allowed me. I'd slam my head against the floor and kill myself rather than be a mindless creature they could manipulate as they willed. . . .

But I couldn't free myself. I was helpless to avert my fate. The vicar lifted the lid to release numbing mist, and I twisted frantically to evade the curls of vapor snaking into the air, but it registered dimly in the back of my mind . . . a slight tingle of familiarity.

The gas billowed all about us, a self-propelling cloud of yellow-brown that hit the air in a swell, and then instantly bloomed again, again. . . . I had seen this, I knew it. Fustian, Pasus, his servant, and the pair of Excess—they knew it too. Everyone but the Emperor leaped back from the very sight of it.

Not Tyrus. He just stood there as the dark cloud swelled about him, his calculating gaze flickering up toward the open air vents leading to general atmospheric circulation. Then the screams began and confirmed what this gas was.

It was Resolvent Mist.

# 44

RESOLVENT MIST was an intelligent bioweapon. It registered atmospheric density and confined itself to deploying within those layers of an atmosphere where breathing, living mammals might dwell, rather than floating up to be dispersed in space.

Each spore self-replicated until it reached a certain saturation within an area, and then those spores moved elsewhere to repeat the process in the next accessible area. It "marked" each area it had been so as not to fill the same chamber twice. In such a way, the fatal bioweapon grew denser, thicker until I could not even see anyone else in the Great Heliosphere, and then it thinned.

My eyes picked out Pasus's fallen servant and the two dead Excess who'd been restraining me. They were both on the ground—blood fountaining from their eyes, their ears, their noses, their mouths, ejected by their lungs as they liquefied.

I propelled back from them and crashed into Tyrus.

His hands caught my waist. "Shh."

I turned to look at him, and the detached and indifferent Tyrus who'd been pleased to have a nice green shirt, who'd been eager to be rid of me . . . He was gone. Replaced by this person who appeared carved out of stone, even as the last of the bioweapon's tendrils snaked into the vents.

To general circulation.

Which would expel it *everywhere*.

Pasus stood paralyzed, looking at the dead Excess. Fustian loosed a cry and dashed for the door. . . .

"I don't understand. What—" Pasus said.

"I always thought the Emperor Amon had a difficult task, slipping a poison to so many people without being discovered," Tyrus said to Pasus. "I think we've had a few late-night discussions, pondering that. Well, having now secretly distributed a substance myself—a counteragent to those I chose as today's survivors—I can tell you it's quite easy. Once the *Atlas* fattened my pockets, I simply paid people to obtain it and do it for me."

Fustian began to scream. My gaze shot to him. He was standing before the open door, gazing into the main promenade of the *Valor Novus*. The murky fog was there now, and through it were faint figures, and so many screams, a virtual cacophony from them.

*Sweet Helios*, I thought. Fustian closed the door and plunged to his knees, huddled there, murmuring to himself. Tyrus's cool, appraising eyes were fixed on Pasus, who seemed to now understand the implications of this.

"The entire Chrysanthemum has interconnected atmosphere. You will . . ." Pasus realized it then. He realized that an enormous number of people were about to die. He tore back his sleeve and shouted into his transmitter, "The Emperor unilaterally deployed Resolvent Mist.

I don't know who has fallen. I didn't plan this. I had nothing to do with it. . . ."

Tyrus stroked a hand through my hair, regarding Pasus with faint amusement.

". . . bring space-sheaths," Pasus was shouting, desperate to prove he'd had no hand in unleashing the Mist. "Bring med bots. And . . . and . . ."

"Why waste your breath, Alectar?" Tyrus said. To me: "All this time tying his bonds to me and he thinks he can truly disavow what I've done."

"No. You are going to pay for this, not me," Pasus said. "This is all on you! Do you know how many masters of those vessels have family here?"

"They don't anymore," Tyrus said coldly.

I looked between them, the implications sinking in: those ships were not allies in on a secret deal. Tyrus had not brokered anything in advance, and Pasus was right in thinking they would retaliate. So Tyrus had struck a blow, and now those ships would avenge those who'd fallen about us. Very well.

I could accept doom.

Even take advantage of it.

"Pasus," I said.

Pasus turned to me. I drove my foot into his groin, doubling him over. My hand tangled in his hair, and I might've hurt him in earnest if Tyrus hadn't said, "Stop!"

"Why?" I almost growled.

"Not yet," Tyrus said. "Give me his transmitter."

I drove my boot down onto Pasus's hand, ignoring his shout, and tore the transmitter off, flung it at Tyrus. Then I let my heel grind those bones. Since I wasn't at full strength, he managed to dislodge me, to propel me back.

But I smiled in savage promise at Pasus's chalky white face, as Tyrus's voice rippled out behind me:

"This is your Emperor. I see you have heard Senator von Pasus's transmission and you are moblizing in response." He looked at those ships, so vast in number, so overwhelming. They could have formed their own superstructure with that power among them. "What the Senator told you is true. I have just killed a massive number of people. Stand down and retreat, or join them."

The words were an empty threat. The ships did not withdraw, but were close enough now that I could pick out the individual lights of windows from even the farthest of the ships. Soon they'd fire tethers into the Chrysanthemum, force open the airlocks, spill in wearing space-sheaths, armed and ready to take revenge.

"Oh well." Tyrus tossed aside the transmitter. "I tried."

My blood raced with fire. Heady anticipation mingled with fear for him, and I moved to his side. "We will grab weapons. We'll fight to the end. We can take many of them with us. But first . . ." I cast Pasus a ferocious smile. "I will enjoy knowing you meet the same fate we do."

"I disavow this," protested Pasus. "I had nothing to do with it. Surveillance will show them as much! They watched it through their windows. They *must* have seen my surprise!"

"No, they saw you covered in fog," I said with cruel enjoyment. "They saw you standing after it cleared."

"They will see reason," Pasus insisted.

Tyrus regarded him with icy amusement. "You put too much faith in the rationality of human beings."

"I put too much faith in yours!" spat Pasus. "The Venalox was supposed to remove that foolish sentimentality. . . ."

"Ah, and it did," agreed Tyrus, prowling toward him. "I once had such hopes for this Empire. I would unite people to address a common existential threat. Now I see those were childish delusions. People do not unite for a common cause when faced with disaster. No. That's the last resort. That's what happens only after they've clambered over each other to loot the corpse of their civilization."

"There is no saving you."

"I believed that for a while," Tyrus said. "Then I broke the hold of the Venalox—exactly as I told Nemesis I had in the oubliette—and I saw clearly at last your desperation for validation only I could give you. I used it. I embraced you. I invited you to dwell in the Imperial Chambers. You were so taken, you made every transmission, conducted all your business, right within my reach, right where I could see your every movement and gather every weapon I needed. Alectar: I watched your back-and-forth with the vicars. I learned all their identities through you."

Pasus drew a sharp breath.

"Men and women of faith," jeered Tyrus," but their Living Cosmos could not protect them from the question I had put to them: lose a head, or lose a hand? And what do you know—those vicars always preferred to lose a hand! The very one with the diode that gave them power over my scepter, allowing those diodes to be reimplanted in any mercenary I chose. Those mercenaries were glad to speak any words I wished for a cut of the *Atlas*'s profits."

"You can claim the scepter," I breathed.

Tyrus traced his finger over his arm, just where he'd placed that sliver of metal. Outside the starship, the vessels were aiming their tethering guns. "I already have. A bead of blood in the oubliette, and I've felt it growing louder in my mind with every heartbeat since. Shall we test it now?"

A frantic hope soared in my heart, for he could make these ships come to a dead stop now. . . .

Tyrus flicked his hand. The lead vessel of the armada flared into a brilliant ray of light . . . as though it powered up for a hyperspace jump. Then it split open. It was no explosion. A crack, a rupture speared out from it like the space had been sliced open by some invisible hand. The fault line snaked in all directions and each vessel in its path spilling shining innards into the pitch black of the void, fire flowering out from its engines, but not receding. . . . No. Thickening the gash of light until it grew so bright it left an imprint on my eyes. The wound rippled, blossomed, heaved, devouring more and more. . . .

I was aware of Pasus's cry, of my heart thundering in my ears. A ribbonlike gash of white began to assume a horrifyingly familiar form.

Pasus stumbled back from the window, but Tyrus just stepped closer to it.

He placed his hands on the window. His silhouette was stark black against the great rupture gulping the starships now trying to fly away, failing.

Stars save us all.

Tyrus had just created malignant space.

# 45

FOR AN INSTANT of transfixed horror, the wound in the universe glowed in my vision, and it seemed almost sated . . . hanging in the void with an odd stillness. . . . The smallest pinpricks of white bled from it in all directions. The intact peripheral vessels tried to change course, but their momentum carried them to their doom. They disappeared into the tendrils of devouring brightness. Abruptly in a spasm, it resumed hemorrhaging with an urgency to consume more. . . .

"This can't be. This isn't real," Pasus said at last, his voice empty, toneless.

The denial settled tonelessly on the air scented with Resolvent Mist. So close to us, the very fabric of the universe itself was a mutilated wound rupturing itself wider with every passing second to spill a lethal band of light that destroyed all it touched. I found myself at a curious distance from what I was seeing, for surely this was not real, as Pasus had said—this was not malignant space spreading in the six-star home system of the Domitrians.

"You can trust your eyes, Alectar," Tyrus said, tracing his palm over the window. "Turns out, it's very easy to create malignant space. Just a few conditions going awry when a ship tries to leap into hyperspace . . . And there it goes. It would be a shockingly cost-effective light show for future imperial spectacles . . ."—he looked back at us with a jaded twist of his lips—". . . if I knew how to stop it."

He had no way to fix it. The realization shocked me.

He'd created something he couldn't destroy.

I stepped back from Tyrus, because the wrongness of this blared at me. Tyrus was illuminated by the brilliant, garish glow of this malignancy he'd vowed to fight, as he mused: "How many people on those starships laughed off the threat of this? What do you suppose they are thinking right now?" He let that sit there. "Well, I imagine they're not thinking. They're probably screaming."

The malignancy had ensnared the nearest star—and that's when I realized the six-star system was now doomed. More of the ships were plunging in, vanishing into the brilliant depths of the light, and Tyrus had made this happen. He'd created this. He had to be using the scepter even now because the distance between the Chrysanthemum and that rippling white death mounted even as the destruction grew. Yet nothing changed what he'd done. He had knowingly created malignant space in his home system with no means of ending it.

It was unfathomable to me that Tyrus had deliberately done this. My whole being rejected the idea that this was truly reality. Surely I would awaken soon. Pasus abruptly bolted toward the door. That snapped me out of my daze. I surged after him—and Tyrus said, "Don't bother."

"Tyrus . . . ," I protested, whipping around.

Tyrus just looked at me. Pointed to his own eyes. "There's nowhere he can escape me now."

The words were meant to reassure me.

They chilled me.

He calmly closed the distance to me, took my hand, and drew me toward the door. I accompanied him in a daze out of the Great Heliosphere . . . and into the *Valor Novus*, its floor strewn with bodies.

The great windows showed the Chrysanthemum, reflecting the eerie light we cold not see from this angle. These docked vessels, afflicted by Resolvent Mist and not malignant space, appeared like loosely hewn limbs jostling back and forth against the background of light and emptiness where there had been so many lives just minutes ago.

On the floor—bodies. So many dead. And kneeling amid them, a subdued and silent Alectar von Pasus.

"You didn't get far," Tyrus remarked. "Did it dawn on you at last that you did exactly *this* on Lumina to *billions* of people? Far more than my number today."

"What do you mean to do to me?" said Pasus hoarsely. "Torture me? Cast me into a black hole? Oh, I am sure that's your intent. You must've been anticipating this for ages."

"Once, imagining this was my foremost pleasure," Tyrus admitted. "I fantasized about repaying degradation for degradation, and making you wish for death before I gave it to you. . . . But we are long past that, are we not? Dear Alectar, in the grand scheme of things, you've done me more good than harm. I have enjoyed years of total impunity. The Venalox ensured I could pin all my misdeeds on you. Even this day's calamity, I'll conceal behind my trusty human shield. The surviving Grandiloquy will be told this was you. All the data will show you financed it. And I will escape unscathed from a day when I've obliterated the entirety of my political opposition. This is our hour of victory! Look to the window. I wish to reward you."

The proud Senator von Pasus seemed a broken and defeated man. He obeyed—and looked.

There was an event called the Awakening, spoken of in hushed voices. It was the moment the Chrysanthemum responded to its new master, and now I saw it. All those loosely joined starships began to contract like a muscle. Lights long gone dim flared to brilliant vibrancy again. Machines that had been drifting languidly through the void for several years abruptly snapped to alertness, powering up, aiming gun barrels in tandem. Flashes of metal and light swarmed our view, and the configuration of starships—so jumbled—began to take form into that organized Chrysanthemum shape once more.

"You saw my uncle do this and it altered the course of your life," Tyrus said. "It's only fitting you die with it fresh in your mind."

Pasus looked at his Emperor's back, a presentiment of doom twisting his features, and a moment later a security bot whipped down from the wall and fired a single, perfunctory slash of light at him.

A disgraceful, unceremonious end to a man who wished to be a legend.

And Tyrus, his executioner, did not bother to watch.

Instead he gazed at me with a warm, dancing anticipation. "I have something for you, Nemesis. I've longed to give this to you for years—and now it is yours. Look there." He nodded . . . at one of the bodies.

When I didn't move, he stepped over to the young boy, moved his head with his boot. "See?" At my blank face, "A Servitor."

"You're giving me a dead Servitor?" I managed.

"*All* the dead Servitors." He smiled broadly. "Look about us, my love. You will not find a single living, breathing Servitor in the Chrysanthemum, and the vast majority in the Empire were here—or on those ships. Consider them banned." He tapped his finger to his temple. "I remembered."

It was the most ghastly offering I could have received.

"Oh, Tyrus" was all that escaped me.

Swept up in the moment, he missed my expression, my tone. Instead, he gave a flick of his hand, and the humming of the neural suppressor snapped off. The resurgence of strength to my body did not reassure me. . . . It merely emphasized the total power he'd just gained over me.

Over everyone.

He stepped over the bodies of his victims and approached the window so he could gaze out upon his work. The superstructure about us began to retreat more swiftly from the terrible threat of malignant space as it devoured its way through the six-star system, tearing at a second star now.

The hypergiant Hephaestus. The very star that burned through the Great Heliosphere and propelled us into the hardships that followed.

And soon it would be destroyed as well.

# 46

"ENOUGH."

Keening. Sobbing. The whimpered words, "Monstrous . . . It's monstrous . . ."

"Yes, yes. Now stop."

My eyes were closed. I forced them to open and Tyrus was sitting on his throne, and around him, immediately filling their roles—like cockroaches reproducing their numbers at once—were the new men and women. Those spared. Those to be elevated. Sly, calculating, greedy, or too debauched to care that the Emperor had just killed their predecessors to make way for them. Most had known beforehand it was coming; I could tell with a glance. All pretended to believe Pasus had done this. As they'd trickled in, they began eagerly discussing the territories they expected to receive.

And now I stared at Tyrus, feeling like I was gazing at him from another world as Fustian nan Domitrian lay on his stomach on the floor at his feet, in a pathetic display of tears. He'd literally been kicking and screaming when he was dragged in here.

"Fustian," Tyrus said, rolling his eyes up toward the ceiling, "I don't know just how much of this is affected and how much is real emotion. You are a vicar and you are on hand. Tell me now if I can use you or if you should simply join the others."

The tears stopped at once. Fustian visibly trembled.

"I could use a vicar at my side tonight. I am going to broadcast a gala to reassure the Empire that all is well." He steepled his hands. "I will speak, and I will require words by the Interdict."

Fustian's mouth wobbled. "But . . . the Interdict . . ."

"Is not dead, nor is the Sacred City destroyed. Who will say otherwise?"

"But . . ." Slowly Fustian connected the words. The despicable opportunist in him overrode the holy man. He positioned himself on his knees, and oh—how his face burned with eagerness. "There . . . there is not an Interdict here. Unless . . ."

"Unless what, Vicar?" Tyrus drew it out, wanting him to ask for it.

"Does Your Supremacy mean . . . Do you mean . . ." He was searching Tyrus's face, desperate for him to end the suspense. "Do you mean to appoint . . . *someone*?"

"The Interdict is the supreme leader of the faith. The words of the Interdict are those of the Living Cosmos, and they are to be obeyed by all. The Interdict is dead—but for all intents and purposes, I think there is an Interdict."

"I don't understand. . . ."

"Fustian." Tyrus rose to his feet, eyes like ice. "Who do you think is your Interdict?"

That was the moment the vicar caught on. And he was aghast, which made Tyrus smile in a distinctly predatory way. He absolutely despised this man and never needed to conceal it again. Fustian was too terrified to say anything but, "You. It is you, Your Supremacy."

"That's right." He stepped over to Fustian, took his face in his hands. "And who will move his lips to the true Interdict's words and issue his decrees, and in turn receive all the wealth, reverence, and honors due to that Interdict?"

"I—I will do so. I will gladly speak and decree as my gracious Emperor commands."

"Yes, I thought you would agree to it. You are a good little puppet. I have seen that again and again, and I will make you fat with honors. . . ." He dropped his voice to a lethal whisper only I could hear. "And I will enjoy watching you die if you give me cause to regret choosing you."

"Thank you. I thank you, I thank you. . . ." He kissed Tyrus's feet. As Pasus had forced Tyrus to do before him in the Great Heliosphere. Tyrus watched Fustian with bare contempt for a lingering moment, before shoving his face away with his heel.

There was no more disdainful gesture, but Fustian burbled his thanks for it. And I couldn't bear another moment of this sight, of any of this. This was power. Naked and unvarnished authority in its purest form. It was revolting.

I was halfway down the corridor where I'd been clamped to the wall and forced to watch Tyrus's downfall, when a voice rippled from the speaker.

*"My love. No good-bye?"*

My heart raced wildly. I twisted about, and the surveillance cameras were trained on me. *Helios devoured!* His eyes were looking through those, weren't they?

"Do you see me?" I said.

"I do."

A low chuckle from the speaker on the wall. *"I'm not even talking, just thinking this. You know—I have the right mind for this. All one needs*

343

*is focus, self-control. . . . Grandmother was born with the mind for this. Not like my uncle. How frustrating for her."*

His uncle had never been able to do this. Randevald had had no self-discipline, no control over his own thoughts, his mind, so he'd been clumsy with the machines. He'd tried to kill us once. He deployed a missile, trying to frame it as a freak accident that ruptured a sky dome in the *Alexandria.* He'd blocked the oxygen from the repressurization closet. That was his best attempt.

Tyrus would never have failed. His mind was a blade honed diamond sharp.

*He never will fail again,* I thought with a cold shiver. *He will gain more and more control, and in the future, any he wishes dead will die when he chooses.*

"I must go rest. Stop watching me," I said. Then, "Please."

The security cameras sank down.

*"Don't let me detain you. Sweet dreams, my love."*

I wasn't sure I'd ever fall asleep again. The only thing I thought to do was look in on the one Grande whose welfare I had the slightest interest in. Gladdic had been inoculated before the Lumina tragedy, but that was years ago, and I wasn't certain whether it had protected him from today's Resolvent Mist.

Gladdic's last location had been on the *Socrates,* a smaller starship where the doddering old Senator von Eustace often held colloquiums, gatherings of intellectually-minded Grandiloquy and Excess. They were open to anyone, apolitical and philosophical in nature. The only requirement was a commitment to dispassionate, emotionally detached reason while in the space, and total sobriety. The refusal to allow intoxicants rendered the colloquiums quite unpopular. Eustace's eccentricities did not help. He never used false-youth and enjoyed mocking his contemporaries who did. He was fond of critiquing power but refused any opportunities to advance himself—even when Tyrus tried luring him onto the Privy Council.

Today's colloquium had likely been intended as a viewing of my Ritual of Penance, followed by a discussion of its implications. The holographic projection ring in the center of the chamber still displayed the Great Heliosphere's interior, now emptied out but for a pair of fallen Excess.

Many of the potential debaters were dead on the floor.

Gladdic sat at one of the great round tables, arms hugging over his body. He was just sitting there so still, alone at the table, he seemed as dead as the corpses about him. My gaze roved around the chamber, a low priority for service bots, so bodies were still sprawled about where they'd tumbled out of their chairs. There were plates of food, half-eaten, without corresponding diners to go with them, so there must have been more who were spared and fled.

No sight of the old Senator von Eustace.

"Gladdic," I said.

He just stared at the table. Two seats over, a man had vomited blood over the cloth before slumping over in his meal. Across from Gladdic, a woman's leg jutted into the air from where she'd tumbled back in her seat.

"Gladdic." I seized his shoulder, clamped my hand down, shook him.

Nothing. I raised my hand to slap him lightly, then thought the better of it when he abruptly spoke. "Nemesis."

His voice was calm. Eerily so.

"What is it, Gladdic?"

"Is . . . is this real life?"

He'd seen this happen on Lumina. The realization struck me, and I cast a gaze about to take in the full horror of what he'd just witnessed. He'd been on Lumina and now, once again, it had happened. He must have had nightmares. Over and over, and here it was happening again.

"This is all real," I told him.

And the words I spoke settled into my own conscious mind. That's when I finally broke out of the numbed stupor of shock and looked around with clear eyes. Really *looked* at what Tyrus had done. There were no windows in here, so I couldn't see the malignant space now devouring the six-star system, but I *felt* it. It crackled in my awareness, that thing, that festering sore on the universe that Tyrus had devoted himself to ending. That he'd just created. He'd planned this all in advance, prepared it as soon as I resurfaced, knowing the cost it would exact. It must have required time and care and effort. He'd known just how much destruction he would wreak and he did it anyway with absolutely no pity.

*That's not Tyrus.*

And I knew it in my heart, in my soul. It clutched my throat in a terrible hand, but I couldn't ignore the truth. How cruel the hopes had been, when he'd declared he loved me still in the Solarbliette. When he told me he'd freed himself of the Venalox—and he had. He'd done it.

Just not in time. He never saved himself.

My hands curled into fists. I knew just what I had to do.

"I have a way out of here," I said to Gladdic. "I'll help you leave."

He dragged his sluggish gaze up to mine. "You do?"

"There's a transponder frequency in my possession. It will put you in contact with someone with a ship who can save you. You can escape. I need something from you in return. Can you get it for me? I need thermite."

He stared at me.

I checked the pockets of the dead until I found a discreet-sheet, and jotted down Neveni's transponder frequency. He gazed at it dully.

"Contact this ship. Get out of here. But first, find me thermite."

"I don't know what that is," he said.

"It's a substance that can destroy a machine." That was all I knew. "Please. This is more important than you know. Ask someone. You must have wealth. Pay someone. I have nothing else to offer, but I can't get this myself. . . ."

"Please. I don't . . . Nemesis, right now, I just . . . I can't deal with this. I can't."

"For once in your life," I snapped at him, "just one time, do not be a pathetic weakling, Gladdic! This is important!"

A choked noise. Nova blast me, he was about to cry.

He was so useless! I ripped back from him, ready to tear something apart. I couldn't even enjoy insulting Gladdic. I just looked around and thought of what it would be like, growing up a sensitive person amid the Grandiloquy. His father threw him away for power, knowing he was likely to be executed. Then his father was murdered by an Emperor who went on to terrorize him, trap him, and force Venalox on him; and now after all that, he had witnessed this Resolvent Mist kill everyone around him for the second time. I'd been born with a core of hard diamond and struggled to soften, just in the slightest. . . . But Gladdic was yielding and gentle and weak, thrust into a universe shaped by those more like me.

I rubbed my palms over my eyes. At times like now, I wished I had not learned to empathize with others. It was so burdensome.

"I'm sorry," I said to him.

Then I walked back over to him, and I did something I'd been trying very hard to avoid. I put my arms around him in a gesture of comfort.

The hug made him tense, and then he began to shake.

"There, there," I said. My voice was too clipped to get the intonation right, but I'd tried. His body softened, accepting the emrace.

347

I pulled away and Gladdic still gazed at me in an entreating, lost way. He would not help me fix this. It would all be my task. I left him, my thoughts still swirling over that mysterious substance. Thermite. It would destroy that scepter and remove that hideous power from hands I could no longer trust with it.

It would break Tyrus's hold over this place forever. He would be enraged over the betrayal, yet the true betrayal would be to do anything else.

In my heart, I knew something with total certainty. The Tyrus who'd asked me to be his wife that day on the *Alexandria*, that boy who stood on the sky with me in his library . . . he would have been horrified to see the future and know it led here.

He would have died sooner than become a tyrant.

So I would stop him.

# 47

WORD spread rapidly of Senator von Pasus's dreadful attempt at a coup—a public narrative of his actions this time. And the very next day, Tyrus organized a great spectacle to demonstrate unity in the face of the devastation Pasus had wrought upon the six-star system of the Domitrians.

He also did it to spread the myth that the Interdict was alive. Later in the ball dome—with a view of the writhing white of malignant space—those who were now a part of the new order hastily donned their finery. I endured the attentions of Shaezar with bewilderment.

I couldn't think of frivolity. Not now. Not with the task I'd set myself, the one I had no means of fulfilling yet: securing thermite, destroying the scepter, and saving Tyrus from himself. Tyrus met me in our viewing box, his hair thicker than usual in the absence of gravity. He drew me into my seat, then steered down into his own.

"You and I will go out there. Fustian will frame what happened yesterday," Tyrus murmured, "and I'll speak to address the rumors, to reassure everyone. You need only appear at my side—the new Empress. Then our part is done."

Good. I couldn't think to do anything else tonight.

He added, "I mean to make it very explicit to everyone just how events must proceed from here. People need to have expectations in place early."

Then, applause. I looked down to see Fustian gliding out in the finery of the Interdict. . . . And wearing a close approximation of Orthanion's face. The sight froze me, for how obscene it was to realize he'd been altered to wear the guise of a man who'd died. A man so much better than he ever could be. The starlit robes rippling about him looked all wrong with the bright glare of malignant space. Tyrus, at my side, closed his eyes a moment. . . . And the optics of the windows shifted to dim the view so Fustian could seem to glow with starlight, as intended.

Fustian nan Domitrian's voice had more of a rasp, but still did not quite sound like the real Orthanion's as he said: "As you know, I have spent many centuries dwelling in the Sacred City."

My gaze slashed to Tyrus. Tyrus was focusing intently on Fustian, and I wondered if he'd told him beforehand what to say, or if he was *thinking* it to him somehow now. Perhaps Fustian had a device in his ear with words being piped to him.

Tyrus had chosen his puppet well. Too cowardly to use the live feed to defy him, versed in all the lingo and mannerisms, and vain enough to exult in the attention.

"And tonight, in the wake of this great atrocity wrought by the heathen Senator von Pasus, it is more important than ever that we reaffirm our faith in the Living Cosmos. And our love and reverence for our Emperor."

That was the cue.

Tyrus took my hand, and we propelled ourselves out of the box and into the ball dome. The rippling silver of my gown floated about me, but something was wrong with the steering rings. I tried to flex them, to adjust my momentum. . . .

They weren't in my control.

Tyrus was controlling them.

So small a thing. So small, and he was probably doing it without conscious thought . . . but my determination to destroy that scepter burned brighter still. I couldn't tolerate this.

Tyrus spoke the words as though he'd rehearsed them in his mind for years, a denunciation of the Senator von Pasus who had seized power—and a mixture of some truths and some lies of Pasus's doings over the years.

"But now this enemy of our galaxy has been torn down, and we will come back from the tragedies of yesterday," Tyrus pledged. "His co-conspirators are already being identified and dealt with. We will be avenged on all who sought to take this Empire from its people."

And a vast swirl of security, medical, and service bots zipped into the dome with us, a whirlpool of them, a display of might and spectacle that set the crowd roaring. Then Tyrus turned to me amid the gleaming vortex and took my waist. He pulled me into a kiss, and my eyes were open and . . . and so were his. . . . Until a subtle pressure of his hands, the insistence of his lips parted mine, and abruptly the encircling bots soared in all directions, and Tyrus and I spun upward in the chamber back to the box.

Now, a performance. I couldn't look at him without pain in my heart. So I tried to focus on the feathered dancers gliding onto the floor. The first threads of music from the Harmonids rose in the air. . . .

And then familiarity struck me.

I sat up straight and threw an incredulous look at Tyrus as the King's Immolate began. "You banned this. You yourself banned it."

"I was overhasty," he said, threading his fingers together. "I overlooked the symbolic importance of the performance. It will send the proper message."

"You want all to see that you are just another Domitrian."

"I want them all to see that I must be obeyed." And when he looked at me, there was something that made me wonder—was that aimed at me?

The trained birds soared out, followed by the performance's Immolate. . . .

All seemed to go quiet about me. For I knew this Immolate. And I knew why Tyrus had been looking at me in quiet expectation, and I knew why he'd spoken of this sending the right message.

Gladdic von Aton.

Tyrus told me, "I mean to make this very clear to you: I miss nothing, Nemesis. Do not conspire against me again."

# 48

I WAS out of my seat, but the lack of gravity nearly sent me hurtling upward. My hand flew to the ceiling of the box to anchor me in place. The entire rest of the universe seemed to be teetering.

"Sit back down," said Tyrus.

"I will not," I said furiously. "You are going to kill him."

"Yes. I am."

"You can't do this."

"I disagree. Why thermite?"

I didn't speak.

"Gladdic looked it up after your conversation. Strange inquiry. I noticed. Then I sifted through all the surveillance of his recent hours and saw what put that word into his vocabulary. Tell me, do *you* know what thermite is? I recall mentioning it to you—in a specific context. And how did you intend to get the scepter? Chop off my arm?"

"I . . . Tyrus, no . . ."

"It's not there anymore. It's tiny but it felt rather like a long metal splinter. I had it taken out." He pulled out a case for a vapor rod, but I drew in a sharp breath to see him extract the familiar sliver of metal. "You wished to destroy this scepter."

I stared at it. The neural suppressor was off. I'd seen already he could deactivate it in a thought—so I suspected the reverse was likely. Otherwise I'd tear the scepter from his hands and destroy it any way I could. "Yes. Yes, I did."

"To what end?"

"I'd break your hold over this place."

"To leave me defenseless before my enemies?" With a twist of his lips, a bite in his voice, "Again?"

"No. No, I meant to spirit you away. By force if it were required. I shouldn't have given it to you. Look what you are doing with this power. Look outside! Look at all the absent faces! And Gladdic . . . He's innocent. He didn't even agree to help me!"

"No," roared Tyrus, "he didn't agree—and I would care about that if I gave a damn about him, but I don't. This is entirely about *you*. Stars ignite, Nemesis, you are the single person I never expected to betray me!"

"This was for you."

"Don't you dare," he warned me. "You once made a very important decision on my behalf that I never agreed to. I've had to live with the consequences for years. That is never going to happen again. The unilateral decisions are all mine. I may love you far too much to hurt you for this, but Gladdic von Aton has no such claim. He dies. Watch it happen, and know that this will be repeated with anyone, Nemesis— *anyone*—you try to use against me. As for the scepter?"

He looked at it, and with a disdainful flick of his wrist, sent it sailing forward, spinning through the air. A pair of security bots abruptly zipped down and sliced their lasers at it. My every muscle jerked, but the steady beams of the lasers melted the supercomputer.

"There you go. It is destroyed." He waved his hand and the bots departed, and my stomach dropped.

*He still commands them.*

"The scepter fires up a link. That's all. Then it waits until I'm dead so it can link another. Now, I've melted it, so there is never going to be another Domitrian to claim it." He leaned back in his seat, a silent, dispassionate challenge on his face. "Tell me, my love, do you wish to break open my skull? Killing me is the only way you end this now."

"No," I breathed. "I wanted to take the power from you so I could save you."

His eyes flashed unpleasantly. "I've seen your idea of saving me, and I'll have none of it. Not ever again. There is no going back. All we can do is move forward." Then his gazed dropped, releasing me from the chokehold of his scrutiny. "I hope I've made my wishes clear. We needn't ever do this again."

"We needn't do this today. I . . . Tyrus, I see what you are trying to tell me. Let him go. Please." I stared down at the dancers, my heart pounding. "This isn't *you*. Don't you see, none of this is *you*? Nova blast me, you killed thousands of people yesterday and that gives you no pause?"

"I acted out of necessity. I won't apologize."

"You *created* malignant space! Malignant space, Tyrus. All you once cared about was fixing that!"

He pinched the bridge of his nose. "Yes. I did. I decided upon it when I had the simplistic mind of a child. I've accepted now that the universe has no design, no meaning, no arc toward justice."

"You will enforce justice!"

"Children seek fairness," he shot back. "I sought out that Excess man I knew to be my father, and then I despised myself for leading the wolves to his door. He died because I'd been forced to tell my uncle that he'd been hiding me. That haunted me. I made sense of it by trying to rationalize the tragedy as one step toward greater good. How much easier, to blame a simple natural phenomenon for destroying it all—rather than to realize my father was a fool who brought his death on himself."

I stared at him.

"They all did. Those Excess who stayed on that planet, knowing what was coming, deluding themselves into thinking they would stop it. . . . I told Arion. I *told* him, and I wept, and he hugged me. He reassured me it was all going to be fine, and little idiot that I was, I let myself be lulled by his words. It was intoxicating to feel protected."

"That . . . that wasn't foolish, Tyrus. You were never allowed to be a child." Neither of us had been.

"I nearly destroyed myself again seeing this galaxy like one!" he said bitterly. "Do you know what I would do in that situation now, Nemesis? I would blow up their oxygen tanks, their water supplies, their granaries. Then if they still refused to leave, I would strand them there to meet the fate they'd chosen. I've wasted enough time raging against the wind."

"Tyrus, you don't hear yourself. You don't see yourself—"

"You're the one who isn't seeing," he said, suddenly frustrated. He surged out of his seat and floated toward me, planting his arms on either side of me. "You say I committed an atrocity? Well, I would do it again. I may do it again. Because I may have to. I created malignant space. Yes. All that time I devoted to stopping it was a waste! The ability to destroy a star system is a *superweapon*, and I could do so much with that in my arsenal! And *you*"—he had fury in his eyes—"have no grounds to condemn me for this. Once you would have done this in my place!"

"You have no remorse about what you've done! That gives you no pause?"

He gave a wild laugh. "Of course I have none. I have passed years waiting for this. To see the malignant space I created devour my foes . . . That was a time of sweet and glorious ecstacy the likes of which I have never experienced. If their terror in those dying moments was a draft, I would drink of it deep and never tire of the flavor. Why would I feel the slightest remorse?"

I couldn't look away from him. He had to be saying this to make his point, to rub it in. Surely he couldn't mean this.

"Now, it's all over," he said. "It's done. We are safe. We are secure. We will only stay that way if we move forward as *I* plan, so that's what we'll do. If today I must kill an innocent man so you never seek another to use against me, I will do it. I'll do it gladly."

"And is my distress another draft you could imbibe without quenching your thirst?" I said quietly.

His hand flew up and for a disbelieving moment, I thought he'd strike me. But his shaking palm hovered just next to my jaw, and did not touch. "I love you to the very depths of my soul," Tyrus noted quietly, "and sometimes I truly hate you for that." Then with a push of his arms, he propelled himself away from me, and dropped back toward his seat.

I stayed there with my back to the wall. This was how it would be. This would set the tone for everything going forward. If I accepted this, I had to accept everything.

He meant to leave me no choice but to accept it.

The dance was entering its final act, and I could see that Gladdic had finally been granted freedom of movement. He arched his legs to drive himself as far as possible from the people he knew would soon try to kill him, panic blazing on his face.

He had to know there was no escape.

I stared down at Gladdic. Soft, weak, well-meaning, fearful Gladdic. He was just one person. It was just one life. It was just the tiniest fragment of the atrocities yesterday, and yet it was the one that meant everything.

Tyrus had asked when we'd poisoned Devineé—when was one life taken a death too many? And now I knew the answer.

It was this one.

Today.

"This is being your Empress," I said to Tyrus. "This is how it will be from this day forward. You mean to kill him and I cannot stop you."

Tyrus closed his eyes a moment, pinching the bridge of his nose. "You are amplifying the significance of this. Gladdic dies. We move on. We wake up tomorrow and move on as though this never happened."

But that wasn't me. It wasn't.

"Do you recall telling me what it was you loved about me?" I asked him. "You love that I *act*."

And with that, I hurled myself onto the floor to save Gladdic.

# 49

**I SHED** the steering rings before Tyrus could use them to drag me back, and the dancers were stunned into stillness by the sight of me, carried into their midst by my momentum. I grabbed the first one I encountered, ripped the sword right out of his hands, and told Gladdic, "Get over here!"

He aimed for me, near to weeping with his gratitude. I only half paid attention to him. I was watching one person.

For a long moment, in the sudden hush, the Emperor Tyrus stared down after me like a stone effigy. I expected to hear the hum of the neural suppressor activating.

I did not. I hugged the trembling Gladdic to my back, holding him as close as I could. It wouldn't stop a security bot from slicing at him with a laser, but I knew Tyrus wouldn't risk shooting me. . . . And I would be too close to take that risk. One by one, the recording bots sagged down. This whole thing was a propaganda broadcast. I'd just interfered.

Tyrus glided down before me, like ice. "Remove yourself from the floor. I'll devise a means of portraying this as part of the performance."

"To explain sparing the Immolate?" I said challengingly.

"No. Desist, Nemesis. This will accomplish nothing."

"I disagree. You will pardon him. If you don't, I will protect him unto death. Against you."

He had presented his terms for me, the way he envisioned us moving forward: he wanted me to sit passively by and turn a blind eye to what he did.

These were *my* terms.

For Tyrus had too much power. He wasn't the person he'd been. I couldn't let him continue unchecked. I *had* to know I could stay his hand.

If I could not, then I would not sit at his side and be his Empress and pretend all was fine. I'd meant to destroy his scepter, to stop him. I couldn't. So now I would find another way to stop him.

"Why," he said between his teeth, "do you care so much for him?"

"I care for *you*. That's why I saved him from you. Tyrus, pardon him."

My heart thudded wildly. If I could just do this now, then there was hope. There was hope I could stop him the next time he decided to sweep a mass of players off the board. The next time malignant space would be convenient to deploy, the next time Resolvent Mist was an option, the next time he could simply slice a foe apart with security bots . . . My voice would mean something. He would hear me. He would listen. That's what I had to establish today—my influence over him. If not today, then I would never have it again.

Tyrus beckoned a dancer over, took the man's sword, then gave him an offhanded shove to send him far from us. He raised the blade before him, letting me see its gleam in the bright rays spilling in the window from malignant space.

"Let me present it to you this way, Nemesis: I'm not going to turn on the neural suppressor. I'm going to let you retain your over-whelmingly powerful strength. So it's in your hands what you do next—for you see, he dies. At my hand. To stop that, you will have to kill me."

No.

Tyrus didn't give me more time to think. He surged toward us, lashing out with the blade.

I thrust Gladdic away from me, far from the blade, and I seized Tyrus's leg as he propelled himself past me, for I had to rely on momentum outside myself. We neared Gladdic as he rebounded off the wall, and Tyrus drove his sword point toward him. . . .

I hurled Tyrus away. He hit the wall hard enough for the sword to slip out of his grasp, and I caught it when it rebounded toward me.

Tyrus recovered. Then—then he beckoned over another of the dancers. I shook my head, but he had another blade in hand. He arched his brows, tilted it toward me in lethal invitation.

"Don't," I said.

"Gladdic. Me. Who perishes, Nemesis?" And then he was on me.

My sword crashed into his, blocking it, but the momentum sent me sailing back from them. Tyrus, undaunted, shifted his arms and legs to stalk after Gladdic as I sank downward, raging with frustration. Then my legs touched the diamond-and-crystalline wall, and I kicked off with a powerful thrust. Just as Tyrus reached Gladdic, I slammed my blade into his. Tyrus's face contorted with the pain of impact, but he kept hold of the sword.

He shot toward Gladdic, and I reached out to seize his ankle. . . . But it was a feint, because he whipped about at the last moment, driving a kick into my chest that sent me reeling down toward the clear diamond wall. The wall forced the breath out of me, but I had the presence of mind to shove off even as I tried to fill my lungs.

The inability to steer was a dreadful handicap, and each time our swords clanged, I flew back across the ball dome. I doggedly kicked off the walls to return, and stopped Tyrus again and again from sinking his blade into Gladdic. Finally, exasperated, Tyrus focused on me, not Gladdic. He kicked himself forward, following me as I was driven back, and then our swords met and his elbow lashed out, pinning me in place against the wall. I grabbed his arm but did not wrench it out of place, did not shatter it.

*How easily, how easily I could break him apart right now if this were anyone else. . . .*

He used his steering rings to crush me then.

"What do you think will happen here?" he raged. "You can't stop this! Make your choice!"

"I am *not* a vicar! There is no hand or head to choose between, Tyrus. I will fight you to my last breath and keep him alive and I will not kill you! That's my choice. If you would just *trust me*—"

"Trust you?" He smiled bitterly. "As I did on the *Tigris?*"

The words stole my breath. The moment seemed to grind to a halt about me as my thoughts spiraled back to that decision, that moment.

We were floating back from the wall, but all I could see were his pale, shadowed eyes.

"I made my choice," Tyrus said quietly. "I would free the woman I most loved and serve those people of my Empire, and it was all I wanted. I trusted you to let me decide, and you knocked me unconscious and left me with them. I chose and you took that from me."

My vision darkened a moment as understanding crashed over me, where the trust had been shredded for him. That decision to thrust him into Pasus's hands, to remove him from danger.

"I—I couldn't let you die," I stuttered.

"So instead, you left me in the hands of enemies whose relatives I'd just helped kill in massive numbers. What outcome did you envision from that?"

"I'm sorr—"

"*Do not* apologize. You made your choice and chose not to listen to me, and now you ask for the same courtesy you never gave me?" He drew toward me and abruptly seized the blade of my sword. I could see the blood floating out as he tightened his fist, eyes burning into mine. He pulled the gleaming tip to his throat. "This is the choice I'm offering you. It's the only choice. Kill me. Kill him. If we must battle a century, you are going to make this choice."

Let Tyrus murder Gladdic.

Or kill Tyrus.

It wasn't a choice. I released the blade. It floated from my hand.

His hands closed on my waist. He drew me to him.

"Tomorrow," he whispered, "all of this will be the past, and we will move onward." And we were floating, floating toward the box, and the dancers were heading out onto the floor again. The transmitting devices powered up and resumed the broadcast, and Gladdic's face grew dumb with terror as he realized his reprieve had ended.

I looked at Tyrus, a stranger after three years enduring the consequences of a choice I'd taken from him. Three years for this quiet anger to build. A great wave of tenderness welled up within me.

"Tyrus, I am sorry for what I did," I murmured.

Then I struck the Emperor of this galaxy with one abrupt, treasonous swing of my arm, and the momentum was enough to knock him back and send me into the center of the ball dome so all might see, all might hear, as I pointed at Fustian nan Domitrian.

"That man is an *imposter*. I know he's not the Interdict—because I killed the Interdict Orthanion when I destroyed the Sacred City."

# 50

TYRUS CUT OFF all the transmitters with a curse, but it was too late, it was too late—the words were out there, and he whirled on me with crazed horror, shouted, "What are you doing?"

"Isn't it obvious?"

"Take it back. Say it was a joke. Say it!" His voice was ferocious, and I waited until he was convinced I'd obey. He turned the transmitters back on.

I said: "I slit the Interdict's throat and rammed the *Hera* into—"

"ENOUGH!" roared Tyrus as the transmitters cut off again. "You've gone mad. What in the hell are you thinking?"

"I know exactly what I'm doing."

He looked like he wanted to hit me. To combust. He soared to me, seized my arms, and drew my face toward his. "You told the galaxy you killed the Interdict! They'll believe you!"

"I know. That's why I said it."

"Black hole devour you—to what end?"

"I'm setting," I told him, my eyes boring into his, "my own terms for how we move forward. Now you have them."

He shouted out in frustration, threw me from him, and I drifted with the momentum, still watching him as he scraped his hands through his hair, clearly trying to think of a way to salvage this. The Empire was in his hands. All the technology in this sector obeyed him. But he couldn't erase what I'd done.

And he knew it.

Then, "Why?" His voice was a deathly whisper, but I could make it out.

I neared the far wall, so I shoved off it to float back toward him. The audience in the ball dome was watching us, rapt. Gladdic was holding on to the edge of a box, heaving himself into it, desperate for his escape.

"Surely you realize . . . ," Tyrus began.

"That I've condemned myself? Yes. That's the point." I caught his arm. Very gently, I pressed the hilt of my sword into his palm. "You could use this. The honor of an Empress's death must surely go to her husband. It will be your duty to carry this out."

He stared at the sword blankly, then looked at me. His momentum kept him with me as I listed to the side. I was only half-aware of every screen in the boxes all about us going opaque as Tyrus blocked us from their view.

"I don't understand you," he said.

"You should. I am the same as I have always been. Yours. And desperately in love with you. I won't sit here and watch you become what you hate. I thought perhaps I could influence you, but I clearly can't. I can't be your conscience. You hoped I would learn to live with turning a blind eye, but I won't. Even if I were capable of that, I could never do you such a cruelty. So here is your new set of choices, Tyrus."

"Choices?" he said between his teeth. "There are no choices anymore. You've made sure of that! You've eliminated every choice but the single one I *cannot* make! You mean me to kill you."

"On the contrary, there are two choices: you may choose me, or you may choose power." The cold certainty of the words registered in my mind. "Your grandmother once said there is a single choice for a Domitrian. Are you a Domitrian? Or are you Tyrus, the one I love— the one who will choose me?"

He just stared at me. I was aware of several Grandiloquy who'd managed to force their screens back to translucence. . . . Tyrus was too focused on me to shield us from them again.

I cupped his hot, dry cheeks in my hand, stared into those bewildered eyes. "The Emperor of this galaxy has a duty to avenge the Interdict. Emperor Tyrus has to kill me. But Tyrus, my husband, the love of my life—he can decide otherwise. He can save me."

"How," he rasped, "can I possibly save you from this?"

"You'll take me away from here. I wanted to save you, but it's not in my power now. So you'll save me instead. We'll aim for the black hole. We'll emerge in a time when no one knows us. How easily you and I might disappear if we wanted to, and they may even think we flew right into malignant space . . . or something else. We can take any of these ships and jump into hyperspace until we are so far away, the Empire is a distant memory."

He gave a crazed, hopeless laugh. "The idea is ludicrous. You've now confessed to killing the Interdict," he said, "and I have decimated much of the Grandiloquy. I am not invulnerable, Nemesis. I am only now learning how to control these machines. Do you truly think we will get that far?"

"We will run fast. If we are cornered, we will fight hard. No force in this galaxy can stop us."

"And this Empire?"

"Leave it behind! Tyrus, your family is deemed royal, but they don't rule this place. They have been *chained* to it for thousands of years. You can break those chains. You've ended the line, so free *yourself* from it. Escape with me, my love."

Tyrus's eyes glinted. "You've never called me that."

"Have I not?" I murmered, my heart pierced not just by the realization I hadn't—but by the fact that he'd noticed. "My love." I pressed a kiss to his lips. "My true love. Love of my life."

He gathered me closer, heedless of how this had to look after my confession. "Why do you keep doing this to me?" His voice was thick like he'd caught back a sob.

"Helios help me, that Venalox wasn't strong enough. It didn't do enough. I would gladly poison every fiber of my heart that beats for you if I could be free of you. You are the only one who can hurt me."

"I don't want to," I said. "Tyrus, I can't imagine myself without you."

He looked at me with a torture in his eyes I hadn't seen in the worst torments of withdrawal. "No. But . . . I can."

Then he buried his sword in my chest.

# 51

HEARTBEATS felt like ages. An eruption of bright, blazing red, the world blasted on a wave of pain, and between our bodies swirled a haze of crimson roses, but then the iron tinge in the back of my throat betrayed the blood I was seeing hemorrhage from my veins. Heat drained from my limbs in one gasp, but arms caught me, clasped about me. My vision saw something strange, a part of me that couldn't be *me*, punctured, split as it was, with steel buried in my flesh.

"I hate you," said the voice, so close, and with a wrench it tore out of me, a slash of his arm casting the blade, end over end, to the far reaches of the ball dome. "Oh, how I hate you for this."

Air strangled me. I choked, heaved it in, but there was not enough, my own breath was drowning me. . . . And the distant crowd floated into my vision, their shouts and raucous voices flooding, pounding the air.

So many animals. Two-legged creatures with their sharp teeth and clawing hands and the fog descended thicker and thicker over them.

My head sagged back against something warm, solid behind me, and a voice whispered, "Shh. Shh." His voice dropped, grew bitter. "This will never be their show."

He twisted us about, and then all we could see was vastness beyond clear diamond windows. Fingers threaded through my hair, tingling across my scalp, the nape of my neck, over and over as brilliant light flooded my vision.

"There." The breathy whisper. "Just look there."

Closer we glided, two faint, ghostly reflections gleaming against the malignant space. Though my vision slid out of focus, the brilliance remained, bright, effervescent, radiating at me until it hummed through my soul as life slipped from my veins.

"Breathtaking, isn't it?" A hoarse voice. Choked. "Never in my life have I seen such terrible beauty."

The fog descended.

# 52

SHE STOOD too close to the edge. Sidonia pointed to something, but I couldn't make it out. She was wandering ever farther, and every bit of me thrilled with warning.

"Donia, Donia, you shouldn't go into that water. . . ."

A moment later, the absurdity of the words dawned on me. . . . Though why they were out of place, I could not say. Donia just looked back at me, a smile glimmering over her lips, a soft, tender warmth in her dark eyes.

"Oh, Nemesis," she said. "I'll take care of you. That's painful."

I knew what she was talking about. My gaze dropped to my bare feet, scorched and lacerated where they bled on the jagged stones beneath me.

Her hand closed about mine, and then she tugged me from the pain to the velvety sands that pooled between my toes. A sigh escaped my lips, and she smiled.

"Look," she said, and then dipped a toe into the water, a clear glaze reflecting darkness wild with stars. "It's very warm."

I followed her lead, but when my toes touched the water, they met ice. Perplexed, I watched her take another step, another, the rippling starscape over the liquid vibrating with her steps. It was so easy for her. But for me, it was impossible.

"Donia, I can't . . ." I tried to explain it. "I . . . I've forgotten something."

I couldn't think of what, but she knew the answer and there was a sweetness and purity of love to her face as she told me she understood me as no one had ever understood me. As I'd ever known myself. "I'll be here."

And then I was choking, my chest heaving, vibrating, and a blare of a voice, too loud, "Oh, good. Now we just have to hope she's not brain-dead."

The voice . . . That voice . . .

I gasped out and tore up from where I was sprawled, but arms tangled with mine, driving me back down, and she skittered back from me, fingers splayed, hands up.

I had to look at her a long moment to make sense of her. . . . To make sense of Neveni, so altered, with most of her hair gone, an angry, thick scar across her face as though someone had tried to cross her out . . .

Then her hand shot forward and tightened on mine. Not small and soft as Donia's was, but Neveni's hard, rough one. "Do you know who I am?" she said.

Of course I knew her. I knew pain throbbed through every single fragment of me and an unfamiliar ship hummed about me, the fluorescent lights overhead blaring into my eyes and Donia was gone, and Tyrus . . .

Neveni.

Neveni—who had stranded me.

A scream ripped from my lips and I surged for her. She reared back, lips blazing in a feral grin, but a pair of enormous arms, heavy with muscles, locked around me.

Oh. Oh, him. Anguish.

"Yeah, she remembers me," Neveni said, leaning against the far wall.

"What's . . . What is . . ." I cast about for understanding. Then I heaved myself forward, and Anguish abruptly released me—sending me plunging to the ground. Pain banged up my knees, and Neveni started forward as though to help me, then halted . . . rethinking that.

And then . . .

Then it was all there blaring in my mind, and my hand flew down. . . . Tender flesh over my rib cage.

The blade . . . The blade!

"I was . . . He . . . ," I gasped.

"Let me help you up."

Her voice rang in my ears, but I couldn't seem to understand it. Neveni's arms wrapped around my waist, and she hoisted me up with an *oof.* I sagged there dumbly, and then Anguish grabbed my arm to help her out.

I looked at her, at him, and I couldn't . . . I couldn't . . . What was wrong with me? "How did I get here?"

"Gladdic of all people contacted me. It was the oddest thing, but he gave me a heads-up where we could find you. Let's get her to a chair." Anguish nodded.

I hung there between them as they eased me across the room. "G-Gladdic?" What? What about Gladdic? What was going on?

"He told us what had happened," Neveni said. "Long before we actually caught the transmission ourselves. I think he wanted us to spirit him away, but I let him know there'd be a price for it. You. He paid us. Whether we pay him back or not, well . . . Maybe if it's convenient one day." I blinked at her sluggishly. Yes. I'd given him her frequency. I recalled that suddenly.

"I don't . . ." My mind fought to untangle as they settled me in a chair. "I'm not . . ."

"Hypovolemic shock." Anguish's deep voice drew my attention to him. He gazed down at me. "It's happened to me before. We don't respond as they do. Great blood loss, and we go into a sort of hibernation. Easy to mistake for death."

"Gladdic also injected an oxygen pellet into your bloodstream to keep you from suffocating while you weren't breathing." Her mouth curled in an uneven smile—with that scar slashing over the corner of both lips. "You think you know a guy, and then he surprises you by not being thoroughly useless. . . ."

Death.

Hibernation.

What?

"Then it was just a matter of trying to make sure we caught up to your tomb before you woke up . . . if you did. Gladdic tweaked the navigation, too. He must have, or you'd be ashes."

I stared at her, and I couldn't understand it. It made no sense. It just . . .

My mouth was like sawdust. My eyes were sliding in and out of focus, but when I looked down at the floor beside me, an ugly shock jerked through me.

A crystalline enclosure.

A tomb.

I'd been in there. I had been inside it. I'd been trapped inside, stranded in bare space. If I'd awoken and never been found . . .

She caught me when I keeled over, but nothing escaped as I dry heaved.

"Yeah, it's rough. Anguish told me it would be," Neveni said.

Waves of ice swept through me, chills prickling over my skin. I looked at the coffin again.

"Welcome back from the dead," Neveni told me.

She reached back to retrieve a glass, offered it to me. Desperate thirst gripped me. I drew in a great mouthful, then gagged.

Not water.

Not water—whiskey.

"Unless you prefer water," Neveni said.

I didn't. I dumped the glass down my throat, and the burn of my esophagus seemed to be the only point of me thawed from ice.

"Should I give her more?" Anguish said.

"She was dead. Give her the whole bottle," Neveni said.

Numbness pervaded my very soul, the hum of the starship about me seeming to vibrate my bones, my skull, threatening to shake loose those muffled thoughts in my mind. I vaguely saw the bare walls of the chamber I'd been led to.

There I sat on a bed where the springs dug into me, and I lifted my shirt to see my chest. . . . Taut flesh over my rib cage with a smear of toneless white a shade brighter than the skin about it, where my life had almost been preserved by a med bot. Or someone had chosen to fix it up for disposal of my body in a star.

Nothing felt real, nothing was as it should be. I had a fog in my head that would not recede, a heavy cloud cover. Anguish and Neveni returned. She plucked up the empty glass bottle, studied me. "So I once got him to drink a whole bottle, and I swear, he was giggly. Can you imagine? A bit scary, actually. You?"

I couldn't process her words.

She let out a breath. "I really hope you don't have brain damage, Nemesis. I'm not sure what I'll do with you then. Actually, I am. I'll probably kill you. I can't afford to deal with that."

Brain damage.

There was a warning in the words, and it didn't matter to me in the slightest. I pressed my hands over my ears. Tyrus's eyes were looking at mine in the ball dome, and I screwed my lids shut to block the image, but it was inside me, the image of that gaze just before . . . before he . . . I couldn't tolerate my memory veering back to that.

I didn't hear whatever else she had to say, her voice lost in the mire of thoughts swirling in my head. I plunged into dreams of those two distant, remote, cold eyes and awoke chilled in my bones.

Something hard pressed the back of my head.

Neveni stood above me where she'd yanked my pillow out from under me.

"Enough. Anguish said it's a bit of a shock to . . . well, to come out of shock, but you've had time. Now you need to be awake. Get up."

When I did not move, she scowled at me, the red line of the scar tracing a lurid path across the corner of her mouth.

"Enough of this," she muttered. She unsheathed a glinting dagger. Then she slashed it down at me.

I caught her wrist, anger spouting in me. "I am not a feeble old man taken off guard!" And to emphasize this, I ground her bones together. I hurled her away from me, suddenly furious. "Desist unless you want me to slice the rest of your face!"

But she did not come at me again. "There you are," she said breathlessly, clutching her arm. "You're still very strong."

"Would you have killed me?"

"Only if you'd let me." She shrugged, sheathed the knife again.

S. J. KINCAID

"Remember how you told me once I'd feel better soon? This was soon after I found out everyone I knew and loved had been murdered. . . ."

I looked at her flatly. Yes, I saw now how insensitive that was.

"It's the last thing you ever want to hear, but you turned out to be right," Neveni said. "Blowing up the Sacred City and becoming the greatest heathen in the galaxy really did cheer me up. So did getting this ship. So did grabbing you before you burned up. Think of it: the whole galaxy knows their Empress killed their Interdict. Imagine how terrified they'll be when you come back from the dead for real this time and say you're going to kill more than that."

I closed my eyes. "What do you want?"

"I want to tell you that I know what you're feeling. I lost everything. You loved Tyrus so much, you went back to certain death, and what did he do? He married you, and then as your brand-new husband, he *killed* you."

She'd said it, she'd given voice to that thing so unbearable to think about, but now I had to. Now I did. I pressed my hand to the new skin of my chest and turned the concept about in my mind, again and again.

Tyrus had killed me.

Tyrus. Killed. Me.

He'd done it. He'd truly done it. He killed me.

"There's only one way to bounce back from this, and you know what it is," Neveni said, her eyes glittering savagely. "Find him and return the favor. And tear down his Empire around him. I know you want this. If you don't yet, you will soon. I'm sure of it."

Just listening to her excited voice made me feel lousy.

"I know what you're thinking," Neveni said. "How can three people do anything? But we're not any three people! The strongest man and woman in the galaxy—and the greatest terrorist! Nemesis, you're a Galactic Empress publicly murdered by her husband who will come right back from the dead. The Empress who isn't Grandiloquy, the Empress who killed the Interdict . . . You think there's no use for that? You're a legend. We all are—and imagine what we can do!"

I imagined nothing. Later, after she'd left, I moved mindlessly to the washroom on legs still aching, sore from disuse. I beheld a reflection, the ruins of a person I'd been days ago donning a gleaming silver gown, determined to salvage what had already been lost.

My gray eyes ran down over that frame, honed into a version of itself acceptable in an Empress, a Grandeé. A Diabolic who had squandered her purpose twice. It took me a moment to notice that wisps of my hair were bound up. I reached back and unlatched the clip holding it . . .

And an ugly pain wrenched at me as I examined it. The very clip Tyrus had retrieved from the nitrogen fountain. The gift he'd offered me for our wedding. How much hope this had given me . . .

My fist tightened on it, a wild urge to break it all apart tearing at me. I raised my eyes to meet a pair of savage, feral gray ones, glaring at me above a nose so fashionably uneven. Donia loved it that way. So did Tyrus.

Then I decided something: I didn't love it.

I despised it.

It wasn't perfect. I could be. I was symmetrical and lethal and powerful, and this intentional and unnecessary mar needn't even be there. I was done with it. With a gritting of teeth, I balled up my fist over the clip and positioned the sturdiest of its gems right where I wanted it.

Then I smashed it over the bridge of my nose.

Pain burst before my eyes, bright, welcome. I struck again, again. . . . Blood dripped down to splatter about my feet. Red-hot waves of agony reverberated through my skull, but it didn't matter, none of it did. I flung the clip away, seized the broken bridge of my nose, and then arranged it. I twisted, yanked, pulled it until it was exactly where it was meant to be—dead center, tugged into straightness. Exactly as it should have been all along.

Any other girl—any ordinary person—would be crying. I hadn't blinked. I was more than a person. I was a Diabolic.

Blood still seeped, so I raised the corner of my shirt to blot it away, then blot it again. If the swelling receded and the nose remained crooked, or uncorrected, then . . . then I would simply break and correct it again.

Neveni startled awake when I kicked the foot of her bed—and next to her, Anguish opened his eyes lazily, a subtle tension in his great muscles that told me he was poised to spring and break me apart if necessary. . . . But for now, he wanted to lounge in bed.

They'd somehow carved some happiness out of the ashes. I saw that, gazing down at them. My heart felt hollow, like I would never feel anything again.

"Whatever you want of me," I told Neveni, "I don't care. I'll do it. I am alive because of you. I'll repay the debt. I'll destroy anyone you wish."

I whipped around to leave them.

"Nemesis," Neveni called after me. I turned to see her sharp, intense gaze. "Anyone?"

I knew what she meant. She only cared about one person. Just one.

Rage and hurt boiled within me, and I hated that I felt them at all. All I wished was to turn to stone, to ice.

My voice, when I spoke, held a remorseless certainty.

"Anyone."

# ACKNOWLEDGMENTS

I'm keeping it short this time! If I leave out anyone, my apologies in advance. I really am overflowing with appreciation for everyone who has made the experience with *The Diabolic* happen.

Thanks, Justin, for having such faith in these books, and Holly, for being such an amazing representative.

Thanks, Meredith and Mom, for the first reads! Rob, Dad, Matt, Betsey, and the kids for being awesome.

My gratitude to everyone at Simon and Schuster Books for Young Readers, especially Audrey, Alexa, Dorothy, Lizzy, Nick, Chrissy, and Chava for all the back-and-forth.

Thank you also to Dana Spector, David Manpearl, and Ryan Doherty.

Thank you to my foreign publishers, particularly Arena. Anna, it was wonderful to meet you in person! Thanks to Elena and the others as well for an incredible experience.

Thanks, Jamie and Jessica. Thanks to the Schaumburg folks, including Toddery Barn.

THANK YOU to children's librarians, to children's booksellers, to bloggers, readers, and every single one of you who has read this series, passed it on, and talked about it. You guys make this all worthwhile.

S.J. Kincaid originally wanted to be an astronaut, but a dearth of mathematical skills made her turn her interest to science fiction instead. Her debut novel, *Insignia*, was shortlisted for the Waterstones Children's Book Prize. She's chronically restless and has lived in California, Alabama, New Hampshire, Oregon, Chicago and Scotland with no signs of staying in one place anytime soon.

Join her on Twitter @sjkincaidbooks